A TAPESTRY OF BRONZE NOVEL

Titles in the Tapestry of Bronze series:

JOCASTA:
THE MOTHER-WIFE OF OEDIPUS

NIOBE AND PELOPS:
CHILDREN OF TANTALUS

NIOBE AND AMPHION:
THE ROAD TO THEBES

NIOBE AND CHLORIS:
ARROWS OF ARTEMIS

Learn more about the Tapestry of Bronze series at
www.tapestryofbronze.com

JOCASTA
THE MOTHER-WIFE OF OEDIPUS

VICTORIA GROSSACK
AND
ALICE UNDERWOOD

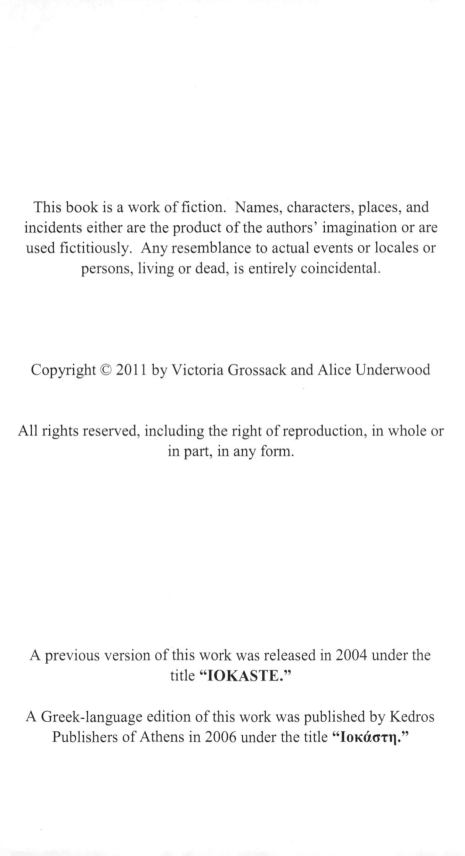

A previous version of this work was released in 2004 under the title **"IOKASTE."**

A Greek-language edition of this work was published by Kedros Publishers of Athens in 2006 under the title **"Ιοκάστη."**

THE CITY OF THEBES

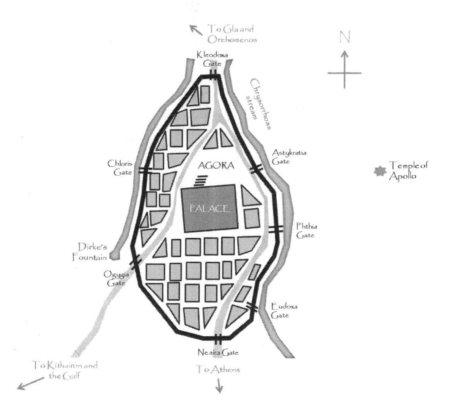

To Gla and
Orchomenos

Kleodoxa
Gate

Chrysorhoas stream

N

Chloris
Gate

AGORA

Astykratia
Gate

Temple of
Apollo

PALACE

Phthia
Gate

Dirke's
Fountain

Ogygia
Gate

Eudoxa
Gate

To Kithairon and
the Gulf

Neaira Gate

To Athens

PROLOGUE

"I don't want to die."

"But you will die, Sister." Creon's voice is firm, unyielding. "Your only choice is how. You can either take the poison I have brought you – quick and painless – or you can wait for the people to come and pull you to pieces."

I shiver and feel the blood drain away from my veins. Thebes has ripped apart its rulers before: Pentheus, Labdakus, Amphion. I do not want my own name added to the list.

My brother continues. "The soldiers and the priests will be here in the morning. If you are not already dead, they will drag you out of the palace into the agora. The people will scream curses at you; spit in your face; call you unnatural, a whore. They'll strip off your fine clothing, take a lash to your soft skin. And, finally, they will tear you limb from limb."

I look around my room in the palace where I have lived the last forty years. I imagine the mob forcing its way inside, smashing the ancient wooden clothes-chest and intricately carved chairs, knocking over the braziers and setting the building afire. Blood – mine – seeping into the tiles, staining the wool and linen of the cushions, spattering on the tapestries and the wall-paintings.

Like the blood on my dressing table: my husband's blood, spilled by his own hand.
I slam my fist against the table, toppling a small ivory statue of the god Hermes. "It's not fair! I'm not a criminal!"

My brother rights the god and then pushes the vial in my direction. "If I were you, Sister, I'd take the poison."

"I have been a good queen! I have taken care of Thebes my whole life – struggled and fought and nursed these people, this city, this land. Together my husband and I ruled Thebes for nearly twenty years. And I ruled Thebes for more than twenty before

1

that! Now, in a single day, it's all ruined! Why – why does this have to matter?"

Creon takes my hands and stills them. "Because it does matter. The priests and the people say it's unnatural, against the laws of the gods. They want a royal sacrifice, to cleanse the curse. And you, Sister, are the most royal – and the most cursed."

I pull away and step toward the door, then turn to look at him. "Can't I escape?"

"The priests have watchers everywhere, even among the palace guard. You would never make it out of the city."

"But—"

"Jocasta, they know the truth."

He's right. The secrets of my life are now plain for all to see. And they are not pretty: like the last dregs in a golden cup, after the wine has drained away. And yet – and yet – I'm still healthy, still called beautiful. I'm too young to die.

"The question is, how long have *you* known it?" Creon asks.

I realize he is suspicious and angry, but I ignore the question; there are more urgent matters. "Maybe they're not yet decided. If we speak to them…"

He shakes his gray head. "They're waiting for morning," he repeats. "The priests plan your punishment to take place in the light of day. They want to make an example of you for everyone to see." Then, as if to soften the blow, Creon strokes my shoulder, my cheek. His fingers are dry and warm; lamplight glitters off the amethyst of his signet ring. "But you're right. You have done so much for them, and they have forgotten in an instant. Perhaps someday they will remember that you, Jocasta of Thebes, were their greatest queen."

"You speak as if I were already dead."

"You are. I speak to your ghost." His voice becomes matter-of-fact, and I know now he will not help me. "But your ghost has until sunrise to depart. This poison works quickly."

"Till sunrise." The sun has already set. How many hours are left to me?

Creon stands and pulls his cloak around his shoulders. "I'll be back before dawn. Keep the vial at hand; you'll need it. Good-bye, Jocasta."

He opens the door into the corridor and walks through it; I will never see him again. My own way is blocked by two soldiers. Up until yesterday they would have given their lives to save mine; their stony expressions tell me their allegiance is gone. But beyond the renegade men stand two women: Merope, the patient maidservant who has attended me all her life, and my younger daughter Ismene.

Merope walks calmly past the guards into my room; my daughter gives them a nervous look and darts through. Merope, usually so quiet, speaks. "My lady, we did not want you to be alone."

My daughter, her face shiny with tears, slips into my arms. "Mother? Is it true?"

I hold her a moment, a precious moment, and think: what should I tell her? But if I must be dead by dawn, what is the point of lies? I look down into her blue eyes, so like my own, and say, "My darling, I'm afraid it is."

"Then, Father—? How could you?"

How could I? That is the question. "Do you really want to know?"

Ismene's voice is soft. "Yes, I do."

I search her face. She, too, is an unwitting victim of Fate. Wouldn't she be better served by truth? Besides, I am tired of lies, tired of keeping silence; and these hours of night are my last chance to talk.

"Come." I take her by the hand, and lead her to the bed that I shared with her father and her grandfather. We sit down together on the striped coverlet and I put my arm around her slender shoulders. Merope quietly pulls up a stool and sits where she can listen easily, but so that her scarred face is shrouded by darkness.

"Listen," I say, as I open my chest of long-suppressed memories. "Listen, and I will tell you."

CHAPTER ONE

"Wake, child," said Hydna, shaking me gently. "Jocasta, it's morning – you must get up!"

I reluctantly opened my eyelids. The scent of spring rain hung in the air, and in the courtyard outside a dove called his song. My limbs felt like marble, too heavy to move. Why was I so tired, and why was my nurse rousing me before dawn?

Then I remembered.

Despite retiring early, I had tossed and turned all through the night. I was anxious over what this day might bring.

She held a flickering lamp near my face, inspecting it. "Did the gods send you a vision of your husband?"

I rubbed my eyes, shook my head.

She patted my cheek. Because my mother had died giving birth to me, Hydna had done the work of raising me. "Never fear, little one," she said. "You'll soon be a bride!"

I sat up and pushed the rough wool blanket from my body. "I'm not betrothed yet," I said. "And we don't even know whether I will be."

"You will be, you'll see." Pulling me from my bed, she ushered me toward the bath. "You'll be chosen."

"I'm only fourteen."

"You're as tall as any maid of sixteen," she replied, slipping the nightgown away from my body, exposing my skin to the cool morning air. "And beautiful: Prince Alphenor won't be able to resist you."

"There's more to it than that." I said, shivering. I stepped quickly into the basin and knelt in the steaming rose-scented water, scooping it up to warm my chest and arms. "The gods – Apollo, that is – will decide." I did not tell her that I was not sure that I wanted the gods to choose me.

"Apollo will want you, too – how couldn't he?" asked Hydna, washing my back with a soft sponge.

Merope, a younger serving woman whose face bore burn-scars from an accident in the kitchens years ago, entered the room with a steaming pitcher. She poured the warm water over my head and began scrubbing my hair. Her vigorous motions and the splashing water made conversation impossible; I kept my doubts to myself. Trying to relax, I breathed in the sweet scent, but the tension in my neck and shoulders remained.

Might the gods choose me because of my good family? But if lineage was what mattered most, then why did the usurper Amphion rule in Thebes, and why did so many people of impeccable heritage come to horrible ends? King Pentheus, one of my own relatives, had been torn to pieces by his own mother and a mob of women generations before. And in Hydna's youth, angry citizens had pulled King Labdakus limb from limb.

"You shouldn't think about such things," chided Hydna.

"What things?"

"Whatever it is that's making you frown." She took my hand and pulled me to my feet so that the water could drip down into the tub. "Think of Prince Alphenor!"

I caught my breath. It hardly seemed real. I was being prepared for my betrothal. For my *possible* betrothal, I reminded myself.

After toweling me off and combing my hair, Hydna and Merope dressed me. First came the multi-tiered skirts of yellow and blue. Next I shrugged into my best open-fronted jacket, made of blue-dyed leather, and held my breath while Hydna pulled the waist-laces tight and knotted them fast. My garments were stiff and heavy, making it difficult to move, but while my maids worked on me I needed to keep still anyway. They next turned their attention to my damp hair, combing up the curls and twining them with bands of beaten gold. After this Hydna dabbed my lips, cheeks, earlobes, and the tips of my breasts with alkanet rouge; she put perfume on my wrists and neck. Finally she placed a short cape around my shoulders and pinned it at my throat with a silver fibula.

Merope retrieved an ivory pyxis that had belonged to my mother and offered it to Hydna. My nurse lifted the lid and withdrew matching bracelets of gold inlaid with lapis lazuli. She fastened them about my wrists, then took a step back. Circling me, she inspected every detail in the growing light.

"My butterfly – you're a woman now!" She flicked tears away from her eyes, then cleared her throat. "You've had no breakfast – we can't have you fainting at Prince Alphenor's feet! I'll fetch a tray; Merope, let her father know that she's almost ready." Both serving women left the room.

Alone for the first time that morning, I grasped the hippopotamus-ivory handle of my mirror and surveyed my reflection in the square of polished bronze. What would Prince Alphenor think of me?

And what did I want him to think of me?

"You *are* beautiful, Jocasta," said a male voice.

I whirled around, to see my brother emerge from behind the curtain separating my room from the bath. "Creon!" I exclaimed. "How long were you watching?"

A grin spread over his seventeen-year-old features. "Long enough to know that the Fates are smiling upon Prince Alphenor."

"You are my *brother!*"

"That doesn't stop me from seeing that you're the prettiest girl in Thebes. Or at least you will be, once your breasts grow."

I lifted the cape to examine my breasts with their freshly rouged tips. Were they really too small? But then I saw the mocking expression on my brother's face.

"You – you satyr!" I cried, throwing a comb at him.

He dodged, then went on: "And you'll soon be queen of Thebes."

"That depends on what the *gods* think of me. Not you, you worm!"

"What the gods think! The gods think whatever the strongest warriors think, or the cleverest politicians."

Creon, thin and tall and still growing, demonstrated little skill with weapons but always seemed to understand the lines of power behind the scenes. But this time I found his cynicism appalling. "Even if you think that," I hissed, "you should not say it aloud."

He seated himself on a stool. "All right: let's turn it around. The strongest warrior *is* the strongest warrior only because the gods have made him that way. Therefore, what he wants must be what they want."

I shook my head slowly. His words sounded reasonable, but I felt in my heart that his argument must be flawed.

"To think anything else," he went on, "*would* be blasphemy! As if the gods were powerless, or indifferent – or as if they didn't exist at all!" He uttered this last in a half-whisper, shaking his black curls. Then he drew a breath, and continued in a stronger tone. "But we know they *do* exist, that they *are* powerful, and that they are *not* indifferent – so the strongest warrior must enjoy the gods' favor. And since you are the most beautiful girl in Thebes, and Father is one of the most powerful men, the gods must favor you. Therefore, you will be chosen."

At that moment Hydna returned, bearing a tray. She clucked her tongue when she saw Creon. "What are *you* doing in here? It's not proper." Hydna placed the tray on a low wooden table and motioned that I should seat myself on the couch. "Eat, Jocasta. Today, of all days, you need your strength."

My brother surveyed the tray. "Goat cheese, raisins, barley bread – peasant fare! Is this food good enough for the next queen of Thebes?"

"What do you think they eat up at the palace, nectar and ambrosia?" scolded Hydna, mixing a small bowl of wine and water for the bread. "This is what your *sister* likes. And when the spirit is anxious, familiar food comforts the body."

I rarely had trouble eating – only that time I fell ill with autumn fever had my appetite vanished completely. Yet this morning, as I contemplated the day's events, my mouth was dry and my stomach rebellious. But Hydna was right; I needed to eat. I dipped my bread in the wine, then took a bite and smiled in surprise.

"What is it?" asked Creon.

"Honey," I said.

"Honey!" He reached out for the next piece but Hydna slapped his outstretched hand.

"That's Jocasta's. She needs her strength today."

"She doesn't mind sharing." He grinned and appealed directly to me. "You don't, do you?"

I was grateful for the distraction of his company and conversation. I tore the small round loaf into two parts, and gave him one. "Let him stay, Hydna." I reached for the dried figs. "Look," I reassured her. "I'm eating!"

"Good. Drink something, too." She poured me a cup of barley-water from the pitcher on the tray. "Your father expects you shortly – it's almost time to go up to the palace."

If Hydna was too fond of me, my father Menoeceus evened the scales with indifference. My mother had been dead for fourteen years, but Father had not remarried. As a child, I thought this a sign of respect for her memory, but later I realized that his mind and heart were simply elsewhere. He cared less about his descendants than our ancestors. Instead of embracing the mortals around him, he devoted his life to understanding the gods. He had even moved us from our home in the middle of Thebes, near the palace and the agora and the other well-born families, to a house he had built near the recently constructed Eudoxa Gate. The new location lay closer to Apollo's temple, on the large hill beyond the gate.

Father waited for me in the courtyard. He was also dressed formally, wearing a cream-colored kilt with gilt at the hem and a dark blue cape over his shoulders. Although gray streaked his reddish hair and beard, his tall frame was lean, his chest muscles not gone to flab like those of many older men.

He surveyed me solemnly and then gave me a rare smile. "You're beautiful, Jocasta," he said. "Like your mother on the day I took her to wife. Perhaps that's an omen. Don't forget: through me you are descended from the Spartoi, the men who sprang from the holy serpent's teeth sown by King Kadmos in Theban soil. Your mother's blood comes from Kadmos himself."

I glanced briefly at Creon, who rolled his eyes. With Father around, forgetting our ancestry was impossible. And, though Father would never admit it, our mother's claim to be the great-granddaughter of Kadmos was questioned by many.

Father continued: "There's no prouder heritage than yours, Daughter. May Apollo smile upon you, and may you make our family proud."

"I'll do my best, Father."

He frowned at my empty hands. "Where's your offering?"

Merope, as if she had been listening, entered the courtyard with a bouquet of narcissi. "Lady Jocasta, your gift."

My father nodded as I took the white-and-yellow flowers and positioned them in the crook of my arm. I would present them to Queen Niobe, the mother of Prince Alphenor.

My father walked on my right while my brother took the place at my left. Accompanied by several retainers, we passed through the courtyard's heavy wooden doors out into the main road.

I walked in Thebes nearly every day. But today, the sun's bright rays illuminated the city as if an artist had touched up a familiar old wall-painting, adding luster to faded colors and slipping in fresh details. Cracks in the whitewashed stucco walls and shadows among the terracotta roof-tiles formed patterns I had never noticed before. A serving woman was beating a brown woolen rug with a stick; the dust that she sent into the air with each stroke sparkled in the sunlight. In a nearby doorway sat an oil-merchant's young wife, nursing her newborn; the last time I had seen her, she had not yet given birth.

Not only was I more aware of the city – Thebans seemed to be more aware of me. The farmers pushing their carts of vegetables, the women carrying baskets of laundry down to the stream, the builders trundling blocks of granite and marble for King Amphion's next building project – they all paused in their tasks to watch us pass.

"They're wondering if you'll be their next queen," said Creon in a low voice. "They could all be your subjects one day."

I tried to take a deep breath, but being laced into my clothes so tightly I had to settle for several shallow ones.

Father spoke mildly. "Creon, you're making your sister nervous."

"I may not be chosen," I said. "I'm not the only maiden."

Father grunted, as if he could not imagine the gods not choosing *his* daughter.

We threaded a narrow street and entered a particularly smelly portion of the city, where cattle hides were turned into leather. I hurried my steps and lifted my perfumed wrist to my nose.

Creon spoke again. "Father, if King Amphion *is* a usurper – not being of Kadmos' line – then why are you willing to offer your daughter to his son?"

"Creon, you ask too many questions," Father said.

"Besides, the gods will decide," I said. Then, curious, I asked: "Father, do you know exactly *how* the gods will make their decision?"

"You'll find out soon enough," Father said, which I took to mean that he knew but was not planning to tell me.

"But Father, if you know, don't you think you should tell Jocasta?" my brother persisted. "It might help her prepare."

Creon's persistence did not persuade our father. "There's nothing more she can do to prepare," he said decisively. "But, Jocasta, if the gods choose you," he continued, "you must do your utmost to be a *good* queen."

I gathered up my skirts to make sure they did not brush against a vat filled with urine to be used by the tanners. "What does that mean, Father?"

But Creon was the first to answer. "Making Thebes great; putting the city before yourself. Judging disputes fairly. Doing your duty even when you're tired, and don't feel like it."

This time, Father did not admonish Creon, and I was impressed by how much my brother had thought on the subject. I wondered how he – with the same lineage as mine – felt about my chance to help rule Thebes by marrying Prince Alphenor. Well, Amphion and Niobe and had many daughters; perhaps Creon would marry one of them.

"Father," I asked, "are Amphion and Niobe good rulers?" They had been king and queen my entire life; they were all that I knew.

"Neither is descended from Kadmos," was Father's predictable first response.

One could not help one's ancestry, I thought, stepping to the side to avoid treading on the tail of a dog sprawled before a leatherworking shop. I persevered, saying: "But in their actions? In what they do?"

Again, Creon answered. "King Amphion built the Temple of Apollo and the walls surrounding the city. And Queen Niobe has produced many children, and she has brought trade to Thebes with her festivals and her family connections."

"Amphion has never shirked his duties," Father conceded. "And they've kept us out of conflict, although sometimes at a price."

I wondered what price Father meant, but I did not ask, for we had finally reached the marketplace. The agora was always busy, with merchants displaying their wares and women shopping and weaving and gossiping, but today it was so full I could not even see the far side. As we made our way across the cobblestones I felt dizzied by the crowd's energy; once I stumbled on an uneven spot in the pavement, and Creon caught my elbow to steady me.

Many ceremonies were held outside in the agora, so that all Thebans could participate, but King Amphion had decided to hold today's event indoors. So we went to the agora's southwestern edge and walked up the palace stairs. The enormous cedar-wood doors were open, but on either side, next to the thick red-painted columns, stood guards with bronze-tipped spears. They nodded at my father and allowed us to enter. Father, usually undemonstrative, crooked his arm for my free hand and we passed inside. Creon walked behind me; our servants came after.

The megaron – the palace's throne room – was a large space with a great circular hearth at its center; above the hearth, windows in the chimney-tower admitted beams of bright sunlight. Even the corners of the room were lit today by oil flames burning atop tall bronze tripods. A small crowd had gathered already: primarily the better class of Thebans, but also a few visitors from other cities. The many children of Amphion and Niobe also helped fill the room. But my view was directed towards the thrones, towards the king and queen of Thebes.

A man of fifty-five, King Amphion wore his curling white hair gathered in a tail at the back of his neck. He was tall and fit, but deep wrinkles etched skin burned dark by the Theban sun while he supervised his many building projects. On a special table to his left rested his seven-stringed lyre.

Queen Niobe sat in an ivory-inlaid chair only slightly lower than the king's marble throne, drumming her fingers. She was about fifty, her stature short and her figure round; her skin was dusky, her hair thick and dark. I wondered if Thebes, with our farms and herds, seemed provincial to her: her brother, King Pelops of Pisa, was famous for his Olympic Games in the west, while her father King Tantalus ruled the wealthy kingdom of Lydia across the eastern sea.

I approached her and bowed low, then offered the narcissi.

A servant took my gift on the queen's behalf. "Jocasta, daughter of Menoeceus," Niobe acknowledged. Although she had a clear command of the tongue of Thebes, her accent proclaimed her eastern origin. She looked at me through narrowed eyes and then waved her hand. "Go sit with the others."

Feeling the gaze of everyone present, I crossed the tiled floor to take my place with the other young women: my rivals. I knew who they would be; Theban nobility was not so numerous. There were three others, all wearing their finest: Rhodia, a slim brown-haired girl and the daughter of Thebes' midwife; Pinelopi, of excellent family but very plain; and Melanthe, who always held herself a bit above the rest of us because her mother came from Aegypt, a faraway land famous for its abundant crops, skilled sorcerers, and enormous monuments.

My palms grew damp as I took my place at the far end of the semicircle of chairs. I sat beside Rhodia.

"Do you know what's going to happen?" I whispered.

"No," she whispered back. "I thought that *you* would know."

I tried to speak to Melanthe, but she pretended not to hear me, a smile playing on her lips. She gazed unabashedly at Prince Alphenor, as if she were confident that he would become *her* husband. Even though I had seen him many times before, especially when I came to the palace to weave with the princesses, I found myself studying him too. He stood on the far side of the hearth, talking and laughing with some of his many siblings – King Amphion and Queen Niobe boasted a total of fourteen children, seven sons and seven daughters. Prince Alphenor's younger brothers pointed at me and the three other young women, and snickered. Evidently, to them, the occasion was more amusing than serious.

I clenched my fist and sat straighter; the desire to win surged within me. Not because of Alphenor's bright smile and broad shoulders – suddenly, as though by the gods had instilled the desire inside me, I discovered I *wanted* to be queen of Thebes. I wanted to be a good queen, a great queen, who led her people in good times and bad.

This feeling gave me purpose, and I surveyed my competition with a calmer eye. True, I was younger than the rest; but that might not bother Niobe, with her foreign ways. The only girl who rivaled me in looks was Melanthe: she had emphasized her enormous dark eyes with kohl, and wore her thick black tresses in a thousand tiny gold-capped braids. I had only spoken with Melanthe a few times, but I knew she was ambitious – or seemed to be, with her air of Aegyptian superiority.

Surely Amphion and Niobe preferred a girl of pure Theban blood, to meld their line with the city's long heritage? A woman with impeccable ancestry, instead of this golden, exotic creature of foreign parentage?

But it was not up to them, nor even up to Prince Alphenor. It was up to the gods, my father had told me, and I still did not understand how the gods would choose among us.

"We are ready," said the king.

A hush fell as a tiny woman, her eyes bound with black linen, entered the room. Barely leaning on the bulky manservant who served as guide and protector, her firm strides seemed to deny her blindness. In her right hand she held a long cornel-wood staff; its taps on the tiled floor echoed in the silence. Her plain dark robe hung straight from shoulder to floor, without any of the ornamentation that embellished the clothing of every other person present. Her gray hair, bound by a single leather thong at the nape, hung lank down her back.

"The Tiresias!" whispered Rhodia.

"May Apollo choose me!" prayed Pinelopi.

"No, me!" said Rhodia, her eyes raised toward the beam of sunlight slanting in from above the central hearth.

So *this* was how the god would choose Prince Alphenor's wife. I thought it unseemly to bicker for the deity's favor, so I kept silent. I glanced at Melanthe; in her face I read scorn. Was she indifferent to Apollo and Athena? Did she prefer other gods? Her attitude annoyed me, and I returned my gaze to the prophetess.

She was called the Tiresias: a special prophet who served Apollo, Athena and Thebes through the generations, for whoever assumed the role gave up his or her own name and identity in order to serve the gods. But loss of one's name was a small sacrifice in comparison to the other requirement – the surrender of sight.

Each Tiresias was blind.

If not already blind, the newly chosen prophet's eyes were put out; the absence of the first sight was said to strengthen the second. It was supposed to be a great honor to serve the gods in this way – although there were whispers that once or twice in the city's history, the initiate had been less than willing.

The thought made the hairs on the back of my neck prickle: how could anyone make such a sacrifice?

The crowd fell silent and made way as the guide led the blind prophetess to the center of the room.

"Tiresias!" said the king. "You honor us with your presence."

My father had told me that although the Tiresias was from Thebes, she had spent little time here since Amphion assumed the throne. Of course, Father considered this evidence that Apollo was not pleased with Amphion's kingship.

The prophetess bowed slightly in Amphion's direction, acknowledging the comment but not bothering to reply.

"May we offer you refreshment? Wine? Figs? Syrian dates, perhaps?"

Finally the Tiresias spoke, and the room hushed to catch her words. "Amphion, I may not break my fast until I have performed the prophecies." Her casual way of addressing the king surprised me.

Amphion's shaggy eyebrows went up, but he seemed more amused than annoyed. Niobe's displeasure was evident in her curling lip and creased forehead. After all, her father, King Tantalus, claimed to be the son of mighty Zeus himself.

Amphion stretched out a calming hand to his wife and spoke again to the servant of both Apollo and Athena. "Very well, then, are you ready to begin? Should the maidens be brought to you?"

"Yes. Start with her," said Tiresias, and although she was blind and her eyes covered with cloth, she pointed her staff directly at the girl sitting furthest from me. A murmur ran through the crowd: was this coincidence, or did she truly "see"?

The guide left Tiresias in the center of the room, and went to fetch Pinelopi. Pinelopi was thin and pale, her teeth small and crooked; her makeup did not hide the blotches that marred her skin. To be sure, she was the descendant of a Sown Man, but did Prince Alphenor want her in his bed?

Pinelopi trembled as the guide brought her to the handmaiden of Apollo. All eyes were fixed on her, but the Tiresias appeared almost bored as the girl drew near.

"Kneel," ordered the prophetess.

Quaking, graceless, Pinelopi dropped to her knees. The golden spangles sewn into her many-layered skirts clanked against the floor.

The Tiresias reached out to touch the girl. She ran her spotted, gnarled hands over Pinelopi's face. We all waited breathlessly, transfixed, wondering what the seer would say. The blindfold obscured most of her face, but her mouth remained visible, demonstrating concentration as the colorless lips pursed, frowned, and finally positioned to speak.

17

"This creature is of no consequence," pronounced the Tiresias, dropping her hand and turning away.

The crowd gasped at the bluntness of this statement. Pinelopi's shoulders shook as if she had been struck; she stumbled when the guide pulled her to her feet and escorted her back to her seat. She pressed her lips together, as if trying to repress a sob.

How terrible, to be dismissed so thoroughly and publicly by the servant of the god!

Then a cold wind swirled through me: would Tiresias discard me so casually and completely?

No, I told myself. If the divination for me proved that indifferent, I would fight it. I would not lie down and be ignored.

Melanthe looked my way, one eyebrow raised; her full lips twisted into a sneer. Didn't she believe the prophecy? Or was she only mocking Pinelopi?

My musings ceased as the next candidate, Rhodia, knelt before the seer. The Tiresias stretched out her gnarled hands again, and on this occasion took more time.

Rhodia was also a descendant of the Spartoi, and her widowed mother was a priestess-midwife who served Artemis, the goddess of childbirth. Rhodia was short and stocky, but then so was Queen Niobe, With her bright eyes and chestnut curls, the midwife's daughter might be acceptable to the prince. But was she acceptable to the gods?

The Tiresias spoke:

She will serve her mother's mistress,
But a mother never be
She will help others bear children,
But her own babe never see.

Rhodia returned shaking to her chair, her face ashen. The prophetess had just declared she would never bear children! Not only would she not marry the prince, no man would now take her to wife.

I grasped the edge of my stool: what dreadful fate did the Tiresias have in store for me?

The guide came next for Melanthe. I leaned forward, more interested than ever; Melanthe was a more intriguing person than either Pinelopi or Rhodia. Those in the room seemed to agree, for all whispering stopped and people's very breathing sounded hushed.

Melanthe, her face proud, sank fluidly to her knees before the seer. She held her body straight, throwing off her short cape and holding back her shoulders so that King Amphion and Prince Alphenor could see her full, dark-tipped breasts to best advantage. I wilted a bit: how could I compare with this voluptuous creature? I glanced around the room and caught my brother's enraptured stare.

"Satyr," I muttered, feeling annoyed and betrayed.

But the Tiresias could not see Melanthe's rich dark locks, her kohl-rimmed eyes, or her luscious figure. She stretched out her right hand; her fingers slipped over Melanthe's face, and this time they lingered, as if there were more to be discovered from this maiden's features.

Then the Tiresias spoke:

Not of Theban woman born,
No seed of Theban man
This child of Aegypt rich in corn
Will rule Thebes if she can
Her words may wound and they may mend,
Her words a new day show
She could become the city's friend,
Or else a dreadful foe

As the servant of Apollo removed her hand, the crowd mumbled and shifted. The guide brought Melanthe back to our small group while all eyes stared.

"It's not true!" cried Melanthe's father.

"What's not true?" asked Pinelopi, her eyes dull and red with tears.

"The simplest interpretation of the Tiresias' comments is that I am not my father's daughter," said Melanthe. Her self-assurance surprised me, but when I took another look I saw that even she was perturbed by the seer's pronouncement. Although Melanthe's voice remained calm, her hands shook, and her golden skin looked a shade paler. I glanced over at her father, a sunburned man whose solid, thickset bulk was topped by a shock of sand-colored hair. Certainly she bore him no resemblance.

"*Are* you his daughter?" I whispered, wondering if she knew the truth.

"What does it matter now?" she asked, her voice sharp. "Whether I am or not, my reputation is tainted forever."

"But the rest of the prophecy," I said. "Are you to be queen?" The meaning of the verse had not been clear, but it certainly seemed that Melanthe would have power of some sort.

"Not likely," Melanthe said, her voice full of bitterness. "I wish I'd refused to come today."

If brave Melanthe regretted her prophecy, what would happen to me? I shifted in my seat, seeking escape. The crowd was still muttering about the Tiresias' last words; even Amphion and Niobe spoke to each other in low urgent tones. Everyone seemed distracted, and for a wild moment I thought: perhaps I could slip unnoticed through a side entrance?

"Silence!" said the seer, her voice awful. "The last remains. I must read *her* future." And with her staff she pointed directly at me.

There would be no reprieve. I rose as the guide approached me, and accompanied him to the center of the room.

The room hushed once more as I knelt before the blindfolded prophetess. I tried to keep my posture erect, to arrange my skirts gracefully and without noise. After all, I told myself, what was there to fear? My ancestry was impeccable.

Like Pinelopi – a creature of no consequence.

The dry, aged hands reached out to me. I closed my eyes and remained still. It was a strange sensation, having my face explored by a blind person. The touch seemed more intimate than being wrapped in Hydna's arms. And why shouldn't it be? The Tiresias was reading my very life: not only my past and my present, but my future.

No, I told myself. I did not want to have my fate read. I did not want to know. I wanted my life to be my own! I struggled to open my eyes but the seer's fingers held them closed, gently but firmly, inexorably.

Yes, I seemed to hear, echoing in my mind. I was not sure if the old woman had actually spoken. The voice seemed to belong to someone else.

Apollo? I wondered, but the voice did not come back.

Once more the prophetess began to speak, her voice low but measured, so that each person in the room could hear.

> *This head born to wear the crown,*
> *This breast to fill with love*
> *For husband of great renown*
> *From sea to sky above*
> *Many children shall she bear,*
> *And claim them in her heart*
> *Whom fate makes the royal pair*
> *Can no man set apart*

The words were uttered slowly; I could not mistake them. But I could barely believe my ears. After the other prophecies, I had not expected anything favorable.

The Tiresias' hands left my face, and I opened my eyes. Melanthe was forgotten; the people gazed only at me. I felt elated, buoyed by the seer's words.

I caught my father's glance. He was smiling again; for him this was a great day. My brother's joy was even more obvious: he laughed in delight.

Then Niobe spoke, her voice dry and sarcastic. "It appears we have found the next queen of Thebes."

CHAPTER TWO

The guide led the Tiresias away. All eyes remained fixed on me.

As the murmuring swelled I looked around, uncertain what to do next. The ladies whispered together behind bejeweled fingers; the men folded arms across their chests and regarded me appraisingly. I expected someone to come guide me, but the Tiresias' manservant was gone, and no one else moved forward. After a moment I rose shakily to my feet and half-stumbled back to my seat.

Pinelopi watched me enviously through her tears; Rhodia's face showed confusion, and Melanthe shot me a look of cold hatred. But I was too stunned to be concerned with their reactions. Could it be true that I would rank above my father and my brother, and bring glory to our family in my own right? Was this all some massive misunderstanding, or would I really be queen of Thebes one day?

But Thebes already had a queen, and she was not ready to relinquish her position just yet. At first I tried to avoid Queen Niobe's unblinking gaze, but there was a fascination to it, and I could not help but look back.

She waited until the crowd's buzzing died down before she spoke. "Come here, Jocasta."

I rose again and crossed the floor to stand before her inlaid throne.

"Kneel," she told me.

I sank back down to the floor gratefully; my legs were unsteady. The stuccoed surface beneath the flounces of my skirts was cold and hard but nonetheless reassuring, for I knew it was real, solid. Not like the words of prophecy that hung like mist in the air.

Pressing her small, plump hands against the arms of her throne Niobe rose, and stepped closer to me; her sandalwood perfume tickled my nostrils. Her flaxen skirt rustled as she circled round me, inspecting me with as much care as if she were a farmer trading for an ox. I half expected her to open my mouth to check my teeth. What if she did not approve of me? Would she go against the Tiresias? But Niobe said nothing until she had returned to her seat.

"What do you think, Husband?"

Amphion smiled indulgently. "My dear, if *you* have no objections..." he let his sentence trail off.

"Alphenor?"

I looked up at the man who would be my husband. Prince Alphenor was tall, with a fine square chin shaved clean and smooth; a wide leather belt circled his narrow waist, and his short kilt showed strong legs to good advantage. His one fault was his hair, which held its curl poorly; but it rested on strong brown shoulders that my slender brother no doubt envied.

Looking up at the prince, my heart beat more quickly – but out of nerves, not because I felt any affection or desire for him.

It surprised me that what I felt was – nothing.

After what the Tiresias had said, how could this meeting arouse no emotion in me? How could the prophecy be right, when the sight of my husband-to-be evoked nothing but emptiness?

But Prince Alphenor appeared pleased by what he saw – rather than disappointed, as he might have been, that the Tiresias had not selected the golden-skinned Melanthe. He smiled – a warm, friendly, encouraging smile – and reached out his hand to me. I took it and let him pull me to my feet. "She is quite acceptable," said the prince, amusement in his tone.

He approved of me, he seemed kind; surely these were good attributes in a husband. Yet still I felt nothing. His touch was warm but otherwise unremarkable. He squeezed my fingers lightly, and released my hand.

I must be dazed, still, from the prophecy – that had to explain my utter lack of interest. I felt as if I floated in a void, removed to some great distance.

King Amphion smiled, his craggy features a weathered version of his son's. "Acceptable indeed! We must celebrate – let there be music!"

The king's musical ability inspired legends; some claimed that his melodies had charmed the stones of the city walls into place. He picked up his lyre and sang the first clear note; then some of his children added their fine voices in harmony. The music was beautiful, and for a moment I could almost forget how utterly my life had changed. But then the song was done. The king set aside his instrument and signaled for food to be brought in. A pair of flute-girls began to play, but now the rest of us could talk and move about freely.

My father came forward and laid a hand on my shoulder. "The gods have smiled upon you, my daughter. A magnificent prophecy!"

Prince Alphenor grinned, his white teeth contrasting with his tanned skin. "Her husband will become one of Thebes' most famous kings; she will love him, and bear him many children. What more could a man ask of a wife?"

"Breeding and beauty," said King Amphion, stepping over to join his eldest son and my father. He waved his hand in my direction. "Qualities your daughter has in abundance, Menoeceus."

Father nodded. "I'm proud of you, Daughter."

I had long wanted my father's approval – but now it seemed empty. What had *I* done to deserve it? Nothing. The praise felt hollow, unmerited.

While Father spoke with the prince and the king, I was approached by several of the princesses. Two of them were twins just my age; they exclaimed over the idea that *I* would soon be living in the palace, while they were betrothed to royalty in other cities and would soon move far away. Then they began giving me advice about their brother. But before they could do more than tell me that Alphenor's favorite dish was boar simmered with mushrooms and wine, a small strong hand closed around my wrist.

"Come with me," said Niobe, pulling me away from her daughters.

The queen led me to a much smaller but more sumptuously furnished room. It, too, had a round hearth in the middle, and rays of sunlight streamed through from above. Servants stood in shadowed corners, awaiting the queen's command. The walls were painted with scenes of a garden, elegant ladies wandering among the flowers and trees. Just below the ceiling and directly above the floor the walls were edged with intertwined spirals of blue and white: symbols of eternity.

Niobe reclined on a thickly padded couch, and indicated that I should sit down on another. "So, you are to be queen of Thebes," she said. Her eyes narrowed, glinting like two sharp daggers. Of course, I could only be queen of Thebes if she were queen no longer.

"The prophecy may not be fulfilled for years," I said.

"Prophecy!" she exclaimed, with a noise that could be best described as a snort. "What is prophecy? A few random words uttered by a blind beggar who claims divine inspiration."

I had heard of Niobe's arrogance, but never before witnessed it. I blinked, dumbfounded to hear even the queen speak so of the Tiresias.

"Prophecy is not achievement," Niobe continued, shutting her eyes a moment and rubbing her temples. "If you become queen, you can't rely on prophecy. It may taste sweet as honey now, but it can quickly sour."

Why did she sound bitter, I wondered, when the gods obviously favored her so richly?

"Think of what she said to those other young women!"

I felt guilty. Pinelopi and Rhodia had to be devastated by what had been said to them. Even Melanthe had been shaken. The gods seemed cruel and arbitrary, blessing me while harming them. And Niobe, despite her reputation for contempt, showed more sympathy than I.

I felt confused and uncomfortable.

The queen waved her hand at a serving girl, then turned back to me. "Do you really think it was genuine prophecy? Or did your father bribe the Tiresias to say those words?"

"*Bribe* the Tiresias?"

A serving girl offered a tray of refreshments to the queen. Niobe reached for a cup of wine; the goblet was gold, chased round with scenes of the Kretan bull dance, and finer than anything my father owned. Niobe barely glanced at it.

"You are young and innocent," she said, and took a sip of wine. "Sweet qualities, in their way. And I suppose your father did not tell you how he bribed the seer, so that you would play your part better." She looked at me, laughing at my confusion. "Come, my dear, if you plan to be queen you must think of these things. Of *course* seers can be bribed."

The extent of her blasphemy appeared to know no bounds. Forgetting that I addressed the queen of Thebes, I exclaimed, "But the Tiresias is the voice of Apollo!"

"She has managed to fool the people of Hellas into thinking that, at least."

"But – how did she do those things? She pointed at us each in turn. I could *feel* her looking at me!"

Niobe looked at me with pity and scorn. "Such things can be arranged. Her manservant could have positioned her in such a way as to make it easy. The Tiresias may have sharp hearing. Or perhaps she's not really blind!"

The Tiresias not blind? But as long as I could remember I had heard how the blinding was done; as children we whispered the gory tale. It was said that this Tiresias, to show her devotion, had wielded the knife with her own hand. How could the ceremony have been a sham? My stomach lurching, I shook my head at the tray of refreshments offered by Queen Niobe's serving girl.

"Bring the Tiresias here," Niobe told another servant. "I want to speak to her." The queen drank her wine and nibbled on stuffed dates, saying nothing more until the seer arrived, this time without her guide beside her.

In this room the Tiresias seemed less like a powerful servant of Apollo and more like a blind beggar. I wondered why – and then realized that the audience was no longer a hushed, respectful crowd but instead Queen Niobe, exuding scorn and skepticism. And crimson pomegranate juice stained the Tiresias' lips: the seer had broken her fast, yielding to her mortal nature.

"Ah, Tiresias," said the queen, leaning back among her jewel-colored cushions. "I've brought you here to answer a few questions. I want to educate this young woman."

"The trance is finished," said the seer. "I am not prepared to answer questions about the future."

"I have no questions about the future just now – what I want are answers about the past. *Without* the rhymes and riddles."

I watched the Tiresias' mouth twist in displeasure at the queen's tone, but still she inclined her head, signaling willingness to listen.

"Did Menoeceus offer you gifts so that you would give his daughter the best foretelling?"

The seer nodded. "His gift was generous. A rhyton made from an ostrich egg, its handles carved with Zeus and a cow dancing – very fine to the touch."

I gasped, doubly shocked that my father would try to influence the prophecy and that he would use the ostrich-egg rhyton to do it. It had belonged to my mother's family, and should have been given to me or my brother one day. The cow represented Io, one of her most important ancestors; the vessel had been in my mother's family since the dawn of time.

The Tiresias turned her blindfolded face in my direction.

"This is Jocasta – the one you pronounced the future queen of Thebes," Niobe said. "I thought you might dispel her illusions regarding prophecy."

The Tiresias spoke to me. "It is customary to offer gifts to the god," she explained. "Apollo must be honored. And without the gifts, how could I live to speak his words?"

The prophet's words seemed reasonable, I thought, and of course every mortal who petitioned a god brought an offering. Niobe was peculiar to criticize the process – yet she had a point. The gifts *were* a sort of bribe.

"But don't those gifts influence your words?" asked Niobe. "Was Menoeceus' offering the best?"

"Best is a word of judgment. I do not judge – Apollo does that."

I stared at the two women. The Tiresias' calm answers amazed me, as did Niobe's persistence in questioning her.

"Then I'll judge for myself. What did the fathers of the other girls give you? Most offerings to gods are presented in public; why shouldn't yours be as well?"

The gray-haired woman shrugged. "A large jar of olive oil, a gold signet ring carved with twined snakes, and a healthy nanny goat."

The queen of Thebes turned to me. "You see, Jocasta, the future can be bought – as can many things."

"Apollo's favor cannot be purchased," said the Tiresias.

"Not Apollo's favor, perhaps, but certainly the favor of his servant. The rhyton was the most valuable of the gifts. And you did not have to ruin those other girls' lives!"

"Not every young woman can be queen. And the prophecies I spoke should make it clear that Apollo's favor was not for sale."

The Tiresias had cold logic on her side, but Niobe seemed more merciful. Mercy was not a quality that I would have ever associated before with the foreign-born queen, but perhaps rulers had to be fierce to protect those who could not defend themselves.

Niobe continued to challenge the prophetess. "Why should we listen to Apollo? What has Apollo done for Thebes?"

"Apollo is the protector of Thebes," the Tiresias replied.

"*Amphion* is the true protector of Thebes! He cobbled the streets and widened the agora, and built our walls with their seven strong gates. It is *my husband* we should be grateful for, not some remote god who never shows his face!"

"You tread dangerous ground," said the prophetess.

"Who should I fear?" asked Niobe. "Why should we honor those who do nothing for us? Amphion has made Thebes what it is, I tell you – *he* is the greatest king this city has ever known! And despite what you once said of me, *I* am its greatest queen: the mother of Thebes. Fourteen children, all living – your precious Leto has only two! Who should Thebes honor more?"

Even I, young as I was then, knew that Niobe had gone too far. The Tiresias drew herself erect and pointed at Niobe with her wooden staff. "You have insulted me, my god, and now his holy mother! You will know nothing but sorrow for the rest of your life!"

"I thought your trance was finished!" Niobe retorted.

"I speak as the god directs:

Niobe, great queen, your hubris offends.
Apollo has seen; his vengeance he sends.
His mother you mock, his might you defame;
He will hunt down your flock and ruin your name."

With a strangled cry, the queen threw her cup at the Tiresias. Her aim proved false, and the cup clattered to the floor, but dark wine lees splashed across the seer's robes and pooled on the floor like blood.

"Get her out of here!" Niobe ordered, dark with rage. Her attendants hurried the seer away.

Silent, shocked, I stared at the queen. Was she only angry, or did she feel any fear? The wrath in the verses was unmistakable.

"You will not speak of what you have heard," the queen commanded, first to me, and then to the servants in their places around the room. She glanced around at all of those present, her eyes blazing. "Do you understand?"

Then she spared me a few more words. "So, you think you want to be queen? As queen you must deal with insults, ingratitude, and enemies who would thrust you from your throne to take your place. Are you my enemy, too, Jocasta?"

It was the first time she had asked for my opinion. Despite my racing heart, I managed to speak calmly. "No, Queen Niobe, I'm not your enemy."

My words seemed to touch her. I wondered why: given her self-confidence, her arrogance, her willingness to taunt even the gods, how could this woman want reassurance from someone like me? But still, as she herself had said of the Tiresias, Niobe was mortal. The daughter of the great King Tantalus, she had ruled our city for many years – but Niobe was also a woman. I looked at the queen and wondered what had given her power for so long. Was it simply because she took the lead, and others were grateful to follow?

For a moment she looked at me uncertainly, suspiciously – and then her shoulders relaxed. Suddenly her face looked lined and haggard, older than her fifty years. She rubbed her temples again, and I wondered if she had a headache – and what it must be like to bear the burden of ruling even when one was tired or ill.

"Perhaps not," she finally said. "Jocasta, you have my permission to wed my son Alphenor – if that's still what you want, now that you know a little of what it means to be a queen. Consider it carefully. You may go."

"Thank you, my lady queen." I rose, bowed, and departed. The servant standing by the queen's door led me out towards the main hall.

Motion and noise filled the megaron; the guests chatted and laughed, drinking wine from silver cups and taking food from the trays carried by servants. As I passed each little knot of people, they paused in their conversation to watch me walk by, as if they wanted me to join them.

But I was tired and my stomach hurt; I could not deal with the stares, the murmurs, the curious faces. The queen's heretical words and the Tiresias' angry prophecy warred in my head. I wanted to leave this place, to go home and retreat to my own quiet room, but first I had to seek my father. I soon found him, still in Alphenor's company.

"There she is!" the prince exclaimed, his hands outstretched. "Your daughter: my wife-to-be."

I accepted his hands and let him draw me close. He smelled of rosemary oil.

My father beamed. "I've come to an agreement with King Amphion and Prince Alphenor. You will wed in five days."

"Five days!" I gasped. It was all so quick.

"Yes, my dear." Alphenor bent his head and set his lips to mine. I thought my father might object, but he did not. After all, this was the crown prince of Thebes and my betrothed.

The kiss was my first, and I was not sure how I liked it. Alphenor's lips were warm, and tasted of mulled wine; his face scratched against my cheek.

I still felt nothing for this man save a vestige of fear, stemming from the words I had just heard from the Tiresias.

Alphenor released me and took my hand, which felt small and lost in his. "Shall we join the festivities, my dear? They're just setting out the feast – and we have the most wonderful delicacies, all the way from Korinth and Pisa."

"My lord prince, I'd prefer to go home."

This did not please my father. "Jocasta, a woman should abide her husband's wishes."

But Alphenor intervened on my behalf. "No, let her go home and rest. Let her be a young maiden for the next few days – great changes lie before her." He looked down at me with understanding. "I will visit you at your father's house tomorrow."

The prince's kindness was a blessing. Surely he would be a good husband.

"Thank you," I whispered.

They were the last words I ever said to him.

Father rounded up our retainers while Creon scolded me for making him miss the best part of the feast. He had grabbed a piece of grilled bread spread with octopus-paste and studded with olives. He bit into it, then offered it to me. I accepted it but one of the palace dogs jumped up, snatched the bread out of my hand and ran off with it. Creon was seriously displeased, but the bread was gone; fortunately Father's return prevented my brother from scolding me.

My father and brother were both annoyed with me for choosing to leave the palace so early – the sun still shone brightly as we walked down toward the Eudoxa Gate. Yet their happiness overcame their irritation. My father repeated the prophecy of the Tiresias, word for word. "The gods are smiling on our family."

Was this really true? The Tiresias' other prophecies had all been so terrible that I had trouble trusting mine. And what of the Tiresias' words to Niobe? These questions troubled me on the long descent home.

When we reached the house, Hydna was waiting for us. At first she was concerned by our early return, but my brother's grin reassured her; then she shrieked and embraced me.

"Calm down, Hydna," said Father, but his eyes twinkled. "Merope, bring my daughter some food; she's eaten nothing."

"Didn't I tell you? Didn't I tell you?" Hydna whispered triumphantly, as we walked down the shadowed hallway towards the sitting room. Finding me tongue-tied, she pumped Creon for details.

My head pounded; I rubbed futilely at my temples. Was I about to be married, or was something terrible about to happen? Would the two merge together somehow? Was my betrothal a blessing or a curse? I did not know. And I could not seek guidance from my brother, my father, even Hydna – I had been forbidden to speak of what had happened.

So I sat silently, watching the linen window-curtains stir in the breeze, while people talked around me. Most of the conversation focused on the preparations for the wedding to take place in five short days. What should I wear? What sort of music would there be? What perfume would be best for my wedding night? My father picked up a wax tablet and stylus, and made notes of the many things that needed to be done and decided.

"Is he handsome?" Hydna asked. My nurse was near-sighted, and had not had a good look at Prince Alphenor in years.

"He's coming here tomorrow," said Father. "Judge for yourself then."

I wished to speak with Creon alone. I wanted to find out what he thought of the proceedings, what impressions he had of the Tiresias and her prophecies, and more of his thoughts about the responsibilities of a queen. But Creon retired before I did, saying he did not feel well.

I went to bed myself, finally taking off the stiff jacket and the heavy skirts. I breathed more easily once I was in my nightshift, but still I worried. I wondered whether Niobe was right, and the gods could be bought – or whether the queen's words were blasphemy, as my father would no doubt have said. And what about Pinelopi, Rhodia, and Melanthe – were they tossing and turning tonight? I decided to visit each of them during the next few days – that is, if they would see me. I was sure that Pinelopi and Rhodia would welcome me, but Melanthe might be too angry.

Then I heard the distant call of an owl, preparing for its nocturnal hunt. The owl was the bird of Athena, goddess of wisdom; perhaps she was telling me that my decision to visit the other girls was wise. That thought was comforting. But Athena was also a warrior, and her owl carried death in its talons: my worries spun free once more.

Somehow I managed to fall asleep, and the next morning my headache was gone. After a night's rest, I felt better able to handle what yesterday had brought. Prince Alphenor was good-looking and seemed kind. Perhaps the life of a queen was not an easy one – but whose life was easy? And I would not be queen for years, but merely a daughter-in-law in the palace. Queen Niobe and King Amphion would teach me what I needed to know.

"Good morning, Hydna," I said, as my nurse entered the room.

"Jocasta! How are you?"

Her question was more than the usual inquiry. Her searching eyes and the edge to her voice demonstrated genuine concern.

"Fine," I answered, sitting up. "Why?"

"Your brother's ill – he's been sick half the night."

"What's wrong?"

"We don't know," she said. "He was fine yesterday – but now he keeps nothing down. Nothing! And his forehead's hot as a brazier—"

"Has a healer come?"

"No! We sent to the Temple of Apollo, but all the healers were gone." Hydna shook her head. "We live so close to the temple, and your father has always served the god faithfully – you'd think they could send us a healer!"

I stood up and started towards my brother's room. "I must see him."

I found Creon lying listlessly on his side. He opened an eye, groaned, and then promptly lowered the eyelid again.

I sat next to him and took his hand. It was burning hot. He seemed to have grown thinner overnight, and his skin felt as dry as a clay tablet. Vomit stank in the chamber pot, and he had stained the linens.

"Are you thirsty?" I asked.

He was too weak to nod, but he squeezed my hand in response. I told Merope to bring some wine and water.

Hydna protested angrily, whispering so that Creon would not hear. "No, little one! He cannot take it – he's too weak."

"If he doesn't eat or drink he'll grow weaker," I argued, imitating some of Niobe's imperiousness from the day before. "See how dry his skin is?"

She frowned, but allowed it. When Merope returned I took the tray from her and carried it myself. I mixed five parts of water to one of wine, then knelt by the bed, holding a flask to my brother's lips. Much of the pale liquid ran across his face and down into the bedclothes, but some seemed to go in. I waited, hoping that it would stay down. After a moment I whispered a prayer to Apollo, then gave Creon another sip. When he had drunk all he could – and it was not much – I dipped the napkin in cool water and wiped his face clean.

"Jocasta," he sighed, almost inaudibly.

"I'm here," I whispered.

I was still tending him when my father found me.

"Come out of there, Jocasta," he said.

"Creon needs me."

"Prince Alphenor said he would call on you today, and you're not dressed." He stepped in and looked at Creon. "I've said prayers for him, and Merope will care for him."

I made Merope promise to do what I had been doing, and then underwent an abbreviated version of the previous day's ablutions. Hydna dressed me, fortunately not pulling the laces quite as tight as yesterday, and did my hair. "Now you look ready to meet your prince," she declared.

There was no question of my going to visit Pinelopi, Rhodia, or Melanthe; with the morning half gone, Prince Alphenor might arrive at any moment – and I dared not leave my brother. I sat on a couch in the dining room, wondering about my future life in the palace and worrying about Creon. Occasionally I ventured into his room; Merope was with him, but he fared neither better nor worse. Father made frequent visits to the household shrine to offer prayers for Creon's recovery.

I waited and waited. Finally, seeking something to occupy myself, I retrieved my spindle and distaff and went into the courtyard. I sat on a bench under the laurel tree that my father planted to honor Apollo. Hydna had muttered at the time that a fig tree would be more useful, but my father had insisted on laurel. Now the scent of the foliage calmed me.

I threw the spindle over and over, gradually turning the saffron-dyed wool into a skein of thread to be woven into cloth. The task of spinning occupied my hands, but still my thoughts intruded. Where was Alphenor? Did he mean to transform my nervousness into longing by drawing out the wait? As the sun passed its zenith and made its way toward the west I wondered if the prince had lost interest in me. Perhaps the Tiresias had been bribed to change her prophecies and now Rhodia would be the next queen of Thebes. Or maybe the king decided I was not good enough after all to wed his son – but how could that be, when I was a daughter of the Spartoi and probably descended from Kadmos himself? I waved away a fly and threw the spindle again, watching it drop spinning towards my sandaled feet. When the thread grew long I looped it into the skein; from time to time I set my tools aside and stretched my arms and back. I went to see Creon again, but Hydna quickly shooed me out, fearing that the smell of his sickness would cling to me.

About mid-afternoon my father joined me in the courtyard, busying himself with honing and polishing his boar-spears. He uttered no complaints, feigning patience, pretending that this was an ordinary day. But he glanced often at the lowering sun, and knit his eyebrows together as he ran an oiled cloth along the spear-shaft. Normally he would have left such a task to servants; unlike most Theban men, Father was not fond of hunting. Each time he finished tending a spear he went to check on Creon and say another prayer.

"Your brother's condition is unchanged," he told me, after my latest inquiry.

I put down the distaff, which I had been dressing with more wool. "I wish he would simply come!" I exclaimed, rising to my feet and stretching.

Father frowned at my show of impatience, but before he could say anything, a knock sounded at the outer door. After a moment a servant announced that a messenger had arrived from the palace.

Why a messenger, and not Prince Alphenor himself? Father and I exchanged a glance, and he put his boar-spear aside. "Show him in."

The messenger was Pelorus, a noble Theban of about twenty-five and one of King Amphion's most trusted men. Father and I rose to our feet as he entered our courtyard.

"Well? Will the prince at last come to see his betrothed?" My father said these words lightly, before Pelorus moved out of the shadows and we saw the dreadful expression on his face.

"My lord Menoeceus," said Pelorus, "Prince Alphenor is dead."

CHAPTER THREE

I swayed, and even Father gaped with shock. Finally I asked: "Dead! How is that possible?"

Pelorus sank down onto the wooden bench beneath the pergola. His face, usually clean-shaven, was darkened by a day's growth; the afternoon's light showed dark circles beneath his eyes. "*All* of the royal princes and princesses are either dead or dying."

"All of them!" Father exclaimed. "What's happened?"

"Shortly after you left, Prince Damasichthon collapsed. And then little Phthia, the youngest, began coughing up blood; she was the first to die, almost before anyone could move. Princess Neaira was next."

Hearing these words, my knees gave way, and I sank back down on my seat by the laurel tree.

"A maidservant cried out that the gods were punishing Thebes for Queen Niobe's impiety, that the queen had insulted Leto and her children. The guests panicked and ran. At first King Amphion wouldn't let them leave: he thought someone was trying to kill his family. He ordered his soldiers to strike down anyone who approached the doors."

"Understandable," said my father, "and yet..." He trailed off without finishing the thought. This was the first time I ever saw Father look confused; I had never known him to be at a loss for words.

"Tell us more," I urged.

"Prince Alphenor came to his mother's defense, praising her as a clever woman and protector of Thebes. He said she would never insult the gods. But before he finished speaking he doubled up in pain and began to retch." Pelorus drew a deep breath. "People are saying this plague is a sign of Apollo's displeasure."

Father nodded solemnly. "That could well be."

"The king and queen are beside themselves with grief," said the young man. "No one else will care for the dying, and the bodies of the dead lie untended."

"What?" I gasped.

"The servants believe it's bad luck to touch them – that they would be cursed by Apollo as well."

I imagined the dead, strewn about the megaron, unable to make their journey to the Underworld. Even worse – the others suffering with no one to help them. "That's appalling," I whispered.

"We must not incur the wrath of Apollo," my father said.

"But the ill must be cared for! And bodies can't simply be left to rot!"

I had never contradicted my father so boldly; his face reddened in irritation. But just then a servant appeared with a tray of refreshments. Father offered Pelorus a cup of wine.

Challenging my father made me uncomfortable and nervous, but our duty was clear. My sense of resolution grew, and I spoke again: "We should go to the palace."

"That's exactly what the king sent me to ask of you," said Pelorus. "For you to come to the palace, and to give such support as you can."

"But that would be to go against the will of Apollo!" my father objected.

"How can we know Apollo's will, except by the things he has told us?" I was astonished at my own audacity, but once I began speaking I felt compelled to go on. "Yesterday he selected me to be the next queen of Thebes. Well, the queen of Thebes must live in the palace, and whether we go there to support Amphion and Niobe or to banish them from Thebes as blasphemers, that's where we should go."

Once the words had fallen from my lips I felt a surge of confidence; I could see that my words had influenced my listeners.

I remembered Niobe's imperial manner, and realized that words spoken with authority had great effect.

Then another thought struck me. "Creon!" I said aloud. "He must be suffering from the same curse!"

Father shook his head. "The Tiresias spoke of a plague upon Amphion's house."

"Yes, my lord," said Pelorus, "but others have been afflicted too. Pinelopi, presented to the Tiresias before your daughter, also collapsed." His voice trembled, and I remembered that Pinelopi was his cousin. "Some are saying that the curse is spreading beyond the royal family to the citizens of Thebes, as punishment for tolerating these rulers so long."

I thought with pity of the pasty-faced girl. "Is Pinelopi dead?"

Pelorus nodded.

I recalled Tiresias' words – *this creature is of no consequence* – and shivered. Poor Pinelopi!

Bright Apollo, lord of healing, I prayed silently, *spare my brother Creon!*

"Have any recovered?" I asked.

"None that I know of. But when I left the palace, neither Amphion nor Niobe had fallen ill. Princess Chloris looked pale, but she showed no other symptoms."

"My son," Father said quietly. "Creon has never respected the gods as he should. I've rebuked him for this many times. But he is descended from the Sown Men, and yet young – I'll ask Apollo for mercy." He stood. "Then, after I have made my prayers, we'll go to the palace."

My father indicated that the messenger should rest in the courtyard, and then he left for the household shrine. I excused myself as well, deciding to visit my brother again.

Creon lay sweating on his narrow cot, a wet cloth draped across his forehead. His face was drawn and waxy, and there were purple bruises beneath his eyes; yet his thin chest still rose and fell.

Merope sat on a stool beside him, worry carving two deep lines on her normally placid brow.

"Is he any better?" I asked her, looking down at Creon's ashen face and listening to his troubled breathing.

"He seems the same to me, my lady, but I've been here all day. Perhaps you'll notice a difference more easily."

I knelt by the bed and lay my hand on his cheek. Still over-warm to the touch, but was he less fevered than before? Or, goaded by hope, did I merely imagine it? Yet he still lived. My instructions to Merope had at least done him no harm.

"Stay with him," I told her. I was terrified that he might die while we went to the palace, but I knew we had to go. I whispered a prayer to Apollo, begging for my brother's life, and then went to rejoin my father.

Pelorus had brought curtained litters to carry us to the palace, each borne by four of Niobe's well-muscled slaves and guarded by another four men: soldiers with tall hide-covered shields, their gleaming bronze swords drawn and ready. Two more guards, armed with spears, stood at Pelorus' side.

"We don't need these," said my father, gesturing at the litters. He had kept his frame lean by avoiding such luxuries. "My daughter and I are strong and healthy – we can walk."

"But the king wishes to show his favor," said Pelorus. "Besides, the streets are not safe. This is for your own protection."

"I think we should, Father," I said. I suspected another reason, but I did not offer it just then.

My father gave me a vexed look, showing that he thought me impertinent, or perhaps that the prophecy had gone to my head, but he agreed. We each climbed into a litter and the slaves picked up the poles.

Although I could see no one, I could hear many: some wept for those who had died, others calling out prayers for those who still lived. There was a stink in the air, too, as if doorsteps had not been swept, chamber pots not emptied; the city reeked of illness and death. I wrinkled my nose, and drew the curtains of the litter to shut out the odor.

As we approached the agora I heard new voices. These people were tense, desperate, and most of all, angry. As the swaying litter drew closer I distinguished their words:

"I beg you, Apollo, spare my child!" shrieked one woman.

"Forgive us, children of Leto!" screamed another.

"A sacrifice!"

"We must make a sacrifice!"

"Repentance! Atonement! Sacrifice!"

From the calls it sounded as if the people had decided that Thebes must make a sacrifice to the gods.

Sacrifice usually meant slitting an animal's throat, then burning its bones and fat on an altar. One could also offer a libation of oil or wine, or a gift of precious gold. But, though I had never witnessed it in my short life, in times of great peril, the gods – or at least their followers – demanded royal blood. When the gods were most angry, only the life of the king appeased them.

A chill traveled down my back.

I remembered the history of King Pentheus, torn apart by the Maenad women in the agora.

Through my mother I was descended from Kadmos himself. Our branch of the family had never ruled, but my blood could be considered royal. Was that why Amphion had summoned us: to offer me to the hungry crowd?

Fear seized me. I began opening the curtains, ready to call out to my father and the guards that we should turn around and go back. But when I peered through the crack I saw it was too late. Before us stood an angry mob, faces dark with rage against the blood-red sky.

"Who goes there?" asked a tall, heavily muscled man.

I recognized him as the quarry master, who directed the chiseling and transport of stones. I had watched him work,

43

impressed by the way he used rope and levers and human muscle to help turn the king's ambitious visions into reality. Now, surrounded by some of his fellow stoneworkers, he seemed ready to use his famous strength for destruction.

I had lost my courage, but Amphion's messenger had not: Pelorus stood his ground. "We escort the noble Menoeceus and his daughter Jocasta. You know they are loyal servants of Apollo and devoted to Thebes."

I felt a wash of gratitude for my father's reputation for unswerving piety.

"True!" called a woman.

There were other shouts of agreement, but then a voice of doubt rang out. "How do we know that they really are Menoeceus and Jocasta? Anyone could be behind those curtains!"

"They could be Amphion and Niobe!"

"Pull back the curtains!"

"Show yourselves!"

I reluctantly opened the curtain of my litter and saw that my father had done the same.

"Good citizens of Thebes," Father called out, "as you can see, we are *not* Amphion and Niobe. And you know that my family serves Apollo faithfully."

There was a muttering of confused agreement from the people in the crowd. They seemed thirsty for blood, but we were not their prey. Besides, men carrying shields, swords and spears surrounded us.

"But why are you going to the palace?" asked someone, and this question was repeated in various forms.

"Hear me!" my father shouted, repeatedly, until the crowd was sufficiently quiet. Then he addressed the people again. "If you heard the prophecy of the Tiresias, you know that my daughter is to be the next queen of Thebes. How dare you threaten her? And where should she be if not at the palace?"

I was surprised, even flattered, that he chose to use my own arguments, and that he could utter my ideas with conviction.

Pelorus, his voice commanding, spoke again. "Citizens, let us through, or we'll fight our way through, and the blood offered to Apollo will be your own."

Bronze swords and spear-tips glinted in the slanting rays of the setting sun, as the king's soldiers pointed their weapons toward the crowd. That decided the people; they fell back and let us pass. Our bearers carried us up the palace stairs, and the guards opened the great wooden doors to allow us entry, then shut them heavily behind us.

The slaves put down our litters and helped us climb out. The soldiers took their places: some went outside to join the watch before the doors while others stayed within, ready to attack should the mob break through.

Pelorus ushered us immediately into the megaron, where the sour-sweet stench of illness and death washed over us. Though he had told us that many of the palace servants fled, still it shocked me to see crusting pools of vomit and red-brown splashes of drying blood on the painted stucco floor. I coughed and swallowed, trying to keep from retching.

King Amphion stood beside the huge circular hearth. In the space of a day he seemed to have aged years: his hair was lank, his face lined with grief. His hands – hands which had played so much music and built so much of Thebes – trembled. Although he wore the same fine clothes as he had the previous night, they were now wrinkled and dirty, stained with the blood and vomit of his children.

The bodies of the dead, from tall Alphenor to little Phthia, had been arranged in a row with evident care and tenderness. The twin princesses lay with their pale arms around each other – now they would never be separated. Flies buzzed in circles over their motionless corpses.

"Thank you for coming," Amphion said. "I feared you wouldn't." His bearing was still erect, and although his voice was full of exhaustion and despair, he spoke calmly. Admiration filled me: anyone else would have been driven mad, but Amphion showed the stuff of true kings.

"I obey the summons of the king," my father said politely, even though he was no partisan of Amphion.

"You still call me that? I thank you, Menoeceus, although my reign is at its end."

"Perhaps this is only a setback," I said. "Like Kadmos when the serpent turned on him and he thought he would be killed."

My father frowned; he disliked my comparing Amphion to the great Kadmos. But Amphion looked at me strangely, as if he were noticing me for the first time since my arrival. A trace of tenderness broke through his hard mask of grief. "Jocasta, you're a sweet child, to think of such a thing – and a brave one, to come to us in this terrible time. You would have made a lovely daughter-in-law, but I have no son left to offer you." He paused, tears shining in his gray eyes. "Soon I will go before the people of Thebes to abdicate the throne. I only have one request – which is why I asked you here."

"To bury the dead?" asked my father. The dead had to be given a proper burial, or their souls could wander forever. Funeral rites were necessary to make sure they went to the Underworld. Even those cursed by the gods were buried, if only to make sure that their ghosts did not remain to make mischief for the living.

"That, of course, but Niobe and Chloris are my first concern. Take my wife and daughter with you. Smuggle them out of the palace in the litters, and then get them safely away from Thebes."

My father stared at Amphion. "If Apollo wants your family to die, then we should not interfere with his will."

"Father!" I cried. "You swore an oath of loyalty to King Amphion."

"And the gods outrank mortal kings. This curse is the gods' own punishment."

"Thirteen of my children have died," said Amphion. "Surely my wife and I have paid the price, whatever our offense?" He gestured to Pelorus. "Bring them here."

Pelorus left and then returned with the two survivors, the queen leaning heavily on her eldest daughter. I would not have recognized either woman. Chloris was paler than bleached linen – from the curse or from fear, I could not tell. And although I thought that Niobe had not been sick, her rich dark braids were gone. Instead her hair – what little remained – was thin and white. Had the gods done this to her? Or were the magnificent plaits only a wig?

Father hesitated; I could tell he was moved by the pitiful sight. Still he said: "They're cursed by the gods. Why should I help them?"

Chloris spoke. "Lord Menoeceus, I have prayed all night to Leto, begging forgiveness for myself and my mother – and to Artemis, who I served so many years."

I felt a surge of hope for my brother. If Amphion's daughter had been spared, my prayers, and my father's, might soften the gods' hearts and let Creon live too.

"Apollo has already spared them," I urged, tugging at Father's arm. This argument, and Chloris' words of devotion, swayed my father. He stared heavenwards, murmured a prayer, and then nodded.

We each took a woman in our litter – Chloris went with my father, while Niobe joined me in mine. The queen's eyes were swollen and red, the black pupils huge, and I did not think she recognized me. Her lips moved continuously, but at first I could hear nothing. Then I caught some of her murmured words: "Alphenor, my first-born! Astykratia, my beauty! Damasichthon, my handsome one! Ilioneus, my prankster! Kleodoxa, my muse! Ismenus, my brave boy!"

The king watched as the bearers lifted us to their shoulders. He ordered ten soldiers – his own personal bodyguard, his most trusted men – to accompany us back to our house. He gave a heavy gold neck-chain and a silver-inlaid dagger to the leader of the men and a turquoise ring to my father. "Menoeceus, I beg you, get them out of Thebes. They have friends who will take them in."

Amphion stared a moment at the two women. He reached out to his wife. "Good-bye, beloved." She mumbled something in response, something that I could not make out; he shook his head and said, "I love you, Niobe. I have always loved you. Remember that."

He took her small, plump hand and kissed it, but she seemed confused, as if she did not know him. When Amphion released her hand she drew it quickly to her breast and began muttering to herself once more. "Eudoxa, my weaver! Phaedimus, my archer! Neaira, my quiet one!"

The king turned to his remaining daughter and handed her a basket that seemed heavy. "This will serve as your dowry. Remember you are still niece to King Pelops and the granddaughter of King Tantalus. You have powerful connections."

"Yes, Father."

He touched her face. "Remember always that your father loved you." Amphion's voice, raised so often in song, broke down. "Think sometimes of your brothers and sisters. Live well."

Her reply was soft and sad. "Father, I will."

Amphion cleared his throat and spoke to Pelorus. "Take them out the side door – I'll go out the main entrance and distract the crowd. Get to the house of Menoeceus and to safety. They should leave Thebes before dawn."

"No," said Pelorus.

Drawn, exhausted, Amphion turned with irritation at this unexpected defiance. "What do you mean, no?"

"You're my king. Let me come with you."

"But I need you to protect my wife and my daughter."

"My lord king, your soldiers can do that. You're an eloquent speaker, but words won't be enough tonight. You can't face that mob alone."

Amphion shook his head. "They'll kill both of us."

"Perhaps – perhaps not. I have an idea." A scream shrilled outside, and there was a frantic pounding at the great double doors. "But, my lord king, we must hurry."

"Very well," said Amphion. "Menoeceus, I thank you. Take them away."

We drew the litter curtains closed, and the bearers carried us through the palace to a smaller set of doors. Cautiously the chief bodyguard opened the doors and the bearers carried us through.

I imagined King Amphion walking out onto the palace steps. Would the crowd be appeased by his children's deaths, his abdication? Or would they demand a king's blood to wash away Niobe's blasphemy? In my mind I saw what I feared: stones thrown with deadly accuracy, brutal clubs and sticks thudding home against soft flesh, dirty hands ripping at clothes and hair, finally pulling at limbs. I imagined blood spilling to the ground in the marketplace.

And then I heard it: a great roar from the agora.

In the litter's gloomy interior I looked at my companion and wondered if she knew what the cries meant – that her husband was letting himself be killed so that she and their remaining child could escape. But Niobe seemed deaf to the screams and the shouts and the stamping of feet; instead, she continued her weeping litany. "Sipylus, my lover of dogs! Ogygia, my teller of tales! Tantalus, my lyre player! Phthia, my little darling!" And when she reached the end of her children, she began again with: "Alphenor, my first-born!"

We moved away from the commotion, the bearers walking calmly but quickly in the direction of our house. Soon the only footsteps were those of our bearers and the soldiers guarding us. I breathed more easily.

Then there was a cry: "Who goes there?"

I heard running feet; had the mob already torn Amphion and Pelorus to shreds? Would it now fall upon us?

I was too terrified to open the curtains.

"Destroy them! Kill the blasphemers!"

"Kleodoxa!" said Niobe. She seemed completely unaware of the danger. "Damasichthon—" I grabbed her hand, trying to pull her bodily out of her mad grief, and then, unable to make her realize that she risked my life as well as her own and the life of her remaining child, I clamped my hand over her mouth and held it shut. She struggled with me at first, her dark eyes wild, but then she relaxed. The tears spilling out of her eyes wet my hand in the darkness. I kept my hand tight to her mouth and listened.

"We guard Menoeceus and his daughter Jocasta," said one of the soldiers. "All Thebes knows that lord Menoeceus is a devout man."

"And he's one of the Spartoi," said another soldier.

"His family is favored by the Tiresias, who says that the lady Jocasta will be queen," said the first.

I held my breath and kept Niobe silent as agreement grew – the acknowledgment that we had passed that way before. With relief I felt the litter begin its awkward swaying movements again, the cries of the crowd growing fainter as we descended toward the Eudoxa Gate.

An eternity seemed to pass before we reached the relative safety of our home. Only then did I withdraw my tear-drenched hand from Niobe's mouth. She resumed her recital as if there had been no interruption. "Astykratia! Ilioneus! Eudoxa!" She paused only when Chloris climbed out of my father's litter and helped her mother out of hers.

"Come, Mother," said Chloris, pulling her mother to her feet.

"Who calls me Mother?" said Niobe in confusion. "Chloris?"

"I am Chloris, Mother."

My father assumed his duties as host. "Come with me, my ladies," he said, offering his arms to them. "Let us take care of you."

While my father led the remnants of Amphion's family to the guest quarters, I darted in another direction, up a few steps and down a hall, where I found Merope. Her head down, she squatted outside Creon's room, a shrouded figure on the floor of the dim corridor. My heart sank: her listless posture seemed to signal defeat and death.

But then Merope looked up at that moment and smiled. Despite the scars on her face, her expression was radiant – and I knew my brother still lived.

"My lady," she said, rising to her feet.

"How is he?"

"Better, praise all the gods," said Merope. "I'm no healer, but he breathes easily now, and can talk. He wanted some privacy to pass water."

"Jocasta?" I heard my brother call feebly.

"I'll fetch a lamp," said Merope, and hurried off.

I stepped into the dark room, which stank with illness. "How do you feel?"

"Terrible," he croaked, "but I'm alive."

I opened the window curtains to allow in fresh air, and then Merope arrived with the lamp. By its flame, dancing in the draft, I surveyed my brother. He looked weak – paler than Chloris, except for the dark stubble on his chin – but he was definitely still alive. He sat up, drank some water, and kept it down.

"Could I have some food?"

I touched his forehead; it was cool and damp. I told Merope to bring broth. She left; I pulled over a low wooden stool and sat next to him. "You're fortunate," I told him, and then described the terrible scene we had found at the palace. He listened closely, sipping from the bowl Merope brought. Halfway through my story, he sat up a bit more; perhaps the broth gave him strength.

"All dead," he whispered when I was done.

"All except Chloris." I squeezed his shoulder. "And you," I added, feeling tears of thanks fill my eyes. I owed Apollo a generous offering for this mercy.

"And Niobe gone mad. Then you'll be the next queen of Thebes quite soon," he said. "But who will be king?"

The question disturbed me. If Amphion was dead, Thebes must have a new king, and presumably I would be married to him. "I'm sure you'll think of someone," I said irritably. *I* did not want to think about it.

Peremptorily I took the bowl away and told him he should rest. I carried the lamp out with me, leaving him in darkness. I was suddenly certain my brother would recover completely, if only so that he could pester me with annoying questions for the rest of my life. But – though Creon's questions were often annoying, they were rarely meaningless. The Tiresias' prophecies about Niobe and Pinelopi had been so accurate: that must mean that mine would also come true. But how could I possibly be queen now? Should I just walk back up to the palace and take a seat on Niobe's throne?

To distract myself, I went in search of my father. He was consulting with Chloris about the journey she and her mother would begin in a few hours. He paused to tell me that a retainer had reported that King Amphion had been stoned to death by the mob in the agora. I swallowed, and glanced at Princess Chloris; she met my eyes with quiet dignity, and I knew that there was nothing to be said.

So I only nodded, and informed Father that Creon's condition was much improved. He closed his eyes and murmured a prayer of gratitude, then told me that Niobe had been given a mixture of herbs and was sleeping in the guest quarters. Then he turned back to the princess.

"You must take several days' provisions," he said. "My servants will arrange for food, water, and wine."

"You're very generous, Menoeceus," said Chloris.

"It's nothing."

"If I can ever repay you, I will."

I had never really known Chloris; she was the oldest of the princesses, and had been away many years among the Maidens of Artemis. But now I perceived her fine qualities – the very fairness and strength that had made Amphion a good king for so many years. "You're an honorable woman," my father said, as if he had been struck by the same observation.

Chloris shrugged: her gesture was elegant and exhausted, full of dignity and grief. "You've risked yourself to take us in."

My father nodded. "May Apollo have mercy on you and yours." He stood. "We should be on our way at dawn. I'll take you as far as the Temple of Apollo."

Early the next morning Chloris and I roused Niobe from her herb-induced sleep. The widow of King Amphion peered at with me with apparent recognition. "You!" she said to me as Hydna helped her put on her shoes. "You are not my enemy," she said lucidly. Then she resumed her mourning, naming each lost child in turn.

It was hard to imagine what Thebes would be like without King Amphion, who had ruled the city my entire life. After my father had left with Niobe and Chloris, I burned some incense in our household shrine as a gift to Apollo and then took my breakfast in the courtyard, wondering what this new day
would bring.

Pelorus returned to our house at about the same time as my father, late in the morning. Father called for food, and a shaky but much improved Creon joined us, as eager for news as for nourishment. Although Pelorus had a few scrapes and bruises, and his kilt was darkly stained with what looked like blood, he was healthy and whole. "I expected to be killed," he said, "but Amphion's own courage saved me. When he saw the crowd's mood he knew his abdication would not satisfy them, and he would not survive the night. But he saw no reason for me to die with him." Pelorus' voice cracked; I saw his eyes moisten with tears. "He ordered me to hold my dagger to his throat, to tell the people that I was bringing them their sacrifice. He told me to say I had caught the coward king trying to escape." He wiped his eyes, and then said: "He just wanted to buy enough time for his wife and daughter to get away."

Father reported that the women were safely on their journey. He added that the entrails of the ram he had sacrificed to Apollo were as fine as he had ever seen, and that the beauty of the sunrise seemed a message from the god that all would be well with Thebes. "It's the end of an era," he concluded. "The usurper and his family are gone at last."

"Yes, they are," said the younger man, his tone flat. Pelorus' family was as old as ours, but it was neither so wealthy nor so devout; he did not seem bothered by Amphion's lineage.

"You've been out on the streets," said Menoeceus. "Is it safe to go to the palace? My daughter must establish her rightful place."

"You'll find another there before you," said Pelorus.

"Who else is there to make a claim?" asked my father indignantly.

Pelorus' words were like a flaming arrow: bringing light, but threatening destruction: "King Laius has returned."

CHAPTER FOUR

"Laius?" I asked.

The name was famous in Thebes, but completely unexpected. Though I knew of him, the man had been gone from the city nearly twice as long as I had been alive.

Laius was the son of King Labdakus, who had ruled Thebes thirty years before – until his death at the hands of the Maenad cult. Stories about the reason for King Labdakus' destruction varied. Some said he interfered with the Maenads' festival in honor of Dionysus; if so, King Labdakus might simply have been trying to keep order in the city, for the disciples of the wine-god were often disruptive and dangerous. Others said that offense against Dionysus was only an excuse; and that the ambitious Lykus, who then declared himself regent of Thebes, had engineered the king's death. The noble Lykus had often raised his voice against King Labdakus over the king's battles with Athens.

But whether or not the Regent Lykus brought about the death of his predecessor, he did not harm the king's young son. At first Prince Laius was raised in Thebes, living at the palace; later he was sent to King Pelops' court in Pisa. The idea was both clever and humane. In the care of the powerful Pelops, the boy would be exposed to learning and culture and the ways of kingship. Yet, removed from Thebes, he could not inspire plots against the regent.

"*King* Laius," said Father. "He calls himself that now, does he?"

"Yes," Pelorus answered. "And he has come with a small army from Pelops' court."

Father had taught me that Lykus never styled himself king, and at first the regent governed well, negotiating a truce with Athens and bringing order among the Maenads. But eventually he had his own set of quarrels, his own set of enemies. People began to ask when Prince Laius would return to claim the throne.

But Pelops did not send Laius to back to Thebes; instead Amphion, Pelops' brother-in-law, came. Amphion overthrew the regent and moved into the palace. Pelops must have found it convenient to have his brother-in-law and his sister Niobe rule a city-state rich with fields and cattle. But now Amphion was dead, as were most of his children.

"Interesting," Father said slowly, and I saw conflicting emotions cross his face. "As the son of Labdakus, Laius *is* part of the true Theban line."

Laius was descended from one of Kadmos' daughters born before Kadmos and his wife departed from Thebes. My ancestor had been born *after* Kadmos and his wife Harmonia left the city. Laius' recent ancestors – Labdakus, Pentheus – had both ruled as kings of Thebes. Over the years, many had suggested that Laius might return, but he had stayed away.

Yet now he was back.

"When did Laius arrive?" asked Creon.

"This morning at daybreak, through the Neaira Gate," Pelorus said, going on to describe the soldiers' tall shields, their boar's-tooth helmets and bronze-tipped spears, and their many chariots and horses, all decorated with bright blue plumes and bearing the horse's-head crest of Pelops.

"But I don't understand," Creon said, cutting off the description of Laius' soldiers. "Amphion died only last night. How could Laius have arrived so quickly?"

I recalled that Pisa and its holy site, Olympia, lay far to the southwest. To come from there one would either have to sail across the Gulf or cross the isthmus at Korinth – either way, several days' journey

"Perhaps he was carried in Apollo's chariot," said my father.

"His explanation is not so marvelous, but still bears the mark of the gods," said Pelorus. "Several nights ago, he dreamed he would return once more to Thebes and become our king. The gods apparently gave King Pelops the same dream; he assisted Laius with men and supplies."

I nodded, slowly, twisting the fabric of my outer skirt between my fingers. That could explain Laius' timely appearance. The gods were obviously taking an active interest in Thebes these days – and so far that did not seem like a good thing at all.

"Well! Well," said my father, resting his hands on his knees. "And, Pelorus? Has Laius brought a wife?"

Everyone turned to look at me.

I gasped as I realized what they were thinking.

"No, he hasn't," said Pelorus.

"Born to wear the crown," said my father.

"The next queen of Thebes," said Pelorus, slowly. "Is *this* what the Tiresias meant? Marriage to Laius? The seer never mentioned Alphenor's name."

"No!" I cried.

Again, all the men stared.

"Jocasta, what do you mean?" asked my brother. "Don't you want to be queen of Thebes?"

"I don't want to marry this Laius."

"Why should you object?" exclaimed my father. "You've never even seen the man!"

"That's exactly why – I've never even seen him!" I stared into their faces, bewildered that they did not understand. "At least I had *met* Alphenor before."

Pelorus said, "I share your grief, my lady—"

"Much better a live king than a dead prince," interrupted my father.

They spoke with confidence, as if they knew my heart and feelings, but they did not understand at all. "I'm sorry Alphenor is dead, but this has nothing to do with him. Do I have no say in this? You offer me around like a plate of stuffed olives, or a tapestry in the marketplace – who will haggle over Jocasta next?" Hot tears welled up in my eyes; I rose to flee the room.

But Pelorus was quicker than I; he leapt to his feet and grabbed my arm. "Jocasta, you're right; you're only part of a tapestry. But that's true for all of us. We are all strands woven into the gods' great tapestry. You want to choose your own place, your own colors. But none of us has that choice – our fates are already decided."

"Well spoken, Pelorus," said my father.

"I'm *not* a piece of thread," I said, trying to wrest myself from Pelorus' grip. "And I won't be used like one!"

"Jocasta, don't be foolish," advised my brother.

I spoke directly to Pelorus. "Let go of me!"

"You might as well release her," said my father. "The Tiresias has foretold that she will be queen of Thebes – so she will."

Pelorus loosed my arm and I ran out of the courtyard – nearly knocking over Hydna, who was bringing a tray of refreshments. Hydna steadied herself, clucked at me in annoyance, and then noticed my expression. "Child! What's wrong?"

I could not explain my desperation to her. Although she loved me, my nurse had also accepted the prophecy. Besides, I could barely explain my feelings to myself. All I knew was that I did not want to passively accept whatever the Tiresias had foretold, even if it meant I would be the next queen. So many horrible things had happened since the seer had made her pronouncements! Niobe was right; sweet-sounding prophecy could turn bitter indeed.

Niobe! At least she and her daughter had escaped. I stepped past Hydna and darted to the door, ignoring my nurse's cries that Thebes was still in turmoil and the streets were not safe. I went to the Eudoxa Gate, through which Niobe and Chloris had fled. Perhaps if I hurried, I could join them and avoid being bartered off to Laius.

But the gate was closed and locked, strange for the middle of the day. I called to the nearest guard, "Let me through."

The man looked at me, his gaze lingering on my fine multicolored skirts, my golden bracelets, my carefully coiffed hair. "I'm sorry, my lady, but I can't do that." His tone was polite, even deferential; nevertheless his words were firm.

"*Can't* do that?" I turned and stared at him. His accent was unfamiliar, and his blue cape decorated with a woven border of white horses. "Who are you, to tell me that the gate is closed?"

"My name is Vassos. I'm in the service of King Laius. The king has ordered that no one be permitted entry or exit until he gives word."

Laius! King Laius again! The gate locked, with me inside and no way to escape. I was trapped. I felt the blood drain from my face.

The guard reached out a hand to keep me from collapsing in the street. "My lady, you're not well. You should go home."

"Home! I have no home," I said.

The man, half a head taller than I, looked down at me as though I were mad. "That can't be true," he said. "Whatever quarrel you've had with your family will be over soon."

He could not know that my quarrel was with the Fates themselves – but he looked kind, and concerned, and for some reason his presence calmed me. I drew in a long breath. "Could I go up? To at least look beyond Thebes?"

He considered my request. Finally he nodded. "I'll take you up myself."

We ascended the narrow stairs, his strong tanned legs before me on the steps. As I neared the top he reached out a steady hand and pulled me up to join him. He kept his hand on my arm, to prevent me from falling or jumping, I suppose. I did not object, because I thought he meant well. Besides, any protest would no doubt have been useless; his grip felt determined.

But I had no desire to jump. I wanted to live.

I wanted to live my *own* life.

Staring out, I could see the stream of Chryssorrhoas, and beyond that, the path heading up to the temple of Apollo. Looking to my right, I glimpsed the road that led towards Athens and Korinth and the Peloponnesus. The hills were steep, the paths narrow and full of stones. Forest and thorny underbrush covered much of the countryside; and in that countryside wolves and bandits and even lions prowled.

Not all was wild. The trees with their new leaves blocked my view, but I knew some of what lay beyond. Cattle and sheep, tended by Theban herdsmen, grazed on fresh grass. Farmers cultivated their fields of barley and wheat, and worked the rows of olive groves and vineyards.

It was all so vast, and much of it was dangerous. I knew it was only a short distance to the temple of Apollo on the top of the next hill – but how much further was Athens? Two days' hard walk, at least – and what would I do once I got there?

I was a fool, to think of running after Niobe and Chloris. How could I ever cross such distances? I did not have Chloris' skill in the wilderness; I would not be safe traveling alone. If Thebes seemed demanding and cruel, at least the city and its dangers were familiar.

I turned to look in the other direction, at the city in which I had lived all my life, protected by King Amphion's thick walls. The narrow streets bustled with activity; up above, beyond the snug homes with their stuccoed walls, I could see the broad, flat roof of the palace. Thebes was my home; how could I leave it?

A spring breeze brushed my cheek. I closed my eyes and breathed deeply.

"Feeling better, my lady?"

Despite Vassos' grip on my arm, I had forgotten his presence. I opened my eyes and looked at him.

He was a stranger, true, and a soldier allied with the new king. But kindness twinkled in his warm brown eyes. He seemed to know that my crisis was over, that I had decided against whatever mad deed I had been contemplating.

"Yes, thank you," I replied. "Thank you for allowing me up here."

"My pleasure, my lady. If you need to come up again, just ask for Vassos."

He helped me back down the stairs and I returned home. To my surprise, Father did not scold me for my departure. He only reiterated that the will of Apollo *would* be done, whether I liked it or not. So I might as well accept it.

Then he told me we were expected at the palace tomorrow.

Once more Hydna woke me early; once more I went through the ritual of bathing, the careful arrangement of my best attire, the fussing over hair and makeup. I was dressed as I had been before, but within, I felt entirely different. Only three days – and so much had happened! Before, I worried about how I might represent the family. Now I thought of what had happened to King Amphion and Queen Niobe, and their children – what had happened to Thebes. What else did the gods have in store for my city – and for me?

I spoke with Creon before departing. This time, still weak from his illness, he did not tease. He thanked me for the care I had given him. "You'll remember me when you're queen, won't you?" he asked earnestly, pressing my hand.

He, too, was so certain I would be queen! And the prospect did not seem to worry him. It seemed to me that he should be more anxious than ambitious, since the curse that had killed so many had nearly claimed his life as well. But I did not argue. "Of course – as long as you promise to take care of me too."

Father called out for me to hurry, and I gave my brother a parting kiss on the cheek. Blue-cloaked soldiers met us at the door, men I did not recognize – except for Vassos, who nodded in greeting when he saw me. I was glad to see him; he gave me a feeling of security as we walked to the palace.

My father and I passed silently through the city. The people of Thebes, a murderous mob two days earlier, had resumed the roles of ordinary citizens. And now they looked to us for guidance and reassurance in this time of transition.

"Long live King Laius!" cried a few voices, but more called out to my father and me. We heard, "Menoeceus, protect us!" and, "Jocasta, shelter us!" "The next queen of Thebes!" was another common refrain; I wished that my ears, like my eyes, had lids so I could block out the noise. Noticing dark stains on the cobblestones, I could not but reflect on how the people had treated their last ruler.

When we reached the palace, we discovered that here too the guards wore the colors of King Pelops. Vassos hailed them in his Pisatan accent; they opened the doors and we entered. Father coughed, and I wrinkled my nose; surely the bodies of the dead princes and princesses had been moved, but still the palace stank of death.

Foreign soldiers filled the megaron, though a few priests and Theban nobles were present as well. In one corner I spotted Pelorus, now clean-shaven and wearing a fresh kilt. The thrones stood vacant; I scanned the many foreign faces to be seen in the megaron. Which of these men was the legendary King Laius? Some I could dismiss at once: one good-looking blond fellow, kneeling down beside a toddler with golden curls, was certainly too young. The young man looked up as I entered; for a long moment he frowned at me. Then he scooped up the little boy and carried him out of the megaron.

Not him, I thought. But there were plenty of other unfamiliar men. Might one of these be Laius?

"Stop it," my father hissed. "Such curiosity is beneath you."

I stopped turning my head and stood straight at his side. My father was right; besides, I was sure to see Laius soon enough. If only he could be like the kind-hearted Vassos who escorted us here!

As if he heard my thoughts, Vassos turned and gave me a warm smile. Then he spoke to my father, asking our names again to be sure that he would pronounce them properly. "I'm sure the king will be here soon," he said.

So Laius was not yet here, I thought, relaxing a little. But my reprieve was short-lived; moments later the crowd hushed as a tall handsome man, dressed in a white kilt and wearing a red and gold cape around his shoulders, entered the room. A bright circlet of gold crowned his head. The man went to Amphion's throne and sat down, then surveyed the group in the megaron.

Vassos cleared his throat and spoke. "May I present Lord Menoeceus, descendant of Echion, and his daughter, the lady Jocasta!"

Laius looked at me, assessing me carefully. His gaze seemed to linger on each aspect of my form, as he studied my face, my neck, and my breasts. His eyes returned to meet mine, and I knew he desired me. It was a new and strange sensation, and I felt myself blush, unsure whether I returned his desire but certainly unsettled by it. My palms felt damp, and I rubbed them against my skirts.

His eyes were dark brown, surrounded by thick lashes that made their gaze seem more significant. A few strands of gray streaked his hair – he was no young prince, like poor Alphenor, but a man of experience. His full red lips made a striking contrast against his beard. His chest bore a thatch of dark hair.

"Lord Menoeceus," said King Laius. He spoke slowly, his words tinged with the same Pisatan drawl that I had heard in

Vassos' speech. "And your daughter, lady Jocasta. I've heard much about you both."

My father bowed; I did likewise. "Welcome to Thebes," said my father.

"It's good to be *home*," said Laius, emphasizing the last word as if to point out that my father's welcome was not necessary. After all, he was *destined* for Thebes – for Laius was the son of the last rightful king. "I've been too long gone from the city of my birth. Through my many years in exile, Thebes has been the center of my life, my hopes, my dreams and prayers."

I wondered about this. If he spoke truth, why had it taken him so many years to return? And if Thebes was the center of Laius' heart, then why did gossip dwell on his amorous liaisons and never mention his devotion to our city?

Laius went on, "When Regent Lykus died, I meant to return to Thebes. But I thought it wise to first consult the gods. And the oracle told me that the next king of Thebes would know nothing but sorrow, and bring destruction to his descendants. So I stayed away, letting Amphion rule in my stead."

The right decision for Laius, I thought, if catastrophic for King Amphion. Impressed by Laius' answers to my unspoken questions, I noticed how he casually tapped the arm of the throne with powerful fingers. In this short bit of time it already seemed like *his* throne. Well, as my father would say, Laius was a descendant of Kadmos.

"My lord king," Father said, "we're glad you're here at last. The city needs the leadership of those who heed the gods."

Laius nodded in acknowledgement and then turned his eyes back to me. His gaze felt hotter than summer sunshine, and my legs seemed to weaken like melting wax.

"I understand your daughter has won the favor of Apollo," said Laius.

"The Tiresias has prophesied she will be queen of Thebes," said my father.

"And have a husband of great renown." Laius grinned at me.

My father must have responded, but I did not hear his words. Looking at the man upon the throne, feeling the strange intensity of his gaze, I could not concentrate. At some point Laius announced, as a casual command: "So she will be my bride."

I had heard the same pronouncement only a few days earlier, and then felt oddly numb to it; but this time my heart leapt in response. When Alphenor looked at me, it seemed like a dream; when Laius announced his intentions, it felt altogether real. I looked into Laius' eyes, and although I could not have described how I felt about him, I knew one thing: we would marry.

"We have much to discuss," Laius said to my father. "Let's speak privately." He snapped his fingers at a servant. "Bring refreshment."

My father and I followed Laius to another room, floored in stucco and lit by a few high windows. Laius drew me over to sit beside him. His nearness disconcerted me, scattering my thoughts. He smelled of cloves and cedarwood. One warm hand lingered on my arm. A golden seal-ring, carved with a pair of mating goats, adorned one finger. "Very pretty," he said, running his fingertips down my jaw. Even as I shrank from his touch, a bolt of heat coursed through me like lightning. My eyes widened.

"I'm in love with her already," he said. He brushed one hand along the curve of my left breast, drawing the fire within me lower. And then he released me, turning his attention back to my father. "Lord Menoeceus, you have a most beautiful daughter."

"Thank you," said my father shortly, and I could not tell whether he was pleased by the king's compliment or shocked by how boldly this stranger touched me in his presence.

One part of me wanted to run, to seek my father's protection. And yet at the same time I ached to feel the warmth of Laius' hands again.

A servant entered bearing a tray of food, and another followed with an amphora of wine. Laius passed a golden cup to me; our fingers met. My hand tingled even after his had gone.

Feeling dizzy, I tried to attend the conversation between my father and the new king. Of most interest to me was *when* we would marry. Naturally my father insisted that we consult the gods, so I received no answer.

And then they moved to other topics. All afternoon Laius questioned my father about Thebes: the ruling class, the Maenads, the level of devotion to Apollo; the health of the cattle herds and the volume of trade with Athens, Gla and Orchomenos. He asked about the wells and crops and the fortifications made to Amphion's walls. The depth of his inquiry impressed me: Laius seemed so wise, and so kingly. I realized that as the next queen, I needed to concern myself with such things as well. Once or twice I actually asked a question; the men paused to answer, Laius indulgently amused by my interest. This made me resolve to learn more about my city and what was important to it – in fact, I was ashamed when I realized the extent of my ignorance.

A woman with hair of gold and eyes the color of grape leaves came into the room and put the used dishes back on the tray. She had to be over thirty, but I thought she was still quite handsome and must have been lovely in her youth.

Laius interrupted his conversation with my father – they were discussing the marble quarries two hours' distance away – to address the woman. "Nerissa, please take Jokar... ah, Jocasta to the women's quarters. As my bride-to-be she should have the chance to inspect them."

I did not want to leave my betrothed, but he had announced that I was his intended, and suggested that I inspect my future home. I ignored his stumble over my name. When I moved to go, he took my face between his hands and kissed me, and the heat of his lips against mine blotted out all thought. My body quivered like a plucked lyre-string: when he released me, and I opened my eyes, I was hardly able to breathe.

"Good-bye, my dear," Laius said. "We'll be with each other soon, I promise."

Reluctantly I followed Nerissa out of the room. My soul seemed to linger behind as I accompanied her up the stairs to the royal chambers; and I scarcely paid attention to my surroundings, although the long corridors and the many rooms were exquisitely decorated with rich colored frescoes.

We entered the queen's megaron, in which I had visited Niobe. I could still smell her sandalwood perfume; the scent lingered in the cushions. My gaze went to where her wine cup had landed when she threw it at the Tiresias. The stain would never wash out; I would have it painted over, but I did not think I would want to use this room myself. After what had happened here, too many terrible memories lingered, and no paint could remove them.

Finally it occurred to me I was being rude – I should at least speak to the serving-woman guiding me. "How long have you served King Laius, Nerissa?" I asked.

"Seventeen years," Nerissa said.

That was more years than had lived. "And what are your duties? I mean, what's your position?"

She looked at me oddly, her eyes seeming to grow larger in her slender face. "I am the mother of Polydorus and Gogos."

I blinked, for to me this was no answer. "Who are they?" I asked, bluntly, without thinking.

She stared at me in disbelief. "They are Laius' sons."

CHAPTER FIVE

Her words were like a dagger in my gut. I had followed her as the sacrifice follows the priest to the altar, unaware of the knife hidden in the basket.

I wanted Laius to belong to me absolutely – present, future and past as well. But he did not. And would not. Nerissa had a part of him that I could never claim.

As I swallowed, feeling sick, I caught the vestige of a smile on Nerissa's face. She must have enjoyed making her announcement. Yet she continued the tour of the palace as if nothing had happened, showing me rooms and objects I hardly noticed. Instead I saw her pale slender hands, her leaf-green eyes, her gleaming tresses. Her gestures flowed with a practiced ease that I suddenly envied. The gray strands at her temples no longer aged her; instead they were silver accents woven among the gold. Fine lines at the corners of her eyes witnessed years of smiles and laughter she had shared with the man who would be my husband.

What a fool I had been, a moment before, to think my youth an advantage! Looking at Nerissa I realized that while youth might be fresh and pretty, a woman past thirty could have as much – even more – to offer than a girl of fourteen.

During the torch-lit descent back to our home I remained silent. My father thought my inability to talk a symptom of joy, excitement, and love. "The prophecy is already being fulfilled," he said, his voice exultant. Pelorus, however, was more perceptive; he gave me a keen glance and shook his head. I did not sob aloud, but I was sure he saw my tears glistening in the moonlight.

Not until I was alone with Creon did I tell anyone of my dismay. I found him sitting in a chair by the brazier in his room, huddled in a blanket.

"You should be in bed," I chided him, and Merope nodded her agreement.

"I've been in bed too long," he replied. "Now, tell me everything!"

I told Merope I wanted to speak privately with my brother, and she left us. Then I made a bargain with my brother: if he returned to bed, I would pull up a stool and tell him everything.

"Of course he's had other women before," he said when I came to the part about Nerissa. "And according to the stories, other men, too. What matters is the future. Do you know how he feels about this woman?"

"No," I replied. I knew nothing of Laius save that he had woken new sensations in my body, and left me quivering from his touch, and that I would not share with Creon.

"Tell me what you do know," Creon said. But I could describe very little about her, other than her looks. My brother waved his hand impatiently. "I'm sure you're more beautiful than this Nerissa. The important thing is her position with Laius."

"He brought her with him to Thebes. And he has two children by her."

"Ah, *children*," said Creon. "Boys or girls?"

"Boys," I said, my mind working. "Maybe that's why he brought her to Thebes: he wants his children with him, and doesn't want to separate them from their mother—"

"Don't be a fool, Jocasta!"

His tone angered me, for I had been congratulating myself on my cleverness. "What do you mean?"

"You're thinking like a lovesick girl. The women he has lain with can be forgotten. The children they've borne are something else entirely. Especially sons."

"Sons," I said slowly.

"They could easily resent you, and any children you give Laius. And they'll be older than your children – by all the Muses, Jocasta, they could be older than *you*."

Laius was more than twenty years older than I, a little old for a first-time husband; he could have been a father for many years. "You may be right," I said slowly.

"Don't let Eros blind you," he said, proving that he knew I had been struck by that god's arrow. "Enjoy the god's gifts, but remember this is no ordinary romance. You must think like a queen."

I frowned, removed a heavy comb from my hair, and shook out my curls. "The Tiresias said I will love my husband deeply."

"Leave prophecies to those who those who have time for such things – like Father. As the wife of Laius and queen of Thebes, you must concern yourself with practical matters. You'll have admirers and power; but you'll also have enemies."

Enemies! Thebes was a secure and wealthy city; my father held a position of prestige among the nobles. Danger had always been far from my everyday life. But now I would be wed to Laius, who certainly had enemies. And as queen of Thebes my position and power would attract envy. Perhaps even the gods would find reason to oppose me, as they had Niobe! She, too, had spoken of enemies.

"It's unpleasant, I know. But you need to think of these things now, Jocasta, *before* you move into the palace."

I sighed and leaned my head on his thin shoulder. "You're right," I said.

I was about to ask him what he thought I should do, when Hydna interrupted us. "It's late, butterfly! You need your beauty sleep, and your brother's still recovering." Creon patted my cheek, and said we would talk again later.

Despite her mention of sleep, Hydna seemed more interested in gossiping about Laius. She bade me sit on the low wooden chair before my dressing table while she combed out my hair, all the time interrogating me about the new king. Nerissa and then Creon had soured my enthusiasm, so at first I gave only curt answers. But as my nursemaid and I talked further her happiness seeped into me, and I remembered again the warm touch of Laius' hands and lips.

When Hydna finished with my hair, I drank the wine Merope brought, lightly infused with sleep-inducing herbs; but after the servants left I lay awake thinking of the nights when I would lie with Laius, his arms around my waist, his lips on mine.

What did I care about Nerissa and her kind? They belonged to his past. Laius' present, his future belonged to me. Together we would rule Thebes. I would bear him many children, and my son – not Nerissa's – would follow us on the throne.

"This head born to wear the crown, this breast to fill with love." Those were the words of the Tiresias. Surely there was no reason to worry.

Yet that night when I dreamed of Laius, golden-haired Nerissa lay naked in his arms. In the dream I stood at the door of their bedchamber, holding a sputtering lamp, unable to move. Suddenly my lamp flame shot up hugely, as bright as a torch. The surprised lovers looked over at me, and laughed.

I woke with a start, my heart pounding. A dog howled in the distance; slowly I realized I was in my own darkened room. It was only a dream. But was it a prophetic dream, or a lying dream?

"Which is it, Hermes?" I whispered. Hermes was the bringer of dreams, but he was also the god of lies. "Are you trying to warn me, or are you just playing one of your tricks?"

The god did not answer. I lay awake long into the night, listening to the guards making their rounds along the city wall.

The next morning I was allowed to sleep late; when I rose, the sun was high and the day growing hot. I heard male voices out in the courtyard: Father, Creon, and another, a man with a Pisatan accent. Merope knew nothing of the visitor, and my curiosity burned. I hurried through breakfast and dressing. At least today no bath delayed me.

"Is it Laius?" I asked when Hydna finally arrived. I tried to keep the eagerness out of my voice as Merope fastened a lapis-encrusted comb in my hair.

"No, child," said Hydna. "The king sent someone with a message."

"A message?" I asked, turning so quickly that the comb clattered to the floor. Perhaps Laius had changed his mind; perhaps it was all a mistake. Perhaps Nerissa – her beautiful face and figure haunted me again, the way they had for the wretched portion of my dreams – perhaps she had talked him out of it. Or some other catastrophe – had not disaster struck the last time I was betrothed?

"Calm down, butterfly," said Hydna. "Your father and brother are speaking peacefully with the man."

"Ah," I said, breathing more easily.

"They're waiting for you in the courtyard," she added.

I sat still long enough for Merope to refasten the comb, and then raced out to the garden to discover that the visitor was none other than Vassos. All three men rose when they saw me.

"Good morning," I said, slowing my step, trying to make my voice low and dignified, as I thought a queen should sound.

Vassos and Creon smiled and replied in kind, but my father was not so gracious. "It's no longer morning," he informed me. "Apollo's chariot has passed its zenith."

Vassos bowed to me. "It is morning if the queen says it is morning," he offered, and his eyes twinkled.

Taking my usual seat in the shade of the laurel tree, I said, "I'm to be queen of Thebes, not the heavens." I did not want to risk offending the gods, especially not Apollo.

"Even so," the Pisatan said good-naturedly. He went on, "King Laius has asked me to handle the arrangements for the royal funerals."

I blinked. Since Laius' arrival, I had scarcely thought of poor Alphenor and his brothers and sisters, dead from the curse –

and of course their father, rent into bloody pieces. At that thought, Creon's words echoed again in my ears: *You will have enemies, Sister.* I shuddered.

"The king," Vassos was saying, "asks your father to lead the sacrifice at the funeral."

I gave Father a questioning look.

"I've agreed to do it," he said. "After all, the man ruled Thebes for many years, and the gods require that the dead, no matter their deeds in life, be treated with respect." Father had resented King Amphion, but he could not resist the chief role in a ritual of such importance. "How many dead are there?" he asked Vassos.

"Twenty. Amphion, of course, thirteen of his children, and six others." He recited the names. Amphion's family, and Pinelopi, I had known about. But the other deaths were news to me. The man we had always believed to be Melanthe's father was among them.

Father shook his head at the news. "I had not realized – what a pity!" He set his hands on his knees, and rose from his seat. "Vassos, if you'll excuse me, I should go to Apollo's temple. I have much to do."

"Of course," said Vassos. "But I must stay a little longer. There is something I wish to discuss with your daughter."

"Alone?" my father asked, looking suspicious. He sat back down.

"No – no, this is no secret. King Laius has decided that your daughter, as the future queen of Thebes, must have a bodyguard." He turned to me. "A group of men, my lady, sworn to serve you and to protect you from harm. I would be honored if you would consider me for the head of your personal guard."

"Thank you," I said, my voice low and, I hoped, charming. "I accept."

The words had already left my lips when I saw Creon frown.

Vassos smiled warmly. "I thank you, my lady. I will do all in my power to ensure you are never disappointed." Then he cleared his throat and said, "I also bring a personal message from the king to his betrothed. He bids me tell you that he longs to see you, but that he is extremely busy."

"Ah," I said, slowly, and slumped in my seat.

I burned to see, to touch, to embrace Laius again. If he felt as I did, how could he wait? Perhaps he was back in Nerissa's arms – or perhaps I meant nothing to him. My heart plunged from confidence to desperation.

"A king's responsibilities are heavy," Creon interjected. "Especially those of a new king."

My father pointed out: "You'll be spending the rest of your lives together."

"I'm sure the king will see you soon," said Vassos.

I struggled for calm, regal words. "I look forward to seeing him when his duties are less pressing."

"Certainly that will be soon, my lady," Vassos repeated, adding, "You are too lovely for him to resist."

Father and my newly appointed bodyguard left – Vassos would start his duties the next day – but Creon remained with me in the courtyard. As soon as the outer door opened and shut, my brother spoke. "That was a foolish thing to do."

"What was?"

"Taking that man as your bodyguard! He belongs to Laius. You should have men you know and trust."

"I trust him," I said, and told him how Vassos had accompanied me to the top of the wall.

"You didn't tell me about that," Creon said.

"I didn't think it was important. Besides, you've been ill," I pointed out. "Anyway, not only do I trust Vassos, I like him. And I think he likes me."

Stirring the pebbles of the courtyard path with his toe, Creon nodded slowly. "You're right. He does like you. A great deal, if I'm not mistaken." We both remained silent for a moment. Then Creon continued, "But he still works for Laius – at least now. You must make sure you win him to your side. His loyalty must be to you, not to Laius."

"What difference is there? Laius loves me." I stood and turned, bending to sniff the hyacinth blossoms, so that Creon could not see how I blushed as I mentioned my betrothed's name. I quivered at the thought of his warm caresses.

My words, uttered to convince my brother, began to work on me as well. How could I have doubted Laius' affection? Of course a new king was a busy man. I needed to be confident, like a queen – not some silly infatuated girl, seeking omens in each of her lover's sighs.

Creon reached for my hand, and I realized that I had been plucking a flower apart. I let the torn petals drop to the ground. "Love is well and good. But still you must make as many allies of your own as possible. So continue to charm this Vassos. And every other man with power."

I thought this overcautious; surely Laius would protect me. After all, he was so concerned that he had sent me a bodyguard! But the idea of charming Vassos was appealing. He might not be king, but he was kind – and handsome in his own way. And although he obviously took his duties seriously, I detected a sense of mirth beneath the surface. He was also much younger than Laius – closer to my own age.

"You're smiling," my brother said.

"Sorry," I said self-consciously, knowing that my mouth was wide and that a smile overpowered my face.

"Don't apologize. Your smile helped win over Vassos. You should practice. You may need to smile when you least feel like it."

"And cry when I least feel like it." I scuffed my sandals over the dirt, covering up the fallen blue petals. "I feel sorry for

Prince Alphenor and the rest of them, but I'm in no mood for a funeral."

"Still, you must go."

I sighed and nodded. "You're right; I must go."

Father quit the house before dawn the next day; Creon and I were wakened not long after. The night before, Father had insisted that I must arrive in time to claim a place at the front of the funeral. "You'll be queen of Thebes," he told me. "It's your duty to lead these functions."

In the gentle light of daybreak we set out; Creon walked at my right side, Vassos at my left. The soldier from Pisa seemed determined to guard me every instant: not just from potential assassins, but from all inconveniences along the way. He kept me from stepping in the droppings of animals that had gone through the city that morning, and from treading on loose stones.

"You don't need to do that," I said, as he respectfully took my elbow and guided me around a puddle.

"It's my duty to protect you, my lady," said Vassos.

"Do I really need so much protection?"

"Think where we're going, Jocasta," said my brother.

The funeral for Amphion and his children. King Amphion had been torn to pieces by his own subjects – who were to be my subjects now. Suddenly I was glad to have a bodyguard. And I would do what Creon had advised, and make sure my guards were loyal. I sneaked a glance at Vassos' face; surely he would not betray me.

"Where will they be buried?" I asked, as we continued through the city.

"On the hill beyond the Kleodoxa Gate," said Vassos. "Where Amphion buried his brother and his family. King Laius had workmen dig the tomb deeper into the hill; the earth there is soft."

We walked on; I admired Vassos as he led us unerringly through the streets of Thebes. "You've been here only a few days, yet you find your way easily."

"A soldier needs a good sense of direction," said Vassos. "He must always know where he is, and where he should and should not go, to safeguard the lives of his men. And the life of his queen."

Perhaps I should have made some polite comment at that; but we were approaching the palace, and the sight of it distracted me. Was Laius behind those thick stone walls? Did he think and dream of me, the way I dreamed of him? I longed to run inside and find him.

Not yet. Not yet. Besides, I would see him shortly at the funeral.

Vassos continued north, and I forced myself to stay between him and Creon. We left the environs of the palace and the agora, and entered the artisans' quarter. Here, the streets usually teemed with people: bare-chested men turning potters' wheels with their feet while their skilled fingers shaped clay into graceful forms. Women standing at tall looms, chatting with each other as they passed skeins of bright-colored wool to and fro among the hanging warp threads. Naked, dusty children swarming everywhere, girls scrambling to keep babies from underfoot while boys strutted and played soldier with sticks for swords. Laughter and youthful shrieks would compete with the ringing blows of the armorers' bronze hammers.

But this was the day of King Amphion's funeral. The few people about worked only half-heartedly, and they ceased entirely as we walked by. Eyes gazed at me, fingers pointed, and though I could not discern the words I knew they spoke of me.

"They know you'll be queen, my lady," Vassos said.

Creon hissed, "Smile at them!"

So I smiled and nodded and occasionally waved. This encouraged the people – not to approach me, but to smile and wave back.

"Bless you, Lady Jocasta," said an old woman, whom I recognized as one of Merope's relatives.

A short plump man, an artisan from the palace, bowed before me. "You'll make a magnificent queen, my lady. Let me adorn your head with flowers of gold!"

"Queen Jocasta will bring peace and prosperity!" called an old woman.

The cheers warmed me as I walked through the streets. These people had already accepted me as their queen. They were ready to admire me, to love me, to turn to me for guidance. Their praise and adulation was dizzying, but also lifted and refreshed me. The very air I drew into my lungs seemed to sparkle. Was this why men strove to become king – not for the palaces, the gold and the women, but for the devotion of their subjects? And I wondered: was this how the gods felt?

"Don't pretend to be a goddess," Creon murmured in my ear, somehow guessing my thought. "The real gods don't like it."

Creon was right. I dared not behave as Niobe had.

The crowds also on their way to the funeral slowed our way through the streets, and again I appreciated Vassos' assistance: his commanding presence helped us push through. When we reached, at last, the Kleodoxa Gate – the furthest from the Eudoxa – he merely waved to the men as they let us through the small door set into the great wooden gate. The city gates were still officially closed, Vassos informed me, and would remain so until the new king was crowned.

We soon joined the throng gathering on the hillside below the tomb, where my father was busy among the priests and priestesses. At their direction, servants were securing the victims that would be sacrificed. Twelve rams, eight ewes – except in time of war, Thebes had never lost so many of the elite in so short a time.

I looked around, hoping to see Laius, but he had not yet come. Of course not. *He* did not have a father who liked rising before dawn and thought the rest of the world should too. That would be another advantage to becoming queen, I thought: sleeping late. The thought made me yawn, and I hid my mouth with my hand.

For the first time that day I found Vassos' presence inconvenient. I could not talk as freely to Creon as I wished. Instead I was forced to stand in quiet dignity, befitting my station. I sighed. The ritual would not be done for hours.

I pulled my cape close about my chest. The sky was growing overcast and the air chilly, unusual for the season. This was a good thing; the chill would keep down the smell of death. But I hoped it would not rain.

Just as my back began to ache in earnest from standing so long, the funeral procession arrived. The dead, carried on litters by slaves, were followed by the living. The people of Thebes drew near to stare at the corpse of the king they had torn apart. Amphion's body was completely wrapped in white linen, concealing his face and form as well as his injuries. But the golden death mask and the gifts the slaves put around Amphion's body – his seven-stringed lyre, his golden wine cup and the royal seals carved in amethyst and chalcedony – made it plain that the shroud contained the remains of the dead king.

Then the other bodies were brought before the crowd: first the thirteen children of Niobe and Amphion, then the others struck dead by the terrible scourge. Glancing at still-pale Creon, I felt doubly grateful that my brother's life had been spared. I gave thanks to Apollo and his sister Artemis.

Others filed forward, bringing gifts to be buried with the bodies: jars full of oil, bright ribbons that had adorned the lovely Astykratia, bronze spears and dirks that had belonged to the princes Alphenor and Damasichthon, clay figurines that I recognized as the toys of little Phthia. I felt sorrow when Pinelopi's weeping mother brought forward an ivory comb her daughter had worn in her hair a few days ago, and pity as Melanthe contributed a model of a ship in honor of the man we had believed to be her father. Her mother had been dead for years; now she had no family at all.

The people's grief was palpable, and tears welled in my own eyes. They were now *my* people. I would do my utmost to ensure we were never cursed like this again.

I searched again for Laius, wondering if he too was touched by the death of so many Thebans. I looked, but did not see him. I watched as other families stepped forward to present their offerings to my father and the acolytes, and still the king did not appear. Where was he? Certainly a new king had many things to do, but wasn't attending this ceremony one of them? Amphion – the only king I had known – appeared at all public events, unless he was away from the city. And this was a crucial time, a time when the city needed atonement, and leadership out of its grief. A time when Thebes needed to see its new king.

After the well-born of Thebes came a few richly-dressed men with faces unfamiliar to me. I assumed they had accompanied Laius from Pisa. They clustered together – all except one tall, balding fellow in a brown cape who said nothing but peered at everything. Next in the procession were the common people: tradesmen, artisans, soldiers, farmers, and merchants. Many of them stole glances at me; some even bowed: more evidence that the news that I would be queen had spread.

Yet where was the king? If not at the front of the procession, Laius should be at the end – perhaps customs were different in Pisa. But the last people came, and Laius was not there.

"Very odd," Creon muttered beside me. "The new king usually buries the old."

My father also seemed to expect Laius, for he hesitated before beginning the ceremonies. The bald man with the brown cape approached my father and spoke in a low voice. I could not hear all the words, but apparently the king was detained on urgent business. My father raised a ruddy eyebrow, a sign of surprise or disapproval, but he did not question the man, and he started intoning the prayers.

So Laius was not coming. What business was more urgent than this?

Was he with Nerissa?

Lost in my thoughts, I was startled when the bearers came forth to pick up the bodies once more. My father and the priests next stepped into line. Vassos touched my elbow to indicate that I should go next. With him at my side, the people let me pass before them. People whispered that my sad beauty suited the solemnity of the occasion. But in my heart I knew my distress had more to do with Laius' absence than anything else.

We followed the priests and the bodies to the tomb cut into the side of the hill. Not everyone could squeeze into the area, but I suspected that many were already on their way to the funeral feast in the agora. The bodies, wrapped in their shrouds, were carried within; the grave gifts followed, with more prayers. My father said the final blessing and signaled the bearers to shut the doors. Then at last we left, only a few mourners remaining behind – Pinelopi's mother was one, Melanthe another – to continue grieving for their dead.

The ceremony was done. As we reached the Kleodoxa Gate, the sun burst through the clouds. It was as if Apollo had forgiven us, and was ready to let us start anew.

Vassos and Creon by my side, I followed my father and the others to the agora; the smell of roasting meats made my mouth water. "I'm starving!" said Creon, still gaunt after his illness.

But I forgot my hunger immediately. For there, at the top of the palace steps, sitting on an ornate chair that had been brought out onto the terrace, was Laius.

How handsome he was! He wore a cloak of red and gold – the colors of Thebes – with a matching kilt. A circle of gold leaves wrapped around his forehead. Talking and laughing with a Pisatan soldier, his white teeth gleamed against his dark beard. He shrugged, and I noticed how strong his shoulders were. I recalled that he was a champion wrestler from the Olympic Games.

Laius looked up, across the crowd. Seeing me, he smiled and waved as if we had parted only moments before. I forgot that my legs ached from hours of standing in the chill, that my stomach was empty. All that mattered was my soaring heart. How could I have doubted him? He loved me. I knew he loved me.

With Vassos beside me, I made my way through the crowded agora and climbed the palace steps. Laius stood and held out his hand to me. "There you are, my dear! By Aphrodite, you're the prettiest maid in Thebes!"

Heat rose to my face. "If you say so, my lord."

"I say so, and I'm king of Thebes, so it must be true." He winked at me. "How was the funeral?"

I was surprised that he spoke so lightly of it. "Why weren't you there, my lord king?"

"I can't bear funerals. And this was for a man who usurped my throne, and a lot of people I didn't know." Keeping my hand in his, he sat back down on the throne, and drew me over to stand by his side.

I asked, "How did you spend your morning, my lord king?"

"Going through old things. We'll come to that later."

I was relieved that he did not mention Nerissa. "The people wanted to see you."

"And they'll see me now. Better for them to connect their king with a feast than a funeral, don't you think?"

I was not sure that this was a kingly choice, and it was at odds with tradition, as Creon had mentioned – but my betrothed had a point. And I was so happy to be with him, his warm hand holding mine, that I would have forgiven anything. The last days of doubt vanished like mist in the sunshine.

He stood, releasing my hand, and stepped forward on the terrace. The people below, who had been chattering as they watched us, now fell silent. Laius raised his voice and spoke so that all could hear. "People of Thebes! You have sorrowed for the loss of your former king – although he never had a right to rule. You have mourned the loss of your loved ones, who died because Amphion's pride offended the gods. Rejoice now: your true king has come. The city is whole, and its gates stand open once more. I am Laius, son of Labdakus, descended from Kadmos. I have returned to my city. Together we will make Thebes great!"

The people cheered. I felt an upwelling of pride and affection for the man I was to marry.

"Before we begin the feast, join me in honoring my wife-to-be: Jocasta, daughter of Menoeceus."

I thought the people had cheered loudly for Laius, but their enthusiasm was even greater when he announced me. Confused, I went to stand by his side.

"You must see, as I do, that she is the most beautiful woman in Thebes. And I have a gift that will make her beauty last." He turned toward the open palace doors and beckoned. "Nerissa?"

So he *had* been with Nerissa, I thought, more perplexed than before. Even if she wanted to, how could Nerissa preserve my beauty? Was she some sort of sorceress?

I did not have long to wonder; Nerissa soon joined us on the steps, her arms full.

Laius gestured at what she carried. "I present a part of my heritage – the robe and necklace of Harmonia!" He took the necklace and held it high, while Nerissa held up the gown.

The people gasped and cheered. Many craned their necks, straining to see the famed necklace. It was exquisite: two serpents of gold entwined with each other, representing love and eternity. The work of a master craftsman.

"This necklace, fashioned by the forge-god Hephaestus, was given by the goddess Aphrodite to her daughter Harmonia when she wed Kadmos, the founder of our great city. Aphrodite herself enchanted it, so that the wearer may have eternal beauty. I will give it to Jocasta, daughter of Menoeceus, on the day we wed!"

The people cheered. "Long live Queen Jocasta, daughter of Menoeceus!"

I had never been happier in my life: Laius at my side, my father, brother and bodyguard all looking proudly on, and the people of Thebes – now *my* people – loudly voicing their support.

Laius held up his hand, asking for silence. The crowd took a while to hush, but eventually their cheers diminished and he could make himself heard. "I am glad you adore her, as I do," he said. "She will also, on our wedding day, wear Harmonia's robe."

Nerissa stepped behind me and draped the antique gown around my shoulders. Its shining blue fabric was unlike any material I had ever touched before: as smooth and soft as flower petals. I tried to imagine Harmonia wearing it – what had she looked like, that daughter of two gods?

A murmur filled the agora, a buzzing that grew until it burst forth with excitement. "A true Theban queen! The daughter of Harmonia! Of Aphrodite!"

Laius again held up his hand. "Now, Thebans, it is time to feast!" He gestured to the food; servants emerged from the palace bearing jugs of wine and water. The people cheered again. Among the crowd I saw several of the Maenad cult, worshippers of Dionysus, carrying thyrsus staffs topped with pinecones; they raised their wine-cups with enthusiasm.

Laius smiled and turned away. In a voice not meant to carry, he told Nerissa to put away Harmonia's things. She did so obediently and discreetly, apparently having returned to her proper role as a servant. Why had I feared her? My husband was a man; of course he had had lovers before me.

The people surged around the food. Creon, Vassos and my father joined us on the terrace. Father beamed at me. "Descended from Aphrodite! Jocasta, you truly are beautiful."

"Yes, she is," Vassos agreed.

Creon winked at me.

"To be sure," said Laius. "And now, let the feast begin! Vassos, check to see whether the banquet is ready in the megaron."

Vassos left, and Laius stepped aside to talk with some of the Pisatans. My father still brimmed with happiness. "Harmonia's robe and necklace – even Niobe never dared wear them. Could one ask for anything more?" Father obviously did not expect an answer; he leaned down and kissed me on the cheek, then walked over to the priests and priestesses who had assisted with the funerals.

Creon grinned, and then spoke in a low voice. "After this, no one can dispute that our mother was descended from Kadmos and Harmonia. You're Harmonia's heir, Jocasta."

"That means you're a descendant of Kadmos too," I murmured.

"Yes," said my brother. He seemed taller as he walked over to join our father.

I drifted closer to Laius. He was speaking to the bald man in the brown cloak, the one who had been at the funeral. "You see?" Laius said. "Pelops has no cause for concern. Thebes is firmly under my control."

The other man pointed at servants bringing out amphorae of wine. "But the cost! This feast is too extravagant!"

"It entertains the people," Laius replied, indicating a group of small children staring entranced at a juggler. "It's a necessary beginning."

"There'll be little joy for you, Laius, if you squander what belongs to Pelops."

Laius shrugged. "Thebes is rich. Pelops will have his tribute."

"He had better–" the Pisatan's glance fell on me, and his expression changed at once. "My dear!" he cried, his voice ringing false in my ears. "What a lovely bride you have here, Laius!"

I let the man take my hand; his palm was unpleasantly moist. "I thank you, my lord...?"

"Okyllus," he said. His hand relaxed, and his smile looked less strained. I hoped he did not think I had overheard his conversation with Laius.

I almost wished that I had not. Our proud city, Thebes – would pay *tribute?*

CHAPTER SIX

The next three months passed with excruciating slowness. I wanted to marry at once, for every day that separated me from Laius' arms felt like an eternity. But the men overruled my objections. Father declared that the gods indicated the sixth day of the year's sixth month as particularly auspicious. And Laius explained that he needed time to arrange for the ceremonies, the feasts and music – and most importantly, to invite the rulers of all the cities across the Hellene lands. Laius meant to show the world that *he*, not Amphion, now ruled Thebes.

I wondered, thinking of Laius' conversation with Okyllus, to what extent that was true. But the talk of tribute I mentioned to no one, not even Creon, because I thought it would make Laius look weak – and because I did not want to remember it myself.

Our messengers departed together but returned one by one, bearing replies from the various foreign kings. The rulers of Gla, Athens and Orchomenos all promised to attend the wedding in person; others would send a son or nephew. Before long an envoy arrived from King Pelops, laden with precious gifts. But the man Laius sent to Krete never returned, and we heard nothing more of his fate. Either his ship foundered on the Great Sea, or pirates captured the vessel.

Always the returning messengers brought news. One of Laius' men reported that the single surviving child of Amphion and Niobe, Princess Chloris, had journeyed safely to the city of Pylos and there married its king. "A beautiful bride, though pale as the moon," he said. "The people wonder if she is ghost rather than woman." The king of Pylos sent rich gifts, fine linen and jewelry inlaid with glimmering sea-shell; he and Queen Chloris would not attend the wedding.

But the messenger brought no news of Niobe. For that we had to wait until our envoy Pelorus returned from his journey to Tantalus' kingdom, far to the east. Tantalus, father to Pelops and Niobe, was fantastically rich and powerful, but had a reputation for bizarre cruelty. The story ran that in one of his rages Tantalus had threatened to serve Pelops for dinner – and raised a sword against his son, nearly cleaving the arm from his body. Niobe and her mother tended the young man's terrible wound, and when he recovered Pelops fled westward with his sister. Here in Hellas, through heroic efforts, he had become a great king in his own right.

Tantalus, although very old, still ruled in the east; and Niobe, after her misfortunes, had decided to return to her childhood home. Pelorus confessed he had always wanted to see that famous court – a desire shared by few, given that king's dangerous reputation. Pelorus returned to Thebes the day before the wedding. Entering Thebes by the Eudoxa Gate near my father's house, he stopped to rest and to refresh himself before proceeding on to King Laius.

I joined my brother and father in the courtyard, now shaded by trees in full leaf, and listened to Pelorus' description of the opulent eastern kingdom. He told us that old King Tantalus' health was failing at last, and that one of his grandsons, another Tantalus, was now regent and was expected to become king any day. Then Pelorus presented me with a gift from Lydia: a carved ivory pyxis filled with perfumed lotion.

I lifted the lid and sniffed; the scent of jasmine and sandalwood reminded me vividly of Thebes' last queen. "What about Niobe?"

"Ah, yes, Niobe," said Pelorus. "I did not see her, but they told me she weeps day and night, sitting on a rock on Mount Sipylus. I heard she has filled a spring with her tears."

"I see." Losing thirteen children in a single day: no wonder that she had gone mad! And yet I thought a ruler should strive *not* to go mad – to stay sane to the end, as King Amphion had done. I put the lid back on the pyxis and resolved to keep my wits about me, no matter what troubles my new responsibilities might bring.

And I would become queen of Thebes the very next day!

The next morning was the slowest and yet the busiest I had ever known. After my bath, in daybreak's feeble light, I picked for a while at a tray loaded with food that I could not eat until Hydna finally gave up and began the elaborate procedure of dressing me. She proved so overcome with emotion that her hands shook, and for once she allowed stolid Merope to arrange my hair, and to apply cosmetics to my eyelids, lashes, lips and nipples.

"More on her eyelids," said Hydna, stepping back.

Merope paused with the vial of kohl, and glanced at me. Neither of us liked to mention Hydna's failing eyesight. "Won't that be too much?" the younger maidservant finally asked.

"People will have to see her from far away," said my nurse firmly. "My poor eyes are a good measure of what they can and can't see."

Merope and I shared another glance, surprised that Hydna would acknowledge what we had tiptoed around for so long. Merope shrugged and I nodded, so she applied more kohl.

At last Hydna was satisfied and we went to join the young women who would walk before me in the procession. Rhodia, my former competitor for Alphenor's attention, stood near the front of the group; so did Melanthe, who had gone to live with the family of her father's business partner. And I thought briefly, sadly, of poor Pinelopi – and of Niobe's daughters, who should have become my sisters-in-law.

The maidens carried gifts: branches of the laurel tree, small baskets brimming with dried rose petals, brightly painted ceramic vials filled with scented oil. These things they would present to Hera, goddess of marriage, when we reached the agora. Female servants such as Hydna, Merope and Nerissa bore my belongings:

clothing and makeup, combs and pins, my jewelry box. The heavier items were already in the palace.

The day before I had visited the shrine of Artemis, the goddess of young girls, giving her my favorite childhood tunic as a symbol of my intention to wed. This morning I carried a bouquet of pale pink roses as a gift for Hera, goddess of marriage. Their scent filled my nostrils, intoxicating, and I thought of what Hydna said as she fussed over the bouquet – that just as marriage would bring both beauty and pain, Hera's sacred roses had sweet scent and sharp thorns. But I had my roses trimmed of thorns; I wanted no pain between Laius and me.

The great wooden doors leading into the street swung open, and the servants leading the procession marched forth. My father and brother led the well-born maidens out of the courtyard; next came my bodyguard – Vassos had insisted, though spears and shields seemed strange in a bridal procession. Finally I stepped out of the shadows into the warmth and light of the noonday sun; additional soldiers followed me.

Applause and cheers greeted me. I blinked and looked around me. There were so many people! Why weren't they in the agora, where the ceremony would take place?

But crowds lined both sides of the road that led up to the palace. It seemed that all of Thebes turned out, and people from all the farms and villages as well – pushing and jostling, craning their necks to stare. They called out to me:

"Bless you, Jocasta, and bless Thebes!"

"You are the daughter of Thebes, and now you will be our mother!"

I continued climbing the hill, my arms filled with roses. The city itself was at its most beautiful: the streets had been cleaned of all refuse, and fragrant pine wreaths and flowers adorned many doors. The wealthier citizens were splendid in their richly dyed clothing and shimmering gold and silver jewelry, and even the peasants wore their best garments and garlands of bright flowers on their heads.

I was about to become queen of Thebes, and already my people loved me.

And I loved Laius. Tonight, at last, I would be in his arms. All night, and every night, for the rest of our lives.

Since the funeral for Amphion and his children, I had seen Laius only six times. When we were together, he was affectionate and loving, but we met rarely. I did not understand how he could bear to be so much apart, but he said it was the only way he could keep himself from taking his husband's rights before our ceremony.

Today that separation would end.

When we reached the top of the hill, I followed Melanthe into the agora, walking the narrow path through the cheering crowds. The merchants' stalls and awnings had been cleared away; only those things that could not be moved remained. Everywhere I saw spires of flowers and laurel wreaths. Laius' soldiers were dressed now in red and gold uniforms; their helmets and bronze spear-points were polished to a dazzling brightness. The women also wore their finest: skirts cascading tier over tier filled the square with riotous color. And then there were the honored guests: among them I recognized a prince of Athens in a snow-white cape, the handsome king and queen of nearby Orchomenos accompanied by their sons, and the king of Gla, his balding head pink and shiny in the sun. Sounds of flutes and cymbals filled the air, and dancers leapt gracefully in and out of our path. The aroma of freshly bread and roasting meat swept past, but I was too nervous for hunger.

We circled through the agora and approached the marble steps of the palace; at the top stood my bridegroom and king. Thrown across his broad shoulders was a long cape dyed in the rich red-purple of Tyrian sea snails, its extravagant expanse proclaiming his status even more than the thick gold cuffs on his arms, the gold-worked leather belt wrapped round his waist. His kilt gleamed white against the suntanned skin of his muscular legs and torso. A wreath of beaten gold leaves circled his head, setting off the darkness of his curling hair. How handsome he looked – how majestic! The sight of him made my knees tremble.

Our eyes met and he smiled at me. I was the most fortunate woman alive!

My father served as the officiating priest. He wore ceremonial robes and laurel leaves wreathed his brow. Standing between Laius and me, he motioned for the procession to stop. Once Father held up his hand the crowd fell silent. When it was completely quiet – I could hear my own heart pounding – he began the ritual questions.

"Who are you?" he asked me.

"Jocasta, daughter of Menoeceus." The first word was difficult, but then I found my voice.

"From where have you come?"

"From the house of my father, Lord Menoeceus."

"And where do you go?"

"To the house of my husband, King Laius."

"Do you go willingly?"

"Yes!" I said, my voice ringing loud and clear.

"And I, Menoeceus, give her willingly, if she be pleasing." My father turned then to the bridegroom. "Are you King Laius?"

"I am," said Laius. "I am Laius, son of Labdakus, descendant of Kadmos, the founder of Thebes."

"Does Jocasta, daughter of Menoeceus, please you?"

"Very much," said the king, his voice loud, clear and confident. He was supposed to say that, of course, but still the words thrilled me; and a ripple of feminine sighs made its way through the crowd. Laius followed up by adding, "Jocasta, daughter of Menoeceus, will you be my wife?"

My father frowned. Laius' question, addressed to me, was not part of the ritual. We were not supposed to speak to each other directly until the priest gave his blessing.

Though Father disapproved, again I heard a murmur of appreciation among the spectators. The chosen daughter of the Spartoi, descended from Kadmos himself, and the legendary, long-absent king. Why should such our match be constrained by ritual?

I longed to cry, "Yes!" at the top of my lungs. But Father held up his hand and stared at me, a warning in his eyes. Accustomed to obeying him, I choked back my reply and beamed silently at my bridegroom. Now I knew Laius loved me. How could I have doubted him?

My father waited until silence returned, then spoke again, still addressing the king. "Do you accept Jocasta into your home and your bed?"

"I do," said Laius, resuming the words of the ritual.

"Will you care for her and protect her?"

"I will," he promised.

"Then, Jocasta, you may cross the threshold and enter the house of Laius."

"Wait!" I cried, my hesitation part of the ritual. "Before I become a wife, I must make an offering to Hera, queen of Heaven."

"That is your right," said my father.

The altar in the agora had been decorated with the symbols of Hera: roses and pomegranates spilled across its surface, and painted terracotta cows as tall as my waist stood on either side. The crowd parted to allow my attendants and me through. Our procession through the agora gave those at the back of the crowd the chance to see the pageantry.

I knelt before the flower-covered shrine; the matron-priestess stood serenely before me.

"Lady Hera, goddess of marriage and fertility, please accept my offering." I handed the priestess the bouquet of roses, glad to be relieved of them, for the wounds on the stems where the thorns had been removed seeped sticky juice onto my palms.

The priestess examined the flowers, then placed them in an alabaster vase. "Young woman, your offering is acceptable. What is it that you seek?"

"I seek Hera's blessing on my marriage."

She placed her hand on my head. "May Hera bless your marriage with children and a faithful husband." Then she helped me back to my feet, my skirts rustling as I rose.

The other maidens presented their gifts as well, each asking Hera's blessing on my marriage. Then we returned through the agora at a stately pace. I longed to run to my husband – *my husband!* – but I compelled myself to walk slowly. Finally I stood again at the bottom of the palace steps.

"Jocasta, daughter of Menoeceus," said my father, his voice loud and clear. "Have you made your offering to Hera?"

"I have, and she has found it acceptable."

"Then you are ready to be a wife. Jocasta, daughter of Menoeceus –" and then his voice cracked, and he was forced to pause. Suddenly, I was able to step outside my own happiness and perceive what a joyful moment this was for my father. "Daughter of Menoeceus," he continued, regaining control over his speech, "you may step over the threshold of Laius' house and become his wife."

Lifted by the cheering voices of the crowd, I ascended the palace steps and walked over to my new husband. Smiling and confident, Laius held out his hand to me. I took it: warm, strong, his hand gripped mine and pulled me close. He hugged me, and then followed with a fierce kiss that turned my insides to melted honey. I pressed myself to him, feeling the warmth of his chest against my breasts. When his mouth finally left mine I felt giddy, overwhelmed by the sweetness of his lips and the scent of his skin, hardly hearing the applause of the people below.

I wanted to dart inside the palace immediately, to fall with him into our marriage bed and be initiated in the duties and pleasures of a wife. He sensed my eagerness and smiled. "Wait, my dear. Just a little longer."

Laius turned and waved toward the open palace doors. Three women stepped out; each carried something precious. The first held the famous serpentine necklace of Harmonia, which she fastened round my neck. The second carried Harmonia's robe; she draped it over my shoulders. And the third woman, Nerissa, set upon my head a golden diadem. Its delicate hammered-gold vines, flowers, and leaves felt light on my brow, and moved like real leaves in the breeze. From the corners of my eyes I could glimpse tiny golden flowers, exquisite and shimmering in the sunlight.

"Behold my wife and your queen!" Laius proclaimed, and the people roared their approval. "Jocasta, daughter of Menoeceus, wife of Laius, and queen of Thebes!"

We stood together, his arm around me, as the people continued to shout their approval. I had never been so happy. I was married to the man I loved, and he was holding me close. I was young and beautiful and wore the necklace with the magic to keep me always so. Not only did my husband love me, but I was queen of Thebes and my people adored me. I was amazed; I had done nothing to deserve it; but I swore I would merit their devotion over time. I would be a better queen than Niobe – I would always honor the gods, and never give my people reason to despise me.

The cheering continued far longer than I could have thought possible, but at last it began to fade. Then Laius, smiling, spoke again. "Bring out the food for feasting! Let the musicians play!"

The flute-girls lifted their instruments and started to blow. Servants came out through the doors, carrying great amphorae of wine and huge platters of food. Most was simple fare: mutton, bread, cheese, and olives; figs and raisins and dried pomegranate kernels – after all, we were feeding the entire city – but it looked and smelled wonderful. There would also be a private, far more elegant feast for the local nobles and the visiting dignitaries.

But I did not want food. I could smell my husband's spicy scent and feel his strong arm around me. I desperately wanted more.

In due time the wine was poured, the food passed out, and at last the people's focus moved away from us. "Now, my dear," Laius breathed in my ear.

I turned to step through the doorway, but Laius startled me by lifting me effortlessly into his arms. I laughed with surprise, and those in the crowd who had not been diverted by the food and drink cheered again.

"A Pisatan custom, my dear," said my new husband, as he carried me easily into the palace. "A bride is always carried into her new home, so that she does not stumble over the threshold and bring bad luck."

The air was cool within the stone walls of the palace, but Laius' arms radiated heat. He carried me up a flight of stairs into a south-facing bedroom, then placed me standing on the floor. The servant women who had given me the ornaments of Theban royalty now surrounded me to remove the diadem, the necklace, and the shimmering, delicate robe of Harmonia.

"I'll take care of the rest," barked Laius. "Leave us."

The servants left, and I was alone – at last! – with my husband. He placed a hand on either side of my face, turned it up towards his own, and began to kiss me.

Such kisses! Slow and gentle and light at first, with a restraint that I could not understand but that coaxed me beyond control. Gradually his kisses grew stronger, more forceful, the slight stubble of his upper lip rough against my skin, his tongue exploring inside my mouth. I writhed, desperately pressing myself against him, but still he kept us standing, tasting my lips, until he paused and I could speak.

"Laius... Husband..." I gasped. I *needed*, and though Hydna had explained to me what passed between a man and a woman, it seemed my body already understood.

Laius grinned at my impatience. "Shh," he said.

He was my king and my husband; I would try to obey. I voiced no more words, but moans of pleasure escaped me. Laius moved his hands to my throat and unhooked the jeweled fibula; my short cape fell to the floor. He explored my neck and breasts with kisses while his sure strong fingers untied the laces of my bodice. Soon the garment lay discarded on the floor. I burned where he touched me, but my back and shoulders felt cool and exposed in the dim room.

He knelt on the floor before me to work loose the knots at my waist. He tugged; my skirts fell to the floor.

Now I was nude, save for my sandals and a few ornaments in my hair. He removed the sandals first, deftly untying one, and then the other. Then he rose again and looked at me, walking around me several times.

"Ah, Jocasta," he murmured, "you *are* beautiful." I was gratified to hear pleasure in his voice.

He brought his lips to mine once more. Still we stood in the center of the room, though the pillows seemed to beckon us and my legs trembled with yearning. His lips brushed across my brow, my earlobes, my neck – every place he kissed quivered in response. Teasing fingers circled my breasts, and then finally he drew one, then the other nipple into his mouth. He knelt before me again, this time tracing a path with his mouth downward from my navel. Grasping my buttocks, he pulled me to his lips. I groaned and twisted my fingers in his hair. At last he pulled his mouth from my body and looked up at me. "All right," he said. "I think you're ready. And I know I am."

With that he released his hold and stood again. He lifted me in his arms and then set me down on the bed. I watched as he quickly removed his cloak, his sandals and his kilt. Then he covered my body with his. He kissed me deeply, moved my legs apart with his knees, and then suddenly entered me.

I ripped my mouth from his, gasping with pain and shock, but then his mouth followed mine and re-took possession. And as he continued inside me, the pain lessened, and transformed into pleasure. I found my own rhythm, moving against him, scarcely aware of anything but the joining of our bodies, the sound of our breath. Finally he shuddered and groaned and it was over.

After a moment he rolled off me and lay on his back, breathing hard. I propped myself up on an elbow in order to study him in the dim light: the dark mass of his beard, the curling hair on his well-muscled chest, his strong nose, the long lashes on his closed eyes. This was my man, my husband.

His breathing gradually became slow and regular, and I realized he had fallen asleep. I felt abandoned – I couldn't possibly sleep just then, not after he had awakened every part of my body. I had never felt more alive. We had just begun! How could he sleep?

But although I was his first wife I was not his first lover; I couldn't expect him to share my sense of awe. I wondered if I, as his wife, might touch him even though he slept. Gingerly I stretched out my hand and brushed the hair on his chest; then I edged closer to him, so that I could rest my head against his shoulder. Strange that I could feel lonely, here in his bed. But nonetheless I treasured the warm closeness, and we lay there together while I counted his breaths and listened to the beating of his heart.

Eventually Laius woke, his eyelids fluttering open, his face turning so that he could see mine. At first he appeared slightly puzzled.

"Husband," I whispered.

"Jocasta," he mumbled, then yawned.

Now that he was awake, I felt comforted. But still I wanted to know that he was not disappointed.

"Was I – am I – acceptable?" I asked, my voice so low I was not sure if he could hear me.

But he did hear me. His response was to laugh, then to kiss me long and hard, and then to laugh again. "Acceptable! My darling Jocasta, you are the most alluring woman in Thebes – perhaps in all Hellas."

I rested my head on his chest. His hand slipped gently down my side, and I hoped we would make love again; but soon he stirred, and reminded me that we had a feast to attend, and the dignitaries from other kingdoms awaited us.

"I'd rather stay here," I told him, kissing his neck.

"Remember, I'm an old man." He laughed, showing he did not believe what he had said, and I joined his laughter. "Come, my dear," he said, sitting up and pulling me along, "we must join our guests."

He dressed himself and helped me put on my clothes. I found a mirror on one of the side tables; dismayed by my appearance, I wiped smeared makeup from beneath my eyes with one thumb, and pushed at my tumbled hair. Laius smiled and told me to leave it. "Tousled hair is a sign of a good marriage," he said, setting the glittering diadem back on my head.

I had never heard this saying before; perhaps it came from Pisa, or perhaps he had invented it for his own convenience. At any rate I put down the mirror and let him lead me out of the room. When we walked into the megaron, where all the nobles and dignitaries were gathered, applause and ribald comments greeted us. I flushed with embarrassment. I did not feel very queenly – but I felt very bridal, as if everyone knew what we had been doing. And, of course, they *did* know. I tried to hide my face in Laius' cloak but this made everyone laugh louder.

"She's a shy one!" called a man's voice.

"Well, you know old Menoeceus would keep his daughter pure!"

"Ah, but Laius will fix that soon enough!" That comment drew a roar of laughter.

"His reputation on that matter is clear—"

"That's just what Thebes needs, a king with some fire in his blood!"

"*And* his loins!"

Amidst the laughter, the priestess of Hera, escorted by Hydna and Nerissa, came out of the corridor leading to our bedroom. They held up a white linen sheet for everyone to see; there was a bright bloodstain on it, sign of my vanquished virginity.

The people cheered, women as well as men. One woman called, "Fiery loins indeed! I'll wager she'll see no monthly blood till her first is born!"

I was relieved when the musicians began to play, and such remarks were drowned out. Laius called for the feast to begin, which soon dampened the coarse joking. I could not manage to eat much, but I drank some wine and nibbled on a honeycake. Laius introduced me to the party from Pisa, old friends of his.

After a while the king stood, saying he needed to stretch his legs, and began to circulate among the guests. My heart skipped a beat when he paused to talk to Nerissa, who held the hand of their younger son Gogos, a boy of three or four. I was relieved to see Laius did not stop with her long. He made his way around to the others, speaking with the ambassadors from Korinth, with Pelorus, and then with my father. I remained silent, watching him lovingly, oblivious to those in my immediate vicinity until another sat in his spot.

I began to object, and then saw that it was Polydorus, Laius' firstborn son.

He was a few years older than I, about Creon's age, and had his father's broad shoulders and strong nose; but he kept his cheeks clean-shaven, perhaps to better display the fine chiseled line of his jaw. His coloring was like his mother's: golden hair and leaf-green eyes. "Let me wish you well, Jocasta," said the young man, picking up Laius' cup and draining it. "Congratulations! No woman deserves more to be queen of Thebes."

"Thank you," I said primly, wishing he would go away.

"So, what shall I call you now? *Mother*?"

"You have a mother," I said, looking over at Nerissa, whose gaze was fixed upon us.

"But you're married to my father, and that makes you my mother, doesn't it? Or at least my stepmother." He wiped his lips with Laius' napkin. He lowered his voice, so that only I could hear. "Of course, you're far too young and pretty to be my mother."

I smiled, until I heard his next words: "Or rather, my father's far too old for you."

I gaped, shocked speechless for a moment. Then I hissed, "He's *not* too old!"

"Maybe not," said Polydorus. "Strange, though, that it took so many years for him to decide that he wanted to be king."

Polydorus then left, and I frowned, trying to understand what he had meant.

Vassos, ever watchful, approached me. "Is everything all right, my lady queen?"

"What? Oh, I suppose so," I answered, not wanting to cause family ruptures on this night, of all nights.

I was confused by Polydorus' behavior. What was he trying to do?

Did he hate his father, and wish to shame him? But that seemed most unwise; only from Laius could Polydorus claim any status – his mother was a mere servant. Did he mean to create discontent in my heart? I thought of the legend of Kadmos and the men sown from serpent's teeth. When Kadmos threw his stone among the Sown Men, they fought amongst themselves until only five, my father's ancestor among them, survived.

"My lady queen?" Vassos said dubiously.

I forced my lips into a smile. "Yes, Vassos, everything is fine. Although I'd like more wine, if you can arrange it."

"As my lady wishes," he said, looking pleased to be sent on an errand.

Creon now slid into the place at my side.

"Sister! Or should I say, my lady queen! Let me drink to you!" He had brought his own goblet, and he lifted it high.

"I'm so glad to see you," I said.

"Something wrong?" he asked, leaning close so he and I could talk more easily.

I recounted my conversation with Polydorus.

My brother bit into a fig. "He's probably just drunk. But remember, it's better to make him your friend if you can. You may need him later." He sipped at his wine. "Although right now, sister dear, you are *very* popular. They're all saying wonderful things about you."

"Like what?" I asked.

"I can't tell you – it would make you too conceited."

"Creon, please!"

His eyes sparkled. "I will tell you, but not now. I'll save it for some time when you're sad. Let me just say that people seem very impressed with you – more so than with your husband, in fact."

I could not understand this. So far I had done nothing. And, from where I sat, Laius was everything. "That makes no sense."

"Well – of course I, as your brother, can withstand your beauty; but everyone else is bewitched. The ordinary Thebans, our nobles, even the travelers. This prince from Orchomenos was saying that you're the most exquisite woman he has seen in his entire life – although he's not that old, so perhaps he doesn't know much."

"But – but right now my hair's a *mess*," I objected.

Creon laughed. "And they all know why it's a mess, and they're all wishing that they had been with you to mess it up."

I wondered if what my brother said was true and felt another blush heat my face. I bent my head down, so that my tumbled curls could hide my cheeks, and reached for a piece of cheese that I did not want. "Could we change the subject?"

"As you like," said Creon. "Let me tell you about the visitors." And he pointed to one traveler, and then another, explaining where they were from and how they had arrived. We had visitors from sandy Pylos and wealthy Korinth and from Athens, our one-time enemy; from the islands of Ithaka and Chios; Tiryns and Mycenae had sent ambassadors as well.

"You remember the man in the brown cape? Standing near Melanthe?"

"Yes," I said cautiously. "Okyllus, from Pelops' court."

"Exactly. You must be especially gracious to him."

"Why?"

"Because he's the power behind Laius, you know."

"That man?"

"Not *him* – but Pelops. Who supplied Laius with an army? Pelops. Who is going to demand tribute? Pelops."

I had never mentioned this to my brother. "How do you know?" I whispered, feeling guilty for having kept that from him, and glad that he had found it out himself.

"I can tell an acorn from a fig." Creon lowered his voice. "Why do you think Laius has spent so much time looking through the palace storerooms, and inspecting the granaries by the gates?"

My mind reeled at his comment. Had Pelops sent Laius? Or had the gods? Or had the gods told Pelops to send Laius? And what had Laius promised, that Pelops would give him preference?

"How did you learn all this?" I demanded.

"I – look who's here!" he said, diverted by an entrance.

I followed his gaze and saw a familiar figure: plain dark robes, long gray hair pulled back, eyes covered with a black cloth. "The Tiresias! I didn't think she was even in Thebes."

"No one wants to miss your wedding, Jocasta. Not even the handmaiden of Apollo!"

We watched as our father went to greet her and offered her refreshment. I was glad to see her accept it: that meant she was not fasting, and so not preparing to prophesize. On the other hand, even when she had eaten she was capable of dire words – I shuddered, remembering the calamity she had foretold before the destruction of Niobe's family.

Yet no one here would willingly offend the gods. And the Tiresias' words to me had been so encouraging.

Creon left my side, and others came to chat: Rhodia and her mother; then Melanthe, boldly dressed in a nearly transparent gown of white Aegyptian linen and drinking wine without any water at all. I grew tired and longed for bed; I had slept little the previous night. Besides, I longed to be in my husband's arms. He was speaking with the nobles and dignitaries, men so important to please – how I wished they would all go away! I shifted restlessly in my chair, and the tenderness between my legs reminded me of what Laius and I had lately been about, and would be soon again.

Although it seemed to take forever, eventually people began to leave. Finally those who were staying with us at the palace began heading to their rooms. I yawned and waved at Laius, who was conversing with my father and the Tiresias. At last he seemed to remember he had a wife and came over to me.

"My dear, you look tired. Why don't you go to bed?"

"I will if you come with me," I said, linking my fingers with his and tugging.

He laughed, resisted, but carried my hand to his lips and kissed it. "I'll come a little later, my dear. You go ahead, and I'll be with you soon."

I felt disappointed that he would not come with me, but I was exhausted. I went to our room and found Hydna asleep in a chair.

"Sorry!" she apologized, stretching and shaking her head. "How is the queen of Thebes?"

"Tired," I admitted.

"And where's the king of Thebes?" she asked, pulling herself to her feet.

"Still in the megaron, drinking and talking," I replied, half in despair.

"Husbands!" exclaimed my nurse, although she had buried hers many years ago. "He'll be here soon enough. Let's get you ready for bed, butterfly."

Hydna seated me on the chair and clucked as she freed the diadem from my tangled hair. She combed it softly, then helped me out of my clothes and into a plain linen shift. "Not that you'll need that," she chuckled. Then she led me to the wide bed and tucked me in.

"I'm just upstairs," she told me. "First door up. Send for me if you need me."

"Thank you, Hydna. Good night."

She took the lamp with her, leaving me in the dark. I did not mind. I wriggled out of my shift so that I would be even more ready for my husband. Then I lay in bed, wondering when he would come, and hugged a pillow close, wishing it were Laius. It smelled like him, I thought, spicy and a little sharp. I remembered how he had touched me and kissed me, how he had filled me so that we really seemed to become one person.

Awash in such recent memories, and full of anticipation, I did not expect to fall asleep. But I must have, waking only when I heard footsteps.

Blinking in the lamplight, I needed a moment to remember where I was. And then I did, and I was flooded with happiness.

"Laius?" I asked, looking at the shadowy figure near the bed.

It was Laius. But this was not the smiling, tender man who had made love to me earlier in the day. His face was dark, his eyes bloodshot, his expression one of unmistakable fury.

"Laius?" I asked again, but this time with apprehension and even fear.

"You whore!" he yelled, and pulled me out of the bed.

Before I could say anything, before I could ask anything, he had dragged me across the room and pushed me out the door. Then he slammed it shut, leaving me naked in the corridor.

CHAPTER SEVEN

I had been dazed with sleep, but the cold air of the corridor shocked me awake. The pair of soldiers standing at the door – one a bodyguard for Laius, the other assigned to me – gaped at the sight of their unclothed queen. The first man averted his eyes, then the second.

But my husband's behavior distressed me far more than my nakedness.

"Laius!" I cried, knocking on the door. "Laius, what's wrong?"

There was no answer. I pounded my fists against the door, and although my throat constricted, I raised my voice further. "Laius, *please* let me in and tell me what's going on!"

"Get away, *porni*!" came his muffled shout.

Tears welled up in my eyes. "How can you call me that?" I cried, splaying my fingers against the unyielding door. "What have I done?"

"Traitor! Demoness! Monster!"

My heart thudded wildly and the tears spilled over. Could this be the same man who made love to me only a few hours earlier? "Laius, please! Will you at least let me have my clothes?"

"You deserve no clothes, *porni*!"

I pushed and pulled at the door but it would not open. Weeping now in earnest, I sagged to my knees, my cheek scraping against the wood of the door.

My bodyguard removed his cloak and draped it around my shoulders. The other man, a grizzled Pisatan, cleared his throat and spoke. "I don't think he's going to be worth talking to tonight, my lady. It's no use staying here at the door."

At his words I sobbed harder. I did not even know my way around the palace. "But where can I go?"

The men glanced at each other and shook their heads.

I pulled the woolen cloak tighter around me, and remembered my nurse. Through my tears I sobbed: "Hydna – my maid – her room?"

Their faces lit up at my suggestion. "This way, my lady," said the younger of the two, and led me up the steep stairs to my maid's room.

Hydna woke at once, but it took some time to make her understand – partly because I was crying so hard, partly because I did not understand myself. "He called you a whore and pushed you out of the room?" she summarized at last.

"Yes," I gulped.

"Oh, child," she said, putting her arms around me and rocking me gently. "Oh, my poor butterfly."

"I don't understand. What have I done?"

She hugged me. "*You* haven't done anything. *He* has done it. Maybe he's drunk. Some men get angry when they drink, you know. Perhaps he heard some terrible lie about you. Maybe both – men believe all sorts of ridiculous lies when they drink."

Her suggestions were not exactly cheerful, but they comforted me a little.

"Now, why don't you creep in next to me and get some sleep? I'm sure everything will be better in the morning."

I slid in beside her. The cushions were less lavish than my own – filled with stiff straw instead of soft wool - but they were thick and clean. I pulled the rough wool blanket around my bare legs.

Hydna murmured gently to me for a while, but then, worn out from the day's events and the rich food and wine of the marriage feast, she fell asleep.

I could not.

Thoughts whirled in my head; tears streamed down my cheeks, and sometimes I could not keep myself from sobbing aloud. I regretted coming into Hydna's bed, because I would surely wake her – then I remembered that I had nowhere else to go. At this thought I buried my face in the pillow to dampen the sound of a wail I could not hold back.

After I had wept myself dry , I recalled how Hydna said that Laius was the problem, not me. But if Laius had a problem, then it must be mine as well: he was my husband.

Was he drunk? Had someone told him vile lies about me? Or was it something else?

Laius had been gone from Thebes for more than thirty years. King Pelops had wanted his own sister and brother-in-law on the throne, so it made sense that he kept Laius confined to Pisa – but might there be another reason?

Could Laius – could Laius be *mad*?

If so, it must be a peculiar kind of madness: before tonight he had always seemed normal. Better than normal – handsome, kind, intelligent. I had heard that King Pelops relied on him to organize the Olympic Games. Only now did his behavior suggest insanity. But the guard had told me to give up on Laius for the night – perhaps my husband had fits of madness, and the guard knew it?

The wine god Dionysus was said to bring madness upon those he opposed, and he had afflicted the descendants of Kadmos before. I resolved to make an offering to Dionysus. Perhaps that would help.

I pulled the blanket over my ear, trying to shut out Hydna's snores. How could this be happening, when the Tiresias had foretold that my husband would love me?

Then I recalled the seer's exact words. She had said "this breast to fill with love" – which meant that *I* would love my husband, not necessarily that he would love me.

I had never done anything to offend Apollo! Why would he send me into a loveless marriage? Or perhaps Apollo wished me happiness, while Dionysus was angry with Laius.

I did not understand the gods, just as I did not understand why Laius was so angry.

Dawn broke before I finally entered the land of dreams, and my stay in that realm was short. But during my brief sleep Hydna managed to find me some clothes, and when I woke she helped me dress. My heart was heavy as I looked around the cramped room with its bare whitewashed walls. I *should* have awakened in the expansive royal chamber, at my husband's side.

"Have you heard anything?" I asked as she combed my hair.

"Only that there was a lovers' quarrel."

Lovers! Were we lovers? Or had everything ended before it began?

A knock sounded at the door, and Hydna opened it to admit Nerissa. The blonde woman carried a tray. "My lady queen, I've brought your breakfast."

I shook my head and turned my face away from her; I didn't want her to see my swollen red eyes or the puffiness of my tear-stained cheeks.

Nerissa insisted gently, "My lady queen, you must eat."

"I'm not hungry," I snapped at her. She wore a beige linen skirt and a green cape that brought out the color of her eyes. Her movements were calm, her attitude poised. She seemed to be everything I was not.

I viewed her with mistrust. Had she been with my husband last night? Had *she* told him something to make him hate me? Or had she cast a spell, and witched his love away?

Nerissa met my gaze. "I'm sorry about what happened," she said. "I know Laius can be difficult at times."

I did not want pity from my husband's former mistress. And certainly not from his *current* mistress! Suspicion swelled like a toxic bubble in my stomach. I felt like throwing up; the sight of the cheese and figs sickened me. "Take it away," I told her.

Nerissa turned and left without speaking, shutting the door behind her.

"That was rude," Hydna admonished me.

"I don't care," I told her. "I can't eat right now. For all I know, it could be poisoned!"

Hydna looked alarmed. "Do you really think so?"

"I don't know," I said. "But I can't face her – she's the mother of his sons. Oh, Hydna, what shall I do?"

I felt ready to burst into tears again, when a second knock startled me.

"May I come in?"

The voice was male and the accent Pisatan. Could it be Laius?

"Enter!" I called, my heart soaring.

But the voice belonged to Vassos. "Excuse me, my lady, but you're needed to receive the envoys from Gla and Athens."

"Am I?" My first thought was: Laius wanted me there! "What word from my husband?"

"The king is indisposed and has given directions not to be disturbed," said Vassos. His look of sympathy intensified my shame: the morning after my wedding night, I was banished to my maid's room and forced to ask about my own husband.

Bitterly I asked, "If the king does not attend, then why should I?" If Laius were indisposed, then so was I – I had barely slept; my chest still ached from sobbing. And how could I appear as queen, with no king at my side?

"Because you are Jocasta, queen of Thebes," Vassos said firmly. "I have chosen to serve you, because I know you will do what needs to be done."

My bodyguard's words reminded me of the things I had pondered the last few months: the duties of a queen, smiling even when she wanted to weep. I had not expected to be tested so soon – but his calm praise encouraged me.

111

"Thebes needs you, my lady queen," Vassos continued. "And if you come it will crush rumors before they begin."

My cheeks burned at the notion of gossip circulating about me and Laius – bad enough that this had happened, but how humiliating to have the people of Thebes *talking* about it! They could be speculating, wondering, even *laughing* about last night's events. Still, I tried to retain some composure. I moistened my lips, and struggled to find my voice. "Tell the envoys I'll be there."

"Very good, my lady." He bowed and left.

Hydna sent for the necklace of Harmonia and fastened it around my neck. It belonged to me now, and would help me look the part I needed to play. The robe of Harmonia was too delicate for any but the most special occasions, so Hydna dressed me in other clothes. But despite her skill with cosmetics my eyes looked puffy and red, my lips swollen. How could I possibly seem convincing as a happy queen and satisfied bride? At last she placed the crown on my head – it was heavy, I thought, and my temples ached already, but it seemed that queens suffered in things great and small.

I was ready. I could no longer postpone facing my public.

When I entered the megaron all talking stopped, and people watched me cross the room to my throne. As Vassos had explained, Laius was not there. But among those milling about, eating and drinking from trays and goblets the servants passed around, I saw my brother. Relieved, I beckoned to him, then lowered myself onto the soft cushions. I was so upset about Laius that I only realized later what I had just done: sat for the first time on the throne of the queen of Thebes. It felt peculiar to be positioned above the people, looking down at them – though lower than the king's throne, the ornate chair that I still associated with Niobe rested on a dais elevated by three steps.

Creon approached me, bowed, and then stepped on the dais so that we could speak privately. "How are you?"

"Terrible," I said softly. "Did you hear what happened last night?"

"Yes. Everyone's talking about it, but no one understands. What's going on?"

"If only I knew!" I said in a choked whisper.

He looked at me with pity and I clutched the arm of the chair, fighting back tears.

Creon pried my hand off the throne and squeezed it so hard that it hurt, so that the very pain distracted me. "We'll find out soon enough. In the meantime, smile even though you want to cry. The queen of Thebes is serene and confident. And now you're the queen."

His voice was kind, comforting. I drew strength from his presence.

"Stay with me now, Creon, please. I need you here right now."

And so my brother remained with me during the next few hours, the most difficult hours of my marriage with Laius. Creon whispered suggestions as I greeted the diplomats and envoys.

"So sorry to hear your husband is indisposed," said the envoy from Sikyon, pronouncing his words salaciously, as if he suspected I had worn Laius out in bed.

"I am sure he'll be up and about soon," I replied.

"Of course, my lady queen. If you would be so gracious as to accept this gift..."

"...we hope you can consider trading the leather from your herds..."

"...the city of Gla would like to arrange safe passage for a shipment of gold from the north..."

Diplomatic requests, business proposals, matters of ritual. I could accept the gifts easily enough, but what should I do in the other situations? I smiled and nodded, thought as quickly as I could, often said I would tell Laius, and always consulted with Creon. Trying to find appropriate responses at least distracted me from my worries.

By midday, although still sick at heart, I felt pangs of hunger. Knowing I must eat, I nibbled at a piece of bread and sipped some grape juice.

I kept a watch for my husband and king, but he did not appear. Nor did the Tiresias, although I was not looking for her. When Father appeared shortly after midday, he mentioned that the seer had already left Thebes.

"But she did not come to pay her respects!" I said, offended.

"The handmaiden of Apollo need bow to no mortal," declared my father, "not even a queen."

"I didn't mean that," I said quickly, although that had indeed been my meaning. "But on my wedding day…"

"And where, Jocasta, is the king?" Father asked, as if I had misplaced him.

"He's indisposed,"

Father frowned but said nothing more, for which I silently thanked all the gods. In the late hours of the afternoon I asked Vassos to check on Laius. It finally occurred to me that my husband could be truly ill. Perhaps some sickness had overtaken him the night before, and I should have sent Vassos earlier.

But the message came back that Laius would see no one. I did not know what to do. Somehow I kept the tears at bay. The day waned; the dignitaries finally departed. Grateful they were gone, I felt exhausted to the core and relieved to be sitting with just my father, my brother, Pelorus and Vassos. While the men discussed some of the visitors' requests, my mind wandered. Where would I sleep that night?

Just then Laius appeared. His hair was wild, his eyes bloodshot, his clothes askew. He stumbled over to his throne but did not sit – instead he clung to it, as if he needed its support to keep from falling.

I leapt from my own throne and ran to him. "Laius! Are you all right?"

He pushed me away with one hand and turned to address my father, who stood before the central hearth. "Take her back!"

"What?" asked Father, stunned.

"You must take her back. She can't be my wife!"

"Why not?" I wailed.

"By the laws of Thebes, you can only divorce her if she's unfaithful or barren," said my father. "A single night of marriage is not enough to determine that."

"The Tiresias. Last night. She told me that our marriage…"

A chill rushed down my back at this mention of the seer; Creon stiffened, and Father took a step closer to the king.

"What exactly did the Tiresias say?" Father prompted.

"She said the gods would strike me dead if I repeat it. It's too terrible!" Laius drew a deep breath. "But I can't stay married to her," he said, pointing at me.

"And you can't divorce her," said my father, slowly but adamantly. "You have taken vows before the gods."

Laius' face darkened with anger at this; he pounded his fist against the side of his throne. "Then let her sleep alone," he stormed, whirling on his heel and heading for the door. "She'll not bed with me!"

When he was gone it was all I could do to keep from bursting into tears. Father frowned gravely and Creon moved to stand beside me. Unable to look into their concerned faces I turned away from them, glancing around the nearly empty megaron, my unfocused gaze sweeping across the bright colors of the wall paintings and the stuccoed floor to rest on the raised lip of the circular hearth. A pattern of red and yellow flames was painted around its circumference. The hearth was the sacred center of any home – but I did not see how this palace could be my home, when my husband the king so utterly rejected me.

Hydna had been right; someone *had* told Laius terrible things about me.

"Why would the Tiresias want to destroy my marriage?" I asked, when I could finally speak. But no one answered.

Laius moved out of our bedroom, so I no longer had to sleep with my maid. I learned that he had gone to Nerissa, who seemed to have escaped the Tiresias' notice. Only *I* was the object of prophecies.

At night I cried, hugging the pillow that still carried traces of his scent, desperate in my loneliness.

During the day Laius and I sat on our thrones, together but separate – Laius never touching me, never looking in my direction, speaking to me only when he must.

"This is torture," I said one morning to Creon, as we completed a tour of the palace storerooms. On wax-coated tablets we had tallied sacks of grain and jars of olive oil and amphorae of wine. Compared to our father's household stores, the quantities seemed vast, but when we reckoned how many the palace had to feed, the amount was paltry. Had Thebes always had so little – or had too much been sent off in tribute? Okyllus had departed for Pisa before dawn one morning; how many carts of provisions had gone with him?

But the problem of tribute disturbed me less than my marital troubles. Despite the unpromising numbers, I had enjoyed spending the morning with my brother, concentrating on something of importance. Now that we headed back toward the megaron, passing through the bands of sunlight and shadow cast by red-painted columns, my stomach tightened. "I can't face Laius again today."

I wanted to go back in time, to say that the past few days had never happened, to return to my father's house. No, that was not quite right: I truly longed for some miracle that would change Laius' heart once more – I wanted the Tiresias to come back and say she had made a mistake, or explain that Laius had misunderstood her. My mind ran rampant with hopeful possibilities. But I saw no way to make any of them happen.

"Jocasta, you *must* face him," said Creon, his voice earnest. "Don't you realize how insecure your position is?"

I shrugged. "What's the point of being queen, if the king doesn't love me?"

Creon's response was harsh. "What's the point of staying alive?"

I clutched his arm. "Do you think – do you think Laius wants me *dead*?"

"He might. We must make sure your position is as strong as possible – so that he's afraid to harm you."

Despite my unhappiness, my position *was* strong and growing stronger. The people loved and supported me, far more than they loved my husband. At first this surprised me, for I could not see what had I done to earn their loyalty. But Creon and I reasoned that I had grown up in Thebes, whereas Laius seemed like a foreigner; despite my youth and innocence, I was the one spurned, prompting sympathy; and, then, the people simply *saw* me far often than my husband – for Laius, morose and brooding over whatever the Tiresias had told him, appeared at few public events. Word gradually spread that Laius was sending Theban treasure to Pelops in Pisa, making him even less popular.

I began to learn about the relative strengths of the leading kingdoms. King Pelops of Pisa, an old friend of Laius', had great influence in the southern peninsula. Athens and Krete dominated trade across the Middle Sea. On the other hand, Thebes had access to northern gold and amber; we had marble quarries just a few hours by ox-cart from the city; and our herds of cattle were the largest and the best in Hellas. We were rich in resources.

More and more I appreciated what Amphion had done for Thebes – especially its strong thick walls and fortified gates. Father told me how when construction started years ago, no one had thought such an ambitious project possible; but somehow Amphion had managed it.

My understanding of royal duties grew through discussions with my father, my brother, Pelorus and Vassos, as well as some of the foreign dignitaries. As Creon predicted, I *could* charm men. A smile, a flutter of my eyelashes, a little flattery – these things went far, and many of the envoys seemed eager to instruct me in the politics of their home cities. After a few goblets of wine, some of them spilled information they should have kept secret – but perhaps they perceived me, this girlish bride, as no threat at all.

I smiled when I wanted to cry.

I made a point of seeking the gods' assistance. I sent Hydna on my behalf with an offering to Hera, goddess of marriage, asking her to change Laius' heart towards me – although Hera's relationship with her own husband was not particularly good. Tremulously asked Father to implore mercy from Apollo: he nodded gravely, and said he would do what he could. Creon went to those who worshipped Dionysus, to plead with that god to take away Laius' madness.

Creon was my support during the day, Hydna my comfort when darkness fell. She combed my hair and rubbed my shoulders, told me she was proud of me. She said that I looked as lovely as ever, and that Laius would certainly return to my bed soon. I listened to her with hope, wishing her predictions carried as much weight as those of the Tiresias.

But after Hydna left for her own room I lay sleepless, my mind full of the many ways that Laius had avoided me during the day. After several nights of this, I finally grew so tired that I did sleep. And then I slept more than ever before in my life. I sank down into the bed each evening, in my exhaustion utterly grateful to be there. Soon I began to wonder how I could possibly sleep so much. Was my longing for Laius making me weary? Or was I ill?

When, over many days, my strength did not return, I began to suspect Laius of administering evil herbs. I did not see how he could manage it, as he never came near me – but the thought made me nervous, and all food tasted terrible. My stomach churned, and I found it difficult to keep anything down.

"Hydna, I'm sick," I told her one evening, as she tucked me into bed. "I'm afraid Laius is poisoning me." Her brow furrowed, she knelt next to me and put her hand on my forehead. She asked a few questions, and I answered them.

But her grave expression gave way to a wide, gap-toothed smile. "My dear, dear Jocasta! My darling butterfly!"

"What is it?" I asked, surprised.

"You're with child!"

I sat up straight, my exhaustion forgotten. "How can that be?"

Her expression became indulgent. "Jocasta, I explained—"

"I know," I said, stopping her. And yet – only once, and still I carried his child. "Are you sure?"

"Your belly won't swell for several months, but the signs are clear. Child, this is wonderful news! It will surely bring Laius back to you."

Joy, which I had thought gone forever, flickered inside me. Could Laius be mine once more? Perhaps the gods had been swayed by my prayers and gifts, and the Tiresias' prophecy of love and fertility would come true after all.

But then I remembered Laius' glum stare from earlier in the day, and doubts arose in my heart. "Do you think so?"

"Of course it will," Hydna said, putting her arms around me. "He'll love you again – you'll see."

My mind raced – would he? He *ought* to, I thought, and yet I could not be sure. He seemed to hate me so much. "I don't know," I said. "I just don't know. I don't want to tell him just yet."

"My dear, you can't keep it a secret for long."

"Just for now. For a few months. Please?"

She frowned and took my hand. "Jocasta, you must visit the altar of Artemis, now and every month until you give birth. My sister died in labor because she ignored this custom – and her child died too."

"I can't tell him yet. I'll make it up to Artemis," I said, although I did not know how I could atone for slighting a goddess. "You could take offerings for me."

With great reluctance, Hydna agreed. Finally she left me to my lonely bed. But now it seemed less lonely, with a baby growing inside me.

Still I could not sleep. What exactly had the Tiresias told my husband? And why had Laius called me *porni*?

Whore was a cruel word for a bride on her wedding night.

For the first time I felt a stirring of anger toward Laius. I had done nothing wrong! As wife and queen I did not deserve such treatment.

I could not decide if my pregnancy would bring him back to me, or if it would drive us further apart. He might hate me even more, since my fertility meant he could never reject me. And what if – what if I lost the baby?

I would not. I *could* not. The spark of life in my womb was our child, my child, and I would protect it with my entire being.

Time that summer seemed distorted: occasionally galloping as quickly as a horse, other times crawling like a lazy tortoise. My days were full and passed quickly, even after the audiences were over, for a queen had much to do – attending festivals and sacrifices, receiving reports on the health of the herds, supervising the weaving room in the palace, learning exactly how hard to press when bartering our goods for Athenian silver or Chian wine. But the short nights of summer dragged on without end. I stared up at the painted beams above my head, trying in vain to recall a single word of kindness from my husband during the day gone by.

Cursed. Why should my marriage be cursed? What confidence could I have in a prophecy from the Tiresias, anyway? To wear the crown – well, yes, I wore the crown of Thebes, but only *because* she had said I would, so where was the marvel in that? In fact, her prophecies contradicted each other: she had told me my marriage would be blessed, and yet told Laius it would be cursed.

I had burned for Laius when we first met, but with each passing day I felt less affection for him. He not only ignored me, but caressed Nerissa in public! My opinion of him as a ruler also sank. I knew he was capable – he had organized Pelops' fabulous games, after all – but he simply did not do the work. A good king would have spent much time away from the megaron: speaking to the men who ran the marble quarry, conferring with his soldiers after their patrols, congratulating the nobles after a successful boar hunt. But Laius huddled in a corner with a few cronies, playing endless games of senet, downing one cup of wine after another. He displayed some interest when we arranged a wrestling match to entertain visiting dignitaries, but afterward sank glumly back down with his drink. He came to his throne late in the morning, so that decisions had to be delayed – or else Creon and I simply made them ourselves. Laius did not seem to care.

In truth Creon and I, together our father, and Vassos and Pelorus, quickly became a ruling council. Father offered political experience and religious knowledge; Creon added sharp intelligence and a keen sense of hidden goings-on. Pelorus and Vassos had traveled much, and knew the foreign kings who were our trading partners, political allies, and rivals. And, though young and inexperienced, my woman's heart understood the needs of the people.

My husband regretted marrying me; his sons and his mistress ignored me, but everyone else seemed to adore me as their queen. People cheered when they saw me; my brother and father praised my increasing poise. I could see real devotion in Vassos and his handpicked men as they escorted me down country paths to visit farmers and vintners, and the temples and altars scattered through the hills. Everyone could see that Laius neglected me; and nearly everyone seemed to be on my side. Even among those who had come with him from Pisa, Laius was not the favorite.

The king grew jealous when visitors bowed lower for me than they did before him. He spent even more of his time with Nerissa and their sons, and glowered at me when people asked, "And what does the queen say?" as if his own opinions were irrelevant. Finally he stopped speaking to me at all, and only sent messages through Pelorus, whose easy-going manner appealed to Laius.

In the meantime, my nipples darkened and my breasts swelled. I drew my cape closer to hide the increasing size of my breasts and used pale ochre on the nipples, but soon my pregnancy would be visible. And I had still not told my husband.

Nor had I made a single visit to the altar of Artemis, and I began to fear her anger. "You *must* make an offering to her yourself," Hydna insisted, and suggested doves, flowers, and hares to placate the goddess.

"But if I go to the altar of Artemis, everyone will know I'm with child."

"Everyone will know soon anyway," said my nurse. "In fact, they're already talking."

I suspected she was one of those doing the talking. But in truth, I had already loosened my skirt-laces. And I was beginning to fear the time to come; childbirth sent so many women to the Underworld. I needed the protection of Lady Artemis.

Though Artemis had never married, nor slept with any male, and was in fact the goddess of young maidens, she was also the goddess of childbearing. Just after her birth, she assisted her mother Leto in delivering her twin brother, Apollo. Artemis held the divine power to protect pregnant women, and she watched over babies and all young creatures. And so, on a clear sunny day three months after my wedding, just as the apple harvest was beginning, I visited her altar to beseech the goddess for my life and the life of my child, bringing an armful of flowers and two white doves in a wicker cage. I did not announce my visit in advance, except to Vassos and my brother, who arranged the sacrifice. But the shrine was some distance outside the walls; before I even left the little wooden temple, word spread.

"May Artemis protect you!" called out a peasant woman working in the roadside orchard, as I returned to the path and Vassos' protection.

"Thebes is blessed!" cried another, gesturing to her basket full of ripe, red fruit. "Look how well the trees are bearing!"

"As fruitful as the queen," agreed her companion. "The prophecy is coming true!"

By the time we returned to the agora, a real crowd had gathered. People shouted and cheered as we crossed the marketplace toward the palace steps. "The queen of Thebes!" "Mother of Thebes!" Others took up the phrases and chanted them wildly.

I climbed the marble steps and stood at the top, my heart soaring. My subjects rejoiced for me, and I reveled in their happiness.

They made so much noise that Laius, though the morning was still young, came outside.

"What's going on?" he asked, blinking in the sunlight.

"My lord king, the people are celebrating," said Vassos.

"I can see that," Laius snapped, although given his bloodshot, puffy eyes I doubted that he could. "What I want to know is *why*."

Vassos glanced at me; I shrugged. There was no point in trying to keep it secret any longer.

"They rejoice because the queen of Thebes is with child."

I expected Laius to lash out at me, to insult me, perhaps even strike me. Instead he whispered: "No!" and then staggered, falling to his knees.

He put his hands over his face for a moment, then removed them and looked up at me, stricken. "How could you?" he asked, his first words to me in months.

"How could *I*?" I burst back angrily. "It's your child too!"

"Not my child," he muttered. "Not my child."

"It *is* your child, no matter what you say."

The people nearest the palace stopped cheering; silence rippled backwards into the agora, followed by murmurs of dissatisfaction. I knew what they felt, because all at once these citizens were an extension of myself. They were mine: my people, my Thebes.

Laius paid no attention to the mood of the crowd. Instead he twisted his body toward the open palace door. "Nerissa!" he called, his cry seeming more a plea for help than a demand for his mistress' affection.

Nerissa must have been standing just inside, for she stepped out immediately. She ran to Laius' outstretched arm and bent down to help him up.

"*Porni!*"

The call rang through the crowd; the happy mood darkened quickly.

"Foreign slut!" called one voice.

"Go home, witch!"

"Why don't you pay attention to your *wife*?" yelled one toothless old woman, expressing the anger I felt.

I saw trouble and worry on Nerissa's features. *Good,* I thought angrily. She might have Laius, but with his bent head and unsteady gait he did not seem that much of a prize.

I, on the other hand, had an entire city.

Someone threw an egg at the retreating couple; it missed, and splattered on the stones. Vassos stepped before me immediately. "Stop that!" he ordered. "Do you want to endanger your queen?"

The people murmured again, their tone uncertain.

I decided it would be best to distract them. "My people – we have reason to celebrate!" I announced. "Let figs and raisins and olives be brought out for all!" I heard my husband grumble in protest but I ignored him. My father and brother, who had come to the palace door, nodded at me with approval. I beckoned to Pelorus, who stood beside my father, and told him to organize a feast. "Simple fare, that can be prepared quickly," I told him.

"Yes, my lady," he said.

"I'll summon the flute-girls," said my brother.

"We should offer prayers as well," said Father.

"A fine idea, my lord," said Pelorus.

Pelorus hurried into the palace, my brother fetched musicians, and Father raised his powerful voice to remind everyone that this was a happy but solemn occasion and that they should all ask the gods to keep their queen safe and healthy. I stood beside Vassos, amazed by the love my subjects were pouring out on my behalf.

"My lady, you're more beautiful than ever," he told me. "You shine like a goddess."

"I'm no goddess," I said hastily. "But today I feel very blessed."

And I spoke the truth. Why had I feared acknowledging the life inside me? It was a part of me, and I loved it already.

When I turned around I could see neither Laius nor Nerissa; they had returned to the shadows of the palace. They stayed there, shunning the feasting and revelry that lasted the rest of the day and well into the night.

But I remained with my subjects, and for the first time since my wedding day, I was happy.

CHAPTER EIGHT

As the days passed my contentment grew. I no longer forced the smiles for my subjects and visitors from other cities. My laughter with Creon was genuine. Even seeing Laius with his arm around Nerissa did not hurt as much.

The people were determined to show their devotion. Maidens brought me late-summer flowers; matrons brought cheeses and cakes, and gifts for the babe. Herdsmen offered their most tender meats, and the farmers presented their sweetest fruit. The musicians who had languished after Amphion's death found new joy in performing for me while the palace artisans fashioned intricate ornaments of silver and gold. Even Polydorus, the elder son of Laius and Nerissa, approached me one evening when the arrival of a messenger from King Pelops required the presence of both king and queen. He shook his head and said: "You look radiant, my lady. My father's a fool!"

"And your mother?"

"Mother's just humoring him." Polydorus ran a hand through his hair, the same golden color as hers. "She's not happy."

I usually avoided watching Laius and Nerissa. At first, the sight had been too painful. If I wanted to keep from bursting into tears, I had to pretend they did not exist; now I was accustomed to looking elsewhere. But after her son's comment, I glanced in Nerissa's direction. Deep circles shadowed her eyes, and her expression was one of tired resignation.

I did not feel sorry for her.

"She hasn't tried to make *me* happy."

"Her position's difficult. You may find this hard to believe, but she likes you. At least, she respects you – my father should have so much sense." Polydorus inclined his head and moved away.

I stared at his broad back as he crossed the room to have his goblet refilled. Why did he tell me this? Did he want his mother's life to be less miserable? Except for the fact that she had Laius and I did not, her life had to be unpleasant. The Thebans hated her for coming between Laius and me. When she tried to shop in the agora, the common folk greeted her with insults and angry looks. Yet why should I help her? She deserved it. I wished that she and her sons would return to Pisa.

Nerissa was a small black cloud in an otherwise perfect sky. Even without a loving king at my side, I adored being queen. I appreciated my brother's political insights, the devotion of my bodyguard, and the conversations with my advisers about far-flung foreign lands. And after Hydna left me at night I did not feel lonely, for my child moved inside me. Lying in bed I sometimes spoke to it, asking if it were a boy or a girl, and what sort of name would befit the new royal prince or princess of Thebes. Eteokles? Antigone? Menoeceus? Ismene?

During this middle stage of my pregnancy, as the nights grew longer and the harsh heat of summer was replaced by lovely blue skies and a cool, life-giving breeze, I had plenty of strength. I often walked through the bustling streets with Vassos and Creon, discussing how best we should rule Thebes. Creon's influence in the affairs of the city was well known; but Vassos too, with his soldier's experience, often gave valuable advice. My father came when there were gods to visit, and Pelorus participated in matters of trade. I toured the local farms and fields, and saw that the olive and pomegranate trees were laden with fruit; barring any late disaster, our harvest of spring-sown grain would be plentiful as well.

Thebes, like its queen, was fertile.

The only real problem, besides the fact that the man who was my king and husband would have nothing to do with me, was the matter of tribute. Pelorus, the king's favorite go-between, brought word from Laius that we must pay Pelops tribute out of gratitude for putting Laius on the throne.

"I thought the *gods* put Laius on the throne," said Creon.

My informal council was meeting on the balcony on a fine autumn day between the rains. From our seats we could see much of Thebes, from the bustling agora where women bartered blankets and cloaks for the winter, to the tiled roofs of homes and workshops, to glimpses of Amphion's walls – and off in the west, Mount Kithairon stretched upwards towards the clouds. We were reviewing the final reports of the harvest and the census of the herds. Thebes had had a good year. There was a surplus of beef and leather for trade, and the olive harvest had been excellent. Now the peasants were breeding their sheep, and fattening their pigs on plentiful acorns. The city should eat well this winter – but our rich year would be much leaner if we sent our hard-earned stores to Pisa.

"The gods were responsible," said Pelorus, "but Pelops claims his due."

"Why should Pelops take credit for it?" Creon objected.

"Laius *is* the rightful heir!" I snapped, and then winced as the babe inside me kicked.

"My lady, I am delivering the message, not creating it."

"I'm sorry," I said, rubbing my belly. "But I don't like the idea of our city in thrall to Pelops."

"No one likes it, Jocasta," said Creon.

"King Pelops is a force to be reckoned with," reasoned Pelorus. "And Pelops fostered Laius at his court all those years."

"And now that he has sent Laius and his friends here to drain our wine-cellars instead of his own, he thinks we should pay even more!"

"King Amphion always sent tribute," Vassos said. He had listened quietly until this point. "That is, he did until the last two years. After he finished the walls."

"That's true," confirmed my father, who had assisted King Amphion with his record keeping, and now helped us decipher some of the scribes' less legible marks.

"And now Amphion is dead," Creon observed. "As are all his sons."

We all paused, digesting this information. Laius might offer little as a king, but change could be dangerous. Especially to those in the inner circle.

My brother turned his attention back to the wax tablets showing the tallies for the barley and grape harvests. "How much does he want?"

Pelorus recited the list, which seemed outrageous: carded wool and finished cloth, leather and leather goods, cattle and mutton and goats' milk cheese, grain and dried fruit by the basketful, jars of oil, amphorae filled with our best wine. I groaned, and my brother asked if the amount could be negotiated.

I reached for a fig, then asked Vassos to tell us more about Pelops.

My bodyguard, more accustomed to describing fortifications than men, knit his dark eyebrows while he gathered his thoughts. "He's a brilliant ruler – canny, clever. He came to Pisa with almost nothing, won the kingdom, and transformed it. He's built a complex of temples so grand that it's a second home for the gods – that's why he calls it Olympia. He's made strong alliances – his daughters are married to kings – and because so many attend the games, most of the rulers of Hellas owe him the debt of a guest. But he has a fierce temper. He punishes those who betray him."

"Does he need our goods?" asked Creon.

"Yes," said Vassos. "All those temples and the games every four years – they don't come cheap."

"We need to know more about him," said Creon. "Find out if he has any weaknesses."

We all glanced at Vassos, who shook his head. "I've told you what I know – the impressions of a guard."

"Perhaps I could visit him," Pelorus offered. "I could accompany the tribute to Pisa and try to learn more."

"Good idea," said Creon.

I nodded my approval, for Pelorus had proved many times that he was a keen observer.

And so Pelorus soon left on another journey, traveling west to the shore where our wagonloads of Theban goods would be loaded onto ships owned by a captain bound for the southern peninsula.

Not long after his departure, on a day when heavy rain kept everyone indoors, I chanced upon Nerissa while climbing the staircase. I had grown indifferent to Laius, and so accustomed to ignoring his mistress that I felt nothing as I automatically averted my eyes and quickened my pace.

"Wait – my lady, please wait!"

I stopped and turned slowly on the stairs, standing above her. "You spoke?"

Nerissa brushed a bright lock of hair away from her face. "My lady queen, I want to say how sorry I am for what has happened."

"For what? For being my husband's mistress?"

"My lady, I – I'm not his mistress."

My mouth twisted. "Doesn't he spend every night in your bed?"

"He does, but...." She bit her lip, and to my surprise, blushed.

For such a conversation I had little patience. "But what?"

"Eros is not there."

I needed a moment to understand her meaning, then blurted: "What? Why not?"

"My lady, the king's suffering – I don't know why. He won't tell me. I think he can't." She looked at me, her deep green eyes pleading for the man she loved. "Please – be kind." Then she bent her knee to me and hurried down the stairs.

Nerissa wanted *me* to pity Laius! But I could not, not when he refused to speak with me – and kept flashing looks of hatred in my direction. Anyone could see he loathed me and obviously wished we had never married. And what had I done? *Nothing!* Biting my tongue to keep from calling undignified insults after her, I turned and continued awkwardly up the stairs.

The next time I was alone with Creon, Vassos, and my father – we were sitting together after the departure of two Maenad leaders, who had come to negotiate for their portion of the new wine, and discuss plans for the festival to honor Dionysus after the winter solstice – I revealed Nerissa's secret.

Vassos spluttered wine from his mouth and started to choke. Creon's eyes opened wide, and my father reacted with a long drawn-out, "Ah."

"Why do you all look that way?" I asked, shifting uncomfortably in my chair. I had expected this bit of gossip to make them laugh.

The men glanced at each other, as if wondering how much they should tell me. "Daughter, you're young," began my father, "and still inexperienced in many things. You can't know how terrible it is for a man to lose his…"

"Potency," supplied my brother, as my father searched for a suitable word.

"Especially for my lord Laius," said Vassos. "His lusts were legendary." Laius, he explained, was famous for his erotic adventures with all sorts of beautiful partners: women and boys, nymphs and goddesses.

"He's been with a goddess?" I had always been curious about my husband's prior experience but never found the courage to ask.

"So some claim," said Vassos. "Others say it was just a particularly attractive sheep."

We all laughed at that, even my father, who normally disapproved of such remarks.

"You've changed, Vassos," Creon observed. "When you first arrived in Thebes you would have never said such a thing about Laius."

"I am the *queen*'s bodyguard," he replied, his voice suddenly serious. "That's my first duty."

Vassos turned his face in my direction, and our eyes met. I felt a spurt of warmth rush through me, and I realized that – although I was heavy with child, and had been spurned by his king – he wanted me. Despite everything, he wanted me. And I wanted him. My lips parted in surprise and delight, and in response a slight smile lit his handsome face.

"Pelorus should return within the next few days." Vassos addressed the others, in order to cover our unspoken exchange. The mood shifted, and we talked of other things.

Vassos, who knew the route himself, was right; Pelorus did return soon, half a month before the winter solstice. Pelorus described Pelops' palace with its beautiful rooms, the musicians and acrobats who entertained the king – and the magnificent temples. Creon hung on every word, and I knew that he longed to make the journey himself.

Pelorus also delivered a message from King Pelops. "He took me on a tour of his stables – he made certain that I saw all his horses, his chariots, and weapons. Then he told me that the quality of what we sent was acceptable, but that the quantity was not."

"What?" cried Creon. "We sent what he demanded!"

"He expects twice as much next year."

"Twice as much! Impossible!"

Pelorus shrugged. "My lady, I tried to explain that myself. He pointed out – rather crudely, I thought – that he has a large army of hungry soldiers. If they don't receive enough food to eat they'll go out and collect it themselves."

"Would they do that, Vassos?" I asked.

My bodyguard nodded. "They might. But *we* will find a way to defend Thebes, my lady. You have other things to do."

As the child inside me grew, I became more uncomfortable. Walking hurt my hips and back, and so I traveled less; the journey to Artemis' shrine was the longest I made. Even that seemed to grow longer as I grew larger. At least the cool winter weather brought me some relief: during the summer months I had felt like a tripod filled with coals.

"You've only a month to go," Hydna assured me, as the days lengthened and the peasants began pruning and staking the grapevines, while the winter-sown grains pushed their green stalks upward.

"A whole month!" Each day seemed to last a year, and I did not see how I could endure growing larger. The lambs were being born, and the calving was just starting; surely it was time for me to be delivered as well. "I'm ready to burst now!"

"Ask Artemis that the babe remain with you for the entire month," my nurse instructed me, her face serious. "For the sake of the child. He's not yet ready to come out."

I raised my eyebrows. "He?"

"I can tell it's a boy," said Hydna. "From the way you walk." She said this matter-of-factly, not hinting that she would prefer a boy to secure the royal succession. In truth I think she wanted a girl – she always favored me over Creon.

I waddled gracelessly, but still I made my pilgrimage to the goddess of childbirth, escorted by my father and my bodyguard, and carrying a small ivory figure of a pregnant woman as my gift. I went early in the morning, to escape any heat the day might bring, and because if I went later I would be greeted by citizens wanting my attention. My Thebans were kind, but dealing with them exhausted me further. I leaned heavily on Vassos' strong arm as he helped me up the hill, and told him how weary I was of my pregnancy. "Hydna says it will be only another month. But what if it takes longer?"

"Then I will have the pleasure of walking here with you again."

"But my back aches. And my head."

"Your head? Hmm – maybe the babe will try to come out that way, like Athena through the forehead of Zeus! Have you noticed him moving upwards, lately?"

"Vassos!"

He stopped and surveyed me. "Really, my lady, I think he may be riding a bit higher these days. But we'll notice if he crawls up through your neck – that's sure to make you cough!"

I pinched his arm, laughing, and by the time we reached the shrine my headache was gone. Vassos and my father took their places outside; men were not permitted to enter. Father planned to consult with the priestesses afterwards, and Vassos would escort me back to the palace.

I did not pay close attention to the now familiar ritual; while the burning incense produced perfumed swirls of smoke, my mind wandered to the pain in my back and the child's kicking. The shrine's stone floor was hard beneath my knees; I longed to be back at the palace lying on soft cushions. But I followed Hydna's suggestion, making a special request that the child stay inside me until the proper time. I had to force myself to utter these words. What if the goddess heard me, and decided he should stay in me for two more months, instead of only one?

At least the babe would not come full-grown through my forehead! Vassos' jest still made me smile.

"The ceremony is ended, my lady," said Theora, senior midwife and priestess, interrupting my meditations.

"Oh! Oh, of course," I said, looking up at her.

"Let me help you, my lady." Although she was thin, her arms were strong and she pulled me to my feet.

"Thank you." We walked to the entrance, and I hoped that this would be my last visit, that in a month I would hold my child in my arms.

Rhodia stepped forward, and touched her hand to her forehead. "A blessing on you, my lady queen." After the Tiresias' cruel words to her last year, she had come to serve with her mother Theora in the temple of Artemis, and to apprentice as a midwife.

"And on you," I replied.

My father nodded at me and approached Theora. I beckoned Vassos, who came to my side.

"Ready, my lady queen?" he asked.

"Very." We started down the path that led to the Astykratia Gate.

"You're tired."

It was a statement, not a question, but I still responded. "Yes."

He offered me his arm and I took it, grateful to lean on him as we descended the narrow path, and happy to have a reason to touch him. We walked in silence for a while, stealing small glances at one another from time to time. Then abruptly he stopped.

"What is it?" I asked.

Vassos pointed ahead. "There."

A snarl of branches barricaded the path, precisely at its narrowest point.

"How strange," I said. "That wasn't here when we came through this morning."

Instead of moving forward to clear the debris, Vassos drew his sword and edged back, pushing me up the hill behind him.

"What is it?" I asked again, instinctively whispering.

"Go back to the shrine," he hissed. "Hurry! Run, my lady, run!"

My heartbeat quickened and I turned to flee up the hill. But at that moment, two men with hunting spears crashed through the thicket. They wore ordinary kilts and sandals, but the side flaps of war-helmets concealed their faces.

"Run!" yelled Vassos, tackling the man closest to me.

I did my best to obey, but running uphill was difficult, and I was eight months with child. I heard deep-pitched yells behind me and felt a spasm of terror.

"Jocasta!" cried Vassos from below. "Look out!"

I turned to see that the other man had almost reached me. I dodged the thrust of his spear, which clattered against the stones, but then the man flung himself upon me. I fought as well as I could, but he wrestled me to the ground and pulled out a knife. Just before the blade struck home, Vassos somehow pulled the assailant away.

"Run, Jocasta!" he commanded, struggling with the man. Blood streamed down Vassos' face, and a jagged tear gaped crimson and ugly across his side.

I scrambled to my feet and staggered toward the shrine. My mind blanked until, panting, stumbling, shaking, I finally reached it, where my father conversed with Theora and Rhodia.

"They tried to kill me!"

Bewilderment and astonishment crossed their faces. Then my father asked: "How many were there?"

"Two. I saw only two. Vassos is down there with them – he's hurt, Father, he's hurt! We must do something!"

"Vassos is a soldier, Jocasta – he's trained for this. And you must get to safety. I'll take you back into the city a different way – but we must disguise you, in case more assassins are about."

Rhodia pulled off her own long cloak and handed it to me. "Take this, my lady," she said. I draped the plain gray cloth around my body.

"I'll go down and see what happened," said Theora. Her face was ashen, but she squared her shoulders and spoke with firmness. The disciples of Artemis dealt in women's problems, not warriors', but they knew something of healing. "Rhodia, fetch my basket."

Rhodia ran into the shrine where the supplies were kept. I sent a silent prayer to Artemis asking her to help save Vassos, if she could. But could she help him? In my heart I formed another plea, this one to her brother Apollo, the healer.

Theora started down the main road; my father led Rhodia and me along a back path, narrow and twisting and full of stones. The wind picked up and it began to rain; the stones grew slippery. Rhodia told me I was bleeding.

"Am I?" I asked, looking down, and saw blood mingling with the raindrops dripping down my arm.

We stopped so she could examine the wound in my left shoulder and press a cloth against it. "A clean-edged cut," she pronounced. "Given time, it should heal properly."

She bandaged the wound and we continued along the rocky path. But, as if the injury had only appeared when she noticed it, now my shoulder seemed on fire. Our brief stop made me realize how tired I was. I grew light-headed and sank to the ground. The child kicked inside me so hard that it hurt. I began to cry.

Rhodia took my hand and tried to pull me up.

"The baby," I told her. "The baby's coming!"

She knelt next to me, wiping the rain from her eyes, and put her hand on my abdomen. The child kicked at her touch as if in protest.

My father squatted down beside me. "Jocasta, we must get you to the palace."

Another kick, or something worse: pain shot through me, an agony I had never before experienced.

"A contraction," said Rhodia, observing my belly.

"It's too soon," I objected. "I asked Lady Artemis…" The pain stopped me from finishing the sentence.

"I'll ask the goddess now," said Father, and he prayed to Artemis and then to her twin brother Apollo to have mercy on me.

Then the pain stopped, and once more I could breathe. "It's over," I said. "Father, she must have listened to you!"

"It may not be over," Rhodia warned. "The pains start and stop. But you have some time until the next one, and we must get you to safety."

They helped me to my feet. "Please, Artemis, not now," I prayed, I begged, as we continued down the muddy path. I told the child that he could not enter the world just yet; that he did not want his mother the queen of Thebes to give birth anywhere but in the comfort of the palace.

The goddess seemed to hear my prayer, for we reached the Phthia Gate without another pain gripping my belly. After hearing our tale, the guards sent a group of men to investigate. They also arranged a litter for me, and an escort to go with us to the palace.

Word spread quickly, more quickly than my bearers could ascend to the agora. By the time we reached the top of the hill a pair of healers had come to greet us, and despite the rain the people of Thebes swarmed around, buzzing with curiosity and anger and relief.

"Is she all right?"

"We'll avenge you!"

"Bless us, the queen of Thebes lives!"

The presence of my subjects should have helped relieve my fears; but the terror I had failed to feel when the men appeared out of the brush rushed upon me.

Creon waited on the palace steps and ran to us as soon as he saw us.

"Your sister was attacked," Father said tersely.

Creon took my hand and helped me out of the litter. I shook with sobs as he half-carried me inside. Pelorus, his wiry frame hunched with worry, stood just within.

"The child?" asked Pelorus.

"All right, as far as we know," said Rhodia.

"But Vassos!" I cried. "Vassos was hurt."

139

Pelorus straightened up. "I'll find out what happened."

"We've already sent soldiers from the Phthia Gate," said my father.

I did not hear the rest of their plans, for my brother helped me up to my room, pulled off the rain-drenched cloak and wrapped me in a warm blanket. "Who could have done this, Jocasta?" he asked, after I sank down on my couch and he brought a cushion for my back. "Do you have any idea? Any clue?"

I shook my head. "Their helmets hid their faces. Oh, Creon, they were attacking *me!* Who hates me so much?"

His eyes narrowed as he looked at me. We already knew the answer. And suddenly the palace, which was supposed to be my home, no longer seemed safe. "Do you really think so?" I whispered.

My brother's tone was grim. "Who else could it be?"

"Bandits?" I hazarded, but I did not believe it myself.

Hydna ran in, followed by Rhodia with a basin full of water and clean cloths. "My dearest! Are you all right? No, don't tell me; I'll look for myself. Lord Creon, move aside, I must take care of your sister."

Creon squeezed my hand and stepped back. Hydna barked out an order for someone to bring wine, and then pulled the blood-soaked bandage from my shoulder.

Creon's face blanched at the sight. "I'll find out who was responsible." He moved in order to go.

"Don't leave me, Creon," I pleaded.

"I'll be back soon," he promised, and went through the doorway.

"My darling girl," said Hydna, as she wiped the wound with water. "Does it hurt very much?"

"Yes."

"This will help," Rhodia said, and handed me a goblet of wine infused with herbs.

I drank, tasting the sweetness of honey mingled with the richness of the grape and a hint of sharp herbs, and felt the mixture's soothing effects immediately. The pain throbbing in my shoulder ebbed away, and even the kicks from within subsided, as if the child had drunk as well. I realized that my belly had not clenched again since that time on the path. "Will the baby come now?" I asked.

Rhodia brushed a damp curl back from her forehead. "I'm not sure; but I don't think so. Not yet. In a moment of fear or excitement, the contractions may start and then go away until the proper time."

Hydna put a bandage to the wound. "Your shoulder should be all right, butterfly; I've washed away the ill humors."

"I will pray to Apollo for your health," said my father, appearing in the doorway.

Creon pushed his way past him. "Jocasta, you must go outside."

I stared at him through a fog induced by wine and herbs.

"She needs rest," said my nurse.

My brother was blunt. "The people are saying she's dead, that Laius has killed her."

"But they saw me arrive. I was outside just a little while ago!"

"They think that Laius has killed you since. They may storm the palace if they don't see that you're alive and well."

"She's *not* well," Hydna protested.

"And in their haste and eagerness they may kill her, you, and anyone else they find."

"I can do it," I told Hydna. I pushed her aside so that I could get up.

"Good girl," said my brother, and he gave me a hand.

Father and Creon and a reluctant Hydna escorted me through the halls of the palace to the megaron, where Laius sat on his throne. He was talking to the king of Tiryns, an old drinking companion from the Games at Olympia as well as one of King Pelops' many sons-in-law. The Tirynian king was visiting Thebes with his son, a tall, broad-shouldered youth a year or two younger than I.

My husband turned away from his friend and spoke. "You were attacked."

After so many months of being ignored, it shocked me to be addressed directly. "Yes," I said simply.

"Are you all right?" The question came from Nerissa, standing a few paces away from the king's tall throne.

"Yes." I spoke with surprising calm – due, no doubt, to the wine and herbs.

"And the child?" Laius asked. His voice shook, but I could not tell whether with hope or with fear.

"Also well, but no thanks to you!" These angry words burst from my nurse.

"Hydna!" said my father, in the voice he used to remind her that however familiar she might feel with us, she remained a servant.

"I did not try to kill you, Jocasta," Laius told me, his dark brown eyes meeting mine for the first time since our wedding day.

"Didn't you?" I snapped

"No, I did not. But…"

"But what?" asked my brother quickly, trying to discover what Laius had left unsaid. "*You* did not try to kill her, but you told someone else to?"

"I told no one to kill her! She's my wife!"

I was his wife. That which I had longed to hear for so many months was now painful, not soothing. "Then why don't you speak to me? Why do you sleep in her bed instead of mine? Why did you try to give me back to my father on our wedding day?" Indifferent to the shocked stares of the visitors from Tiryns, I demanded answers to the questions that had gnawed me for the last eight months.

"Jocasta..." His voice trailed off awkwardly. For the first time since the day we married he looked at me and seemed to realize what I felt – what he had done to me. "It's not you. It's the child."

"What about the child?" asked my father.

Laius only shook his head. Before we could press him to explain, Pelorus burst through the door. "The people are restless – my lady, you must go out and calm them!"

"I'll go with you," said my brother, pulling my hand through his arm.

"I'll go too," said Laius, rising.

"My lord king, for you it's not safe," said Pelorus.

I leaned against my brother's arm, not turning to see if Laius followed. The guards escorted us into the cool air of late winter. The chill rain still fell, but despite the weather, the agora was packed, and the people surged against the foot of the palace steps.

"Thebans, here is your queen!" announced my brother.

The muttering slowed. Those nearest the steps stared upwards, and others jostled them, trying to catch a glance. But their doubts were not allayed. I heard someone ask: "Is that really her?" Another voice wondered whether I might be a spirit.

"I am Jocasta, queen of Thebes," I told them. "I am alive – I am healthy – and I love you!"

The words that issued from my mouth surprised me. But whatever the source, their effect on the people was amazing. "We adore you, Jocasta!" they called.

"Bless our queen!"

Their cheering lifted me up; but then their good spirits darkened, and angry muttering began again. I wondered why, and turned to see that Laius had also come out onto the palace steps.

"Murderer!"

"Assassin!"

"What sort of husband are you?" yelled an old woman, a leader of the Maenads.

"I am the king, who loves his queen – just as you love her," said Laius, and he stepped over to put his arm around me.

I was astonished, and even in my exhausted state my feelings must have shown on my face. Why had he refused to touch me for so long – and how dare he touch me now?

He turned my face up to his, and kissed me on the cheek. "How are you feeling, my dear?"

"All right," I said, more baffled than ever. Maybe he *did* have nothing to do with the attack on me.

I glanced at my brother. Creon's face was dark with mistrust.

A man in the crowd called out: "Where's Vassos?"

Vassos! How could I have failed to find out what had happened to him? My pain, my fear and confusion about Laius, even the numbing herbs were no excuse – he had risked himself to save me! Desperation surging inside me, I turned to Pelorus and repeated the question. "Where is Vassos?"

The crowd hushed, waiting for the answer. All faces, all eyes, turned toward Pelorus, who clearly wished to be somewhere else.

"Vassos gave his life to save yours, my lady. I'm sorry, but he bled to death on the path."

I burst into tears, and my knees gave way; Laius caught me as I crumpled in grief. Pelorus continued his report, explaining that another man, Schedius, had also been found dead, but I scarcely heard him. Laius addressed the people. "I must take my wife inside; she's distraught." He put began to lead me back into the palace. Creon came at once to my other side, and the two of them assisted me to my rooms.

"Vassos – dead!" I wept, as they helped me lie down on the bed. "Poor Vassos!"

Creon spread a blanket over me and then looked up at Laius. "What have you had to do with all of this?"

Laius spoke hastily. "I? Nothing."

My brother took my hand and squeezed it. "How can we believe you? For months you ignored my sister – worse, you insulted her by parading your mistress in public. Then one of *your* bodyguards, Schedius, tries to kill her. Once you realize the assassination attempt has failed, because you know the people adore her and despise you, you try to redeem yourself by acting the part of a concerned husband. And in case an archer in the crowd has an arrow ready for you, you stand behind my sister and use her as a shield."

Laius' voice shook. "That's not true. You don't understand..."

"What doesn't he understand, Laius?" My father's voice surprised me, for I had not noticed him enter the room.

"I don't want anything terrible to happen to Jocasta. She's a sweet girl, and works hard for Thebes. She's a better ruler than I – don't you think I see that?"

These words of praise, after so many months of being despised by my husband, came too late. I was too worn out to speak, and tears trailed down my cheeks. Poor Vassos was dead.

"I'm glad you do," said my father. "You should realize how much the people love her. And if anything happens to her, they'll rend you limb from limb. As they tore apart Amphion, the last king. And Labdakus, your father. And Pentheus, who insulted Dionysus. Thebes has a way of ridding herself of unworthy kings."

Laius paled beneath his beard but continued to speak. "I've never tried to harm Jocasta. It's not she who troubles me, but the child she carries. The child is cursed."

Stillness fell on the room; even my tears were checked.

His voice serious, my father asked: "What sort of curse? And how do you know?"

145

"The Tiresias told me, on the night of the wedding, that any child of our union would – I can't say, she forbade me to say."

"The Tiresias *was* here that night," said my father.

"She didn't stay long," added Pelorus, "but I remember her speaking with the king."

My brother put his hand on Laius' arm. "What sort of curse?"

Father intervened. "Creon, he's not allowed to say."

"I want to know if it's a curse that only involves him, or him and my sister, or all of Thebes."

"A fair question," said Pelorus. "My lord king, can you tell us that much?"

Laius covered his face with his hands. From behind them he spoke. "It's terrible. But yes, it involves me, her and all of Thebes. The child will destroy us all."

I felt a kick inside me, and moved my hand across my belly to soothe the babe. "What could my child do that's so terrible?"

The king dropped his hands from his face and stared at me. "I can't tell you that. But any child we have would have the same fate – would bring the same destruction on us all."

"This is terrible," said Father, white-faced. He shot a look at me and then turned his attention back to Laius. "We must decide what to do."

"What to do?" I asked, panic rising in my chest. "What is there that can be done?"

"Hush, my dear," he said. "Daughter, you have had a shock, and you have been hurt. We must leave you to rest."

Creon remained when the others left, helping me rearrange the pillows, trying to find a comfortable position. "I don't understand," I said. "How can a child be cursed before it's born?"

"The gods can curse anyone," said my brother.

"But – but how can the gods tell me that my future will be glorious, that I will be a wonderful wife and mother and queen, and then tell my husband that our child is fated to bring destruction on us all?"

Creon took my hand in his. His hand seemed so warm – or was I cold? At last he replied, although he had no answer. "I don't know. Perhaps Laius is lying."

"Do you think so?"

"I don't know what to think. The Tiresias spoke only with him. Perhaps the curse only involves him – not you and the rest of Thebes."

I stared at the lamp on my bedside table. Its yellow flame sent a thin black thread of smoke trailing up into the darkness. "He didn't look at us when he told us that the child would bring destruction on Thebes."

"No, he did not," said Creon. "And I find it difficult to believe that he—"

"That he what?"

"That he didn't know Schedius would try to kill you today." My brother's voice sounded grim. "Jocasta, I'm spending the night here. You must make sure you're never alone, at least not until the child is born."

Hydna came back into the room just then, carrying a tray. Creon made room for her and she knelt in his place, helping me sit up and then lifting a cup to my lips. I drank gratefully, and ate some bread and cheese. Then I sank back, barely noticing as she probed my shoulder. My mind was on the fate of my child. What could the gods have said? Or was Creon's theory right – had Laius lied?

But whether or not the king wanted me dead, his attitude towards his child was clear. He wanted it destroyed. That was plain.

I felt as if the babe within me were calling out, begging me for protection. And I knew that I would sacrifice my life for the child, just as Vassos had given his life to save mine. "I'll protect you," I promised him, although I did not yet know how I could.

And then the mixture of herbs, wine, wounds and sorrow overcame me, and while Creon and Hydna kept watch, I slept.

CHAPTER NINE

Vassos was dead. Never again would I see his crooked smile, hear his voice caress my name, feel his hand steady me along rocky hillside paths.

I wept in the arms of my nurse, in the shadows of my chambers.

I wept, too, in the late winter sunlight, as his body was lowered into the cold ground: Vassos, always so vital, now reduced to a linen-wrapped corpse. Despite the jars of olive oil and wine provided to comfort him in the afterlife, and the extra thick cloak and kilt to keep him warm, the narrow grave shaft looked dark and terrible. I wondered whether he would think of me, in the Underworld.

At least Schedius received no place in the royal tomb. Creon and Pelorus managed to convince my husband that this was necessary – for Laius' own safety, since simple justice seemed not reason enough.

"If you honor the assassin," said Pelorus to the king, "Thebes will believe that you wanted the queen dead, and they will never forgive you. They will think the two men acted on your orders."

The other man was never caught. Creon suspected he made his way back to the Pisatan court, or else joined a group of bandits.

A middle-aged temple attendant led the sacrifice, an unblemished black ram, to the altar outside the tomb's tall doorway. The priest, a man who had come with Laius from Pelops' court, intoned the ritual words, offering the life of the animal to Hades and begging the god's favor for our lost soldier. The animal let out an angry bleat; when the priest raised the axe I turned my face, unable to bear the sight of more blood. At least the Pisatan's hand was practiced; death came cleanly at the first stroke. My father could have done no better.

Father was not at the funeral. He had left Thebes in order to seek out the Tiresias. We had heard she was at Gla, and on her way toward Delphi, but Father wanted to persuade her to alter her course toward Thebes. The curse on the child troubled him deeply. Since Laius would not talk, the Tiresias was the only person who could explain what the gods had revealed about my child's fate.

The curse disturbed me too, but not because I believed it. How could I believe anything that the seer said? Yes, Niobe's children had died shortly after Tiresias cursed them – but Niobe had insulted the gods. I had done no such thing. No matter what I sometimes thought, I served them faithfully. Besides, what the Tiresias had prophesied for me was completely wrong. I did *not* love my husband. And Laius was certainly not the greatest king of Thebes. In my fifteen years Thebes had known two rulers, and it was clear to me which one had been better.

And why would the gods curse a child not yet born? How could the babe have offended them? The gods themselves had sent Laius to be king of Thebes, and Apollo had chosen me as the city's queen – it made no sense for them to be angry with our unborn child.

The Tiresias was old; she was blind; she was more than a little strange. Couldn't she have misinterpreted something? Or – couldn't Laius, in his drunkenness on our wedding night, simply have misheard her?

Yet even if I did not believe in the curse, others did. And that was why Schedius attacked me, why Vassos was now dead.

With a final prayer to Hades, the priest threw the ram's heart and liver onto the smoky altar fire. Beneath the cloudy sky, servants shoveled damp earth into the grave. I wiped a tear from my eye. "Farewell, Vassos," I said, loud enough that others could hear.

Laius shot me an angry look but he said nothing.

The walk back to the city had never seemed longer. My husband put out a hand to help me along one steep part of the path, for my gait was very awkward now, but I pushed his arm away and leaned on Creon instead. Bitter wind chilled my damp cheeks, numbing my fingers as I clutched my brother's arm.

"You should be more polite to Laius," Creon said, as we passed through the Eudoxa Gate back into the city proper.

"Why? His man tried to kill me. And he wants me dead."

"Quiet!" he hissed. Creon gestured toward one man in the crowd, a brawny fellow who stared at me and then cast a narrow-eyed glance at Laius. My brother lowered his head, and put his lips to my ear. "Do you want to stir up the mob? Thebes needs unity."

I shrugged, then leaned more heavily on Creon's arm. "I suppose you're right."

So in the name of unity Laius and I ate together in the megaron that evening, in the company of the visitors from Tiryns and some of Thebes' prominent citizens. Creon and Pelorus also attended, serving as a buffer between the king and queen.

I missed Vassos. I had not realized how much support his presence gave me. With him dead and my father away, I felt unprotected in the palace. Creon stayed by my side, but like me he was young and inexperienced – and certainly no soldier. And with Nerissa, Polydorus and little Gogos surrounding Laius, I felt unwelcome, unnecessary.

Appetite failed me; all I could manage were a few figs and some bread. I sipped instead from my goblet of well-watered wine; and even that seemed too much for my stomach.

In the past few days my swelling body had become more and more uncomfortable, and I had trouble paying attention to the dinner conversation. Letting my eyes wander around the room, I found Laius looking in my direction. He looked not at my face, but at my rounded belly, and his expression was one of loathing and calculation.

I shivered. He might not be planning to kill me – after the hostility the Thebans had shown him on the palace steps, he had to know the danger of that course – but he certainly wanted my child to die.

How could I protect the baby?

When my time came – and it would be soon – I would be weak, helpless.

Laius knew that. He had to be counting on it. He raised his gaze to meet mine, and I read the threat in his face. He wanted the child gone. And I – I certainly presented an inconvenience. Perhaps he hoped I would die in childbirth. That was something the Thebans might understand; many women lost their lives that way.

Perhaps Laius meant to ensure that his wife was one of them.

My hand shook as I raised my goblet not to drink, but to hide my face. What could I do to save my life – and the life of my child?

I thought and thought but found no answer.

In truth *I* could do nothing. I needed protection; I needed help.

Who could help me?

Surreptitiously I glanced around the room. My brother Creon was an obvious choice – too obvious. Laius might have him watched, and send someone to kill both Creon and the babe. Father... Father was away, tracking down the Tiresias; but even if he returned in time I was not sure he would choose to protect the babe, if he thought it cursed by the gods. Hydna loved me and my unborn child; but she was only an aging maidservant with failing eyes.

I looked at my new bodyguard, Demochares, a young fellow with a booming voice who was one of Rhodia's cousins. So far he was satisfactory – he had a great reputation as a hunter – but I did not know how far I could trust him.

I could think of no one.

The child inside me kicked. I did not know how it could; there seemed to be no room left. That morning Theora had told me that the babe's head was down, and my time was near.

Time was so short! I had only days – perhaps just hours – to arrange my child's survival. What could I do?

The plates were cleared; Laius and Nerissa left and then the guests drifted out, chatting among themselves. Even Creon departed, deep in conversation with Tiryns' young prince. Theora laid a hand on my shoulder, and said that she and Rhodia would return in the morning. I remained behind with my worries, staring at the fire in the hearth, knowing that I would be as uncomfortable in my bed as I was on these cushions. Yellow flames danced over the coals, casting shadows across the wall painting's procession of dark-haired maidens bringing offerings to the gods.

Perhaps I should ask a god to help me. But which?

Asking Zeus for help would be bold, but would Zeus help a woman outwit her husband? His wife Hera – she might have pity on my plight, but she had a vengeful side. Besides, she was enemy to Leto, mother of Apollo, the protector of Thebes.

What about Apollo? His prophetess had blessed me, but she had cursed Niobe's children to death – I was reluctant to appeal to Apollo. Then there was Dionysus, whose mother came from Thebes. He had many followers, but their maddening riddles and drunken orgies did not inspire confidence. How could I entrust him with an infant?

"If only there were someone!" I whispered.

"What troubles you, my lady queen?"

I twisted with difficulty to look over my shoulder. Pelorus stepped out of the shadows into view.

Pelorus, with his wiry build and cunning expression, always reminded me of the god Hermes. The last king, although devoted to Apollo, had also revered Hermes, inventor of the lyre. In Amphion's old music-room was an ivory carving of the god.

Pelorus was not musical, but in other ways he resembled the god of merchants, thieves, messengers and liars: he was clever and quick with words.

Pelorus squatted beside my chair, and spoke in tones too low to reach my bodyguard's ears. "Is there anything I can do to help, my lady?"

Hermes, I thought, was a tricky god: not just clever but sly. Pelorus had somehow gained Laius' confidence as well as my own – how had he done that?

"I don't know," I said slowly. I searched his brown eyes, shining in the firelight. He appeared kind and concerned, but I was sure he could appear that way if he chose. "I don't know if I can trust you."

"You have to trust someone."

I looked down at my swollen belly. Pelorus was right; I had to take a chance. We spoke quietly, so that even Demochares could not hear. What Pelorus agreed gave me comfort, although not enough to banish entirely the dread I felt for my child and myself.

That night, before I went to my bed, I went to Amphion's conservatory. The little ivory Hermes still stood on the table, just as I remembered. With a finger I traced the lines of the god's friendly, smiling face. He was covered with dust -- had he felt neglected and lonely since Amphion's death?

As I wiped the dust off the carving, I remembered a story told about Hermes. When the god Dionysus was born, Hera had tried to kill him, for Dionysus was yet another bastard son of her faithless husband Zeus. Hermes braved Hera's wrath and delivered the child to safety; Dionysus grew up to be the god of wine and revelry, with the Maenads as his followers.

I felt as if a burden had slipped off my shoulders.

I picked up the small carving of Hermes and took it with

me to my room. "Please," I whispered, pleading with the god. "Please, help me if you will."

In a few days spring arrived, all of a sudden, and everything was green and full of blossoms. But I did not enjoy the new season's energy or its beauty. The sun's rays felt too strong and hot, and the child within me seemed to generate heat of its own. I stayed inside, praying each day to Hermes. I had thought time slowed as I waited to be married; now I knew what it was truly like for days to creep with snail-like lethargy.

And I could do nothing but wait. Wait for my father to return, with or without the Tiresias. Wait for time to heal the aching grief I felt for Vassos. And wait, always wait, for the baby to be born.

I was frightened: women died during childbirth. But my nurse and the priestess of Artemis reminded me that I was healthy and strong. "Some women have no trouble at all," said Theora. "The last queen gave birth as easily as spitting out a pomegranate seed!"

"Yes, but how did Niobe feel during her *first* childbirth?"

"You'll be *fine*, Jocasta," Creon snapped as he entered the room. He was nearly always at my side, despite the fact that my bodyguard, Demochares, was usually there too. Creon was keeping his promise to protect me, and I appreciated it, but it was wearing on us both. As I could now move very little, he was confined as well – compelled to listen to my worries and fears, and endless women's talk that either bored or sickened him.

Now returning from one of his many short breaks to visit the megaron – where he learned what he could of what was going on – Creon's ill humor was so obvious that Hydna and Theora exchanged a look and left, taking Rhodia with them.

"What's wrong?" I asked. His mood seemed particularly foul.

"Nothing," he said, his tone sharp. Creon grabbed the jug of wine from the side-table and poured himself a goblet without bothering to add water. He settled himself in his usual spot, a chair in the corner, and drank. "Father's returning to Thebes."

"Is he bringing the Tiresias with him?" I asked.

"Pelorus said she doesn't want to come."

"Pelorus is the one who told you?"

"Yes. Laius sent him on an errand to the far cattle pens, and he learned it from a trader." I was certain that my brother would much have preferred a journey to the dirtiest cattle pens to sitting in close rooms with his pregnant sister. I yearned for fresh air and freedom myself. Freedom from the relentless ache in my back, from feeling like a bloated wineskin filled to bursting, and most of all freedom from my fear for the child and myself.

"Why doesn't the Tiresias want to come to Thebes?"

"I don't know." Creon wiped his mouth with the back of one hand. "Jocasta, I'm not sure we can trust Pelorus."

His words cut through my discomfort, for I *needed* to trust Pelorus. "Why do you say that?"

"Because he's such a favorite of Laius these days."

"He's just running errands for the king, that's all," I said, my voice more confident than my feelings. "Someone has to, and Pelorus is reliable."

"Is he?" Creon leaned forward, resting his arms on his knees. "Do you remember the night Amphion died?"

"Of course." So much had happened since then, but it was only a year ago, and that night was chiseled into my soul.

"Remember how Pelorus said Amphion sacrificed himself? That the king said to hold him at knifepoint and offer him to the crowds – so that they would take only the king's life, and spare his servant?"

"Yes," I said, shifting the pillows behind my back as I searched in vain for a comfortable position. "One of Amphion's most noble moments, don't you think?"

"That's what Pelorus wants you to think. But one of the servant girls – the plump one with the mole on her chin – tells a different story. She says that Amphion made no such suggestion. Instead Pelorus really pulled his knife on the king and forced him out before the mob. She says it was never Amphion's idea at all – that when Pelorus unsheathed the knife, the king cursed him to eternal darkness."

The idea that Pelorus was capable of such treachery sickened me. But I clutched at anything that might give me hope. "Isn't that what Pelorus and Amphion would have wanted the maid to believe?"

Creon shrugged. "Think what you will, Jocasta. At the very least, Pelorus often wears a mask. We need to be careful around him." He took a large swallow from his wine-cup and slouched back in his chair.

Panic swelled inside me, gripping me, causing real and terrible pain. And it did not go away.

"What is it?" asked Creon, as my wail roused him.

I needed a moment before I could speak. "The baby. It's time."

The baby was coming. Hydna and Theora confirmed that, and herded me to the birthing-room, where they helped me into a loose linen shift. Though I could hardly stand upright, Rhodia held my hand and urged me to pace back and forth across the straw-covered floor. Only when I cried out with the pain did the midwife let me stop, and rest on the childbirth stool. "A few more hours," she said, although we all knew of women who had labored for days.

Creon peered occasionally into the room. In truth he should not have done even that, as childbirth was the province of women and men were supposed to stay away, but Theora understood his agitation and my need to have him near me. Sometimes he stood with Demochares outside the door; when the waiting grew too long he left and walked around the palace. Thus he was able to report, in the middle of the night: "Father has returned."

"Has he?" I gasped, for a long contraction had just finished.

"Yes. And he has the Tiresias with him."

So she had come, after all! "Tell her I must see her."

Creon hesitated. "Do you think that's wise? You can't order about the handmaiden of Apollo!"

"Phrase it however you want, but make her come here!" The child was on its way; I had to know the truth.

Creon opened his mouth but shut it again without speaking. He went to fetch her, perhaps deciding that in the circumstances it was best to humor me. Or maybe he was glad for a reason to leave again so soon.

Caught in the vise of another contraction, I did not notice anyone enter the room. But when the pain ebbed, I looked up to see the Tiresias.

She was dressed as always: dark robes, cloth bound over her eyes, long gray hair tied at the back of her neck. Yet somehow she seemed different: less certain, diminished. Perhaps she was just tired; it was past midnight. She came alone, without her guide. He had to be tired as well.

"Tiresias?" I asked.

"Who speaks?" she asked, turning her face in my direction. The left side of her mouth sagged, and a thin line of spittle trickled down her chin.

For a moment, astonished, I could not find the words. "I – I am Jocasta, Queen of Thebes."

"Ah," she said, as if that information was unimportant. Then she added with more energy, "The daughter of Menoeceus?"

"Yes," I said, wondering why she seemed more impressed by that fact than my royal title. "Leave us," I said to the others. "I wish to speak to the Tiresias alone."

"But, my lady–" Theora objected.

"You just said it will be a few more hours, and that there's nothing you can do to ease my pain."

Theora nodded slowly and departed. Hydna gave me a questioning look, but I waved her and the other women away.

I brushed sweat from my face and stared at the seer.

"You are the Tiresias," I said to her. "And you have said much that I don't understand."

She limped towards me, leaning heavily on her wooden staff. Her left foot dragged behind her, leaving a path of bare tiles amidst the matted straw. "All ways will be made clear," she said. "All ways are dark."

I did not understand this at all, but decided to press on anyway. "On the night of my marriage you spoke with my husband."

"Your marriage? I was at your marriage?"

"Yes, last summer, my marriage to Laius."

"I nearly married," she whispered, "but then Apollo called me. I was young once – now I am old."

"Yes, you've had a long life," I said, trying to keep my patience. But I was tired, in pain, and desperate to know what she had told my husband. "On my wedding night, you told Laius there was a curse on our child."

"A curse?"

"Yes, a curse!" I shouted. I knew the Tiresias deserved more respect, but I could feel the pains coming on again and I could not understand her.

"Where am I?"

"You're in the palace. Don't you know that?"

"How could I know that, child? I'm blind!"

I stared at her, a blind old woman, leaning on her staff in the middle of the room. What had happened to the Voice of Apollo?

"What city is this?" she asked.

"This is Thebes!"

"Thebes?"

"By all the gods, yes, Thebes!" I cried, in pain and exasperation. Then I grew concerned at her evident confusion. "Are you all right?"

She spoke:

"Thebes, the city great and fair
Thebes, the home of my despair
Here I gained my second sight
Now my gate to endless night."

"Are you talking about yourself?" I asked. "Or someone else?"

She said nothing, but took a shuffling step forward.

The pain swelled, stabbing through my belly like a blade of bronze. I gasped, and gripped the wooden arms of the birthing-chair with all my strength. When the pain was over, I tried again: "You told my husband something about our child being cursed. I must know what you said to him."

"Cursed?"

"Listen, old woman, I'm giving birth! I need to know if my child is a monster!"

I wanted to take back the words as soon as I had said them, for I risked the wrath of Apollo. Even so had Niobe erred –

But the Tiresias only tottered forward, the linen blindfold dropping off her face to reveal her scarred eye sockets.

She was truly blind.

"A curse? There was something about a curse and a child. But now all is dark..." Her arm slipped on the staff, and she collapsed.

Somehow I was able to catch her. For all her power she weighed nothing: thin, dried out, as light and brittle as a twig.

"Help!" I screamed, and Theora burst into the room and took her from me.

"She's dead," pronounced the midwife.

The Tiresias: dead, to be replaced by the next Tiresias.

Tears of pain and frustration rolled down my face. Unless Laius talked, I would never learn the truth. And even if he spoke to me, could I believe him?

But I could worry no longer about such things. The baby pressed hard upon me now, and I pushed and pushed, as Hydna held my hand and wiped my brow. Rhodia gripped my shoulders and encouraged me: "Breathe deep, my lady, deep! Now push, with all your might!"

I was barely aware of the bustle in the rest of the room: two maidservants removing the body of the Tiresias; my brother's white face at the door, wincing at the sound of my screams; Rhodia scattering fresh straw to soak up the blood. And then the room grew quiet, except for my own groans.

"Is it here yet?" asked a male voice with a Pisatan accent.

"Nearly, my lord," said Theora. "But, my lord king, with all respect, Artemis forbids men to enter the birthing-room –"

Laius was here!

I could not give birth now! He would take the babe away and kill it!

Yet I could not keep the child from coming.

"I can see the top of the head now, my lady," said Theora. "You must push!"

I screamed and pushed and felt something tear.

Where was Pelorus? Was he outside?

Another push, and pain beyond belief, gasping for breath, pain sharp and searing hot, the smell of blood and a woman's cry of triumph as something slipped between my legs. Theora's strong hands pulled the child from my body, and I leaned back, exhausted. They told me to continue to push, and so I did, until the afterbirth fell out. Then Theora cut the birth-string with a sickle-shaped dagger. Rhodia took the knife and handed the midwife soft cloths; Theora wiped the infant clean.

I lay back, panting like a dog after the hunt, drenched in sweat and blood.

"A boy!" declared Hydna, her voice ringing with happiness. She looked to the king and said: "My lord king, you have a son!"

But Laius turned his face away. "That is not my son."

"Please, let me see him," I begged.

"No," said Laius.

"My lord, what harm would it do for her to see the child?" The soft voice of Pelorus came from just inside the door.

He had come – all glory to Hermes; Pelorus was here!

Laius relented and Theora brought the child to me. Rhodia approached with a lamp and held it high, so that I could better see. A male child, large as newborns go, but nevertheless an infant, tiny, vulnerable. I was exhausted and the light was dim, but to me he looked perfect.

"Hello, my son," I whispered.

He did not cry the way newborns were supposed to but nestled close against my breasts, as if he knew me from without as he had from within. His small red mouth opened and closed as if he wanted to tell me something.

Holding him, I suddenly knew what true love was. How could I have ever thought I was in love with Laius? That was a trick played on me by Eros and my body: not love but lust. The bond between this child and me was real, pure: deeper than anything I had ever felt.

"My sweet child," I whispered.

I heard a sharp hiss, and remembered that others were in the room. Laius. Pelorus. Creon.

Theora wrung her hands, disturbed by the presence of so many men in the birthing chamber. "My lord king–"

Laius waved an angry hand in her direction. "All of you – get out!" he barked.

The women obeyed, although I could see from the frown on Hydna's face that she was reluctant, angry.

"You, too," Laius said to Creon.

Laius radiated anger and power. He was a tall man, well muscled, a former champion wrestler at the games in Olympia. My brother, only eighteen, still thin from growing, never much good with weapons, appeared pitifully weak beside the king.

Yet Creon clenched his fists and stepped between Laius and me. "I won't leave my sister."

"I will not harm her."

"You tried to kill her!"

Laius shook his head. "I did not give that order – Schedius acted on his own."

"Creon, you should go." This came from Pelorus, in a reasonable, disinterested-sounding voice, as calm as if we were discussing how much barley rations for the peasants. "The king won't hurt her."

Laius spoke. "I swear by Apollo and his holy mother Leto, your sister will not be harmed."

These words seemed finally to persuade my brother. But perhaps more persuasive was Laius' hand on the hilt of the knife at his belt.

"Jocasta, I'll be just outside the door," said my brother. Then Creon and Pelorus left the room.

Fear filled me. This was the first time my husband and I had been alone since our wedding night.

"Jocasta, I must take the child."

I looked at Laius and saw that he had a rope in his hands. Was he planning to strangle the babe? "No!" I said, holding my son closer to my chest.

"It must be destroyed."

I was weak and exhausted; blood dripped warm down my legs. "He's your son. Our son!"

"Jocasta, any child we have will bring destruction on us all. Not just on me, but on you, and all of Thebes. He is a monster."

I looked at the infant, who was quiet in my arms. "How can you say that? Look at him – have you ever seen anything so beautiful?"

"Jocasta, he will do terrible things. He must be destroyed. For the good of us all." And with that he pulled the child from my clutching arms. He sat down, put the infant on his lap, and used the rope to bind the child's ankles tightly together. The babe shrieked in protest.

Tears spilled out of my eyes. "What will you do with him?"

"Pelorus will expose the child on Mount Kithairon. We will not be responsible for his death – he will starve, or be destroyed by wild animals. Pelorus will wait and watch to make sure he does die. Then he'll report back to us."

He called for Pelorus, and handed him the child as soon as he entered the room. "You know what has to be done."

"Yes, I do. My lord – my lady." He nodded to each of us, then turned to go. He did not glance down at the face of his tiny charge, but I saw that he held the babe with care.

And then Pelorus was gone, with my son.

Which one of us would he serve? Laius, and let my son die? Or me, and let him live?

I did not trust him, but he was my only shard of hope.

And even if my son survived, I would never see him again. I would miss his first smile, his baby steps, his first words. My womb ached: empty, bleeding.

I burst into tears.

Laius came near, and rested a large hand on my shoulder. I had not been so close to him since our wedding night, and I had no desire to be close to him now. I tried to move away, but I had no strength, and nowhere to go.

"Jocasta, my dear, I'm so sorry this had to happen." He pulled me up from the birthing-stool, wrapped me in his arms. "I know I haven't been a good husband to you."

I sobbed, thinking of my baby, my small weak child to be left defenseless on the mountainside.

"I'll do better in the future. Now that the danger is over, things will be better between us. You'll see."

"What danger?" I finally choked out. "What is so dreadful that you would destroy our child?"

"The Tiresias forbade me to tell you."

"What does it matter what the Tiresias told you? She's dead, isn't she? Oh, please, Laius – go after Pelorus and bring him back! Tell him to bring him back!"

I felt my husband hesitate, as though he were actually considering calling back the child. His own face was white, as if he finally understood a small measure of my grief, but still he shook his head. "My dear, I wish I could, but I can't. I can't."

He pulled me tight against his broad chest. And, having nothing else to lean against, I leaned against Laius, and wept.

CHAPTER TEN

Pelorus had told me he would give my baby to some family to raise; he had told Laius he would expose the child on Mount Kithairon and wait until he was sure it was dead. He returned on the second day with my son's linen swaddling – sodden from the relentless spring rains, ripped and bloodstained.

"A lion," Pelorus said to Laius.

"Then it was quick?" asked the king.

"Yes," said Pelorus, his face somber. "Mercifully quick."

I turned my face to the wall and sobbed. My husband reached over to comfort me but I shook off his hand. My only consolation – my one slender strand of hope – was a nod from Pelorus. He caught my eye, then inclined his head in a single quick movement. At first that stopped my tears and filled me with happiness; later I wondered if I had imagined it. For Pelorus never confirmed what I thought he had told me with that gesture, never told me that my child was safe and healthy and being cared for by good people.

The Thebans had witnessed their queen's pregnancy. They knew I had given birth, but no name-day was announced, no son or daughter introduced to them from the palace steps. Some whispered that the child had been stillborn; but word of a swaddling cloth bearing a lion's bloody footprint spread through the city.

Hydna was not shy in asking questions. "What did they do?" she hissed at me while she combed out the tangles in my hair. "How could you let them take the child away?"

"How could I stop them?" I asked. I could not reveal my hope that my son lived; to do so would betray Pelorus, even endanger him, for Hydna had a loving heart but a loose tongue. "What could I do?"

166

She yanked on my hair with the ivory comb. "I would have stopped them!"

"You would have tried," I contradicted her. "You would have failed, and they'd have killed you too. Then I would have been without my baby and without you, and I couldn't have borne that."

Her arms relaxed as she realized the truth. She was silent a while, and when I looked around there were tears running down her face. "I'm so sorry. You're right, I couldn't have stopped them. But – that monster! May Hera and Artemis curse him – and his harlot Nerissa!"

Nerissa. Her sons, unlike mine, were safe. Perhaps Laius had promised her that Polydorus would be king, and that little Gogos would share the riches of Thebes. Perhaps *her* sons were why my son had been taken away and left to die. The curse must have been a ruse; anyone who had seen my infant knew he was no monster.

I whispered my suspicions to Hydna, and she stamped in anger. "How dare he? Why, your father is descended from a Sown Man! And you – you can trace your line back to Kadmos himself! Nerissa is – Nerissa is nothing!"

Perhaps Hydna shared my suspicions with others, or perhaps the Thebans arrived at this idea themselves. But on the last, rainy day of my seclusion, I was reclining silently on the cushions, staring at the fire and wondering what it would be like to hold my child to my breast when Creon burst into my room and told me Nerissa was dead.

"What?" I asked, sitting upright. His words were a pitcher of water on the hearth of my hatred. "How can that be?"

He said no one knew exactly what had happened, but that her muddy, strangled corpse had been found lying in one of the back streets of Thebes. Beside her lay the body of her younger boy, Gogos – his neck broken.

Creon knelt by the fire and held out his hands to dry them, then turned to face me. "Jocasta, look at me. Did you have anything to do with these deaths?"

"I? I've not left this room for four days. How could I have anything to do with them?"

"I know you didn't kill them yourself! But did you ask anyone to do it for you?"

"No!" Though I had hated Nerissa, I had not asked anyone to take her life. And I could never have countenanced the death of the child. My stomach twisted, to think of his fragile young body lying broken in the street.

"All right. Then someone must have done it for you, thinking it would please you. Your feelings about Nerissa were obvious to everyone."

"*My* feelings! Laius shouldn't have brought his mistress with him to Thebes! Even if I hadn't resented her, the people would assume I did! You should be talking to him, not to me."

"Vassos. Nerissa and Gogos. If you don't make peace with Laius, there'll be more. In the long run, Nerissa's death may make things easier for us, but for now we need to keep tensions from growing worse."

I stared silently at a glowing ember. Creon had not numbered my infant son among the dead. The child had never reached his naming-day; as men count things, he had never been truly alive. Men did not understand the love a woman felt for a child that she had carried for nine months beneath her heart.

But I drew a long breath. I had been queen long enough to understand the importance of what Creon was saying. Nerissa's death meant little to me, although I hoped that it had been quick. I pitied her innocent child – and Vassos' absence was an ache in my heart. Who would die next? Hydna? Attempts might even be made against Creon, my father, or me.

"Very well," I told my brother, finally looking up from the hearth. "I'll try."

Creon came close and put his arm around my shoulders. "I'm proud of you, Jocasta. Laius may be a wretched king, but you are a true queen."

So Laius and I started appearing together before the people. He had also been warned, either by Creon or Pelorus, that our enmity had to end; and he made an effort. "You look well," he told me, as we started down the palace steps together.

"You don't," I said. His face was haggard, his eyes swollen and bloodshot.

"I can't sleep. In my dreams the Furies come to remind me of my guilt." He uttered the last few words in a half-whisper, as if he could not say them louder.

I looked around me to see if anyone could overhear us. Pelorus and the guards walked a few paces ahead; Creon had gone to the temple earlier. "And what do they say?" I asked.

Laius stepped over a puddle. The rain had stopped, but the ground was still soaked. "I should never have made her come here. Now she and Gogos are dead, and it's all my fault."

I felt my face flush with anger. Why didn't he mention *our* son, who he himself had ordered to die? If Laius had not sent my son away, no one would have taken revenge on his mistress.

Then I saw Polydorus, grief for his dead mother and little brother plain on his face, and remembered what the young man had told me about her. Nerissa had never tried to harm me; she had simply been there, and now she was gone. And Laius had known her since before I was born. She had been a part of his life for many years, whereas he had only seen our son for a brief moment.

I finally understood Laius' sorrow, and my anger towards Nerissa died, as if it burned with her and her son's body on their funeral pyre.

I listened to the rhythm of our footsteps as we walked on without speaking. Gogos, Nerissa, and Vassos were dead. My child, even if he lived, I would never see again. These events were past, already woven into the fabric of fate; I could do nothing to unravel them. In the meantime, Laius was my husband, for good or for ill. I was queen of Thebes, with a city to rule – and lining the streets to see my first appearance outside the palace since the birth were my people, who called out wishes for my good health.

My brother was right. The hostility between Laius and me had brought turmoil to the city. I loved my subjects, who had supported me through such a terrible time. I did not want anyone else to be hurt. So when Laius took my hand in his, I did not pull back, but let him help me up the hill.

At the top we reached the broad marble-tiled portico of the temple of Apollo. Creon was already there; he gave a nod of approval when he saw Laius holding my hand. The three of us took our places at the side of the terrace and waited.

The ritual that day was one I had been trying not to think about: the selection of the new Tiresias. A priest representing Apollo had arrived from Delphi; a priestess of Athena had come from Athens, that goddess' favorite city. Together they would select and initiate the new Tiresias.

A new Tiresias, to take the place of the one who had collapsed and died while I was in labor. The one who had convinced Laius our child would be a monster that had to be destroyed; who had cursed Niobe's children to their deaths. Melanthe, Rhodia, Pinelopi – their lives had been ruined by the last Tiresias' terrible prophecies. Pinelopi was dead. Rhodia would never marry. And Melanthe's relatives in Thebes – her father's family – claimed that she was no relation, being the bastard daughter of some other man. People said she was running wild with the Maenads, and I always expected to learn that she had been killed by bandits or lions, or that she had died from taking too much of some dream-inducing herb.

It seemed to me the world would be better without any more visions.

But I would not raise my voice against the gods. The gods, the priests and the people all demanded a new Tiresias.

A ram for Apollo was brought to the front of the temple, and barley-meal sprinkled over its head and gilded horns. A single cut across the throat, and the animal collapsed: a quick death. The stomach was slit, the bloody entrails examined; then the priest nodded and announced: "Apollo has received the sacrifice and the omens are promising. The new Tiresias is acceptable."

Athena's priestess would play the role of the goddess in re-enacting the initiation of the first Tiresias. Her attendants carried a huge bronze basin, embossed with images of owls, to its place at one side of the temple and filled it with water. Into the fire of the hearth at the temple's center – the fire that was never allowed to die – they placed a small sharp dagger.

The priestess removed her robe and stepped naked into the bath. Apollo's priest sang:

> *Athena, virgin goddess,*
> *Bathes in the wilderness.*
> *She thinks herself unobserved.*
> *Tiresias is out hunting,*
> *And wanders near that night.*
> *He sees her in nakedness.*
> *For this he must be punished,*
> *And she destroys his sight.*

The Tiresias-to-be crossed the tiles of the temple floor until he reached the center. I stiffened as I recognized him.

Father!

I should not have been surprised. His devotion to the gods, especially Apollo, was enormous. For him this was an honor, not a punishment. But I gripped the hand of my brother, who stood at my side.

171

Our father knelt in the center of the terrace. The priest who had come from Delphi to perform the ceremony stood behind him, gripping his shoulders tightly. The priestess playing the part of Athena emerged dripping from the bath. Still naked, she went to the fire and removed the dagger.

With two quick thrusts of the knife she put out my father's eyes.

The watching crowd gasped. Father did not cry out, but he flinched and shuddered. Blood ran down his cheeks and dripped onto the tiles.

The priest turned my father to face the people.

Tiresias' world is dark
But he brings others light;
Apollo shows his mercy
And gives him second sight.

The priestess had put down the dagger and donned her robe. Then she came back to the new Tiresias, carrying a strip of dark cloth and a wooden staff.

When the priest from Delphi took the cloth and wrapped it around my father's eyes, I felt I could breathe a little. Watching them bleed was too terrible to bear.

The priest's voice rang out again.

Tiresias keeps the cornel-wood rod
Now and forever ready to his hand
He may become woman, he may be man
But always he hears the voice of the god.

The priest from Delphi and the priestess of Athena helped my father to his feet. The priestess placed the staff in Father's unsteady hand. He straightened his shoulders and made a visible attempt to stop shaking. The priest took his other hand, put it upon his own arm, and led the new Tiresias out of the temple. Together they began the journey to Delphi, where Apollo's newest servant would be trained as a seer.

My father departed without saying good-bye. I had never witnessed this ceremony before, so I learned only later that the new Tiresias had to remain silent until reaching Delphi. As he left, a feeling of emptiness settled upon me. My father was not dead, and yet he was gone; he would return to Thebes, but as an itinerant servant of Apollo and Athena, not as my father.

I turned to my brother, uncertain what to say. Creon smiled wryly, then bent his head to whisper to me. "I only hope he can persuade the gods to favor us!"

The gods did seem to give us their blessing. In public, Laius and I presented the appearance of unity. Word spread, however, that he did not share my bed. Common gossip had it that he was impotent, which galled him – perhaps all the more because it was true. But as the people saw him treat me with respect, they were dutiful toward him. Our harvests were good; the city was at peace. As queen I had much to do: organizing processions and festivals, conducting diplomacy and negotiations, hosting feasts and celebrations, leading ceremonies and supervising contests honoring the gods. My days on the throne of Thebes passed quickly into months and then into years. People said that Harmonia's magical necklace had blessed me with eternal youth and beauty – and although I myself did not believe I would be young forever, my health remained excellent and the mirror stayed kind.

Creon's lanky frame and sparse beard filled out. He sold the house near the Eudoxa Gate and moved into the palace so that he could be nearby to advise me. Always he was at my side in trade and treaty negotiations with foreign envoys, and each year he helped inventory and distribute the harvests – a task that bored Laius utterly.

About ten years into my reign Pelorus married a plain girl named Chrysippe. Her best feature was her wealthy father, Naukles, who spent much time traveling and trading; Pelorus happily accompanied him. Some whispered that Pelorus was more interested in his father-in-law's journeys than in his new wife, who waited impatiently for her husband to return.

My father, or rather the Tiresias, spent much of his time at Delphi but also journeyed throughout Hellas: stopping to worship in the sanctuaries at Pylos and Sikyon, visiting Athens, Korinth and Pisa to advise their kings, and everywhere offering sacrifices to Apollo with the local people. He made fewer disturbing prophecies than the previous Tiresias, and what he did say had nothing to do with Thebes or me. I grew used to the sight of him with bandaged eyes, leaning on the arm of his guide.

Hydna remained angry with Laius. As desperate as a would-be grandmother, she wanted me to have children; but my husband shunned my bed. Hydna tried to keep her anger to herself, but now and again I heard her mutter a curse against the king. When she fell sick, and the illness turned grave, even that she blamed on Laius – though I myself never believed that he had stooped to poisoning her. Old Theora paid many calls to Hydna's sickbed; she and her daughter Rhodia could not stop the disease eating at Hydna's vitals any more than the healer-priests of Apollo, but at least their herbs eased her pain. When Hydna died, Merope took her place as my chief maidservant. She was just as devoted to me, even more thorough, and very quiet – a quality I came to value ever more over the years.

Melanthe had joined the Maenad cult, devoted to the god Dionysus. As the son of Zeus by one of Kadmos' daughters, Dionysus had local origins; and the Maenads held that Dionysus, not Apollo, should be the patron god of Thebes. Having Apollo as our protector posed certain problems – the prophecies of his voice, the Tiresias, had wrought dreadful changes in my life, to be sure. But Apollo offered many wonderful gifts: light, music, the arts of the muses. Moreover, his rites were orderly. We went to the temple, sang hymns, offered an animal in sacrifice, and chanted appropriate prayers. Dionysus, god of the vine, was young and unruly.

Vineyards covered many of our hills; Theban grapes, raisins, and wine nourished our people, and were of great value in trade and tribute. So I, along with the rest of Thebes, was ready to honor Dionysus. But celebrations in his name often became mad orgies: his devotees sang and danced their way through the countryside chewing ivy leaves and drinking unwatered wine. In these drunken riots men and women were killed, houses in the fields destroyed, whole crops ruined when the Maenads took what they liked by the light of the moon.

The number of Maenads waxed and waned; in lean harvest years more Thebans joined the cult, seduced by strong wine and the thought of simply helping themselves to the fruit of the fields instead of waiting for their apportioned share. In one such year, after a rash of destroyed crops, Laius, Creon and I summoned Melanthe – now their leader – to appear before us. I expected that, as usual, Laius would feign interest, but Creon and I would make the real decisions.

I had been queen now for more than twenty years; I was well into my thirties. Melanthe, two years older than I, was no longer the girl who had vied with me to become the bride of Prince Alphenor. Her lithe body radiated strength and power gained from a life spent outdoors. She carried a long thyrsus, the vine-wrapped staff favored by Dionysus' followers. Instead of normal women's clothing she wore a short tunic, and used a lion's skin as a cape. Some said Melanthe killed the lion herself, and wore the skin as a trophy. Others said it reflected her Aegyptian heritage, where the merging of woman and lion had a powerful significance, and therefore called her the Sphinx.

She appeared much changed, and yet the same. Her eyes remained dark, rich and mysterious, with only a few wrinkles at the edges to hint at her age. Her figure, although it had lost some of its softness, still offered curves enough to draw my brother's eye.

Melanthe crossed the megaron to stand before the hearth, her bare feet padding lightly on the tiles. Her slight, quick bow reminded me more of a creature preparing to spring than a subject showing respect. Tucked into the broad leather belt that cinched her tunic I saw the ivory handle of a dagger.

Her eyes appraised Laius and me, and then my brother, who stood next to my throne: each of us in turn, as if trying to determine who was in charge.

"Thank you for coming," I said.

"No need to thank me, my lady." She flicked her head toward the armed men we had sent to fetch her, causing her many gold-capped braids to rattle. "Your soldiers are very persuasive."

Laius leaned forward, his well-fed belly making the movement difficult. "We brought you here for a reason. You're the leader of the Maenads."

"We Maenads have no leader," Melanthe responded. "Only Dionysus, and he speaks to us all."

I wondered briefly at the idea of a god who would actually speak to all his worshippers – even the drunken rabble that made up the lowest rungs of the Maenad cult. How typical of Dionysus! Dignified Apollo was more selective.

"But he speaks to some more than others," Creon rejoined. "Especially to you."

Melanthe only lifted her chin and looked at him.

Creon continued. "The Maenads are destroying too many fields. This year the destruction is worse than the last, and the harvest of the summer barley is already thin. People will go hungry if it doesn't stop."

Her eyes flashed. "The Maenads *are* the people. We take what we can before the harvest, because we certainly won't receive it later."

Creon colored: he worked hard each year to inventory the harvest, and supervise its storage and distribution. "Everyone receives his fair portion."

"And who decides what is fair?" she challenged. "You, living behind your sister's skirts? Or that one, the tool of Pelops?"

I could almost smell the anger of the men on both sides of me. Melanthe's insolence seemed to know no limits, but we needed her help. "King Pelops?" I asked, partly to change the subject, and partly because I wanted to hear her thoughts. "What does he have to do with all this?"

She folded her arms and looked in my direction, cocking her head to one side. "He controls Thebes, doesn't he? We send oil and cattle and wine to feed his court; we send marble and gold to beautify his palace in Pisa and his temples in Olympia. Our king—" she almost spat the word, "—grew up in his court, and Pelops ordered him to Thebes to assume the throne. No doubt he feels a certain loyalty. Or perhaps he's simply afraid that if he stops the tribute Pelops will send someone to poison him, just as Amphion's children were poisoned."

"Poisoned!" I stared at her, then turned to look at my husband.

Laius' eyes remained fixed on Melanthe. "I had a dream," he stammered. "A dream, which told me to return to Thebes."

"How convenient," said Melanthe. She turned back to me. "I remember the banquet. My own father died that night. Since then I have studied all kinds of herbs. I say the octopus paste was poisoned – I believe it was brought by the envoy from Pelops – and that was what caused so many deaths."

Creon drew a sharp breath. I knew he was remembering, as I was, how ill he had been. I remembered, too, how a dog had stolen the bread with octopus paste out of my hand.

"Herbs?" asked Laius, and there was hope in his voice. "What sort of herbs?"

"All sorts." Melanthe took a step in the direction of the aging king and her voice lowered to a purr. "I even have something that might help you, my lord king."

Despite Melanthe's rebellious attitude, we offered to provide food and clothing from the palace stores to those Maenads in need; in return, Melanthe agreed to persuade the cult to leave the rest of the fields undisturbed until the crops were safely gathered.

The next day was filled with athletic contests in honor of Demeter and the harvest: wrestling, racing, archery and throws of the discus and the javelin. One curly-headed young man cast his javelin nearly twice as far as last year's champion. The crowd stamped and cheered, and I myself tied the victor's ribbon around his forehead.

Creon and I did not return with Laius in his chariot. The king, after a day of drinking too much wine and too little water, was always bad-tempered: urging his horses on recklessly, yelling and cursing at any peasant unlucky enough to be in the way. Instead, Creon and I chose to go on foot. The early fall air was warm and fragrant with pine, and after a day of watching so much exertion I had the urge to be active myself.

"Interesting, what Melanthe said yesterday," Creon said in a voice that reached only my ears.

"She said a great deal."

"Yes, but I mean about Amphion's banquet."

"Poison! Do you think...?"

Creon was grim. "It would explain a lot."

"But – why? Niobe was Pelops' own sister! And all those children – they were his nephews and nieces!"

"Yes. And there were so many of them." Creon helped me over a fallen branch. "Think it through. When Pelops first established Amphion here, Amphion was just his brother-in-law. An ally, grateful for the support, more than willing to send grain and cattle to the west. But after years as king of Thebes, Amphion grew tired of his master. He wanted to keep the wealth for himself, make alliances in his own name, be a power in his own right. And he had enough children to make alliances with all of Hellas!"

I pondered his words as we navigated the descent toward the Kleodoxa Gate. "And by that time, Pelops had so many children of his own that he did not need – or want – Amphion's any longer."

"And look at that." Creon pointed at the towering fortifications. "Amphion built the wall and the gates – these very gates that bear his daughters' names. He *must* have perceived Pelops as a threat."

I stared at the blocks; Amphion's walls were thicker than Creon was tall, and looked strong enough to stand a thousand years. The soldiers posted at the gate bowed as we entered the city. A small girl darted forward from the crowd to give me a bouquet of late roses. "Thank you, Daphne," I said, touching her soft cheek.

The girl smiled and ran away.

"Pretty child," observed my brother. "Pelorus' daughter?"

"Yes," I said, holding the flowers to my nose to savor their sweet scent. "But about the poison – I don't understand. The Tiresias cursed Niobe and told her that Apollo would strike her children down. Pelops wasn't there."

We climbed the steep road to the palace silently, both pondering this last bit. "I don't know," Creon said, as we finally reached the agora. "Perhaps the old Tiresias was controlled by Pelops, too. Or maybe the gods' plans and Pelops' plans are one and the same."

"Perhaps," I said, remembering how Creon had always maintained that the gods preferred the strongest. And though warm from climbing the hill, I shivered.

"Jocasta, what's wrong?"

"Maybe I should be glad I have no children. How terrible, to lose them that way."

We stopped, staring into the nearly empty agora. I was thinking about that long-ago banquet, and judging from the expression on my brother's face, so was he. But his memories were different from mine; he had nearly died. I put my hand on his arm and tugged him in the direction of the palace. "Speaking of children, when are *you* going to have some?"

"When I marry, I suppose."

"And when are you going to do that? It's past time. You're thirty-seven, Creon. You're the most eligible bachelor in Thebes. Every well-born family with a daughter of marriageable age is throwing her into your lap – I've seen them, at the banquets!"

"But the most beautiful woman in Thebes is already married." My brother pulled my arm through his as we climbed the palace steps. "And before I settle down, there are at least two things I want to do. First, I plan to visit the court of King Pelops."

"What's the second?" I asked, handing the rose bouquet to one servant as another came forward to remove my cloak.

Creon waited until the servants had left. "To learn all I can about poisons."

Creon did visit the Pisatan court the following summer, as sponsor of the chariot team Thebes fielded in the games at Olympia. When he returned and we could speak privately, he detailed all he could about King Pelops: his palaces, his character, and his all-too-excellent health. "It does not appear as if he's going to oblige us by dying anytime soon."

I put down my spindle and stretched my arms. "If Pelops takes after his father, he'll live a long time. What about Pelops' sons?"

Creon smiled wryly. "There are plenty of them! None of those I met show their father's ability, but some have his ambition."

"And what can we do to end this perpetual tribute?"

Creon leaned back and closed his eyes. "I don't know, Jocasta. Send a poisoner of our own? Raise an army? Appeal to the gods for help?"

"Do you think any of those things would work?"

He shook his head, then opened his eyes again. "We could always ask the king," he said, his voice caustic with sarcasm. Then he turned serious again. "What's wrong with him lately, anyway?"

"Our Sphinx," was my curt reply.

Laius had turned to the Maenad leader hoping that one of her herbal mixtures could restore his potency. He ate and drank what she told him, invited her to his bed at night, and caressed her in public. When she was not with him he stared dully into the air – not with the expression of a man dreaming about his lover, but a man whose spirit was simply gone. I suspected Melanthe was giving Laius drugs that only bewitched him into *believing* he was a masterful lover once more, and that during the nights they spent together she slept undisturbed.

"He must be fifteen years younger than Pelops," commented my brother. "But he looks older."

"I tried talking to him, but he wouldn't listen." I shrugged. "Does it matter?"

"Perhaps," said Creon. "Do you think if I spoke with Melanthe it would help?"

"You can try." I sighed, then said, "I think you should speak to some *other* girls, and choose a wife."

"Ah, yes," said Creon, and closed his eyes again.

I did not let it rest, as I had done so many times before. "Creon, I'm serious. You just told me about Pelops' many sons.

Well, Thebes has *no* royal princes. And will have none, unless you take a bride and get her with child."

His lids lifted, and he turned wary eyes upon me.

I continued my arguments. "Laius won't live forever, even if you can convince him to stop swallowing Melanthe's potions. Then what? Do you want that bastard Polydorus on the throne?"

"No," he said, and the corners of his mouth turned down. "But, Sister, those girls – they're all such foolish, giggling creatures."

"Then it doesn't matter which one you pick."

He nodded slowly. "I suppose you're right."

And in the next month he did pay closer attention to the daughters of the prominent citizens at palace banquets – though he still pinched the bottoms of his favorite servant girls. Before long he settled upon Eurydike, a girl who was healthy, pretty, well-connected, and always in good spirits. She was only fifteen, and my brother insisted on waiting until her sixteenth birthday before they married.

"She won't understand so long a wait," I said when he told me the news. "She's in love with you." I had invited Eurydike and her parents to an intimate supper at the palace, during which the girl's gaze scarcely left my brother.

"I'm not sure that's an advantage," said Creon. But even if he was not passionately in love, he treated Eurydike with kindness.

Despite Creon's procrastination, the day of the wedding finally arrived. The procession of maidens reminded me of my own marriage ceremony. How much I had hoped that day – and how thoroughly my hopes had been destroyed. The Tiresias had arrived too late to stop my wedding from happening, but soon enough to ensure the marriage would never be happy.

Well, that Tiresias was dead now, I thought, as I heard the priest put the ritual questions to Creon and Eurydike. And in all his years as the Tiresias, Father had burdened us with no terrible curses. Today he stood at my side in the dark robes of his calling. What little hair he had left was entirely gray.

"They are wed," I told my father, as the couple entered the palace.

"Finally," he said, his tone sour. Then his expression brightened. "Does that mean it's time for the feast?"

"Yes, it does," I answered, and pulled his arm through mine.

"The servant of Apollo is supposed to be unconcerned with such mundane matters as food," said the blind old man. There was strength still in his arms, and he used me only as guide, not support. "However, I'm here today not on behalf of the gods, but to witness my son's wedding. So I plan to eat well."

I laughed, and led him inside the palace. Melanthe sat at Laius' right hand, Pelorus at his left. Further down the table, Polydorus looked up and favored me with a leer. With Creon off enjoying his new bride, the company was weighted in my husband's favor. But at least I had my father with me.

"Who is here?" he asked, after I put a goblet in his hand.

"Don't you know?" asked Melanthe, flashing him a look of scorn he could not see.

"Apollo tells me what I need to know," said the Tiresias. "I know that those who are present should show him more respect."

"And why should we do that?" growled Laius. "What has Apollo ever done for me, except curse me with your daughter for a wife?"

I tensed. Laius had not insulted me for so long that his words took me by surprise. Pelorus frowned, and touched Laius' elbow, murmuring something.

The Tiresias rose from his seat. He put his goblet down easily, without first feeling for the table, then lifted his staff and turned toward Laius. And although his eyes were bound with black linen, he seemed to stare directly at the king.

The son you fear comes ever near
You'll meet your fate within the year.

Then, without eating a bite, the Tiresias turned and left the room, striding as easily as sighted man of thirty.

Laius put down his own goblet with a clatter.

Melanthe scoffed. "The old fool! As if—"

The king interrupted her. "Be gone!"

"What?" asked the dark beauty. "My lord..."

"I ordered you to leave!" Laius barked, with a fierceness that matched her own. The woman in the lion's skin stared him down for a moment, then rose and went in the same direction my father had just taken, her back straight.

"The curse – the curse has returned! And I have neglected Apollo!" The anger he displayed a moment before had vanished. Instead the king's face was ashen; his hands trembled. "What can I do? What must I do?"

Pelorus and I stared at each other a moment, then returned our gaze to the king. "My lord king," Pelorus began, his voice as always calm. "If..."

Laius interrupted him. "You! I thought you said the child was dead!"

"The infant born to you by the queen? He *is* dead – unless some god took him out of the jaws of the lion, put the body back together, and returned him to life."

I looked quickly down at my plate. Pelorus' brutal words crushed out the tiny flame of hope I had nourished all these years. After so many years, hearing about the death of my child still hurt.

"Then I don't understand," said Laius.

I found my own tongue. "He – he is not your only son."

Polydorus' face flushed and he rose from his seat. "Watch your words," he hissed at me.

Laius shook his head, motioning for his son to sit once more. Looking at Polydorus, his face took on a brooding expression; but he said nothing, and turned his attention to his wine cup.

After that Laius refused to have anything more to do with Melanthe; and soon he spent less time staring vacantly into the air. His eyes grew clearer, his color better. But he was a frightened man. He rarely ventured outside. And after a minor argument with Polydorus, he banished his son from Thebes.

Month after month slipped by. "Within the year," Laius muttered one evening at dinner. We dined alone, as we generally did these days; since the Tiresias' prophecy, Laius admitted few into his company. And, to my increasing irritation, each night he spoke of his fears. "The olive harvest is past, and soon they'll be bringing in the spring-sown grain; the year is nearly gone."

I slammed my fist on the table. "And how have you spent these past months?"

Laius started at the sound. "I—"

"You've wasted them! Perhaps the prophecy is wrong, and you'll be alive at year's end. Perhaps the prophecy is right, and you will be dead. What difference would it make? You've let fear keep you from living!"

He picked up his goblet of wine. "You don't know it's like to live with the threat of death."

"Laius, we're all mortal. How long have you been living with this threat? Ever since we married! Twenty-three years! And you've spent those years drinking instead of living. You might as well renounce the throne of Thebes and go cower in a cave."

The king stared at the goblet in his hand. He slowly put it down on the table, its contents untasted. "The prophecies..." he began, but left his sentence unfinished.

"The prophecies!" I repeated, further raising my voice. "Do you even understand the prophecies?"

"I'll go to Delphi," he said at last. He straightened his shoulders. "I am king of Thebes; I have as much right as any man to consult the oracle. I'll go to Delphi, and ask for guidance."

Such determination in Laius was rare, but he insisted that only the Delphic oracle could untangle the web of prophecy. Two days later he set off for Delphi. He took with him only a pair of guards, his charioteer, and Pelorus.

As I had found before on those rare occasions when Laius traveled, I was far happier without the king in residence. His absence affected palace business not at all, as my brother and I had always run things; but with him gone I somehow felt lighter, and the air tasted sweeter.

A few days later, Creon and I received the latest ambassador from Pelops. Nikippes, a tall, thin, scowling man of forty, arrived during the festival in honor of Hephaestus and Athena. At this time the crafts of our best artisans were displayed in the agora, accompanied by delicacies from the fall harvest. Nikippes clearly enjoyed inspecting our beautiful tapestries, pottery, and finely-wrought jewelry, and the locals basked in his praise – unaware, perhaps, of the fact that he was planning to haul as much back as possible to the Pisatan court.

"It's a shame that Pelorus is away," whispered Creon, frowning as he watched Nikippes hold a golden necklace up to catch the light. The artisan described how he had worked the delicate beading, pride ringing in his voice. "He might have been able to deal with this man."

I bent over a tapestry depicting a lush garden scene with two kneeling griffons. "We'll find a way."

Demochares, who no longer served as my bodyguard but had become the palace herald, pushed through the crowd to interrupt us. "My lady queen, a messenger says he must see you at once."

I looked up from the cloth I had been inspecting. "From where?"

"From Delphi."

"Let him come forward," I said.

The crowd packed the agora shoulder-to-back, so it was not easy for the mud-stained traveler, a thickset fellow wearing the leather wristbands of a charioteer, to reach us. But the citizens edged back to make space, and slowly he made his way forward.

He bowed politely, took a deep breath, and then spoke.

"My lady queen – King Laius is dead."

CHAPTER ELEVEN

"Dead?" I asked blankly. "Laius is dead? How do you know?"

The messenger took a small item out of a leather pouch. "This ring was found upon the body."

At first my eyes would not focus, but I compelled myself to look. A golden signet ring with mating goats carved into the face: it had belonged to Laius. I nodded, then tried to pass the ring to Creon; but my fingers shook, and it fell with a clatter on the stones.

Creon put an arm around me. "A chair for the queen!" he ordered, and in a moment I was seated on a stool belonging to one of the weavers.

Someone picked up the ring and handed it to my brother. He examined it, then gave it back to me. "Definitely the king's," he said, his voice tight.

Laius had left only three days before, and had been in as good health as any man of sixty who exercised too little and ate and drank too much. How could he be dead?

I looked around the agora: the people clustered at a respectful distance, but there were gasps in the crowd as the news spread, while stillness fell on those near us. Laius had been their king for twenty-three years.

When I spoke, my own voice seemed distant, like an echo. "What happened? Can you tell us?"

The muddy traveler began his tale. Laius and his attendants had been found near a narrow, rocky trail. The chariot was overturned; the horses gone. The messenger mentioned bandits – visitors to Delphi were sometimes attacked. Pilgrims made tempting targets, as they often brought precious offerings for the oracle.

As he mentioned this possibility, the messenger flicked a wary glance in my direction, as though he feared I would blame him and his masters for not keeping the temple roads safe enough for the king of Thebes.

I felt no anger. I had yet to understand the news. Laius, dead? My husband, gone forever? I felt strange, shaky, dazed, as if I had been kept in a cave for years and was only just emerging into the light.

A single half-hysterical laugh escaped me, but I forced it into a cough. Creon placed a hand on my shoulder, his tight grip warning me to keep my self-control. The people knew that Laius and I did not share a bed, but they were used to us as king and queen. I could not laugh at news of my husband's death here in the marketplace, in the plain light of day, in front of the festival crowd. Given my loveless marriage, some might wonder if the bandits had tasted Theban gold before they attacked the king.

I coughed again and Creon beckoned for someone to bring wine. A cup was poured for me, and I drank deeply. The taste was sweet and mellow; the late-fall air smelled of the fruits of the harvest; in the yellowing afternoon light the whole agora seemed to glow. Everything was too beautiful, too full of life, for us to be talking of death.

Silence overtook all; everyone watched and waited for me to react. I moved my lips but could form no words.

"Traveling," Creon finally said, "is often dangerous. I warned the king to take more men."

Demochares, who was Creon's most frequent companion, raised his voice in support. "Yes, my lord, you did." Agreement rippled through the crowd, for Creon had indeed given this advice. But Laius, wanting none to overhear the questions he planned to ask at Delphi, ignored it.

My brother turned back to the mud-stained messenger. "Go on. Were there any survivors?"

"Only one; he was carried to the temple but his condition is poor."

"Which man?" called a woman, her voice shrill with panic. She was the wife of Laius' charioteer, and we waited as she pushed her way through the crowd. Her dark eyes opened wide, swollen with desperation and hope. "What is his name?"

The messenger turned his head. "We don't know. But he was about my height, lean, with streaks of gray in his hair."

The woman collapsed into the arms of a plump matron at her side: her husband had been short and bald.

Creon squeezed my shoulder, then spoke quietly, his question addressed only to me. "Pelorus?"

I forced myself to think, trying to remember who else had gone on the journey. "It must be." I beckoned to Lilika, one of my young serving women, and told her to help the widow of the charioteer home and to send her family baskets of food and wine. Creon ordered another servant to notify the wives of Laius' dead guards.

The messenger from Delphi waited while the woman was led away and his information wended its way through the crowd. Then he continued. "The survivor has not spoken, and his injuries are severe. He will probably die. Without his witness we have no means of identifying the murderers, unless we find them with Theban gold."

"And first they would have to be captured," said my brother.

The messenger nodded. "No easy matter, in the hills."

I drained my cup down to the dark lees.

An old man's deep-pitched voice broke through the quiet. "The killers must be found and brought to justice! The murder of the king of Thebes – chosen by the gods – must not be allowed to go unpunished!"

My father the Tiresias, leaning on his servant's arm, moved through the crowd until both prophet and guide stood before us.

He spoke again. "Letting the guilty escape would offend the gods."

Creon and I shared a look that our father could not see, and I was sure we thought the same thing. The mortal King Pelops, and no god, had placed Laius on the throne of Thebes. Besides, Thebes had murdered her kings three times before, all without divine retribution – unless one counted twenty-three years of Laius' rule as punishment. Creon and I had done well for Thebes: the city had never been more prosperous. If only we could avoid Pelops' tribute, we would have plenty for even our poorest citizens.

But the Tiresias was both the servant of Apollo and our father, so my brother spoke with respect. "Of course, Tiresias. We will do all we can to bring Laius' killers to justice."

"Perhaps you can tell us who killed him, Tiresias?" I spoke quickly, out of curiosity, without intending to make my words a challenge. But Father shook his head and he gripped his staff tighter.

"The god has not yet revealed that information," he said. "But unless the murderer is punished, Thebes will suffer."

I let out a soft hiss. His words sounded too much like a curse.

Creon spoke quickly. "Messenger, can you tell us anything more?"

The man shook his head. "Not unless your man recovers."

"Then," said Creon, "he must have the best care. We'll send an offering for the oracle and a healer from our temple."

"What about the king's body?" I asked. "And the others?"

"They are being brought here, my lady queen."

My brother and I made what arrangements we could: we ordered soldiers to meet the bodies, an escort befitting the king of Thebes. We also arranged for a local healer, as well as Pelorus' pregnant wife Chrysippe and their daughter Daphne, to make the trip to Delphi, bringing gifts for the oracle and protected by a large contingent of guards. The Tiresias chose to go as well; Father preferred to spend most of his time at Delphi, and even the prophet of Apollo valued protection on the road. Finally we offered the messenger refreshment and shelter.

"I'll take the queen inside," said Creon. "Serve the feast, Demochares; the food is ready, and our harvest meal now honors Laius as a first funeral banquet."

"Of course, my lord," he said.

My brother took my hand and helped me to my feet; together we crossed the agora. Despite the crowd and the clutter of tables and looms, the people managed to step back, allowing us space to walk. We climbed the palace steps and went inside.

I crossed the megaron to my throne and sat down, then looked at the throne beside mine. Laius had sat there only three days before.

Could the messenger have been mistaken? I examined the ring once more. There was no question that it belonged to Laius. No question but that he was dead. Yet I had trouble believing it. I expected him to come in at any moment, to rattle the pebbles of his senet board, and then snap his fingers for a goblet of wine.

A goblet of wine. The wine I had drunk in the agora had been comforting; I wanted more. I waved my hand; a slave girl darted forward, and soon I had a fresh cup in my hand. I swirled its contents and drank.

A queen often had to smile when she was sad, to weep when she was happy. How did I feel now?

I did not even know. My heart was numb. Like hands exposed too long on a winter night, no sensation remained.

"My lady, can I get you anything?" Merope whispered.

I looked up, surprised to see her. Then I held out my cup and she poured me more wine. Drinking reminded me of Laius. I glanced around the room: I was not alone. Besides the guards and servants, several prominent citizens had come, drawn to the palace megaron at this time of change.

Melanthe stood among and yet apart from them, staring at me with glittering dark eyes.

My brother stood next to his pregnant wife. Eurydike looked both shocked and sad; Laius had been king for her entire life. Creon's expression was harder to read. When he saw me glance his way he spoke to Eurydike, then crossed to the front of the room.

"May I sit down?" he asked.

He gestured at the king's throne. Laius had never permitted anyone else, not even his son Polydorus, to sit in it: but Laius was gone. Even Polydorus was gone, banished by his own father. I shrugged, then gestured for my brother to sit.

Creon lowered his spare frame onto Laius' wool-filled cushions. "So this is what the view looks like from here."

"Different?"

He put his head to one side, considering. "It's the same room, but it seems different."

"Perhaps it has more to do with the way others see you than how you see others," I said.

"Very perceptive."

"I've sat here for twenty-three years; I've had time to think." I downed more wine. "You deserve to be on that chair far more than Laius. You've done much more for Thebes! And you are also descended from Kadmos."

Creon shrugged. He dropped his voice, and tilted his head toward mine. "Jocasta, you weren't happy with Laius. Did you do anything to arrange this?"

"No," I replied, surprised. "Did you?"

He shook his head. "I'd never do something so drastic without consulting you first. If I didn't do it, and you didn't, then who did? Pelops would never get rid of Laius – Laius was his man."

I remembered that it was my outburst that had persuaded Laius to go to Delphi. If he had not gone, he would still be alive.

To wash away this thought, I drained my cup down to the lees. "Perhaps it really was bandits," I said, my tongue sluggish. "They do exist."

"Yes," he said slowly, his dark brows drawing together. "But if bandits were responsible, why didn't they take the ring?"

I looked at the ring still in my hand. "Maybe they were rushed. Or they found enough gold in the chariot."

"Hmph," Creon grunted. "Speaking of bandits, here comes one now."

The guards had admitted Nikippes, the envoy from Pisa. The former Olympian champion runner crossed the room with long strides and bowed his head. "My lady, let me tell you how sorry I am for your loss."

I nodded in acknowledgment. "It is a terrible shock."

"Indeed. And Pelops has lost a great friend – a great ally. Laius was like a son to my king." Nikippes fingered the fibula that fastened his cloak; its agate head was carved in the shape of a horse's head, the emblem of the Pisatan court. The envoy then turned to Creon, and spoke firmly. "Isn't it tactless for you to sit on Laius' throne? The body's not even buried."

Creon's hand gripped the arm of the throne so hard that his knuckles turned white. "I am consoling the queen of Thebes, my sister."

"That gives you the right to be near her." Nikippes brushed back his cloak, straightening his shoulders. "But this is not Aegypt. Theban queens do not marry their brothers. You will never have the right to sit on the throne of Thebes!"

I could feel the fury of Creon's stare. Nikippes' meaning was plain enough: his master Pelops would not allow Creon to rule in Laius' place. Pelops had to be in his seventies; but he had a horde of ambitious sons whose influence had spread throughout the southern peninsula – they now called it the Peloponnesus, the land of Pelops.

Creon slowly rose from his seat, his face drawn tight to control his anger. He moved to stand at my shoulder, and took my hand. He opened his mouth to say something – but just then Melanthe called out: "Why should she marry again at all? Why does Thebes need a king?"

Both men stared at Melanthe. Creon was accustomed to her outbursts, but Nikippes' jaw dropped. "Of course there must be a king! Whoever heard of a woman ruling alone?"

"As if Laius ever contributed anything to governing Thebes!" she spat. How quickly she dismissed the man who had invested so much hope and gold in her!

"He was an ally of Pelops," Nikippes said coldly, "as well as the rightful heir to the throne."

"You name his friends, his ancestry. But what did he ever *do*? Organize a few wrestling matches? Send cattle and gold to Pelops? He did not take care of his people."

Nikippes retorted: "And who are you, woman, to judge the merits of a king?"

I watched the two of them glare at each other, relieved that their quarrel drew attention away from Creon and me. I drained my cup, gave it to Merope and then stood. "I will retire now."

The Maenad and the envoy broke off their argument. Nikippes bowed with more grace and respect than before. "Of course, my lady queen, you must be very distressed. I will leave you to your sorrow."

Melanthe's lips twisted, as if she doubted any distress or sorrow; but she said only: "I wish you good night, my lady queen."

In my chamber, Merope helped me undress. I asked her to bring more wine. I sank back against the couch pillows, and let my gaze wander to every corner of the room: my vanity table strewn with containers of cosmetics and jewels, the ivory Hermes standing on a corner table, the painted ceiling-beams high above, the pair of braziers that brought light and heat to the chamber. I looked carefully, seeing each object anew.

I had become so accustomed to this room that I no longer noticed its contents. Just as I had grown so accustomed to being queen of Thebes that I no longer questioned my right to rule. But with Laius' death, everything changed. His body was not yet buried, not even yet returned to Thebes, and those with influence were already quarreling about whom I should marry.

Melanthe's words appealed to me: why should I marry at all?

At fourteen I had longed to marry. I had believed in – had expected – love.

At thirty-seven my outlook was different. I knew a few happy couples; I knew far more who were not. I no longer expected marriage to bring love.

Twenty-three years!

If I could only unwind the skein of my life, and be that girl of fourteen once more!

But I could not.

I sipped from my cup, feeling the warm haze of the wine settle over my thoughts. Was this why Laius had drunk so much – to forget his unfulfilled dreams? To forget what he had hoped for, and what had been denied him, despite the promise of his youth? He had been born a prince, with every advantage and promise for the future: handsome and wealthy, educated in the greatest court in Hellas – yet he had never been happy, at least not since I knew him.

I had despised Laius' lethargy, his drunkenness. But now that he was dead, I felt I could finally empathize with what he must have felt. The Fates had dangled joy before him and then had snatched it away.

Again I lifted the pitcher and filled my cup. A few red drops splashed over the rim of my goblet, glistening on the floor-tiles like fresh blood. I stared at the red stain as I set the pitcher back on the side-table. Poor Laius! I hoped his death had been quick.

Strange that the fellow-feeling should come so late. If I had experienced it sooner, could we have mended our marriage? Or would we simply have drunk ourselves into oblivion in our separate corners?

I filled my mouth with wine, then swallowed.

The next day Creon and Eurydike came to my rooms before I had risen from my bed. I blinked at them. "Go away," I said. My mouth was dry and tasted foul. "It's too early."

Creon looked down at me. "It's nearly noon!"

"Noon?" I asked, glancing toward the curtained window.

"Merope, bring water," called my brother. Without waiting for an invitation, he settled his wife at one end of my favorite couch and seated himself at the other.

"My lady queen, I want to tell you how sorry I am for your loss," said Eurydike.

Her high-pitched voice was like a stone scraping along my forehead. I groaned and covered my ears.

"How terrible, to be widowed," she continued. "But of course a lady of your years—"

"Hush!" said Creon, not crossly, but firmly. They remained silent until Merope returned with a pitcher. Creon poured, made me sit up, and then pressed a silver cup into my palms. I held its cool surface to my cheek for a moment, then drank thirstily.

"It's too dark in here." Creon rose and opened the curtains. I groaned again when the light struck my eyes, and turned my face away.

Eurydike moved so that the sunbeams washed across her completely. She was so very young, with her pink cheeks and her unlined eyes!

I had never felt so old.

197

Creon, sunlight bringing out the strands of gray in his dark hair, stood before the window exuding energy. "We must start making plans for your next husband at once."

I rubbed crust from my eyes. "The first one's not even buried!"

"Do you think Pelops will let you mourn long? Not that any of us expect you to mourn *much*, Jocasta."

My head throbbed. I swallowed, and set the cup down on my bedside table beside the empty wine-pitcher. "I – I cared about Laius."

"If you say so," said my brother. "But that doesn't matter. As Nikippes pointed out last night – if you remember – the man who marries you will become king of Thebes. You'll be highly sought after, my dear. Most likely Pelops is grooming a suitor for you now. So, get up, my darling sister, and join us in the other room."

Creon ushered Eurydike into the antechamber, giving me some privacy.

Merope handed me a damp linen cloth, which I pressed to my brow. I rose heavily and stumbled over to the chamber pot. When I was done, Merope helped me don a robe, then she opened the door and I joined my brother and his wife.

They were sitting on the couch, and breakfast had been brought in: bread, dried figs, soft white goat's-milk cheese rolled in dried herbs. The pungent smell of the cheese, which I normally enjoyed, turned my stomach. Swallowing back bile, I took the seat furthest from the food.

"Pelops chose my last husband – I won't be pushed into that again," I said, continuing the conversation where we had left it.

"And I won't let Pelops force my sister into a marriage she doesn't want."

Eurydike giggled and tossed her dark curls. "Creon, you're so *gallant*!"

He ignored her and went on. "Especially when such a marriage would mean another Peloponnesian puppet. Some fool like Laius who thinks he knows better than I – and my darling sister – what is good for the city. Who thinks that what is good for *Pelops* is good for Thebes. Our city has seen enough of that: first Amphion, who was Pelops' brother-in-law; then Laius, who was raised by him. Both of them sending our best cattle and half our harvest to Olympia."

"Then how do we stop him?"

"I'm sure your passionate refusal will win over the people of Thebes. But it won't defeat Pelops' army. That's what has kept me up all night."

Eurydike touched his arm. "And I thought *I* kept you awake last night, Honeycake, not that old Pelops!"

Creon did not so much as glance in her direction, and Eurydike pouted. She opened her mouth and looked my way, as though appealing for support on the grounds of our common sex; but she started when her eyes met mine, and said nothing. Impatience and headache must have made a fearsome-looking combination.

Didn't she realize this was serious? Deadly serious?

"The people of Thebes will support you," Creon continued, "but that's not enough. We need a *reason* for rejecting Pelops' man."

"Why must I marry at all? Melanthe had a wonderful idea last night – a queen and no king!"

Creon continued speaking to me. "Jocasta, there's no choice. Thebes is like a meat-pie left to cool on a windowsill. Every ambitious dog in Hellas will be sniffing around. Pelops will send his cronies and their sons, but they won't be the only ones." He laughed. "The city will swarm with suitors. You'll have to beat them back with a shield and spear, like Athena."

Eurydike sat up, her eyes bright. "How romantic! It's just like in the stories. Remember the princess who had so many suitors that her father didn't know what to do, and he finally said he would give her to the man who could yoke a lion and a boar to a chariot, and drive them around the race-track? And then there was Atalanta, who declared she wouldn't take a husband unless he could outrun her. Even Pelops himself won his wife in a chariot-race!"

She paused, because Creon was staring at her.

"What, Honeycake? Don't you know the story? The old king had no grown sons, but his daughter was very beautiful; and he didn't know which of her suitors she ought to marry; so he said any fellow that wanted to marry her would have to defeat him in a chariot-race; but he was so good that none of the young men could win; and when they lost he killed them; but then Pelops came over from Lydia, and they're wonderful with chariots there, so he won the chariot race and the hand of the princess." She smiled, like a child expecting praise after correctly repeating a lesson to her tutor.

"Pelops may have been good with a chariot back then – and he had superb horses. But he didn't rely on just his driving skills." A sly look spread across Creon's face. "He bribed the king's charioteer to replace the bronze lynchpin with one made of hardened wax. When the king got up to speed the wax melted, his chariot wheel fell off, and he was dragged to his death. Then Pelops killed the charioteer to keep the story from spreading."

Eurydike's eyes and mouth opened wide.

"Didn't know *that* part of the story, did you?" He chuckled, then caught my eye. "It's true, though."

I rose, went to sit before my dressing table and picked up a comb. "If Pelops killed the king's charioteer, how did *you* learn this piece of information? I can't imagine that Pelops himself told you."

Creon crossed the room and took the ivory comb from my hand. Gently he began to untangle my hair. "I had some very interesting conversations when I went to the games at Olympia a couple of years back. One was with the granddaughter of the charioteer himself. She smelled of horses, but still she made a warm armful—"

"Creon!" Eurydike's voice was full of reproach.

"What a snarl you have here," said my brother, slowing down to work through a knot. "Anyway, that just goes to show that with Pelops you have to watch your back. But, you know..." his face grew thoughtful. "Maybe Eurydike has a point here."

Little Eurydike? A point? That seemed unlikely.

He drew the comb through my hair, smoothly this time. "If the next king of Thebes had to pass a test, that could prove very useful."

"Do you expect me to run a footrace? Or do you plan to challenge Pelops' men in a chariot?"

"No, of course not. Too much chance of getting hurt!" He set down the comb. "Eurydike, dear, aren't you supposed to see the midwife this morning?"

"Yes, but—"

"Go on, it's rude to keep Rhodia waiting. I'll meet you for lunch in a little while. I just have some things to finish up with Jocasta. Merope, would you escort my wife back to our apartment?"

Eurydike rose with obvious reluctance, and the two women left.

I turned to my brother, curious.

He looked back towards the door, which Merope had carefully shut behind her. "No chariot races," he said at last. "We'll come up with something else. But we *will* arrange to get rid of Pelops' men."

"Get rid of them?"

"Yes." His tone was unyielding and left no room to doubt what he meant. "This is no time to be soft-hearted. Besides, if we make it clear that the contestants are risking their lives, maybe Pelops will think twice about sending anyone he really values."

Distasteful, perhaps dangerous. But he was right. I slumped back, leaning against the edge of my dressing-table. It cut into my ribs, and I shifted. "What if I don't like the winner?"

"We'll make sure you do. *We'll* control the lynchpins this time."

"What if Pelops sends an agent here to poison us?"

Creon's eyes narrowed. "We'll have to make sure that doesn't happen."

"And what if he sends an army instead?"

"Jocasta, this will be *ordained*. By Apollo. Officially. Pelops can't fight that, can he?"

I saw where he was going, and shook my head. "Father will never agree," I said. "He really believes the god speaks to him." I did not point out that Father, as the Tiresias, had accurately predicted when Laius would die, but we both were thinking it. "Father won't falsify a prophecy."

Creon frowned, then resumed combing my hair. He didn't want to admit it, but he knew I was right. "Then we'll find another way. Another god."

"Another god?" I said. "Creon, I don't know…"

"Melanthe and the Maenads. We'll use them."

"Melanthe," I repeated, staring at the wall painting, with its procession of maidens carrying sacred offerings. "Perhaps; but—" I hesitated. "Won't that offend the wine-god?" With my current hangover, I had more respect for the power of Dionysus.

"We'll ask his priestess," Creon assured me promptly. "If she agrees to cooperate, then we can assume she has his blessing." Creon smoothed his hand over my hair and added thoughtfully: "Or if he is displeased, then his wrath will fall upon her."

"Perhaps," I said cautiously, liking my brother's arguments.

"She'll make a wonderful spectacle, with that lion skin she wears. The people know her; and many believe she works the will of Dionysus." He laughed. "The Maenads love riddles. We'll make it a contest of wit. That will protect *me*, at least, from any dirty tricks with chariots! And *you* from getting a fool for a husband. Jocasta, we can make this work!"

He grinned, turned me around in my chair, and kissed me on both cheeks. Instead of the care-worn administrator with streaks of gray in his beard, I saw my mischievous brother once more. His exuberance was as irresistible as when he was seventeen.

"It might," I said, confidence growing within me.

The next morning my young maidservant Lilika dressed me in a plain skirt and jacket of unbleached linen. Though I knew I did not look my best, I refused to let her apply makeup, and I left my golden diadem and the necklace of Harmonia in their chests. I forced myself to eat the bread and cheese Merope brought, then went to the megaron. The body of Laius had been brought back to Thebes.

Many of those who had known Laius came to pay their respects. Already several locks of hair, shorn in token of mourning, had made their way into the funeral-wreath. I approached and accepted a small knife from the priest of Hades who stood nearby, and cut a black curl from my own head; the priest accepted it with a nod, and tied a white ribbon round before fixing my offering in among the branches of pine. Then I turned to see the body of my husband.

His body lay on a bier. He seemed whole but there were dark spots where blood had flowed and later dried. The face seemed different than I remembered, his expression more relaxed. Was it because he was afraid no longer?

Rhodia stood nearby. "His neck was broken, my lady," she volunteered quietly. "You can't see it from his position now, but I'm certain that's what killed him. It must have been quick."

"Goodbye, Laius," I said calmly. "May Hermes guide you safely to the Underworld."

Demochares approached me and bowed slightly. "My lady queen," he began, "we'll move the body out to the foot of the palace steps this afternoon, so that the common people may pay their respects. Creon says the funeral will be tomorrow."

I nodded. The people needed to see that their king was truly dead – and we needed time to make ready the royal tomb.

"Are there personal objects, my lady, which the king would want with him in the Underworld?" asked Demochares.

I considered. "His jewelry, certainly. His wrestling trophies from the games at Olympia. His senet board – and his favorite wine-cup, the one with handles shaped like dogs' heads."

"Very good, my lady queen. I'll take care of it."

That afternoon I watched from the palace windows. The agora was completely changed, all traces of the artisans' festival gone: today the mood was somber, and no jugglers or merchants plied the crowd. Soldiers, wearing boar's-tooth helmets and carrying spears, stood at either side of the bier, guarding the king better in death than they had in life. The gray skies and cool drizzle suited the musicians' dirge.

I remained inside, not caring to show my grief – or lack thereof – to the public. I also refused all visitors, with the exception of my brother. Creon was away most of the afternoon, but in the evening he came to my rooms. We talked at length, imagining myriad things that could go wrong, and at last hammered out a plan. We had to act quickly, for there was much to arrange and the threat was real. Laius had already been dead for days; it was all too likely that King Pelops knew.

In the morning Demochares and Creon gave orders to move the stores from the outer granaries into the palace. We consulted with Melanthe and with the captain of the guard.

Then it was time to put Laius and his treasures to rest in the royal tomb of Thebes. The populace was subdued during the funeral feast. A few people wept, because Laius had been king for so long. Most did not, because they knew that Creon and I ran the city.

More than anything the people's mood was one of simmering anticipation. What would happen to Thebes? I did not doubt that my people loved me, and wanted me to continue as their queen; but I sensed a tremor in the air, a desire for change, for excitement. I even overheard one man wonder if Polydorus might return to Thebes, and claim his father's throne by marrying me.

"That's ridiculous," I whispered to Creon. "I can't wed Laius' son."

"He might try to take over Thebes without you," Creon said. When he saw my grimace, he added hastily, "But he wouldn't succeed. The people would never allow it. They'd rip him to pieces first."

We spent the whole night putting our plan into action. Demochares toured our seven gates and then made a report.

Shortly before dawn, Merope and Lilika dressed me in my favorite outfit: the skirts bright blue and the jacket white, all edged with gold. They fastened Harmonia's necklace at my throat, and set the crown of golden leaves and flowers upon my head. Despite having lain awake all night, I felt wonderful: more alive, more full of hope than I had been in years.

"You're lovelier than when you married Laius," my brother said when we met for breakfast, and kissed my cheek.

"Flatterer!" I said, and kissed him back.

"Suitors will come from all across Hellas," Creon declared, giving my shoulders a squeeze. "I guarantee it!"

I tried to laugh, but could not. Who would try for my hand?

CHAPTER TWELVE

Every night my soldiers closed Thebes' seven great gates; but this morning the gates would not open.

Many Thebans left the city almost every day: men to hunt hare and deer in the nearby hills, women to wash their laundry in the streams of Chryssorrhoas and Dirke. Today the guards would warn them: those who passed through the small, narrow doors set into the great wooden gates could not return. We would all have to eat from the city stores; the women would have to use the wells inside the walls. Thebes' springs and wells offered plentiful water, but those living near the gates would add a steep climb to their daily routines.

Others expected to enter Thebes: herders bringing cattle, sheep and goats; men from the quarries delivering marble; coastal traders with carts of salted fish. These would meet a closed city. My soldiers would allow trade goods through the gates only after close inspection, or not at all, and would turn the traders themselves away. I trusted some to react calmly; others might argue and curse, but certainly, word would spread.

I only hoped our actions had been quick enough, so that any agents sent by Pelops were shut outside. To be sure, Pelops' envoy Nikippes was within the walls, but we knew who he was; we would have him watched.

Finally feeling the effects of the night without sleep, I drew a deep breath and whispered a prayer to Dionysus, asking him to protect his mother's city. But he was a fickle god; the whole scheme was a gamble. Father would not approve; he would tell us to ask the gods first, and to then act upon their advice. Instead we had put our plans into motion and only now sought the gods' blessing. I felt relief that my father the Tiresias had departed just after Laius' burial to spend the winter at Delphi, his reprimands locked out with the rest of the world. When he finally returned to Thebes, his rebukes would be too late: success or failure would already be ours.

As dawn broke, Creon and I walked out onto the palace steps. A crowd stood gathered in the agora; news of the closed gates had already spread. I glanced at Creon; he nodded. I grasped my vine-wrapped Maenad staff in one hand and slid my other arm through my brother's; we descended the steps and crossed through the throng in the agora to the shrine at its center. During the night, the Maenads had decorated the altar with vines and pinecones.

At the altar stood Melanthe, wrapped in her lion-skin robe, the beast's head topping her dark braids like a cap. This morning she had strapped to her shoulders huge wings fashioned from wicker and covered with feathers. From a distance she appeared strange, even alarming. Up close she was even more terrifying, with her grim expression and the casual way she fingered her daggers.

I was glad Creon stood between Melanthe and me.

The late autumn sun shone bright that morning, the sky a clear pale blue with puffs of white cloud just over the distant hills. A breeze played with my hair and the air tasted sweet from the harvest. Beautiful weather: a good omen? Surely all would be well. But I gripped my thyrsus, the staff that I held in tribute to the wine-god, until my knuckles turned white.

Demochares began the announcement, his rich voice booming across the heads of the crowd. "People of Thebes! The city gates are shut! And they will remain so, until a new king for Thebes is found!"

Hearing this, the people stirred. Then they quieted, waiting for more.

The herald continued: "In accordance with the will of Dionysus, as made known to us through his servant the Sphinx Melanthe: the new king of Thebes will be chosen through contest of wit! The contest will take place in three months' time, on the last day of winter; and the marriage will occur eight days later! These are the words of our regent, lord Creon! And of the god Dionysus!"

Silence held for a moment; then a ripple coursed through the crowd. Soon the common folk began to cheer; we had captured their interest. The contest would offer drama and spectacle, the wedding feasting and merriment. I relaxed my grip on the thyrsus. The peasants would no longer mutter that Thebes needed change: we were giving them change, by the will of a popular god – but this change we could control.

Among the wealthier Thebans I saw approving nods. Even Nikippes appeared intrigued, although the lift of his eyebrow let me know he was skeptical. Only a few of Laius' old drinking-companions grumbled among themselves. I wondered if any among them would be fool enough to enter the contest.

Creon stepped over to Melanthe, and urged her forward as the cheering continued. My brother's voice was good, but not as strong as Demochares'; the crowd hushed to hear him. "Let all know, any well-born man may present himself to be tested by the Sphinx!"

He paused, and Melanthe slowly raised her arms away from her sides, spreading and lifting high her false wings. Her narrow fingers stretched wide apart, like eagle's talons. "Come forth, you who dare – but do not think to deceive Dionysus!" she cried, her voice high-pitched and keening. "Pretenders will be purged." She slowly lowered arms to her sides once more.

Creon spoke like an interpreter. "Any well-born man may present himself! But no man should come forward lightly. Success means great reward: Thebes is a rich and powerful city, and my sister a woman of beauty and wisdom. But failure will meet with disgrace and death!"

This brought a murmur from the well-born, and a cheer from the peasants: more drama than they had expected!

"Now," said Creon, "bring forth the sacrifice!"

The animal, a large brown sow, was led to the altar. She came willingly, tamely, which the people considered a good omen; but I knew she had been fed calming herbs. As she neared the altar and Creon hefted the great double-headed bronze axe, I stepped back several paces.

I loved appearing before my people in my finest clothes; I adored addressing them and leading them as their queen. I was relieved, though, that the task of sacrifice fell to others: when not the priests and priestesses, then the king, or in this case Creon. We needed to honor the gods, of course; but I preferred keeping my own hands unstained. In truth, although I had witnessed many sacrifices, I did not think I could kill an animal.

The blade flashed in the morning sun as Creon swung it overhead and down; the animal fell without flinching. The crowd clapped at this sign of good fortune. Melanthe let out a cry – triumph? delight? – as the temple servants turned the twitching carcass over to expose the belly. Creon passed the axe back to the chief servant.

Had this sacrifice been to Apollo, Creon or one of the priests would have drawn the next task as well; but, as the offering was to Dionysus, Melanthe stepped up to the dead sow, holding her scythe-shaped silver dagger high. For a moment, it glittered as brightly as the sun; then, with a sudden jerk, Melanthe plunged it two-handed into the beast. Bright red blood welled up around her hands, adding more stains to the tawny lion's pelt. A few swift moves with the knife, and she held the glistening liver. One of the Maenads took the dripping knife as Melanthe kneaded the organ.

I held my breath; what would she say? In the privacy of the palace, Melanthe had provoked; here in the agora her words could prove dangerous. Would she say again that Thebes needed no king – and then add that the city needed no queen? Thebans had turned on their rulers before.

Yet Melanthe had fallen in with our plan, agreeing to combine forces with us to throw off the Peloponnesian yoke. If we ended the tributes to Pelops, her followers could receive more of Thebes' yearly harvest. And she had to realize that she and the Maenads, though they might bring down a queen, could not hold off Pelops' army.

She needed us as much as we needed her. But did she understand that?

Melanthe threw the liver into the holy fire – and I discovered I had been holding my breath. Smoke poured upwards, and the smell of burning meat unsettled my stomach. Usually the scent roused my appetite, but this morning I was too full of nerves.

Melanthe raised her blood-smeared hands to the sky, then spoke:

The king of Thebes shall be that man
Chosen by Dionysus' plan
The heir to Kadmos' throne will be blessed
By the people — and they, with the harvest.

I felt, rather than saw, Creon's twitch of disapproval; I knew he did not like the implication that Melanthe might control distribution of the harvest. As for me, I wondered at the confidence in her words and her bearing. Had Dionysus truly spoken to her? Or had she spent half the night composing what verse she would say?

The gods had never addressed me personally. From time to time I thought I sensed a god's presence, but I had never heard one speak. I sometimes wondered why. I was a descendant of Kadmos; descended through his wife from Aphrodite herself. My own father was the Tiresias. I had performed rituals and ruled Thebes for more than twenty years. Didn't I deserve even one holy vision?

Perhaps Creon was right, and the gods kept their own counsel; men only tricked themselves into believing that they heard divine voices. Or perhaps the gods knew my feelings of ambivalence and resented them. I remembered Dionysus' mother, reduced to ashes by the too-glorious sight of her lover, Zeus. Perhaps it was best to keep the gods at a distance!

Melanthe lowered her reddened hands and walked away from the fire. With Creon in the middle, the three of us led the way out of the agora.

We toured the city. At each gate we left a contingent of Maenads to support the soldiers. Some of the soldiers looked with scorn at the worshippers of Dionysus, who were mainly women, shaking their heads at the ragged clothing and ochre-painted faces. Others leered, for some of the Maenads were shapely and scantily clad, and all were known to be lusty. We would have to keep a close watch on this strange alliance between the soldiers and the Maenads, but for now we had no choice. We needed them as much as they needed us.

At each gate we ascended the walls, making the same pronouncements to the frustrated, shut-out travelers. They listened, stared, then turned around to return in the direction from which they came – and to spread the news. At the last gate, the Eudoxa, which guarded the road to Athens, Melanthe remained, pacing back and forth along the wall. Creon and I descended the narrow stairway; at the bottom, I turned to look up at the Sphinx. She squatted on her haunches atop the wall, staring out into the distance. From my vantage point so far below, the lion skin masked Melanthe's form and the feathered wings seemed real – transforming her into the monster she claimed to be.

I was grateful to return to the palace. There I visited the private royal shrine, asking Dionysus once more for his blessing. Creon and I had an understanding with Melanthe; I hoped we had an understanding with the god as well.

Our alliance with the Maenads proved difficult. Although zealous, the wild women lacked discipline. Three times they attacked carts at the gates, stealing the trade goods and keeping them for themselves rather than inspecting them and sending them to the palace for distribution. Two of the traders were injured; the third was killed.

"Your rabble will frighten merchants away! Thebes *needs* commerce," Creon yelled at Melanthe after the third incident. "It's necessary for the city's prosperity."

The winter rains were cold and heavy, and Melanthe – wearing her lion's skin but not the false wings – dripped water on the floor. She looked thinner, her skin taut. But her posture was defiant as she stepped towards Creon.

"You mean the prosperity of the palace and the privileged," she countered.

A muscle in Creon's cheek twitched; I could tell he was furious. But he tried to lower his voice. "Goods are to be brought to the palace for distribution."

"And how much would you have given us? The ration is as unfair as it has always been."

"There would have been plenty, if you and your followers had not destroyed so much of the last harvest!"

"We would not have needed to plunder the harvest, if you had not sent away so much in tribute!"

"Creon! Melanthe! Stop this quarreling! Creon, we can give more to the Maenads." I shot a warning look at my glowering brother. "After all, they're helping to defend the city."

Melanthe broke in: "We deserve more!"

"That's what I just said." I peered at her, wondering whether she understood me, or had even heard my words. Had she been drinking too much of her god's wine lately?

Melanthe appeared slightly embarrassed. "You're right, my lady."

"The Maenads at the gates must be cold and wet; it's no surprise they are hungry." I saw her shoulders sag a little, and she glanced at the fire. She could not deny she was drenched; but would she admit she was cold? "But keep away from the traders. Whoever attacked them must be punished. I don't want to hear of this again."

"It will be as you say, my lady queen." Melanthe, her face once more a mask, bowed, and Demochares escorted her out of the room.

"I loathe that woman!" Creon practically spat as soon as they were gone.

"I know."

"She doesn't understand that we need order in the city!"

"Or she doesn't care."

"She lives for the moment, without thinking about tomorrow!"

"You may be right."

"Jocasta, how can you smile? This is serious!"

I had been remembering how infatuated Creon was with Melanthe in his youth; with her luscious curves, her large dark eyes, and her skin of gold. But I repressed my smile, and touched his arm. "You rarely express your feelings with such – such vehemence. I know she and her people are causing problems, but it won't last much longer. Winter ends in another month."

"Do you think she'll give up power now? Jocasta, in order to rid ourselves of one enemy we have yielded Thebes to another. We're captives!"

I bit my lip: I, too, wondered what Melanthe would do. She was the wild element in our scheme, and the role she had to play was large. I spoke slowly. "She has cooperated so far. Remember, her control of the Maenads is not perfect, and they may have acted without her direction."

Creon's eyebrows knit together.

"We always knew this course had risks," I reminded him.

He shrugged. "And there are more risks ahead. We have yet to see who will come to seek your hand."

I said nothing, but my expression must have showed concern, for this question gnawed at me. Creon took my hands in his and squeezed them. "Don't worry, Jocasta. There will be someone suitable among them."

Creon and I needed to meet the suitors, to determine which of them we preferred. So we invited them and their retinues, as well as some dignitaries and envoys from other cities, to attend a banquet a few days before the contest. Four suitors, Laius' son Polydorus among them, entered the city; as they passed through the gate, Nikippes announced that he also planned to present himself as a potential husband. A horde of common folk, with time to waste at the end of winter and more tolerance for camping in poor weather than the well-born, clamored to enter Thebes as well; but we refused to admit them. My soldiers could not hope to watch so many, and any one of them might be an agent of Pelops.

Five suitors: Haralpos, Doran, Tassos, Polydorus, and Nikippes. Which of them would I marry?

Haralpos of Orchomenos I had met before; politically he had advantages. His city lay just north of Thebes, and an alliance would strengthen our position in the region. But the thought of him as a husband left me cold; he was a dull fellow. The Tirynian, Doran, was young and handsome – and clever; but we were certain Pelops had him on a leash. Then there was Tassos, a relative of the king of Pylos. I disliked him at once. He spoke with a stammer, and his skin was blotchy.

By the time we started the banquet my discouragement was complete. While a flute-girl played, I slumped back against my chair. What had I expected? The sudden swift touch of Eros? I reminded myself I had experienced that before, and the union into which it had led me had proved disastrous.

Creon, who had been speaking with Demochares, returned and resumed his place beside me. I thought of my brother's wife, Eurydike. Creon was fond of her, but not captivated – and certainly not faithful! Why should I expect anything better?

"Have you decided, sister?"

We kept our voices low, the surrounding conversation masking our words.

"I'm certain who I *don't* want to marry!"

"That's easy – Polydorus."

I nodded.

"Tell me that you don't want Nikippes, either."

"Of course not." I chewed my lip. "Nikippes is a snake, but he's clever. What if he wins?"

Creon patted my hand. "He won't. Melanthe hates him. What about Tassos?"

I made a face. "His skin is bad. And his breath smells." My brother laughed, but I was serious. I would have to marry the man. "And he seems weak, somehow."

"That could be an advantage," Creon countered. "We don't want someone with too many ideas of his own."

"Or bad skin," I said firmly. "I suppose it will have to be Haralpos." The fellow from Orchomenos did have a talent for games and riddles. He would drone on at dinner every night, but I doubted he would give Creon and me any trouble about our decisions in governing Thebes. Not a bad-looking man, but not handsome, either. I sighed.

A plump serving girl set a bowl of bean stew before me, and bent to light the lamp at my elbow. Next she moved to Melanthe. In the golden lamplight the glass eyes of Melanthe's long-dead lion glittered harshly. Beneath the lion's fixed snarl, Melanthe's own eyes gleamed like obsidian, intent on someone across the room.

I followed her gaze.

"Look at our Sphinx," I said to Creon.

"What?"

"When did she last have a lover? And don't count Laius."

"Who knows? Some peasant at her last orgy, no doubt. Why do you ask?"

I gestured with the hand that held my wine-cup, first indicating Melanthe's stare, then its object: a tall young man with broad shoulders and russet hair. At that moment, he turned my way; meeting his calm blue eyes so suddenly unnerved me. He smiled, showing good white teeth. For a moment I froze, my hand extended, intrigued and startled by his boldness. To cover the awkward moment I lifted the cup to salute him, and when the drink met my lips I found I had returned his smile.

With effort, I detached myself from the compelling gaze and turned back to my brother. "Creon, who is that fellow?"

My brother raised his eyebrows, then threw his head back and laughed. I did not know why, and yet in an instant I was laughing too.

Creon drank down a swallow of wine and passed the back of his hand across his mouth. "Jocasta, he's too young for you!"

I pinched my brother's arm. "I only asked his name!" Yet my eyes wandered again to the youth, who continued to stare back at me. This time he did not seem so very young; I sensed wisdom in his gaze. His face was clean-shaven, the skin paler than a man's complexion should be; yet it suited the reddish hair. His waist was narrow, his belly taut; his arms were shapely with muscle, and a heavy gold bracelet adorned his right bicep.

"That," said Creon, "is the only son of King Polybus of Korinth."

"Does he have a name?"

"They say he was named for a problem he's had since birth – something to do with his feet."

I knew my brother enjoyed teasing me, but I persisted. "And? What is he called?"

Creon satisfied my query at last. "Oedipus."

CHAPTER THIRTEEN

Oedipus, prince of Korinth! That explained the costly jewelry, the finely made kilt. Korinth guarded the narrow isthmus connecting the northern lands, where Thebes and Athens ruled, to Pelops' southern domain; the city was of great strategic importance. If Thebes were to become independent, a Korinthian alliance could prove valuable. But this man had not entered as a suitor. "What's he doing here? Is he here just to see the spectacle?" Certainly we were offering the best entertainment in all Hellas, better than even the famed Olympic Games.

Creon ripped a piece of bread into two. "He seems to have nowhere to go. They say that King Polybus disowned him. Or that Prince Oedipus has renounced his father. Some falling-out over a girl or a hunting dog, I expect."

While my brother spoke, my eyes sought the youth again. As though I had tapped his shoulder, he turned and stared my way once more.

Creon tugged my arm gently. "Come, sister, people will talk. Remember, you are to marry in a few days. If you want the lad, call for him later."

"Call for him? I couldn't!"

"Why not?" he asked, as a serving girl set a platter of mutton before us. He picked up his ivory-handled knife, and carved thin slices for himself and for me. "You are queen. You were married to that useless Laius for more than twenty years – and you are about to make another political marriage. This may be your only chance. Why should your bed stay cold?"

I speared a bite of meat. Despite the shortages behind our closed gates, the cooks had done well: the mutton was spiced with cumin and coriander, the sauce fragrant with wine.

I chewed slowly, wondering if I dared be so bold. Creon knew what I wanted, perhaps better than I knew myself. But could this young man be attracted to me? And if so, what was I supposed to do about it?

Creon laughed at some hunting story Demochares was telling, and a flute girl began a lively tune. The tension from the day had dissipated; even Melanthe seemed to relax. I stared into the flames dancing on the hearth, trying to ignore the heat in my own flesh.

Creon could take any willing wench to his bed; Melanthe indulged in her Dionysian orgies. But I had been queen of Thebes for more than twenty years, and I had not had a lover since my wedding night.

Once, long ago, I had thought of Vassos. And he paid with his life.

I had not dared think of another man since.

Exactly how did one go about taking a lover?

As if he heard my thought, the russet-haired youth nodded at me and rose to his feet. When the musicians stopped, he crossed the tiles to stand before me. His slight limp somehow added to his grace rather than detracting from it; he carried a staff, but did not lean on it.

A lyre-player started a new piece, a merry song of how Hermes made off with Apollo's herd of cattle, but I scarcely noticed.

The youth bowed. "My lady queen. My lord Creon."

I inclined my head. "And you are...?" I knew his name, of course, but I wanted to hear what he would say.

"A wanderer, my lady. And everywhere I go, I hear tales of the greatness of Thebes, and the beauty and wisdom of its queen. Yet the stories fall short of the mark."

The flattery was common enough, but heat flushed my cheeks.

Creon grunted. "What favor do you seek, young man?"

"One thing, my lord. To win the heart of the queen."

Now this was different. He made no claim to his royal heritage. He did not mention the challenge of the contest or the riches of the city.

Instead he said he wanted my heart.

Were his words just a ploy to win my favor? Or – and for the first time I allowed myself to think it plainly – did he in fact desire me?

I circled the edge of my cup with my finger, in my imagination tracing the lines of his hard muscles instead. Allowing my gaze to cross the span of his torso, I felt a thrill course through my body. I looked up into his face, and to my surprise I saw earnest longing there.

For me? I could understand Tassos, or Nikippes, or even Polydorus wooing me, but the man before me embodied youth and beauty. He had a right to ask for perfection as well.

And yet – and yet – it was said the women of my family had always aged well. My courses still came regularly with the moon. My breasts remained high and firm; the mirror revealed few lines in my face, and my hands and feet were supple and soft. Good fortune, good breeding, Harmonia's magical necklace, or the inheritance from Aphrodite – whatever the reason, I looked far younger than my thirty-seven years.

What would it be like to have this hard-muscled youth in my bed?

My brother squeezed my elbow. "You wish to win her heart – that would be a gift from her to you. What can you offer my royal sister? Should she consider a young nobody for her husband?"

The Korinthian stood tall, and his strong chin pulled up. "My lord Creon, my family is as proud as your own."

"Is it?" Creon challenged.

The young man raised his chin. "I am Oedipus, son of King Polybus and Queen Periboea of Korinth."

"A proud family indeed, Prince Oedipus." I was relieved that my voice did not tremble. "You say you wish to join the contest. Why didn't you present yourself with the others?"

"My lady, trying for your hand means risking my life. Will you forgive me when I say I wanted to meet you first?"

Privately, I thought this very reasonable; I had insisted on meeting the suitors myself. But I could not reveal this thought publicly. "And?"

"And now I know you are a prize worth dying for – although I intend to live, and become your husband."

Bold words from a bold young man! My heart felt light within my chest. "Then may the gods smile on you."

A frown rippled across his features, then vanished. "May they smile upon us both, my lady." Prince Oedipus bowed and turned on his heel, returning to his place near the musicians.

I hated the distance between us. I wanted him beside me.

How could I manage it? Others had experience in such matters, but not I. Besides, my suitors and the servants watched everything I did.

"Ouch!" I gasped, for Creon had pinched my arm again, hard.

"Don't stare at him so!"

I forced myself to look in Creon's direction. "What do you think?"

"It's certainly clear what *you* think, Jocasta." Then my brother's attitude changed from teasing to serious. "A Korinthian alliance could be what we need. The boy seems presentable. Young enough so we can shape his ideas, if necessary."

"I'd like to spend more time with him."

"I'm sure you would."

"I'll go to my rooms. If you could speak with him first, and then send him to me…"

Creon smirked.

"I only want to talk to him again."

"Of course," said my brother, rising. "I'll send him to you in a while, so that you can *talk*."

I waited until Creon had reached the Korinthian prince. Then I stood, and all those seated rose to their feet. "I thank you for coming this day," I said. I nodded to the suitors: a total of six, not five. "May Dionysus choose well among you." Then I turned to leave; in the silence, the rustle of my stiff skirts and the clink of their golden ornaments seemed loud, but no louder than the beating of my heart. I was conscious of my movements, aware of the tautness of my gilded nipples, and I wondered whether Prince Oedipus' glance lingered on my narrow waist as I departed from the hall.

Merope and my bath-attendant Lilika joined me in the corridor. I told them that I expected the Korinthian prince to join me in my rooms soon. "Merope, a fire, but not too bright," I said. "And wine."

"Music?" she asked.

I adored music, but with music came musicians. "No, not tonight."

"As you wish, my lady queen," said Merope, and she left to fetch the wine.

Lilika and I headed to my apartments.

"What preparation does my lady wish?" whispered Lilika. "A bath? A fresh jacket and skirts?"

I nodded to the guard as we crossed the threshold into my suite. Once the wooden door thumped shut behind us, I passed through the antechamber into my bedroom. Oedipus had seen me already tonight in the clothing I wore. To change would send the wrong message. I was Jocasta, queen of Thebes, one of the most powerful women in Hellas. Why did I think I had to impress this Korinthian prince?

But if these were my true feelings, why did my palms grow damp? And why was my stomach so unsettled?

221

"No," I told the girl. "Just refresh my hair and makeup. It would be rude to keep the prince waiting."

In truth, it was I who did not wish to wait.

When Lilika was finished, I left my bedroom for the outer chamber. This room had once belonged to Niobe but was now wholly mine. I had chosen the bronze tripods, the small Kretan lamps, the cushions with their covers of crimson and purple. The air smelled of rosewater, not sandalwood. The effect was regal, but warm; inviting.

A servant brought Oedipus just as Merope was mixing the wine.

"Prince Oedipus of Korinth," announced the servant.

Without glancing up, I waved to Merope to bring him wine. I took my own golden cup with both hands, and examined its raised decoration: a Kretan girl bull-dancer caught mid-leap, her expression ecstatic as she threw her body over the bull's deadly horns.

Why was I so nervous?

I did not look in his direction, but rather sensed him as he walked across the room to my side.

"You intend to match wits with our Sphinx."

He drew close; a musky scent rose from his flesh. "My lady queen, I have some skill with riddles. I believe the gods will give me victory. Perhaps Dionysus himself will whisper the answers in my ear."

I glanced up, a retort on my lips; for if Creon and I decided to make this young man king, *we* would give him the answers. Yet when my eyes met his, the words drained away like water from a broken jug. I could do nothing but search his eyes, captivated by glimmers of silver in the blue, and the midnight-dark rings round the edge of his irises.

Perhaps he thought my gaze sharp; he broke the silence with a conciliatory tone. "Lady Jocasta, I don't mean to presume. I can claim no special favor with the gods. But I do hope to win."

My voice returned at last. I said carefully, "That is in the hands of Dionysus." I sipped at the wine, my fingers skimming the backward-bending arc of the bull-dancer's body.

The prince tasted his wine as well. Mercifully, the strange moment was gone; my tongue and my thoughts were again at my command. "Come," I said, gesturing to the balcony. The woolen curtains were drawn open to admit the night's breeze. As Oedipus followed me, I flicked a hand at Merope, indicating that she and the other servants should leave.

The tiled surface felt cold beneath my bare feet, and the night air was cool; but I did not chill. Leaning against the balustrade, I looked out at the scattered lights of my city. Torches flickered on Amphion's walls; out there were my soldiers, the Maenads, and the rest, all depending on me to make a union to counter the Peloponnesian threat. I tried to put aside the heat I felt at the Korinthian's nearness; never mind my wants, how could I best guard the interests of my people?

"Did King Polybus send you to Thebes?" I asked. "Does he seek an alliance between our cities?"

Oedipus turned his head toward the southwest: the direction of Korinth. "I don't know his wishes, for my father did not send me. I have left his care and his house, and while I believe he still loves me, I can never return."

I remembered Creon's words. "Have you and your father quarreled? If so, then with time—"

"My lady, there was no quarrel! I could never have argued with my father – I love him too much."

"Then you and your father are on good terms? Thebes and Korinth could make an alliance?"

"I'm sure my father would welcome the alliance. But as your husband, I would agree to it only on one condition: he and I must never meet."

As my husband! The prince spoke the phrase so easily, as if it were meant to be. "Why? If there's no ill will between you, why must you never meet?"

"My lady, I was recently at Delphi. And the oracle told me that I must never see my parents again."

My stomach churned. One prophecy had made me queen of Thebes; another had ruined my marriage to Laius. Was my fate about to twist again, and send me this handsome youth as a husband? Prophecy had far too much power in my life. Trying to banish my fears, I asked: "And what did your oracle say of the queen of Thebes?"

"Nothing, lady. But everyone else speaks of you. Tales of your beauty, wealth and wisdom are on every trader's lips."

With those words Oedipus stepped closer; I held my ground. "Wealth," I said, my voice husky. "Thebes is rich. Do you need to find a fortune, now that you have abandoned the throne of Korinth?"

He set his cup on the balustrade. "My lady, I trust the gods to provide what I need. But only a fool does not strive for what he wants."

I swallowed the last of my drink, and set my cup beside his. "And what, Prince of Korinth, is it that you want?"

With his left hand he covered my right. "To win your heart, my lady," he said, repeating his words from the megaron. Then he twined his fingers with mine, and slid his other arm behind my back. I turned my face up to his; and when our mouths touched, our flesh melted together, obliterating all separateness.

My first kiss from Alphenor was pleasant but unremarkable; the touch of Laius' mouth had seemed dangerous and strange. But Oedipus' lips fit perfectly to my own, and I could think nothing, nothing but that I wanted this man as I had never before desired anyone. He moved to kiss my cheek, and then pushed back my hair to brush his lips along the rim of my ear. Feeling his breath warm against my neck, I shuddered.

"I – I've never..." I began, and stopped, for I did not know what I wanted to say.

But he paused to listen. "Never what, my lady?"

"Invited a man here." My words were barely a whisper.

Oedipus' expression became thoughtful, and he brushed a strand of hair from my face. Then, my hand in his, he led me back inside, through my audience chamber to my bedroom.

He had lain with a woman before, and not merely some shepherdess in a rough wool shift, for he knew how to work loose the laces of a lady's jacket. He knew, too, the ways of a woman's body, and gave me pleasure before taking his own. Afterwards, he touched my cheek with his fingertips. "Tell me one thing, my lady. Have I won the queen's heart?"

I stroked his brow. "Yes."

Oedipus drifted off to sleep, but I did not. I wanted to store away each moment, in case they were the last we ever shared. I longed to kiss him, to run my hands across his chest, to make love again. But I dared not. He needed his hours of slumber, for he needed to keep his wits about him.

The lamps in my bedroom burned low; but there was light enough. I studied the prince who shared my bed: the thick reddish hair, the straight nose, the wide mouth, his lips slightly open and relaxed in sleep. He had a recently healed scar on his hip. His chest rose and fell with each slow, peaceful breath. He seemed so familiar, like a part of me.

In his slumber he stirred, then pulled me to his side without waking.

I fitted myself into the curve of his arm. Oedipus was the perfect choice. With Korinth's position on the isthmus and its strong sea presence, we would fend off any Peloponnesian threat.

Nothing could be better. Then why was my stomach so tense?

I thought again of Laius; and then of Vassos, who had risked his life for me and lost. Twice I had been full of hope; twice had my hopes ended in catastrophe. And this time the outcome was so uncertain. The contest: we would do our best, but would Oedipus win? I prayed that we had enough influence with Melanthe, and that Melanthe had enough with Dionysus. Or would some other god interfere?

This man could die! And it would all be my fault!

My heart thudded wildly; I drew in a long breath, and tried to convince myself that Oedipus would be safe. Creon and I had planned this all so that we, not Pelops, could choose the next king.

I whispered a prayer to Dionysus, and thanked him for sending Oedipus to me.

My prince did not sleep long. Dawn was still far away when I glanced at his face and saw that his eyes were open.

"Not sleeping, my lady?"

"I don't want to waste a moment of our time together."

He took a lock of my hair between his fingers and kissed it. "We'll have the rest of our lives together."

Such optimism and confidence! I took his hand in mine. "I want to know everything there is to know about you."

He shook his head. "My lady, I don't wish to bore you."

"How could you possibly be dull? Tell me, what does a Korinthian prince do for sport?"

He spoke of the games and athletic contests he had entered. The weakness in his feet and ankles, for which he was named, seemed not to embarrass him as much as it might some young men. It kept him from footraces and hunts, but he was skilled in sailing and fishing, the cast of discus and javelin, archery and wrestling. He spoke proudly of the wrestling ribbons he had won at the Isthmian games two years ago, besting the champion from Athens – despite his weak ankles, Oedipus had won by his wits, using his opponent's own strength against him.

"You did not get this from wrestling," I said, touching the newly formed scar on his hip. "Does it still give you pain?"

"No," he said, but he tensed in my arms anyway.

"What happened?" I moved in the bed so I could observe his face better. "Does it have to do with the oracle at Delphi?" I hazarded the question as he had appeared so sensitive on that topic earlier. "Did they hurt you there?"

"At Delphi they don't harm people; they heal them. No, it had nothing to do with the oracle. But it happened near Delphi. A terrible incident, which I regret." Oedipus unwrapped his arms from around me and sat up in bed. "Have you ever been there?"

I shook my head.

"Then you don't know how steep and sharp the mountains are, and how narrow the roads."

"Building wide roads is difficult," I said, thinking of the efforts we put into making the roads around Thebes serviceable for soldiers' chariots and farmers' carts, and how much toil was needed to maintain them.

"That may be. But still, the roads near Delphi aren't wide enough for all the rich fools who come to learn their fates. After I left, I met one fat old bastard full of arrogance and void of courtesy. Our teams came face to face on the narrow path, and he demanded I give way."

I pictured the scene, proud handsome Oedipus facing down some rich old lord. "But you didn't?"

He shook his head. "Though I was headed downhill – which all travelers know means right of way – he was the elder, and I intended to yield. But I wasn't quick enough for his liking; he yelled and sent his man to strike at my horses."

"So near Delphi?"

"Arrogant, as I said. No respect for the holy district. Well, my lady, I don't like telling what came next, but – I'd just learned I could never return to Korinth. All I had in the world was my chariot, my horses, and my groom. How could I let that fellow and his men kill my team? So I jumped down and drew my sword.

"My charioteer held the horses as I shouted at the first man to back off. But he refused; his blood was up and he meant to fight. He charged but I dodged; he came at me again and then I struck him down. He did not rise. Then the other guard and the charioteer let out a cry and rushed us; but my groom and I prevailed quickly. After that I don't know if the old fellow was more angry or afraid – whatever the case, he came after me like a Fury. I didn't want to kill him, but he gave me no choice." He slapped his hand against the mattress. "And by then my groom had struck down his traveling-companions as well."

I was silent.

"But I'm a prince, not a thief. Though his chariot was worked with gold, and his team a fine pair of bays, I left it all. When I reached the next village I asked the headman to send one of his boys up to the sanctuary to tell them of what had happened, to recover the bodies, and offer the things to the god."

An arrogant old man and his retinue. A gold-worked chariot. A team of bays.

Near Delphi.

I tried to keep my voice even as I asked, "When was this again? Last year?"

Oedipus nodded. "In the fall. Before the rains began."

And then I knew with certainty that the village elder had sent no offering to the sanctuary, but told his men to collect the horses and gold for themselves. Like Oedipus, they thought Pelorus as dead as Laius and the others, and left the bodies to rot. Until a more pious pilgrim passed by, noticed that Pelorus was alive, took pity and carried him to the sanctuary.

My handsome young lover was the man who had killed my husband.

During my years as queen, I had learned to mask my emotions. But this news caught me unaware, and I stiffened.

"What is it?" he asked. "I assure you, it happened just as I said."

"I believe you." In order to gain time I slipped out of bed and pulled on a robe. Then I crossed the threshold into the antechamber. I set another log on the fire and poured two cups of wine.

When I returned, Oedipus took the cup from my hand and looked up at me earnestly. "I didn't mean to kill him, my lady. He left me no choice."

"I believe you," I repeated softly. Easy to imagine: Laius, jumping out of his chariot, charging at Oedipus and his charioteer. What a fool Laius had been! His temper had cost him his life.

But now was not the time to think about Laius. Laius was dead. Before me was a man very much alive, and I had to decide what to do.

I sat down on a footstool and drank deeply from my cup. The wine felt harsh and strong in my cold, empty stomach; but my thoughts remained clear and sharp. What would this mean to my plans?

Did I still want to marry the Korinthian? I knew at once that I did.

And aside from my feelings, Oedipus was a good match. Handsome, of royal birth, without ties to Pelops, linked to powerful Korinth, intelligent and healthy – despite the limp. He was young and inexperienced in statecraft, but that had its advantages as well: Creon would not feel threatened.

Nor would Creon care that Oedipus had killed Laius – he might privately thank him.

The man I wanted for the next king of Thebes had killed its last king.

Was that so terrible? Or even unusual? In war, kings and princes slew each other with regularity, the victor often taking the widow to wife. This was no different – except that Laius and Oedipus had not known each other – and that it happened by mischance, and that only a handful, instead of an entire army, had died.

The Tiresias had declared it would offend the gods to let the guilty escape. But of what was Oedipus truly guilty? Nothing! He had acted in self-defense.

"Have you spoken of this to anyone in Thebes?"

"Only to you, my lady. Though of course my groom was there when it happened."

"Is he reliable?"

He drew his ruddy brows together. "Yes, my lady, certainly. Why?"

If the groom spoke, then people might realize the arrogant old lord in the fracas was Laius. "You must not speak of this again, and your groom must also be silent. The Theban people might resist putting you on the throne."

He set his cup on the bedside table with a loud clank. "By the gods, I slew the man in self-defense! And still I stopped at the temple of Apollo outside Orchomenos to cleanse the blood-guilt." So, penance had already been done. Surely the gods would be satisfied with that.

I stood, and laid a hand on his shoulder. "I know. I understand. In my eyes you're blameless, and since you've atoned, the gods must feel the same way. But there is truth, and there is politics. Pelops wants to regain the influence he had once in Thebes. And if he learns of this – this incident he will use it against us one way or another."

I could hear Creon's voice even now. *Jocasta, an alliance with Korinth is precisely what we need. But you can't let the groom live. Arrange for an accident. He knows too much. Think: one man's life to protect the prosperity of our city.*

But Creon had spent too much time contemplating Peloponnesian politics. I did not want to kill the charioteer, a man whose only fault was to happen across an arrogant king who did not understand the rules of the road. A man who might have saved Oedipus' life! My lover spoke of him with fondness – if I ordered his death, Oedipus might never forgive me.

I sat down on the bed, running my fingers down his arm, and took his hand. "Even my brother," I said slowly, deliberately. "Even to him you must not speak of this—"

He interrupted me, speaking quickly. "Don't you trust lord Creon?"

I squeezed the prince's hand and released it. "He's loyal to me, and to Thebes. Never doubt that. But he has his own idea of what is best for me, and the city. He may think you too dangerous, even though the blood-guilt has been cleansed. Besides," I added, "the fewer who know a secret, the better. It's safer so. And you should send your groom back to Korinth. So he can tell no one here."

"My lady, you're as wise as you are beautiful." With a strong arm he pulled me over to him and set his lips to mine.

I reveled in the sweetness of his kiss. No one, not even Creon, would take Oedipus from me!

After another delicious bout of lovemaking, we relaxed again in each other's arms. Oedipus ran his fingers through my hair; I studied the scar on his hip. What man did not bear a few scars? It would fade with time.

Birds chirped outside; dawn was coming.

"I should leave you," said Oedipus.

I kissed his neck. "I don't want you to go."

"We'll be together again soon, after the contest. And then we'll have the rest of our lives together."

I ran my fingers down his arm. "Yes," I whispered.

Reluctantly we sat up and I swung my feet to the floor; then I heard a noise other than birdsong. Someone was in my antechamber. I froze, held my breath and listened.

A familiar voice called my name.

"My brother," I whispered. "Just a moment."

I pulled my robe back on and slipped out into the audience room, pushing the door shut behind me. Creon still wore last night's rumpled kilt, and had his cloak wrapped tightly around his arms. Dark circles stained the skin beneath his eyes.

"Why are you here so early?" I asked. "Did last night's maidservant have to start the bread?"

"I've been with no one but my wife," Creon said self-righteously. "Eurydike thought she was in labor last night, and Rhodia had to come."

"And?"

"The child has not yet arrived." He sighed. "Eurydike was convinced he would come last night; Rhodia was equally convinced he would not – although she assures us the birth will be soon. Rhodia has the patience of a goddess, but last night Eurydike tried even her." He rubbed his eyes, then looked down at me. "I understand that *you* were busy last night as well."

I said nothing.

"And, what do you think of the young prince from Korinth?"

"I like him," I said, and then flushed at my outrageous understatement. "Very much."

"So – he's your choice?"

I nodded.

"I'd like to interview him further myself," Creon said. "It's such an important decision."

"That's a good idea," I said. I put my hand on his arm and tried to guide him toward the outer door. "Now, if you'll excuse me, I need to dress—"

My brother resisted. "He's here, isn't he?"

Creon did not let me deny it, but opened my bedroom door and walked through. I followed quickly.

"Good morning," Creon said briskly. "I understand you've been entertaining my sister."

Oedipus gave a quick start, but sat up slowly and pulled his kilt around himself with some semblance of dignity. He said nothing, but looked at Creon, then at me, and then back at my brother.

"Come now, young prince; my sister and I have no secrets."

"*Few* secrets," I amended sharply.

Creon laughed, and threw himself onto a couch. "Yes, I suppose there are some details we don't share." He shot a glance at the rumpled bedclothes. "But not on things that matter to Thebes!" Winking at me, he said, "Come on, Jocasta, I'll get a cramp in my neck. Sit down."

Creon had sprawled across the length of the couch. I did not like to make the situation even more intimate in my brother's presence, so I seated myself on the wooden dressing-stool. This left Oedipus alone and exposed on the edge of the bed.

Creon pretended to notice nothing awkward. "Tell me, Korinthian: you make no claim to your birthright, and you come without your father's blessing. So you bring us no wealth and you *may* not even bring us alliance with Korinth. What then do you have to offer my sister?"

Oedipus met Creon's gaze evenly for a moment, and then turned to me. "I love her," he said simply.

My throat felt hot and thick; tears sprang to my eyes. Oedipus and I had known each other for less than a day. Yet I believed that his words were no mere show for my brother's benefit. And at the same instant I knew, foolish though it seemed – for in truth as much as I knew now of his body I knew almost nothing of the man himself – that I loved him too.

The realization was amazing, and terrifying, and magical.

I swallowed with difficulty, and as the sound of the sea rushing in my ears subsided, I discovered that Creon was talking. "...a sweet sentiment to be sure, but my sister is the queen of Thebes. Have you experience in battle? Can you lead an army?"

"I've been trained in arms, my lord," he said, and for one heart-leaping moment I feared that despite my cautions he would brag of besting the old man outside Delphi. "But," he said, "I've not yet had the privilege of commanding an army in battle."

Creon's lips twisted downward. "Statecraft, then. Has your father Polybus involved you in negotiations? Has he introduced you to heads of state? Can you offer new alliances for Thebes?"

"I've been at his side on official occasions and have met many people, but no, I have no personal alliances. I'm willing to make them, my lord."

They were like two dogs circling each other, growling and baring their teeth, determining whether they would be friends or foes.

"Expertise in architecture and fortifications? Knowledge of trade?" asked Creon.

"Trade, yes, architecture, no," Oedipus said, calmly. "But I know how to build and steer a ship, under either oars or sail."

"You may have noticed that Thebes is not on the coast."

"I had noticed that fact, my lord. But if I can build a ship that stays afloat on water I can build anything on land."

Creon frowned as if he doubted this, but since my brother knew nothing whatsoever about shipbuilding, he could hardly contradict Oedipus. Creon swung his legs over the edge of the couch and leaned forwards. "Have you any skill with riddles?"

A grin spread over Oedipus' features. "Yes, my lord."

"Let's see," Creon continued, chewing on his lip as though he had just now thought of the idea, though I knew that during the winter he had tried to learn every riddle ever mentioned by Melanthe.

"Very well: what ruler reigns without praise, but falls when hailed?"

Oedipus ran a hand through his tousled curls. "Silence," he said. "Praise it, and the silence is broken."

The riddle was none too difficult; but I was relieved when my prince answered it easily.

"Not bad! Here's another," Creon continued. "This is born in brightness but grows up dark. It can fly without wings and kill without sound."

The prince hesitated, and I turned to watch. Oedipus wrinkled his brow and scratched his chin. Creon waited a moment, then reached a hand to the lamp Merope had set on the table last night. "Sister," he said to me, "you should tell your maids to do a better job of trimming the wicks. Otherwise the lamps put out too much—"

"Smoke!" said Oedipus. "Smoke is born in fire, but is itself dark; it moves through the air without wings and can smother the unsuspecting."

"Very good," said Creon.

"But you gave me a hint," Oedipus objected.

"True, but you understood it. Now I'll give you another: let me escort you from the queen's rooms. We wouldn't want anyone to think she's taken a husband already. Besides, you and I have much to discuss."

Oedipus nodded and strapped on his sandals. He stood and gathered his cloak, then stopped before me and took my hand. "We'll be together again soon, my lady." He bent and kissed my fingers. Then he followed Creon out of the room.

I looked out the window; the sky was growing brighter. I ordered my bodyguard and my maids to mention Oedipus' stay with me to no one. Then I told Lilika to prepare my bath, and luxuriated for a time in the warm, rose-scented waters.

"You shine this morning, my lady," said the girl as she toweled me dry. Admiration showed on her cheerful young face.

"Thank you, Lilika," I said, humming. I felt filled with light. Though I had slept little, my head buzzed with energy and my feet danced lightly across the tiles. I doubted I could feel better had I tasted the nectar and ambrosia of the gods.

Lilika slipped a robe around my shoulders and we went back to the bedchamber. I selected a leather jacket worked with crystal beads, and a many-tiered set of skirts in shades of saffron and purple. I held my arms wide while Merope cinched tight the laces of my jacket.

My maids powdered my face, darkened my brows and lashes with kohl, and rubbed my cheeks, ears and nipples with red alkanet. Lilika curled my hair with hot tongs and Merope tucked each ringlet into place among my golden headbands; just as they finished, Creon appeared in the doorway.

"Good morning!" I said, as if we had not seen each other that day already. "Would you like to join me for breakfast on the balcony?"

We stepped outside, and seated ourselves on folding chairs of carved ebony. A servant brought over a low bronze table; one serving-girl offered cups of sweet barley-water, while another carried over a tray bearing a fragrant loaf of bread fresh from the palace ovens, surrounded by olives, dried figs, dates, almonds, and cheeses.

Creon and I had breakfasted together on this balcony many times before, but never under such happy conditions. The weather was glorious: the sky that luminous blue that only early spring mornings achieve, fragile as the shell of an egg. Not a wisp of cloud was visible, and the breeze felt fresh against my cheeks.

"Try not to glow so much," said Creon. "You'll make the sun jealous. So, have we found the next king of Thebes?"

"I hope so," I said, trying to keep my voice calm.

"An alliance with Korinth. Excellent." He reached for the loaf of bread and tore off a steaming piece. "Almost perfect, in fact," he said, chewing.

"Almost?" I said. At first I was annoyed that my brother did not think Oedipus as perfect as I did; then fear struck me – did Creon know that Oedipus had killed Laius?

"What strange expressions crossed your face just now! Don't worry, I don't want to separate you from your prince. But take care not to fall in love – it's a weakness."

Saying nothing, I watched several women pass below us, carrying amphorae for drawing water from the city well.

Creon's advice came too late.

He picked up an olive, slid it into his mouth, then continued. "The other suitors were not pleased by the attention you bestowed on Oedipus yesterday evening. And they would be even less pleased if they knew you spent the night with him."

I felt a flush creep up my cheeks.

"I know, Jocasta. I encouraged you! But…"

I set my cup on the table. "No one need know. My guards and servants are loyal. They'll keep silent." I tried to speak calmly, but I heard the quaver in my voice.

My brother looked at me keenly. "You have fallen for him, haven't you?" He did not joke, he did not smile; he only reached out his hand for mine. "We'll make sure that he wins. And not just for your sake. For Thebes. I'll talk to Melanthe."

I stared out at the mountains in the distance, trying to keep my fears at bay, searching for balance between euphoria and dread. My feelings were so intense that I did not hear the footsteps behind us. Only when the girl cleared her throat did I turn around and see the young woman, clad in the robes of an apprentice midwife.

"My lady queen. My lord Creon," she said, bowing nervously.

"What is it?" asked Creon.

"Rhodia sent me, my lord. Your wife is in labor."

237

CHAPTER FOURTEEN

Over the years I had learned to avoid having anything to do with women in labor.   Infants, pregnant women: these I could handle.   But childbirth always brought back the memory of my own baby, and Laius wrenching him cruelly from my arms.

Yet Eurydike was my sister-in-law, my nearest female relative; she carried my brother's child.   It was possible – even likely, given my age and childless state – that her offspring would one day rule Thebes.   I could not shun the arrival of her firstborn, so in the afternoon I headed towards the birthing chamber.

Creon occupied his proper place in the colonnade outside the birthing-room, but unlike many fathers-to-be he did not pace or fret.   He and Demochares had set up a senet board in a patch of bright sun shining through from the courtyard and were moving colored pebbles about according to the fall of the knucklebones. My footsteps were quiet, but my skirts rustled as I approached, and Creon looked up and waved.

I glanced at the closed door; only a low hum of women's voices came from within, so Eurydike must be between pains. "How's your wife?"

"Well enough, Rhodia says.   The child could come any moment."   As though on cue, a shriek rang out from behind the wooden door.   Creon raised an eyebrow.   "Perhaps we hear him now."

So many years had passed since the birth of my own child that I felt removed from Eurydike's pain.   Old Theora – who had died recently, leaving her practice to her daughter – called it a blessing from Artemis, this ability to forget the agony of childbirth.

An old soldier once told me that Ares bestowed a similar gift on men: that after a battle was finished and comrades bandaged or buried, the pain and fear was forgotten, while the memory of the exhilaration of arms and the glory of victory remained. Childbirth, I mused, was women's battleground. I wondered whether the sound of war-trumpets had the effect on men that Eurydike's cries worked on me. Though I recalled the pain of my baby's birth it came to me dimly, like the outline of a distant mountain seen through a haze of fog.

Far stronger was the sense of loss, and emptiness, that I had been able to hold him only a few moments. Might Artemis curse Laius' soul! Silently I thanked my lover for ridding me of him forever.

Then it occurred to me that I might be already with child by Oedipus – and that was a warm thought indeed.

Creon had risen, and turned to look at the door; but the screaming soon subsided and no midwife burst through. He shrugged and came to stand close beside me. "I've spoken to Melanthe," he murmured.

"And?" I asked softly.

"She has agreed."

I glanced over at Demochares, who was adjusting a sandal-buckle. "Do you trust her?" I whispered.

"Do *I* trust her? *You're* the one who's been saying we should trust her."

"Yes, but—" A cry from behind the door interrupted me, and besides, I did not want to say what I was thinking.

I did not have to. Creon squeezed my shoulder. "Oedipus will survive, you'll see. I spoke with him some more, and he has a talent for riddles." He left my side and went back to his game.

My brother's words were comforting, but how could he guarantee anything? If Melanthe betrayed us, then the Korinthian prince could die. Dear Apollo, the risk! If only we had never started down this path! Yet if we had not, Oedipus and I would have never met.

"My lady, your brother is trouncing me," said Demochares. His rich voice sounded excessively cheerful; I guessed he thought me worried about Eurydike, and was trying to distract me.

I smiled at him but still my stomach churned, and not for my sister-in-law.

"You throw for me," he said, and handed me the knucklebones.

I rattled them in my hand and tossed, casting the high throw. Demochares chuckled and moved his pieces with satisfaction; Creon joked about being betrayed by his own sister. Though I was wary of omens, this bit of luck pleased me. What if the Fates, instead of frowning upon me, finally decided to smile?

I spoke with the confidence I wished to feel. "Two days until the contest, eight more to the wedding. Ten days: assuming Eurydike is delivered today, that will be your child's name-day; and we'll have a new king to welcome your child into the citizenry. Creon, this means…"

I trailed off, for Creon was listening no longer, merely staring over my left shoulder. As I stopped speaking he rose from his stool once more; I turned to look behind me.

"Father," said Creon. "I see that the Maenads have granted you entry."

The old man, guided by his servant, walked toward us. His black robes and dark blindfold were a gloomy contrast to the late winter sunshine and the brightly colored scenes of the hunt that adorned the walls of this second-floor inner balcony. His weathered face was lined and cracked like old leather, and his long beard an unkempt tangle of gray. He was seventy now, and it showed.

"You will address the voice of the god properly," he said, his voice harsh.

Creon and I exchanged a glance. Our father sounded more cross than usual, but we had expected this ill-temper.

"Tiresias," Creon amended, his tone contrite. "You've returned from Delphi, then—"

"As you see."

"And Pelorus?"

Pelorus! I had not thought of him, but he was the other witness to Laius' death. My heart pounded rapidly, the sound loud in my ears.

"Pelorus remains at Delphi," the Tiresias reported.

"Then he survived?" I asked, hoping my voice did not betray my nerves.

"Yes."

Another scream came from within the birthing-room, and I jumped. We all turned again in the direction of the noise, although we could see nothing but the closed door.

Pelorus, alive! A terrible danger, for he knew the truth and would have no reason to keep silent. Indeed, he might hold a blood-grudge against Oedipus, and work to bring about his destruction! My knees trembled, and I leaned against a pillar for support.

When Eurydike's cries stopped, Creon returned to the subject without losing a beat. "Good news. We need Pelorus; he has served Thebes well all these years."

"He may not be much use to you in the future," said the Tiresias.

"Why not?" Creon asked sharply.

"He's blind. That is why he remains at Delphi – the healers are helping him learn to cope with his condition."

Blind? Then Pelorus could not recognize Oedipus. Relief flooded through me, and I pressed a hand to my mouth to stop myself from laughing inappropriately.

"Blind." Creon shook his head.

"By all the gods," said Demochares, letting the knucklebones drop. "And he so loved traveling, and seeing the world."

Another scream interrupted us, this one louder than all those before, followed by a high-pitched wail and then the sound of women cheering.

So, the child was born! I pushed myself away from the pillar, and with a faint, "Excuse me," I opened the door and slipped into the room.

Eurydike squatted naked and sweat-streaked on the birthing-chair. Rhodia, her chestnut curls straying from their plait, was bathing the child. Meanwhile two apprentice midwives pulled Eurydike to her feet. Standing would help her body cleanse itself and encourage the afterbirth to drop. As she stood erect and smiled weakly, I raised a hand to push damp strands of hair back from her brow.

"Congratulations, my dear," I said. "Creon will be pleased to learn he has a son."

Rhodia gave me a tired smile as she sponged the infant with water from a basin. "A healthy boy, my lady! He's a big fellow – that's what took him so long. But the mother's doing well; she has the hips for it."

"Let me hold him," said my sister-in-law, and stretched out her arms.

"Soon, Eurydike," I promised. "First we must present the child to my brother."

One of the girls held open the door for me; Rhodia and I stepped out of the damp, rank birth room into the fresh air of the colonnade. Creon stood, his sharp eyes locked with mine, and the blindfolded face of the man who had once been my father seemed to fix on me as well. The Tiresias turned in pace with my movements as I walked forward and offered Creon his son.

Suddenly the prophet's deep voice rang out. "Claim the infant as your own, Creon, and you will know a father's sorrow. He will heed not your counsel; he will marry unwisely; and your own words will send him early to the tomb."

Still holding the child, I twisted back, filled with anger. "This is your own grandson! How dare you speak so?"

The old man frowned at me. "Jocasta, the Tiresias speaks only the prophecies given by Apollo. I voice his words, not mine. The truth must be spoken."

"And why should I believe those words are true?" I said. "I am queen as foretold, but no one can claim that Laius was the city's greatest king, nor were we blessed with love and many children."

"Jocasta," said Creon, his voice calm. He reached for the infant and took him from me. "Even if these words are true – as the Tiresias says, it's hardly a curse. What son heeds his father's counsel?" His lips twisted into a half-smile, knowing our own father could not see it. "And what father thinks his son's choice of wife entirely wise? And as for the third prediction – it may come to pass no more than the children you did not have with Laius." He lifted the babe and held it high. "I say now, this is my child! And on his name-day I will speak his name to all."

Creon lowered his son, and Rhodia stepped forward to claim the baby and take him back to his mother's waiting breast. I straightened my skirts and watched Father's face.

At length he nodded. "So be it," he said. "Creon, you have your son; and you have the word of Apollo on his fate."

Before I could open my mouth again he turned to me. "As for you, Jocasta: the Tiresias foretold that your husband will be the city's greatest king, and that you will bear him many children. And yet Laius is dead."

"Yes," I said.

"But aren't you planning, even now, to take a new husband?"

Somehow I felt that he meant more than the contest, which of course was known to all – or even that I favored the Korinthian prince, which many had guessed.

243

Did the Tiresias know how Creon and I had schemed? Did he know that Oedipus' hand was the one that had led Laius to his death?

The silence lingered so that I had no choice but to speak at last. "And?"

Father's face twisted with some odd emotion, and I remembered how the previous Tiresias had been angered by Queen Niobe's arrogance. A small churning fear disturbed my stomach, but I quieted myself. This was only my blind old father, after all. What could he do?

"You have turned to Dionysus rather than Apollo," said the Tiresias, his voice tinged with disapproval. "Thus, not all is made clear to me."

"I see," I said, and secretly I begged Dionysus not to let my father learn the details of what happened outside Delphi.

The Tiresias continued, "Apollo tells me that you are entitled to wed again; such is any woman's right, and certainly the queen's. But the match you consider is an ill one. It will bring only sorrow in the end." With that he turned his back, as none save the Tiresias dared do to me. Leaning on his staff and the arm of his servant, he made his way down the hall until he vanished into the shadows of the far stairwell, his footsteps echoing as he left.

Sorrow in the end – and yet he had also hinted that the prophecy given when I was still a maid would be fulfilled. That prophecy had been full of wonderful things. How could both come to pass?

My brother spoke. "What a joy our father is!" He laughed.

Still feeling uneasy, I took a seat on Creon's gaming stool. With Father gone, I noticed once more warmth of the sunlight and the sound of birds chirping in the eaves. In the birthing-room a servant was sweeping up the blood-soaked straw, and through the open door I could hear Rhodia and her assistants fussing over Eurydike and the baby. My brother had a new son; soon I would have a new husband. These were joyous events for us and for the city. If I became like Laius and spent my time worrying about every prophecy, I would never enjoy the gifts the gods gave us.

A servant brought a large amphora of dark red wine, and I accepted a cup from Demochares, well-mixed with water. Creon, Demochares and I raised our goblets.

"To your son," said Demochares, nodding to Creon.

"To your future husband," said my brother, grinning at me.

"To Thebes!" I said.

Two days later, I sat in my chair on a platform in the agora, decorated this time in honor of Dionysus. At this time of the year, fresh flowers were few, but maidens scattered dried rose petals from wicker baskets, and fragrant pine-boughs brought a cheerful note of green to the dais. Thebans thronged the marketplace, some dressed in animal skins to honor Dionysus, others wearing garlands of ivy. Flute-girls played skirling melodies and acrobats competed for the crowd's attention as we waited for the suitors to arrive. Now and again some remarkable flip or jump drew a cheer, and people clapped and laughed.

Trying to keep calm, I scanned the crowd. Well-dressed ladies gossiped behind gold-ringed hands; their husbands strolled around lifting silver cups to honor the wine-god. A few looked already drunk.

I turned to Creon, who stood behind me. "I don't see the Tiresias."

My brother shrugged. "Probably avoiding anything to do with Dionysus. This isn't the kind of celebration Apollo prefers."

I nodded agreement. I did not mind; in fact, I was relieved. The next few hours would be difficult enough without the frowns and dire words of our father.

There was an excited stir in the crowd, and the people parted to make way. First came a band of young women: each one clad in a short tunic, and each carrying a thyrsus like a spear.

Through the space they opened up strode the Sphinx. Melanthe was dressed as she had been on the day we closed the gates, in her lion's pelt and wings. Today she moved differently: she looked tauter, tighter, ready to pounce.

Melanthe took her place at one corner of the platform, her hand resting on a dagger in a gilded scabbard attached to her belt. I was glad to have my bodyguards beside me.

Next came the suitors, who, with their escort of soldiers and Maenads, climbed the three steps to the wooden platform where I sat. Demochares stepped forward and introduced each man to the spectators.

Tassos and Haralpos were first. As the herald announced their names and origins, the people cheered. But when he came to Pelops' envoy Nikippes, their applause dropped off, and the cheers sounded half-hearted. Doran of Tiryns garnered little more approval; like the Maenads, the common people knew he was another of Pelops' tools. Yet when Demochares announced Polydorus, the people's reaction surprised me: not only were there no cheers, but a few hisses could be heard. I felt relief; as the son of Laius, I had thought he might have his own faction in Thebes.

Polydorus' stance wavered, and a flush crept up his cheeks; clearly he had expected something better as well. Then his jaw set in a line of desperate determination. Pity darted through me; why hadn't Laius' son stayed away?

But any compassion I felt for Polydorus vanished as Demochares raised his resonant voice once more: "Finally, people of Thebes: Oedipus, prince of Korinth, son of King Polybus and Queen Periboea, has also come to match wits with the Sphinx and try for the hand of Queen Jocasta!"

Oedipus stood straight and tall, the sunlight gleaming in his reddish locks like gold inlaid upon copper. He carried his staff, but did not lean on it. A bronze-colored cape swept over broad shoulders, and a fine leather belt circled his waist. His dark brown kilt was edged with gold, and his arm-band was studded with rubies, reminding all of Korinth's strength and wealth.

Hope and fear warred within me: my beloved came forth to claim me at risk of his life. Looking at him, I could not help but remember our night of lovemaking; my heart raced, and heat filled my loins. Blood rushed in my ears with a sound like the sea; and then, when I could hear again, I realized that the crowd was cheering, whistling, shouting encouragement to the Korinthian prince, as if they wanted their queen to be happy at last.

Just then I saw how Melanthe's dark eyes flashed a challenge at all the suitors, not excepting Oedipus.

Demochares led the six men over to my left. When the contest was finished, five would be dead and one would become king.

Suddenly it all seemed too improbable, unreal. For an instant I wondered if I were in my bed dreaming. But the late morning sun felt warm on my breasts and my leather jacket stuck to my skin as I shifted in my seat. The wooden arms of my chair were real and solid against my palms. This was no dream.

Once Demochares had quieted the crowd, Creon walked forward from his place at my side and addressed the six men.

"The will of Dionysus has been made known to all here. He alone shall choose the man to become my sister's husband and king of Thebes." I listened closely to Creon's smooth voice; even though I knew him so well, I detected no hint of irony as he spoke. Creon also said we had the vine-god's blessing for our scheme. Perhaps we did.

He continued. "You submit now to test your wits against the riddles of the Sphinx?" All six signaled their assent. "Very well. Melanthe, come forward."

Two Maenads dressed in goat skins, with wreathes of ivy crowning their long hair and daggers at their waists, escorted Melanthe to the middle of the platform. They removed the heavy wings from her shoulders; Melanthe stretched her frame with

247

feline grace. Her lion-skin cape slid from her shoulders; her many gold-tipped braids swung shimmering as she raised her arms. A deep breath pressed her full breasts against the diaphanous linen of her Aegyptian-styled tunic. I wondered how this looked to the crowd in the square below us: six daring men from across the Hellene lands; the dangerous priestess of the Maenads who would serve as the voice of the vine-god; and enthroned between them, glittering with gold and jewels, the queen whose husband was to be chosen here.

If we succeeded, it would be a spectacle remembered for generations – but then again, it might all go horribly wrong.

I gripped the arms of my chair.

"Praise Dionysus and Thebes!" Melanthe cried; the crowd lifted voices in paean.

I saw Nikippes' mouth twist downward, and watched him shift, as if impatient. Despite the noise of the crowd, I heard him say: "Praise Pelops and Olympia!"

And suddenly there was a dagger in his throat. He stared disbelieving, choked, and then crumpled.

I gasped in shock, and half rose from my chair; but Melanthe was far quicker. She pounced upon the writhing form of the Peloponnesian envoy and wrenched out the knife; Nikippes' dying breath followed the blade. When she slit his neck from ear to ear, crimson blood spattered across her breasts.

Only then did I realize that Melanthe herself had thrown the knife.

We had heard stories of Melanthe's hunting prowess, and the outlandish tale of her besting the lion single-handed, but we had never seen her in action. I glanced at Creon, wondering if he had expected this of our Sphinx; but his eyes were as wide with surprise and shock as Nikippes' had been before he fell.

Melanthe fixed her eyes, burning like black coals, on the remaining five men. "Dionysus will not tolerate treachery," she said coldly.

"Treachery?" I asked.

"He had a knife, and was planning to use it," Melanthe announced with conviction. She nodded to one of her Maenads, who pried open the dead man's fingers. Indeed, there was a small blade hidden in Nikippes' hand! The suitors had been searched before being brought to the agora, yet somehow Nikippes had smuggled in a weapon. My heart pounded wildly: who had he been planning to kill? Melanthe? The other suitors? Even me?

I settled back in my chair and glanced at Oedipus. He stood tall, and his beautiful blue eyes met mine steadily; but his complexion had lost some of its color.

I hoped whichever gods were on my side were watching.

Melanthe wiped her bloody knife on her skirt, and sheathed it again in the scabbard at her waist. She then turned and strode back to where she had been standing before with perfect calm, as though nothing of consequence had happened. Other Maenads dragged away Nikippes' body.

In the agora absolute silence reigned. A raven flew overhead, emitting a harsh cry. Behind me, Creon softly let out a long-pent breath. A drop of perspiration rolled down my forehead; I wiped it away.

Melanthe's bloodstained right hand twisted back and forth, palm open to the sky; her left dropped down towards the wooden platform. Slowly her left hand lifted, index finger outstretched, to point directly at Tassos. "In the darkness of night we come without being called," she said in a husky voice, "but by daylight are we lost without being stolen."

"Aha," Creon whispered from where he stood close behind me. He patted my shoulder. "Cleverly worded, but not so difficult—"

"Wolves," said the man. He swallowed hard; I saw the knot in his throat bob. "They come at night but vanish by day."

A murmur ran through the crowd below us; I glanced up at Creon, who shook his head slightly.

Melanthe stepped closer to the man from Pylos. Her gold-capped braids slithered like the snaky hair of the Medusa, and she fixed Tassos with a stare worthy of that monster. "Tell me, Pylian," she said calmly. "Have you never seen a wolf in daylight?"

Tassos swallowed again; I found that my own mouth was dry as he stammered, "Yes, Sphinx, but—"

Melanthe's knife flashed again; she moved with the sinuous quickness of a striking snake. Was this the result of some herb she had taken? Or had Dionysus truly empowered her? Before I had thought her dangerous, but now she was starkly terrifying.

Tassos' body fell twitching, throat slit wide. As two Maenads came forward to pull him away, Melanthe whirled towards Doran of Tiryns. Flecks of Tassos' blood flew from her blade and spotted the Tirynian's cheeks. To his credit, he did not flinch; his dark handsome features remained impassive as he faced the knife pointed at his nose.

"The stars," he said. "They cannot be seen in daylight but in the dark of night they come unbidden."

Melanthe turned away from him, once more wiping the knife on her red-stained skirt; he must have given the correct answer. The crowd let out a cheer, and in the tumult I looked over my shoulder at my brother. The slight upward curve of his lips told me that he had known the solution already. Silently I gave thanks for his cleverness and the time he had spent trading riddles with Oedipus. I reassured myself that my beloved would be safe. These other deaths were necessary, that Oedipus might prevail.

Melanthe raised both hands imperiously, and the applause ceased. She cocked her head to one side, now regarding Haralpos through just one eye, like a bird. This time both hands remained aloft as she said, "I never was, will always be. Though no man ever saw me, all have trust in me."

Creon whispered nothing this time. I thought furiously: one of the gods? No, Melanthe would not claim a god had "never been," and certainly not all men trusted them.

Haralpos looked at the ground for a moment, his brow furrowed. Then the craggy face rose. "Tomorrow," he said. "It never was, but will always be." He looked Melanthe in the eye, and finding his death not yet there, color returned to his cheeks. He turned his face up to me and smiled; in his relief he was almost handsome.

I returned his smile with a nod, not wishing this innocuous man dead and yet willing him to fail so that Oedipus might live and be mine. Under cover of the crowd's cheering I asked my brother, "Did you know that one?"

"Yes, Jocasta. So did your Korinthian. Stop worrying."

Melanthe dropped both palms towards the ground and thrust her chin upwards, breasts straining against her fine-pleated gown. The crowd hushed its applause once more as Melanthe fixed her kohl-rimmed stare on Polydorus.

"Feed me," she hissed at him, "and I live. Give me water and I die."

Polydorus, despite his bravado, took a step back. He hesitated.

Melanthe dropped her chin and spoke again, her voice fluid, dangerous, demanding. "Your answer, lord Polydorus."

"A moment," he said, holding out a hand.

The silence grew painful; I felt sure the folk standing down in the agora could hear my heart pounding. Then my brother stroked my hair, and I knew that this puzzle was familiar to him as well, and that Oedipus was safe.

Much as I disliked Polydorus, I pitied him when he turned his face desperately to the skies, as though seeking his answer there. His posture reminded me of Laius before one of his rages. But Polydorus was not the king, nor even a prince; a fit of temper would earn him nothing. "Thirst," he finally said.

"Wrong," said Melanthe evenly, and threw the knife.

He dodged, but the knife struck him just above his jeweled belt. Dark blood seeped between his clenched fingers, and he collapsed to his knees. Melanthe took a step forward, as though she meant to draw out the knife and slit his throat as she had twice before; but Polydorus twisted away from her, grasping the knife in his hands. Cords stood out against his forearms and veins bulged at his temples, and with a grunt he wrenched the knife from his belly. Blood welled out freely, and a loop of gut glistened pale in the wound. I felt ill, and had to force myself to swallow the bile that filled my throat. He stared with hatred, not at Melanthe, nor even at Creon — both long his enemies — but at me. "You brought a curse on the house of Laius," he said. "May your children be cursed as well."

I shivered: the curses of a dying man were said to have great power. But Polydorus was certainly no favorite of the Fates; I hoped they would not listen to him.

He turned back toward Melanthe. "No woman's hand will slay Polydorus," he said, and plunged the blade into his own heart. Staggering a moment, he pitched face-first onto the platform and landed with a sickening crunch.

Melanthe, terribly, only smiled. She knelt and rolled over the new corpse. The knife was slick and red; Melanthe's arms were now blood-smeared to the elbow. Still kneeling, she aimed the knifepoint at Oedipus. My mouth went dry.

"You," said the Sphinx. "Korinthian. What is the answer?"

Oedipus' voice was like a cool stream of water slaking my thirst. "Fire," he said with calm confidence. "It must be fed to live, but water kills it." This was the answer; I let out my breath with a sigh.

While more Maenads dragged away Polydorus' body, Melanthe rose to her feet. . She flipped the knifepoint towards Haralpos; flecks of blood flew outward, glistening in the sunlight.

"Squeeze me tight," she said, "and I cry bitter tears. Yet my heart is stone."

"I... I..." stammered Haralpos. Poor man! He had managed well with his first riddle; but now the power of thought seemed to have deserted him. The crowd below muttered ominously. Moisture shone on Haralpos' face. He was a harmless fellow, and only a few days ago I had been almost willing to marry him. Should he die, because I had fallen in love?

The moment lengthened. My voice, when I finally broke the silence, surprised me with its strength. "Sphinx! If this man gives up his ambition for the throne of Thebes and makes a dedication to Dionysus, will the god spare him?"

Melanthe stood and turned toward me, her eyes piercing. We had not discussed sparing any of the suitors, and her blood lust was up. Her dagger was clutched in her hand, ready to throw – would I be her target? My bodyguards apparently sensed the same danger: they moved forward, and readied their shields to block her throw.

Then her gaze seemed to focus, and she surveyed the people. "This man has offered his life to the contest," she said, and my hope fell. "But if he will dedicate the city of Orchomenos to the worship of Dionysus, the god will spare him."

"I swear it," said Haralpos immediately, his voice cracking.

"Then you may go," said Melanthe.

Haralpos, shaking, supported by one of my soldiers, left the platform. He would be called a coward for the rest of his life – but he would live.

"Jocasta," my brother murmured, his tone reproachful, as if he wanted to scold me for changing the flow of events. But Creon had no time to say more.

Only two men stood on the bloodstained platform. Melanthe's strong shoulders turned; still holding the bloody dagger, she raised her right hand to Doran. "Tirynian," she said. "How do you answer?"

I myself had forgotten the riddle. Something about a heart of stone. Such a heart as had had Nikippes, and Pelops, and no doubt this Doran as well. Haralpos had quivered in fear like a hare; I felt sure that even Oedipus, though he hid it well, was afraid. But Doran replied easily. "An olive, Sphinx. Its juice is bitter and the stone is its heart." Though he addressed Melanthe, he turned his gaze toward me. Surrounded by the blood of men freshly dead, he eyed my breasts and leered. My flesh crawled.

And now the turn should fall to Oedipus; he moved expectantly, awaiting the voice of the Sphinx. But, as though she shared my revulsion for Doran, she remained focused on the Tirynian. "Proud, aren't you?" she hissed. "Then you may answer the next puzzle too."

The crowd gasped, and one man protested the unfairness, but a sharp glance from Melanthe silenced him.

"I am never seen, but all see what I can do. My touch sometimes caresses, sometimes strikes. When I howl, both man and beast fear."

Fear. As she spoke the word, her face twisted, and she made some sign with the fingers of her left hand. I felt chill despite the day's growing warmth, and looked at Creon for support.

And what I saw there struck terror into my heart. For my brother seemed confused. Didn't he know the solution?

Sweet Leto, what about Oedipus?

High overhead, a cloud passed before the sun; Doran glanced up wildly. His eyes, so often lit with mocking scorn, grew wide. I thought: this must be some Aegyptian witchcraft.

"Creon," I whispered, panicky, "Creon, she—"

"Hekate," Doran said loudly. "Goddess of witchcraft: she—"

Before he could finish the sentence Melanthe was upon him. This time she did not throw the knife but leapt upon him and struck, her slender arms corded with stringy muscle. He fell backwards; Oedipus jumped aside as Melanthe landed on his opponent, striking again and again. So must the lion take down its prey, I thought; and remembered what the hunters said, the she-lion was more deadly than the male.

She muttered softly, and I heard without doubt the voice of madness. "Such, my Peloponnesian friend, is the caress of Hekate." She plunged the knife a final time into the Tirynian's throat and pulled it free; his body jerked once and was still.

On hands and knees she remained, straddling him, half deadly lover, half beast. I almost thought to see a lion's fangs in her mouth when she spoke. "Korinthian! What is the answer?"

Creon laid a hand on my shoulder; his grip hurt me.

Yet somehow Oedipus was oblivious to the nightmare that had seized us. He gazed steadily at Melanthe and said, "The wind. It is invisible, its touch can caress or destroy, its howl strikes fear into man and beast."

This made sense; but for the space of a heartbeat I dared not breathe. Fear held me fast to my chair, and Creon's fingers dug into my flesh, hard enough to leave marks.

Then, as suddenly as it had come, the cloud blew away from the sun, and we were all free of the shadow. The crowd cheered, and surged towards the temple steps. "King Oedipus!" cried one voice, soon joined by many more. "A husband for our queen!"

I rose shakily from my seat, tears of fear and relief running down my cheeks; but Melanthe leapt to her feet. Wild-eyed, with the blood of four men splashed across her face, arms, and breasts, she was terrible to behold. I gasped in unison with the hundreds of Thebans who thronged the square.

The Sphinx prowled a circle round the body of her latest victim. "Dionysus sends a final riddle," she said loudly, addressing her words to the sky.

I could only stand frozen, thinking: no, he has done it! Let him be! He is mine!

But Melanthe, or Dionysus, cared nothing for my unspoken plea, and the people hushed.

"In the morning," she went on, "I walk upon four legs. When the sun is high stride I upon two. But at sunset my gait is three-legged."

Oedipus hesitated, and ran a hand through his hair. A green stone glinted in his seal-ring. Only two nights ago that hand had rested upon my hip.

Sweet Leto, this could not be happening. I could not lose him now.

Melanthe folded her red-washed arms across her chest – not impatiently, but proudly, as though confident that her final opponent could not now succeed. I saw dismay and confusion on the faces in the crowd.

No, I thought. Dionysus wants me to take a husband. Melanthe cannot kill the last contestant. She will not.

Yet Melanthe had proclaimed that Thebes needed no king.

In the lengthening silence my beloved seemed at a loss. He shifted from one foot to the other. His ankles must have ached from standing for so long; as if he suddenly felt the pain himself, he leaned heavily on his staff. His eyes scanned the crowd, and seemed to light on my father, who had suddenly appeared at the front of the crowd. In his black robes Father looked like Charon the ferryman, come to take my beloved away to the land of the dead.

I shivered, and remembered what the Tiresias had said about bringing the killer of Laius to justice.

But though my father pursed his lips together, he did not speak.

"What is your answer, Korinthian?" Melanthe demanded.

An infant's wail broke the crowd's breathless silence. The mother shushed the babe, and tried offering a breast. When the child would not quiet, she hurried away in a swirl of skirts. The citizens muttered uneasily, the intensity of the mood disturbed.

"Creon, we must do something," I whispered.

Melanthe began to unfold her arms; all too clearly I saw the dagger in her right hand.

But then Oedipus called out: "A man!"

Melanthe stopped, her arm stilled.

The prince laughed, not shrilly in fear, as I might then have done, but in pleasure and triumph at having found the answer. "Yes, a man. In the morning of his infancy he creeps on all fours. In the day of his youth he walks on two feet. But in the evening of old age he leans on his staff. From four legs to two to three."

The crowd now roared without restraint, and my spirits soared. I felt as though I were floating, and doubted my legs could hold me much longer.

Melanthe kept staring at the foreign prince. The applause died off slowly, nervously; all feared what she might do next. For a breath she remained unmoving as a statue. Only when there was complete silence once more did she speak, still without taking her eyes from Oedipus. "Queen Jocasta, my lord Creon," she said evenly, "that was my last riddle."

With that Melanthe turned slowly away. Vanished was the powerful beast-priestess: in her place was only a tired woman painted with Aegyptian kohl and Hellene blood. The huge dark eyes that had flashed so wildly just a moment ago looked flat and lifeless now, as if the magic of Dionysus had deserted her.

I looked up to meet the smiling face of my Korinthian prince.

Oedipus was safe. He was mine.

CHAPTER FIFTEEN

While Thebes had enjoyed the bloody spectacle of the contest, it was not what I wanted the city to remember most. Creon and I planned a splendid marriage ceremony, with a generous feast for all the citizens. Music and dancing, acrobats and magicians; juicy mutton and salt fish and roast beef; soft breads and cakes filled with raisins; honey and wine flowing in abundance. I meant to give my city such a day as even Amphion never had done.

But with the gates still officially closed, arranging the feast was no simple matter. All foods had to be carefully inspected, for until the alliance with Korinth was secure we were liable as ever to dangerous intervention from Pelops. "We don't want to risk a repetition of what happened when you were betrothed to Alphenor," said Creon.

That memory haunted me. Even though I had not witnessed the demise of Amphion's sons and daughters, I had seen their bodies laid out in the megaron. And I remembered Creon's pale, sweating face as his body fought the poison.

"No, we don't," I concurred, and gave the order for the gates to remain shut.

Despite these continued restrictions, the days flew by in a whirlwind of meetings, preparations and pronouncements. We presented Oedipus once more at a banquet in the megaron, this time as my betrothed. How handsome he looked, how well he spoke! Each time he glanced my way I brimmed with joy and desire.

We also sent a courier with a fast team to Korinth, to ask King Polybus and Queen Periboea for their blessing, and for an alliance with Thebes.

The day before the wedding, my seamstress was making final adjustments to the gown of Harmonia when we heard knocking at my suite's outer door. Lilika went to answer it; she came back, frowning. "My lady queen, the Sphinx has come to the palace and wishes to speak with you."

I turned too quickly, pricking myself on a sharp bronze pin. I had not seen Melanthe since the contest; rumor had it she planned to depart with Haralpos for Orchomenos, to take advantage of his pledge to the Maenads.

But I had no desire to deal with Melanthe. I wanted to enjoy the pleasures of preparing for my wedding, to delight in being a bride. "Tell her I'll see her after the ceremony."

Lilika hesitated. "My lady, the guard said she was most adamant."

I started to retort that Lilika should be adamant as well – then I bit back my words. The girl was but my maid, her skills dressing hair and mixing cosmetics. I might be a bride, but I remained queen of Thebes.

"Very well," I said. "Tell the guards to search her and remove her daggers. Then I'll see her in the small audience room. And send word to Creon to join us." I considered inviting Oedipus, then recalled he was touring the gates with Demochares, inspecting the preparations for tomorrow's ceremonies.

But Creon, spending time with Eurydike and their newborn son in their palace apartments, was readily available for an interview with our Sphinx. He stood at my side in the private audience room as a guard escorted her into our presence. The guard watched the Aegyptian warily, his hand on the hilt of his sword.

Melanthe's appearance surprised me. A few days before, she had been a creature of power: graceful, deadly, brimming with divine energy. Now she looked haggard, her dark eyes sunken, her skin dry and sallow. Her movements seemed slow and awkward.

Even her lion-skin cape was bedraggled and dirty, stained with the blood of the men who had died that day.

Was this the price Dionysus demanded of his priestess?

I was willing to honor the vine-god – indeed, I would drink his health forever, in gratitude for sending Oedipus to me. But the gods exacted too high a price for intimacy: Zeus burned his lover Semele, the mother of Dionysus, to ashes; Apollo and Athena required that the Tiresias forfeit his eyesight. I preferred to maintain a respectful – and safe – distance from the gods.

Gaping at the changes in her, I forgot to speak. So instead Creon began the conversation.

"You requested this audience, Melanthe?" His voice was cool.

"I want you to increase the portion of grain allotted to my people."

Creon shook his head. "Not possible. The division must stand as we agreed."

She took a menacing step forward; I was glad I had ordered the guards to confiscate her weapons. "What of the feast being prepared? You have plenty of food for that!"

"Yes," I snapped. "And the Maenads will take part in the wedding feast along with everyone else."

"Without me, there would be no wedding." Melanthe's voice sounded strained and rough. "And if you don't cooperate, we'll refuse to open the gates."

This was nonsensical. "Melanthe, be reasonable," I said. "If we don't open the gates, how can we admit more goods to feed your people? "

"We won't open the gates just to give Thebes to the prince of Korinth!"

I peered at her through narrowed eyes. Just how strong was this "we" of which she spoke? As far as I could tell, the vast majority of citizens, including most of the Maenads, supported my plans. But she could cause serious trouble, and I did not want the start of my new life marred by bloody fights at all the gates.

I studied her, wondering why Melanthe was coming up with new threats now. The matter had been settled! Had she acted upon the instruction of Dionysus, or was she reluctant to give up newfound power?

Or was she simply mad?

I tried speaking evenly, moderately. "Oedipus isn't merely the prince of Korinth. He will be my husband and the king of Thebes. We are not 'giving' Thebes to Korinth; we are making an alliance with them. And Oedipus will be a good king."

"Why does Thebes need a king at all?"

"Sweet Leto!" I cried. "You yourself have been the agent of the god in *choosing* the new king!"

Creon laid a calming hand on my shoulder. "Melanthe, I'm sure that no one, not even the Maenads, wants to disrupt the wedding feast. But you have provided a great service to the city, and if we no longer need to send tribute to Pelops, we should have plenty for all. Why don't you and I meet in the storeroom near the Astykratia Gate to inspect the inventory and see if we can find anything extra for your people?" He squeezed my shoulder. "Say, at dusk? Then we'll see what we can spare."

Before, I had been the one to placate the Maenads with more grain; I was surprised to find my brother taking this tactic. Melanthe, too, seemed suspicious. She stood silent, as if she were weighing my brother's words. Finally she nodded agreement. "At dusk." She departed, the scruffy tail of her lion's pelt dragging behind her. My watchful guard followed her out.

"Thank you," I said to Creon, when she was gone. "By all the gods, I don't know how to make that woman see reason."

Creon's lips twitched. "Isn't that why you need me, Sister? To handle the things that you can't?"

With Melanthe appeased, at least for a while, I returned to the happy business of preparing for my wedding. Though I had worn the golden diadem and the necklace of jeweled serpents regularly ever since I became queen, I had not touched Harmonia's gown, as I feared damaging its ancient cloth. But when we took the robe out of its cedar wood chest, I discovered that the material was sturdier than I had realized, as was its long belt. And now my curves fit the robe perfectly. When Merope held up a bronze mirror for me, I saw with astonishment that at thirty-seven I would look even more beautiful than I had at my first wedding.

I smiled with relief. With each passing day, I felt more secure in Oedipus' love; but still, I wanted to be sure he would be attracted to me. I did not want my young husband to think of the years between us.

At my dressing-table, Lilika was setting out the cosmetics and brushes. "Will you want the malachite paint for your eyes, my lady, or the gilt?"

I considered this, admiring the rich azure of the gown with its gold acanthus-leaf trim at the edge. "The gilt," I said. Lilika nodded, humming as she worked.

Another knock at the door; this time Merope answered it. Demochares stepped inside, and bowed. "My lady, the messenger from Korinth has arrived."

My heart leapt. I could not imagine a reason for bad news – Oedipus assured me his parents loved him dearly – but I still felt a shiver of nerves. "And? Do they agree to the alliance?"

"So I gather, lady. The messenger bears a gift under Polybus' seal, and asks an audience with you."

"Excellent," I said. "Show him to guest quarters in the north wing, and tell him we'll meet him this evening."

The next day we would celebrate my marriage to Oedipus, and all expected the revelry to last well into the night. So that evening when I came to the megaron it was almost empty; most Thebans were resting in anticipation of the morrow's festivities.

But Oedipus was there, standing next to my throne and speaking with Demochares. When I appeared at the door both men smiled; the herald bowed, and announced in his rich voice: "Queen Jocasta!"

The few guests present bowed, and offered a polite murmur of deference. A musician strummed a lyre by the hearth.

I crossed the tiles to my betrothed and accepted his kiss. I wished for more, but had to content myself – for now! – with a chaste embrace. He held my hand as I took my seat on the throne. His fingers were warm against mine.

"Is all ready at the gates, beloved?"

"Yes," said Oedipus. "Demochares and Creon were thorough in carrying out your plans. I'm filled with admiration for the gates and walls of Thebes. You're a remarkable ruler, my lady."

I liked that he referred to me as a ruler instead of a queen; he realized I was more than a decoration on the throne. "I can't take credit for our fortifications. Amphion built them, not I."

"But you have maintained them."

"Ah, if you are *determined* to compliment me…"

"I am, my lady," and he bent down to kiss me. I sensed his reluctance as well as my own when, conscious of our audience, we broke apart. Oedipus glanced around the megaron and asked, "Where's Lord Creon? Doesn't he want to meet the messenger from Korinth?"

Diverted by the wedding preparations, I had completely forgotten the morning's interview with the Sphinx. I glanced up through the opening above the hearth; a bright star twinkled in the evening sky. "I'm sure he'll be here as soon as he can."

Just then, Creon appeared and made his way around the room. He was breathing quickly and his cheeks were flushed; no doubt he had hurried up the hill to be in time for the audience. I opened my mouth to inquire after his conversation with Melanthe, but I closed it again with my question unasked. For in the doorway stood Demochares, and at his side, a richly dressed stranger.

"Lord Mnesikles of Korinth," announced Demochares. Oedipus fairly glowed with happiness: I knew he missed his Korinthian home, and he had mentioned Mnesikles as an old family friend, a man his parents trusted absolutely.

The Korinthian envoy stepped forward and bowed. Although he was completely bald, he had a striking dark beard speckled with gray and his tanned face was not deeply lined. I guessed he was a little older than my brother.

"Welcome to Thebes," I said.

"I thank you, my lady," Mnesikles replied. After the requisite exchange of niceties, he delivered the message we all hoped for: "King Polybus of Korinth and Queen Periboea of Korinth have agreed to the alliance."

I had expected good news; nevertheless, I felt my heart lighten. Creon relaxed visibly at my side, and a boyish grin spread across Oedipus' features.

"Here is a list of the gifts Korinth will send to Thebes as a token of friendship, once the marriage has taken place," Mnesikles continued. He pulled a clay tablet from a pouch at his side and handed it to me; I examined it briefly, noting the seal at the bottom. Dried clay was the most reliable method for sending an official message; the seal guaranteed authenticity and the drying of the tablet meant it could not be altered. I scanned the inventory of precious items above Polybus' royal seal, then passed the tablet to Creon.

"King Polybus and Queen Periboea have but one condition," said Mnesikles, this time staring straight at me.

Creon tensed again and even Oedipus seemed to lose some of his optimism. I asked, "And what is that condition?"

The man smiled, warmth radiating from his brown eyes. "That you make their son happy, my lady."

Oedipus placed his hand on my shoulder. "You may assure my parents that I am happy – and that except for my mother, there's no woman more wonderful than Queen Jocasta."

After that, Mnesikles presented us with a wedding gift – a pair of conical rhytons, two exquisite vessels adorned with fanciful carvings of octopi and fishes, their eyes bright with blue enamel. He added that the king and queen of Korinth regretted their inability to attend the wedding of their only son, but that they would accept the commands of the Delphic oracle. In the meantime Mnesikles would serve as their representative.

"Of course," I said. "As the envoy of Oedipus' parents, you're welcome always."

As we left for dinner, I heard Creon mutter, "A Korinthian spy." But, looking at his face, I discerned more caution than suspicion.

Over the meal, Oedipus spoke to Mnesikles and asked after his parents, and caught up with all the news from Korinth. That wealthy city had fared well over the winter; Mnesikles added, "Your father's joints troubled him as they always do in the cold months, but have improved with the better weather. And your mother misses you."

I realized how my beloved's exile from Korinth must pain him, how he must ache to go home. But when I mentioned my concern later, Oedipus pressed my hand to his lips. "Thebes is my home now."

With these words echoing in my heart, I went to my apartment – alone, but alone for the last night.

I woke early the next morning. I tried to relax in my bath of warm rose-scented water, but my heart seemed to beat faster with each passing moment. At last the makeup was done and each curl in place, and Lilika helped me into Harmonia's gown. Once she had cinched the belt, fastened the famous necklace at my throat, and set the circlet of golden vines and flowers on my head I endured my maids' scrutiny.

"Hydna would be so proud, my lady," said Merope, her voice hoarse and her eyes shining with unshed tears.

"I wish she were here too," I said, and squeezed my serving-maid's hand.

We left my chambers and went to the palace steps, where I surveyed the crowd. The agora was packed with citizens: well-born and peasants, weavers, builders, artisans, merchants, and even a few farmers and herders who had been allowed through the gates with their goods. Mnesikles, serving as witness for the king and queen of Korinth. Rhodia and her assistants, come to wish me well. Demochares and the soldiers. Haralpos of Orchomenos was there, surrounded by Maenads, but I did not see Melanthe. I thought she must be putting the final touches on her own garb; surely she meant to stand out in the throng.

Then I saw a tall figure garbed in black: the Tiresias. I blinked, startled with a sudden memory of how he had stood in much the same place months ago, and demanded that Laius' murderer be brought to justice.

Instead I was about to marry him and make him king of the city.

The Tiresias turned his face toward me, yet he said nothing. He was my father as well as the prophet of Apollo; if he thought what I was about to do would bring a curse on Thebes, surely he would stop me.

The last Tiresias had foretold that my husband would be the greatest king that Thebes had ever known. As she could not possibly have meant Laius, she must have been referring to Oedipus. And how could a man be Thebes' greatest king and simultaneously defile it? That made no sense.

Oedipus had been approved by Dionysus. Creon and I had helped to prepare him, true, but he had passed the test by his own wits. I resolved not to worry any longer. Better to follow the advice I gave Laius – which he did not take – and live my life without obsessing about incomprehensible oracles.

The flute-girls began to play, signaling that I should descend the stairs. Merope handed me the gift for Hera, a pyxis of

Lydian incense, and then I took my brother's arm. Despite my decision to ignore the prophecies, I whispered the words: "Holy Leto, mother to Apollo – if this is a mistake, then stop me now." But, out in the agora, my father only bent his head down, as if trying to catch some words uttered by his guide.

The people tossed dried petals at my feet; I trod across a colorful carpet. Thebans called out their blessings and well-wishes, and I heard whispers about the magical powers of Harmonia's necklace. Creon and I made our way across the square; the crowd parted before us until at last I saw Oedipus. A golden fillet circled his head, and he wore a kilt and cape of creamy white. He looked so handsome that I caught my breath.

The high priest of Zeus, a short man with gray curls, led the ceremony and asked the traditional questions. I broke the ritual at the usual place to make my offering to Hera, the goddess of marriage. As I was a widow instead of a maid, well-born matrons accompanied me. My sister-in-law walked slowly among them, the color returned to her pretty cheeks. I felt a wave of affection toward her: perhaps because I was so giddily in love myself?

After the priestess accepted my gift, I rejoined Oedipus. We crossed the agora to the altar dedicated to Zeus. The sacrificial victims – a pair of bulls – went easily to their deaths; the axe fell cleanly on each neck. "An excellent sign," Oedipus whispered, as the priest set about carving the offerings to be burnt. "Proof that the gods will bless our marriage."

I squeezed his hand. Surely they would. Oedipus had done penance at Orchomenos; he was forgiven by the gods, and my father's warning irrelevant.

Creon stood solemnly at my right shoulder, Eurydike beside him. Their son could not appear officially, since he had not yet been named. But as Eurydike could not endure being parted from her infant long, she had arranged for Nysa, one of Rhodia's assistants, to carry him nearby. I noticed how my sister-in-law kept turning her head in the direction of the girl who held the small bundle in her arms.

Tonight Creon's son would be presented formally, and receive his name. A fitting gesture as the first event of my new husband's reign: a symbol of new life for the city. Thank Artemis and all the gods the child was well! Eurydike looked distracted, but happy. My brother, on the other hand, seemed too quiet, inward-focused. Was he concerned that things would change, now that Oedipus was king? I stole a glance at Creon's furrowed brow. Didn't he know I still valued his counsel in all things?

The priest of Zeus sliced off sections of meat from the thighs of the sacrificial animals. These he doused in wine and olive oil mixed with spices, wrapped in fat and then placed on the altar fire. They sizzled and burned in turn, their scent filling the air; my mouth watered.

"Zeus has found the marriage acceptable!" proclaimed the priest. I sighed in relief and contentment.

Demochares announced: "Let it be known that Lady Jocasta, queen of Thebes, has taken a husband: lord Oedipus, prince of Korinth and now king of Thebes!"

Wild cheering erupted from the crowd, while acolytes stepped forward to prepare the rest of the meat. Oedipus took advantage of the jubilant interruption to place a kiss on the back of my neck. I looked up into his brilliant blue eyes, and my heart swelled. What good fortune, that this handsome wonderful prince had made his way to Thebes!

How near I had come to another empty, joyless marriage – yet instead I had found the other half of my heart.

In place of the typical bridal procession of maidens, we had a courtly promenade of king and queen, giving all Thebes a chance to see the new king – and the king the chance to see all of Thebes. My people had readied their dwellings and workshops in preparation for the day; wreaths decorated nearly every door, the streets were swept clean, and the city sparkled in the bright sunlight.

At each gate we mounted a dais that had been prepared the day before; Demochares introduced Oedipus to the crowd as Thebes' new king, and then the soldiers ceremoniously opened the gates. People surged in, Oedipus and Creon pronounced the city open and the new reign begun, and the crowd shouted its tumultuous acclaim. Thebes had a new king, young and vigorous; Thebes was open at last.

Although I knew the city as well as I knew my favorite spindle, with Oedipus at my side I saw it through fresh eyes. He greeted people of every station in his easygoing, cheerful manner: nobles and soldiers, priests and merchants, artisans and farmers. He praised the walls and gates, the many springs and wells, the health and spirit of the citizens. As we walked arm in arm I pointed out sites of interest, delighted to share with him the history of my city. I explained how the old king Amphion had named the gates of Thebes for his seven daughters. And at the Kleodoxa Gate I pointed out that Amphion, his brother Zethos, and thirteen of Amphion's children were buried on the hill beyond.

"Amphion was destroyed by the people," said Oedipus.

"Yes," I said. "A terrible fate for a king."

"But hadn't he insulted Apollo? And brought a curse upon the city?"

My new husband accepted such edicts from the gods with greater equanimity than I. For this, I decided, I should be grateful: the Delphic oracle had caused Oedipus to abandon Korinth, sending him here.

"Amphion did not offend the gods," I said quietly. "It was Niobe, his wife."

We continued, passing the road to the spring of Dirke. "In that direction lies the cave that held the serpent slain by Kadmos," I told him.

"The serpent of Ares," Oedipus said. "The one from whose teeth the Spartoi sprang."

"Yes," I said, "among them my father's ancestor Echion." I looked up at Oedipus and smiled. "After Kadmos and Harmonia tired of ruling, they left the city and had another son, my mother's grandfather, in the distant north. But another story says that when they resigned the throne, they turned themselves into blue-spotted black serpents. They slithered away, and are supposed to be out there still."

He fingered the snakes of my necklace, and kissed me. "May they watch over us, and bring us luck."

Finally we reached the last gate, the Astykratia. Although this was meant to be the supreme moment of the day, our parade was growing disorganized. After all, our procession was composed largely of ordinary citizens, not soldiers disciplined to marching. The people were growing hungry and thirsty; many looked weary in the bright afternoon light. Creon frowned at the confusion and pushed ahead to restore some order.

Poor exhausted Eurydike lagged behind, but the sound of her child's hungry cry revived her. She went over to the young midwife who was carrying the babe, hesitated, then approached me. Her breasts looked swollen; no doubt they ached with accumulated milk. "I know this is the culmination of the ceremony, my lady, but I'm very tired—"

"Go and be with your son," I told her.

"Thank you," she said gratefully. She turned, then stopped. "But where should I go?"

I looked around. The babe was not supposed to be acknowledged until this evening, and if the queen's sister-in-law nursed her child in public a crowd would surely gather. Yet the area offered few alternatives. The Astykratia Gate was a busy place and the environs were not the most accommodating. She could go to the guardhouse, of course, but it would be full of soldiers.

Then a possibility occurred to me. "Demochares, send a soldier to let Eurydike and Nysa into the granary," I said. It would not be very comfortable, but it would be private, and my sister-in-law could care for her child in peace.

I watched as the soldier led the women against the surge of the crowd and spoke to the guard who stood at the door to the storeroom. He glanced in my direction; I nodded my approval. The guard opened the door, and Eurydike, Nysa and the unnamed child slipped into the dark interior.

Then Oedipus and I ascended the platform, joining Creon and the flute-girls. As we turned to face the crowd, the musicians ceased playing, and Demochares spoke. He repeated the proclamations he had made at all the other gates; by now even his voice was weary. "Thebans," he concluded, "Hail lord Oedipus, prince of Korinth and now husband of Queen Jocasta and king of Thebes!"

The people cheered, though their applause seemed less enthusiastic than before. I was sure that most of their thoughts had turned to the agora, where long wooden tables were being set out for that evening's feast.

I myself hungered to return to the palace with my new husband – though not because I wanted food.

Oedipus, however, would not rush through his kingly duty. He smiled, and began to speak. "Thebans, I thank you for entrusting me with your queen and your city. I will honor—"

"Dead!" shrieked a voice. "Dead!"

We looked down among the people, and saw Eurydike pushing her way toward us, followed closely by young Nysa, holding the baby. Eurydike's face was pale, but panic gave her strength, and she ran up the stairs.

"Dead!" she cried again.

A hand seemed to clutch my heart: the child! "He can't be! He was so healthy!"

Eurydike stared wildly at me, as if she did not understand.

"What happened?" I asked. "An assassin?"

Had one of Pelops' men had gotten past the guard?

"I don't know, but she was dead, on the floor behind the great scale, and her braids lying all in the blood…"

"*She*?" So it was not the child!

Before I could question further, Creon stepped forward and took his wife by the wrist. His grip was tight, his fingers sinking into her white flesh; his voice was low but commanding. "Control yourself, woman; you're making a scene! The people are watching and wondering what this is all about."

Creon was right; a hush had fallen on the crowd; they stared, and I was sure their ears were open wide as their mouths, as they strained to catch our words. But in the distance, back by the granary, another commotion was erupting.

"I'm also wondering," said Oedipus.

Creon stared across the heads of the crowd, at the growing excitement a stone's throw away. "Where? In the storeroom?"

"Yes," she said, nodding vigorously, "behind the grain-scales."

"What were you doing there?"

I interrupted: "*I* sent her there, Creon. So she could nurse the child in private."

Creon hissed at his wife: "You should not be nursing the child out here at all! You should have stayed home with the babe until he was named!"

Eurydike burst into tears.

I pried Creon's fingers from his wife's arm; purple bruises showed livid against her skin. I slipped an arm around her; she clung to me and sobbed into my shoulder.

A cry went up among those near the door of the granary. "The Sphinx! The Sphinx is dead!" some began to wail.

Melanthe: dead, in the Kleodoxa storeroom!

I looked over Eurydike's head at my brother's face, and saw the grim line of his tightly pressed mouth and the glitter of his eyes. A chill went to my stomach, while some of the Maenads shrieked.

"Creon," Oedipus began, his voice dispassionate, "it seems you know something of this matter. What shall we tell the people?"

My brother struggled to regain his self-control. His expression went from icy anger to irritation and then grudging acknowledgment of Oedipus' request. Turning, Creon raised his voice for all to hear. "You are right, my lord king; this matter concerns all of Thebes. Everyone knows our Sphinx, and her vital role in our city and the surrounding lands as priestess, healer, and advisor. This year, Dionysus called the Sphinx to her greatest duty: to serve the god's will in choosing a new king." Creon gestured at Oedipus; the people nodded and murmured their assent.

"Yesterday afternoon," Creon continued, "I met with the Sphinx here, at the Kleodoxa granary, to review the provisions I had made for feeding the city and the Maenads. When she saw the grain-tallies, and knew that the apportionment was fair, she said that she had fulfilled every last command of Dionysus. She had, she told me, completed her final duty to Thebes. Then, filled with the god's power and moving quick as a snake – just as we saw her do eight days ago – she slipped the knife from her belt and plunged it into her heart."

The people gasped in shock. As for me, I experienced a strange mix of feelings. I had known Melanthe since childhood, but had never really liked her – and these past few days I had truly feared her. I was not sorry to learn that she was dead. But had she really taken her own life, or had my brother helped her? I wanted to believe his story, but it seemed unlikely.

Creon raised his hand to indicate he had more to say, and the throng fell silent. "Before the breath left her body, the Sphinx gave me one last message for Thebes. She said that a new priestess of the vine-god would arise, but in Orchomenos. Those who wish to hold the Maenad rites should travel there."

"Why would she end her life *here*?" cried a voice from the crowd. A gap-toothed woman, one of the Maenad leaders, pushed her way to the front. "I think you killed her, lord Creon!"

The woman voiced what I was thinking. Murmurs swelled within the crowd; the Maenads looked angry and menacing. I stared at my brother, wondering what he would say.

He held up his hands and raised his voice. "I'm flattered! I am truly flattered!"

His words were not what anyone expected, including me – and they confused the crowd long enough to bring quiet.

"Although I have done my utmost to serve Thebes all my life, you know I'm no warrior. I have no particular skill in archery or spear-hunting – much less with throwing knives. If you think that *I* was able to overpower Melanthe – the Sphinx you saw kill so many men just a few days ago – well, my friends, I'm flattered!"

The Maenad frowned, and doubt crossed her face. Uncertainty spread throughout the crowd, and even in my own heart. I suspected Creon, but how could he have overpowered Melanthe?

Still the old Maenad was persistent. "She would have come to us, not to you!"

"Wasn't her duty first to the god?" Creon shouted above the angry muttering that followed the old woman's words. "When Dionysus told her that her role was done, and called her to end her own life, didn't she have to answer at once?"

"Surely it is so," called another voice. Haralpos ventured forth from his place beside the platform, and the people made way. "I can attest that Dionysus is no god to be trifled with." Many of the Maenads murmured agreement to that, and the mood grew calmer.

I caught my brother's eye. *This* was why Creon had been so quiet today – but how long had he planned to keep silent?

"I am sorry, dear sister," he said. "This is a great loss to our city." I heard the barest trace of irony in his voice. "And the fault is mine for not coming forward with the news at once. I thought only of my queen, and my young child. I did not want to ruin your wedding day, and my son's name-day."

Everyone was silent, as if they expected me to do something. But I found it difficult to speak. At last I crossed the platform and reached for my brother's hand. He grasped mine so tightly that my fingers hurt. "Creon, I understand, and I forgive you."

My brother relaxed his grip a little, but he kept my hand.

"The day is not ruined," Oedipus declared. "If Dionysus called his servant to end her life, that is his right. Isn't that true, Tiresias?"

Heads turned in the direction of the soldiers' hut, before which Father stood. "We are all in the hands of the gods," said the Tiresias. "We should honor those they have chosen."

I was relieved that Father said no more than that, and that his visions with respect to Dionysus, at least, were blurry.

"This death is no evil omen," my husband continued. "Melanthe has offered her life in homage to the god. The end of one day is the beginning of the next. Our marriage marks a new day for Thebes. Spring follows winter, and life comes again." He smiled, and stretched out his arm to my brother. "Creon, have your wife bring your son up on the platform for his naming ceremony at once! Thebes has lost one life, but gained another!"

Quick as the blink of an eye, the mood of the crowd changed. Among shouts of praise for the wine-god I also heard, "A son of the royal house!" and "Long live our wise King Oedipus!"

Creon released my hand and nodded curtly to my husband.

My heart swelled with pride. Oedipus had taken a potential disaster and found blessing in it, had put the people's hearts at ease. From the start I had sensed that he was the right man to be my husband, and king of Thebes – now I saw my hopes being fulfilled. Surely Creon would feel it too, and be relieved.

275

But his expression stayed distant.

Even when Eurydike laid the squalling babe at her husband's feet and he lifted his firstborn son high before the people to proclaim his name Haemon – surely one of the proudest moments in any man's life – my brother's spirit seemed far away.

As we climbed the hill to the agora – Eurydike now beaming as she held her son in her arms, distress over her discovery of Melanthe forgotten – I went over to my brother. I touched his elbow, and he turned to look down at me.

"Yes, Jocasta?" he asked, his voice flat.

"Melanthe's death is a shock to Thebes, but it removes a problem," I said. "And now the Maenads will move to Orchomenos, and no longer destroy our harvests."

"I'm glad you appreciate that," Creon said.

The tone of voice, the twitch in his cheek, fanned my suspicions. "Creon," I said, lowering my voice to a whisper, making sure no one could hear. "Did you kill her?"

He looked up at the palace atop the hill, then all around us. He did not answer the question directly, and I began to fear he would not answer at all – that I had offended him, and this day, which in so many ways was the happiest of my life, would lead to a breach between my brother and me.

Finally he spoke. "Whatever I do," he said, "I do for Thebes."

As I digested these words, once more my stomach felt chill. I was sure, now, that Creon had somehow arranged Melanthe's death. She might have been more expert with a knife, but her skill with riddles did not make her a match for my brother's wit. Creon had caused a woman's death with the deliberate dispassion of the Fate Atropos shearing a life-thread. Why had Creon not warned me – was he keeping other secrets from me? And what if I, or my beloved Oedipus, crossed him?

I glanced at him uneasily, not yet ready to meet his eye. He was watching me, waiting for my reaction. But the people were throwing dried flower petals at us, making private conversation impossible.

And I did not yet know how I felt. One part of me feared him, wanted to run away. But I had loved and trusted Creon all my life.

He said he had done this for Thebes. Well, I was queen of Thebes. Had he done it for me? Was it possible he had refrained from telling me simply because he wanted my wedding day to be a day of unalloyed joy? Creon was right: Melanthe *had* been a danger to our city.

He had done what was necessary, what had to be done.

My thoughts carried on in their own relentless logic. Surprised at my own ruthlessness, I wondered briefly why he had not hidden the body more carefully. Then I realized he had left her in what should have been a safe place, and would have disposed of the body later. A shame I had sent Eurydike into the stores; the story would have been much better if Melanthe had simply disappeared – said to go off to worship her god in the wilderness.

The procession turned a corner, entering the street of the bakers. The smell of baking bread made my mouth water and distracted those around us, who turned their heads towards the displays of loaves and cakes. I took this moment to speak to Creon. "Do you think Father has any idea? After all, Melanthe was chosen by Dionysus."

Creon looked sourly back at our father, who lagged far behind. "He just enjoys making pronouncements that are enigmatic and ominous."

We walked silently for a several paces; finally, I changed the subject. "Oedipus did well today, didn't he? I believe he has the makings of a good king."

To my surprise, his eyes grew cold once more. "I suppose," he said.

Celebrations intensified again once we entered the agora. People spoke of Melanthe as a visionary, called to give her life to the god. Talk seemed to turn easily from this to the new king chosen through trial with the holy Sphinx, and the wedding, and Creon's new son. Flute girls, jugglers, and acrobats made their way through the square, and the people laughed and clapped as at any festival. The food was excellent: the beef tender, the cheese tasty, and the wine poured generously. The revelry continued outside when my husband and I retired at last to the sweet pleasures of our bed.

Late that night we lay in each other's arms, happily exhausted. Oedipus' russet head rested on my shoulder as I stroked his hair. His voice had that slow, heavy tone that boded sleep any instant. "Creon should not have feared to make it known," he said. "It was the will of Dionysus. The new day for Thebes had begun. The day of the Sphinx was ended. Time for a new day…" A long breath escaped him, and I knew my beloved had entered the land of dreams.

Yes, I thought, *once you and I were married, beloved, the Sphinx had no more use.* She had become a danger instead of an asset.

I wished I could be like Oedipus, and simply trust in the divine. But after so many disappointments and confusing prophecies I could not. Yet in my mind I kept hearing Father's words: that we should honor those chosen by the gods. But Creon had killed Melanthe, the priestess of Dionysus. And Oedipus had killed Laius, the king of Thebes sent by Apollo.

I moved restlessly beneath the linen sheets. My husband turned to lie on his side; I stroked his arm, following the smooth curves of muscle.

Oedipus slew Laius, true, but he acted in self-defense. And in doing so he rid Thebes of an incompetent king, and provided a way to end the tribute to Pelops.

Creon killed Melanthe, but she too had threatened Thebes, with the Maenads' destruction of the harvests and her demands for increasing power.

It was all to the good. Thebes' good. And none of this could have happened without the acquiescence of the gods.

I silently berated myself for worrying. Worry accomplished nothing, and there was no benefit in trying to second-guess the gods.

Another concern was Creon's reaction to Oedipus. Was my brother jealous of the new king? In this first day Oedipus had already proved to be better than Laius had ever been – and by resolving a situation that Creon had created.

When Melanthe's body was found, Creon had been caught unprepared. We could have faced a Maenad riot – we could have been killed, the city thrown into chaos. Creon had spoken well, but it was Oedipus who had averted the storm.

Did Creon resent that?

I loved my brother; I adored my husband. I hoped they would be friends and allies.

I turned on my side, slipping my arm around my husband's chest, fitting my cheek against his back. His breathing was slow, regular; his body warm.

But I shivered, for I could still see the coldness in Creon's eyes.

CHAPTER SIXTEEN

Thebes breathed the cooler air of autumn; the harvest was done. In the hills beyond the city, peasants trod grapes for the new wine and pressed olives between great stone wheels. Oedipus and I sat on wooden folding chairs on our private balcony, facing the south, but with views in three directions. From this vantage we could see the hill where the goddess Athena revealed to Kadmos the sign to found our city; there, olive trees were planted in her honor, and their silvery leaves shimmered in the sun. In the distance beyond, mountains rose against a sky of brilliant blue.

A beautiful countryside; and fruitful, as well. "The barley was successful this year," I remarked, pressing my seal-ring against a wax-coated tablet.

"But the wheat harvest isn't as good," said Oedipus, a hint of a question in his statement. This was the first time for him to study our agricultural reports; and although my husband's agility with new concepts and his skill with numbers constantly impressed me, he did not have my years of experience.

"Wheat is difficult to grow," I explained. "It's more valuable in trade, and the bread is delicious, but we can't depend on it to feed the people."

"At least the figs have done well." My husband's eyes twinkled as he pushed a dish across the table toward me. "Very important, those figs."

Seeing no reason to resist, I reached for a piece of fruit and bit into its sweet flesh; the tiny seeds crunched between my teeth. My craving for figs increased each day.

"Should the servants bring another tray?" Oedipus asked, even though the dish still contained plenty. "We can put a potted tree in the bedroom. And one in the megaron, just behind your throne – why not?"

My mouth was full, so I could not answer, but I grabbed at his wrist when he beckoned a servant as if to give the joking order. But then his face grew serious, and I followed his gaze to see Creon standing in the doorway.

"What a charming sight," said my brother, his voice sharp.

Oedipus chose at first to ignore Creon's bad mood. Disregarding his kingly status, he rose to his feet and welcomed my brother. "Creon, come join us," he called. "Your sister and I are going through the harvest accounts. The queen tells me that this year's crops are far more bountiful than the last."

Creon's sandals slapped across the tiles as he approached; he did not sit down in the chair my husband offered. A scowl distorted his features, and I wondered if my brother resented Oedipus' reviewing the harvest reports with me. After all, Creon and I had shared this task through the long years with Laius.

But my brother cast not a single glance at the tablets heaped on our small table. Instead he stood at the balustrade, blocking the sunshine.

"What is it, Creon?" I asked.

"I understand that not only the fields are fruitful," said my brother.

Oedipus and I glanced at each other; I saw his face lighten once more.

"Yes," said my husband. "We have not announced it officially yet, but your sister is with child." His smile grew broader with each word.

"I'm happy for you both," said Creon, though his tone proclaimed he was anything but. "I just want to know why I had to learn it from Eurydike."

Only yesterday Rhodia had confirmed my suspicions: I was nearly three months along. We had told no one. Rhodia was also attending Eurydike, who was five months into her second pregnancy. The midwife must have seen no reason to keep the news from my sister-in-law.

But Creon had always liked to be the first to know things. I remembered one long-ago autumn day, as fine as this one. I was only seven, but with patience and a bit of luck I had caught a little grass snake; its slender green body flowed like water in my hands. After trapping the creature in a basket I ran to show Hydna, asking her how to care for it, wondering aloud if it could be related to Kadmos and Harmonia. When my brother learned I had shared news of my pet with my nursemaid first, he had sulked the rest of the day.

Oedipus looked searchingly at Creon, then at me. He reached for his walking stick, which lay beside his chair. "I'll have the servants bring some wine. And another chair." Leaning on the staff, my husband left the balcony.

Creon watched Oedipus depart, then finally sat in the vacated chair. "His ankles really do bother him, then?"

"Not all the time. More when it's about to rain."

Creon cast a skeptical glance at the cloudless blue sky. "If you say so." He reached for a tablet, but from his expression I knew he was still cross.

"We weren't keeping it a secret from you. I would have told you the next time we met."

Creon put down the tablet without comment and picked up another. "Pomegranates," he muttered. Then he added, "You didn't tell me before, either."

"Before?" I asked, uncomprehending. And then I realized he meant my first pregnancy – the one I could not bear to remember. Instinctively I looked toward the horizon: the sun hovered over Mount Kithairon, where Pelorus had taken my baby to die.

Blinded by the sun's rays, I could see nothing. Nor could I speak.

"I'm sorry," I heard Creon saying in a gentler tone. "I did not realize how much..." He fell silent, which was just as well, because words were useless to me. Instead he took my hand and squeezed it.

"That time was so different from this," I told him, fighting back the tears. "Just as Oedipus is so different from Laius."

Creon kept my hand in his, twining his fingers in mine, comforting me, somehow giving me strength. "Oedipus doesn't know, does he?"

I sat a little straighter. "I haven't told him. It's not that I'm trying to hide it from him – it's just that I can't bear to talk about it."

"I won't tell him either," said Creon, and his voice held an odd timbre of satisfaction. Perhaps Creon was glad to know something that Oedipus did not – to be in some way still closer to me than my husband. "After all, it was so long ago. And it isn't really important."

A nameless infant, dead for more than twenty years: how could such a thing be important? I lifted my face once more, pretending to gaze at the sinking sun. "I suppose you're right," I said, though the pangs in my heart disagreed. Creon might know what had happened, but even he could never understand.

Creon's mood improved, as if his irritability had metamorphosed into sadness and poured itself into me. As though trying to cheer me up, he spoke amicably about my pregnancy and then started studying the harvest reports in earnest. I allowed him to distract me; I did not want to dwell on my memories either. And so we were calculating the number of new amphorae needed to store the olive oil when Oedipus returned, followed by servants bringing wine, water, a tray of fresh grapes and stuffed olives and an additional chair.

"The harvests are excellent," said Creon.

Oedipus settled into the third chair, his back to the sun, its rays brightening his auburn locks to reddish gold. "So your sister says. Thebes has been blessed."

"And this year we are *keeping* the harvest," said Creon, "instead of sending cartloads off to Pisa."

I took a stuffed olive from the tray, and gestured to the serving-maid that she should pour the wine. "We're sending wheat, figs and leather to Korinth," I pointed out.

"Yes, but they're sending fish and salt in return," said Creon. "Trade, not tribute. With the alliance between our two cities, Pelops has had no choice but to acquiesce. And that we owe to you, my lord." My brother raised his goblet to Oedipus.

I smiled, pleased and relieved to hear Creon acknowledge my husband and what he had done for Thebes. In return I said: "And the Maenads, having moved to Orchomenos, no longer rampage through our fields."

I caught Creon's eye; he gave me a slight nod. Another forbidden subject! It seemed they were collecting, like dark crows roosting in a single tree. But it too belonged to the past. I swirled my wine, then sipped.

The past was dead as Melanthe and Laius. As my first child.

The past was gone. What mattered was the future.

And my future – Thebes' future – had never shone brighter.

"We must make an offering to Demeter," said Oedipus. "A generous one, to show our gratitude."

Creon's gaze flicked in my direction, and he raised an eyebrow. My brother had commented on Oedipus' piety on earlier occasions, wondering whether my young husband would outgrow it with time. I did not think so. Oedipus' heart was so earnest and open; his faith in the gods was as much a part of him as breathing.

"Of course we'll honor the goddess of the harvest," said Creon. "We'll sacrifice to her as we do every year."

"But this year is special," I said, reaching for Creon's hand with my left and taking Oedipus' in my right. "So we should arrange for a special thank-offering."

"Yes, Sister," agreed Creon. His glance fell to my right hand, clasping my husband's. "This year is special."

After the customary sacrifice of swine for Demeter, we held a feast accompanied by music, dancing, and an elaborately costumed enactment of the seasons' change. Those followers of Dionysus who had not journeyed north to Orchomenos joined in the festivities, and we heard no grumbling about the sharing-out of this year's harvest.

Two days later – after everyone had a chance to recover from headache and exhaustion following a night of wine and revelry – I made my first offering to Artemis. The people of Thebes rejoiced with me. No one seemed happier than Oedipus – and he looked especially proud to share the news with Mnesikles, who arrived from Korinth not long after, with ten cartloads of dried fish and one of sea salt.

"What wonderful news!" replied Mnesikles, bowing in my direction. "My lady, felicitations!" He turned back to Oedipus. "This will bring happiness to your parents, my lord."

Outside, a gray rain fell; we were spending a quiet day indoors. All around the small audience room braziers burned brightly, and a musician strummed his lyre. The Korinthian's arrival offered an excellent excuse not to work my loom, which I welcomed – with my pregnancy, standing made my back ache. Creon showed more industry than I; he was down by one of the gates, supervising the distribution of the fish and salt.

"I wish I could tell them myself," said Oedipus, regret plain on his face. Then he summoned a smile. "But I should not complain, even of that. I have so many reasons to rejoice."

"Indeed, my lord," Mnesikles agreed, and in his voice I heard relief. Had the Korinthians worried that Oedipus' bride, more than a decade older than he, would be barren? For a moment anger heated my cheeks; then I dismissed my resentment, for I had asked myself the very same question.

"And how fares the queen?" Mnesikles asked me. "My lady Periboea will no doubt wish to hear all the details."

"Very well, my friend," I told him, and it was the truth. Although I suffered the usual discomforts of pregnancy, Rhodia assured me that my problems were relatively minor – that I had the stamina of a woman half my age. Did the necklace of Harmonia grant fertility as well? Fingering the ornament at my neck, I told Mnesikles of my craving for figs and other details that I thought might interest the mother-in-law I had never met.

"What news of Korinth?" Oedipus asked, avid as always to hear about the parents and home he had had to abandon.

Mnesikles answered, describing new boats under construction and enhancements planned for the harbors, bountiful catches and profitable trade with Krete and the Cycladic isles. Unfamiliar as I was with the world of the sea, my attention wandered, and I was the first to notice Demochares in the doorway. Behind the herald stood a familiar, black-draped figure: the Tiresias.

I shivered: why had Father traveled in the rain? We had expected him to remain at Delphi for the next several months.

Over the years he had increased the time he spent near the oracle, telling us he preferred the company of priests and the deities they served to the ordinary and bustling life of Thebes. His descriptions of Delphi, with its fresh mountain air and sweet flowing streams, sometimes made me wish that I could experience it for myself. Yet the holy district also struck me as a place of ill fortune. Laius had been killed there, and Oedipus cursed. No, I decided, Delphi was a place to avoid.

At a break in the conversation between Mnesikles and the king, Demochares stepped forward to speak. "My lord king, my lady queen: the Tiresias has arrived, accompanied by Pelorus."

Pelorus!

In the whirlwind of events since Laius' death, I had forgotten about Pelorus. But now his name sent terror through me.

Would he realize that Oedipus was the man who had nearly killed him?

Months ago, Father reported that Pelorus was blind. But could the oracle of Delphi have worked some wonder to restore his sight? I wanted to postpone this meeting until I had a chance to talk to Pelorus in private, and assess his condition for myself.

What excuse could I give?

My tongue fixed itself to the roof of my mouth as though frozen there. Before I could think of anything, Demochares led Pelorus and the Tiresias into the megaron, followed by Pelorus' wife and child.

Like my father, Pelorus had a dark cloth wrapped around his eyes. So he *was* blind! My muscles relaxed and I was able to release the arms of my chair, though I could not yet speak.

How peculiar, I thought, that Pelorus' injury should prove a boon to me.

I looked more closely at Pelorus and my father. Their garb seemed identical. That was no surprise, given that both had been made at Delphi. Then a new worry struck me. Pelorus had spent the last year in the holy district. Had he somehow gained second sight?

Or would he simply recognize my husband from the sound of his voice?

Oedipus spoke; I could not stop him. He greeted the rain-soaked travelers, and ordered servants to bring blankets and fresh cloaks, and arrange chairs for them near the largest brazier. Only then did he ask about their journey.

Pelorus moved cautiously, I noted, his hand resting on his wife's arm as she positioned him by the fire. He turned his head in the direction of the various speakers, but he showed no sign of recognition at the sound of the king's voice.

The encounter between Oedipus and Laius had been brief and violent; if my husband had said anything, it would not have been in the calm, regal tones he used now. Slowly I exhaled my pent breath and allowed my eyes to leave Pelorus. I glanced over at my husband and king.

At once I bit my lip. What if Oedipus recognized Pelorus?

My husband still did not know that the man he had killed outside Delphi was the previous king of Thebes. Although that death was brought on by Laius' own bad temper – and certainly no thinking Theban could doubt that the change in kings had improved the city's lot – still, I had not revealed the truth to my husband. On our first night together, when I learned of it, I did not know how he would react. And since then I had not known how to introduce the topic. What could I say? "By the way, my love, did you know you killed my last husband?" There were no appropriate words.

The servants arrived with fresh cloaks. I was especially glad to see them wrap Daphne, Pelorus' young daughter, in a thick woolen blanket, for the little girl was shivering. Oedipus nodded in satisfaction. "Very good," he said. "Some hot mulled wine, too."

I watched my husband's face for any symptom of surprise or recognition, but detected none. Certainly the scene before him had to be very different from that on the narrow road near Delphi. Besides, Oedipus had left Pelorus for dead. He would not be looking for him now.

"How are you, Pelorus?" I asked.

He brightened at the sound of my voice, and turned his face in my direction. "Well enough, I suppose. The healers tell me I'm fortunate to be able to walk again."

His wife Chrysippe spoke eagerly, her voice nasal and too loud. "You should have seen him a year ago, my lady. For months, we thought we would lose him. Only my care pulled him through."

I saw Pelorus' lips twitch below his blindfold. While Chrysippe's homeliness would no longer bother Pelorus, her voice had to be an ordeal. I imagined that Pelorus, although he would show due gratitude to his wife, would find his inescapable dependence tiresome. A curse worse than the blindness, perhaps.

"The healers at Delphi say the gods must have a special role in store for my father." These words came from young Daphne, who at seven showed promise of turning into a real beauty. Unlike her mother's, the girl's voice was soft and sweet; hearing it, Pelorus' mouth curved into a smile. I suspected that Daphne was the reason for her father's recovery: not his wife, nor the healers, nor even the gods.

"Pelorus, what can we do for you?" I asked. "Do you need anything?"

"Besides my sight?" he asked, and sighed. "No, my kind lady queen. I thank you for the gift of gold you and your brother sent to the temple when you first learned of my condition. I merely wanted to see you—" and his lips twitched, as if he realized how odd the phrase sounded, "—to see you once more, and request to leave your service."

"What are you planning to do?" I asked quietly.

"First we will visit my wife's father. The healers say he cannot live much longer, and he is so dear to us both that we must stay until Hermes comes to escort his soul to the Underworld. After that, we will return to Delphi. At Delphi they are accustomed to the blind; life is easier for me there. And the priests have offered to train me in the service of the gods."

Pelorus, ever so practical, devoting his life to the gods! A close brush with death often changed a man; but still, the idea of Pelorus becoming a priest was a strange one.

"Will they teach you the secret of second sight?" asked Oedipus.

"That is a gift from Apollo," said the Tiresias, "not a skill in which one can be trained."

Not for the first time I wondered how keen my father's second sight was. Did Apollo bestow the same level of foresight on all his prophets? Sometimes my father seemed to have no answer.

"You have our permission to go, Pelorus," I said, hoping my voice did not betray the relief I felt at his proposed absence. "We'll send an offering to the oracle with you."

"Thank you," he said, inclining his head. "Now, if you will excuse me, my lady, I will take my wife and daughter to the house of my father-in-law."

"Of course," Oedipus said.

"We hope that old Naukles is comfortable in his last days," I added. "We will send you wine and soothing herbs."

"We thank you, my lord king – my lady queen."

Pelorus held out his hand, and Chrysippe led her husband out the door, young Daphne following behind them. On Oedipus' face I saw kind concern, but nothing like alarm or even curiosity. Mnesikles watched Pelorus intently, but the Korinthian showed an interest in everything, preparing his detailed reports for Oedipus' parents, I supposed.

"Tiresias, will you take some spiced wine?" asked my husband.

"Thank you, yes," said my father. As his servant pressed a steaming cup into his hand, I noticed that Father looked older. Many wrinkles were hidden by the blindfold, but new lines showed in his neck and jowls. He slurped his drink gracelessly, and the hand with which he wiped his mouth trembled.

"Now, seer," said Oedipus, "What wisdom of the oracle can you share with us?"

In early spring, after burying his father-in-law, Pelorus left Thebes – without, to my great relief, discovering who had blinded him. Creon paid him a visit before his departure, which cost me an anxious morning. But when my brother returned to the palace, he seemed none the wiser regarding the accident. Instead he seemed fascinated by how Pelorus' blindness had affected him. Pelorus' newfound willingness to serve the gods sparked our conversation for days.

"He's certainly endeared himself to Father," Creon remarked, and I thought I heard a touch of envy in his voice. "He treats Pelorus like a son."

We sat outside the birthing-room, Creon's senet board between us. Eurydike suffered behind the doors, laboring to bring her second child to the world. I had entered the room a few times to offer my sister-in-law encouraging words and sponge her brow; each time, Rhodia assured me all was going well. As my own girth was increasing daily, I found Eurydike's untroubled childbirth reassuring.

"Father and Pelorus have much in common," I told my brother. Then I hesitated, peering at him. "Come, Creon, you don't want to lose your eyesight and go to Delphi to serve the gods!"

"Of course not." Creon cast the knucklebones and moved his pieces on the board. "Well, what son ever satisfies his father?"

I recalled Creon saying something similar after the birth of his first child; I also knew that Creon still burst with pride each time he showed off little Haemon.

We had almost finished the game when a final scream came through the door, followed by a thin wail: a new child for my brother. Pushing against the arms of my chair, I rose heavily and went inside. My sister-in-law looked pale and tired but managed to smile up at me. "A girl," she told me, and her voice was stronger than I expected. A woman's second childbirth, I knew, was generally easier. Perhaps mine would be too.

But Eurydike was seventeen; I was more than twice her age.

After Rhodia cleaned the babe, I took my niece out to my brother; he stood and carried the child over to view her in the sunlight. "Look at her, Jocasta! She's perfect!"

I enjoyed seeing Creon so happy, so content. Of late we had been drifting apart. This saddened me at times, yet I recognized that it was natural. Perhaps it was strange that we had stayed so close for so many years. But Creon's long bachelorhood and the loneliness of my first marriage, as well as the hours we spent together each day taking care of Thebes – these circumstances had kept us together.

Oedipus came down the colonnade toward us. "I heard that the child has arrived," he said. "Is everything well?"

"Wonderful," I reported. "She's a pretty little thing."

He smiled and put an arm around my shoulders. "It will be our turn next."

"Yes," said Creon, a frown creasing his forehead. He handed his daughter back to me, and I took the child back to her mother.

Creon was gone by the time I came out of the birthing-room; only my husband waited for me. Oedipus took my hands. "How's Eurydike?" he asked, leading me to a bench and helping me to sit down.

"She's fine."

Oedipus picked up the knucklebones and turned them over in his hand. "Your brother doesn't care for me."

I reached over to touch his face. "Of course he does! He knows how much you've done for Thebes."

But my husband would not be placated with a half-truth. "Acknowledging my work for the city and liking me are not the same thing. Was he jealous of Laius, too?"

"No, beloved. But Laius was not a good king, and Creon fulfilled many of his duties. You, on the other hand, have left Creon little to do."

Oedipus placed the knucklebones back on the table, positioning them so that they displayed the high throw. "Then we need to give him something to do – something that I can't."

"But what could that possibly be, my love?"

He looked down at his ankles. "I'll never win a footrace," he jested.

I laughed. "I don't think Creon has any interest in that."

"Well, more seriously, I can't go to Korinth. And as Thebes' king I should spend most of my time here."

So Oedipus and I asked Creon if he would like to journey to Korinth as our ambassador. Creon cocked an eyebrow and said, "Sending me away, Sister?" but his face lit up at the prospect of travel. So, after his daughter Megara was named, Creon left for Korinth, accompanying a shipment of leather and olive oil. He also carried gifts of gold jewelry for Oedipus' parents, and plans for broadening our trade agreements. Creon and the traders, and their wagons filled with great terracotta jars, would first travel west to the shore, then continue to Korinth by sea rather than chance the overland passage along the isthmus. That narrow neck of land was a favorite haunt of bandits. Perhaps someday, now that we had the alliance, Thebes and Korinth could root out the highwaymen, and make the isthmus road safe for travelers at last.

In a way I found life easier once my brother was away: for the first time in years I was free of his sarcastic comments and curled lip. Even Eurydike, although she missed him, was too busy with her children to suffer much from his absence.

Spring waxed into summer, and the child swelled within me. In the growing heat I tired easily, and spent much time relaxing in cool baths. Oedipus was unfailingly attentive; even while I lounged in the bath he sometimes came to sit with me, often using that time to soak his own ankles in warm water infused with herbs and salt. We traded kisses and stories and talked of our dreams for the child. Of course we both wanted a son, an heir; but my love said he would happy, too, with a little girl – especially if she looked like me.

As midsummer neared I made what I hoped was my last visit to the shrine of Artemis – my last visit during *this* pregnancy, I told myself. Rhodia said there was no reason I shouldn't bear a dozen more children. I knew she exaggerated, but still her words pleased me.

All through these months, no one spoke of my other pregnancy, so many years ago. I tried not to think of it; even after so long, the memory of my lost child tore my heart. When, from time to time, remembrance came unbidden, I felt my throat grow thick and my eyes fill with hot tears – but I blinked them back, laid my hands on my rounded belly, and reminded myself that *this* child I would keep. Oedipus wanted the baby as much as I, and would love our child with all his heart.

I had grown too large to move about easily; so, as Creon was away, Oedipus shouldered most of the burden of ruling Thebes. Each evening at dusk we sat together on the balcony to catch the breeze, fragrant now with the scent of hay drying in the fields, and share the events of the day.

"The workers are transporting limestone to repair the wall near the Ogygia Gate," he told me, after an afternoon of chariot riding with Demochares. "It should arrive tomorrow."

"Good," I said. "That was always been a weak point."

"It's amazing to watch, how they hew out blocks of stone and bring them here. If I hadn't seen it myself, I wouldn't have believed mere men could achieve such feats!" Oedipus proceeded to describe how the men employed their chisels and pry-bars, ropes and wheels, teams of mules and oxen to achieve the almost-impossible.

"It is marvelous," I agreed. But to me, my husband's enthusiasm for ruling was even more wonderful. How could it not be, after my years with Laius?

Merope appeared at the doorway. "My lord king, my lady queen," she said, "Lord Creon has returned from Korinth."

"Has he?" asked Oedipus, brightening at the mention of his childhood home. "Send him to us."

Creon stepped out onto the balcony. The sun was just set, the sky a deep glowing blue. Cicadas chirped in the evening air.

The king pulled himself to his feet to welcome his brother-in-law. "Creon! Was the journey successful?"

"No mishaps worth mentioning," Creon reported. "I have brought back many cartloads of fish, dried and pickled. As well as greetings from your parents."

"And?" I asked. From Creon's tone I could tell that he had more to say.

But Creon only took a seat, and asked Merope for some wine. "The most interesting place was Korinth. *Much* to be learned."

I studied my brother, who gazed unblinkingly at my husband. I ordered the servants away. Oedipus moved behind me, resting warm hands on my shoulders. Still Creon did not speak.

"Any news of Pelops?" I hazarded, hoping my question would elicit whatever Creon had to say. "We've heard rumors that his health is finally failing."

"Pelops?" said Creon, his eye still fixed on Oedipus. "Not that I've heard. The old man is like an olive tree. Age only seems to make him tougher."

"A pity," I said, shifting uncomfortably and leaning against Oedipus. "But at least we no longer pay tribute."

"Not this past year," Creon said, folding his arms across his chest. "But who knows about the future? We're rid of Laius, but who's to say that Pelops did not replace one tool with another?"

My husband's fingers tensed against my skin. I turned to look up at him.

"What are you suggesting, Creon?" said Oedipus. Despite the dim light, I saw his cheeks flush.

I whirled to face my brother. "What are you talking about? Oedipus brought us the Korinthian alliance *against* Pelops. Thebes did *not* send tribute to Pisa last year, and he is the reason."

Creon sipped his wine. "Perhaps. But you must admit, Oedipus, that Laius' death enriched you. You took his kingdom and his wife. You didn't bother with his horses or his chariot, but it would have looked a little *too* suspicious if you arrived driving the gold-worked chariot and that magnificent pair of bays."

I caught my breath. Creon knew!

Oedipus' eyes widened. Finally he stammered: "Do you – you mean to say that *I* killed Laius?"

"Do you claim not to know?" Creon leaned forward in his chair. "Did no one point him out to you at Delphi, along with the narrow road where you might arrange his downfall?"

I did not like Creon's accusatory tone. "How did you learn of this?"

Creon drained his wine-cup and set it on the table. "King Polybus arranged for me to see some of the sights near Korinth, and provided a chariot driver for the duration of my visit. A large fellow, with curly hair and a round mole on his cheek – I'm sure you remember him, Oedipus. He asked after you, told me he had once driven you to Delphi. One night over a krater of wine he fell to boasting, and he described a fight with an arrogant old bastard in a fine-worked chariot pulled by a pair of bays. So my question to you, my *king*," and the last word was coated with barbs, "have we substituted one of Pelops' puppets for another?"

I felt a pain along my side, sudden as lightning, but I did not let myself cry out. Instead, I gasped: "Creon, how could he be under Pelops' control? Think how different Oedipus is from Laius. The first thing Laius did was to rummage through the treasury and palace storerooms. Oedipus did nothing of the sort. Instead what we have – *because of Oedipus* – is a mutually beneficial arrangement with Korinth."

Oedipus took his hands from my shoulders and walked around to face me. "The man I killed was Laius, the last king of Thebes?"

Pain struck me again, as if his words were blades aimed at my gut. I shifted, pulling a cushion behind my back, delaying my response.

Creon's eyes glittered as he looked from my husband to me; he slapped the table so hard that his wine cup bounced. "So! The king is genuinely surprised, but this matter is no news to *you*, dear sister. Just the opposite of what I expected!"

Oedipus raised his voice. "You knew, didn't you? Why didn't you tell me? How could you keep this from me?"

Although he put three questions to me, Oedipus did not wait for a single response. He strode back into our chambers; I heard him fling open the outer door. I struggled to rise, then sank back in defeat. I was nine months pregnant. Although Oedipus never walked quickly, in my condition I could not chase him down the stairs.

Terror darted through me; would he come back? Or was this the end of my marriage to Oedipus, as abrupt as the end of my marriage to Laius?

"Creon!" I wailed. "How could you do this without telling me first?"

"How could *I*? *You're* the one who has known about this – *you're* the one who should have told *me!* And I would like to know why you didn't – why you thought you could keep this a secret from both of us!"

I opened my mouth to speak, but could not. Instead a cry escaped me.

"I'm sorry I came between you and your beloved husband, but how could I have known? I thought you told each other everything." Creon's voice was less angry now; he looked at me with concern. "Jocasta? What is it?"

I finally knew, and could speak at last. "The baby – is coming."

CHAPTER SEVENTEEN

My brother sent a servant to fetch Rhodia and her assistants while Merope helped me to the birthing-room. Eurydike joined us later, and in the company of these women, I paced back and forth between the pains.

The wavering lamplight cast distorted shadows on the room's painted walls; each time someone moved the straw underfoot rustled. Between contractions, each moving shadow, each shift and cough caught my attention. Again and again I looked to the door, its heavy wood construction designed to muffle sounds, and listened – hoping desperately to hear Oedipus' voice outside.

The door opened several times, but my husband did not enter, and I caught no glimpse of his auburn head in the corridor. Oedipus was more observant of tradition than I – did he keep his distance because of the custom banning men from the birthing-room? Or did he no longer want to see me?

Oedipus had no ancestral tie to Thebes. Hera help me – if I had offended him greatly enough, he could simply shake the city's dust from his sandals and leave.

But, then, was my silence the main problem? He had in fact killed King Laius, descended of Kadmos, a man who claimed to have been called by Apollo to rule over Thebes. My pious husband might conclude that he had blasphemed, and had no right to the throne.

"It was an accident!"

"What accident, my lady?" asked Merope, sponging my shoulders with cool water.

I had not realized that I had spoken aloud. "Nothing," I gasped, and released my anguish with a wail that coincided with the oncoming contraction.

Was my second marriage now finished?

Laius cast me out after less than a night; the pain of that rejection had been difficult enough to overcome. And that had been only a girlish infatuation with a man who did not merit it. Over the past year with Oedipus I had come to know real love, love for a man who shared my throne and my life as a true partner, a passion that had grown with each golden day and each sweet night.

Never again would I find another man like Oedipus.

Between the thought-obliterating pains of labor my mind raced. I sobbed, not knowing whether any or all of the things I imagined were true. The night wore on, the starlit sky through the window giving way to a gray pre-dawn light which seemed forbidding and cold to me even though the day would surely grow hot. I sweated, paced, and wept, trapped by the child within me.

At last Rhodia helped me into the birthing chair a final time. "This is it, now – push, my lady! Push!"

For a time I knew nothing but the pain; I welcomed it as a release from worry.

"A girl!" Rhodia's announcement was followed by a high, thin cry.

With sweat stinging my eyes I watched the midwives bathe the child in a terracotta basin. Eurydike then took the infant outside for presentation to the king.

She returned almost at once, the babe still in her arms.

"King Oedipus is not outside just now," reported my sister-in-law. "Don't worry, Jocasta – some pressing business, the guards say. I'm sure he'll be back soon." She smoothed the slight frown from her pretty face, and smiled. "Here, my lady. Hold your new daughter."

Eurydike lay the small bundle in my arms. The child was red and wrinkled and weighed almost nothing. How could this tiny thing have made me so heavy for so long?

299

I looked at my daughter and tried to feel love, but could not overcome my crushing sadness. Oedipus should have been outside the door, awaiting the birth of his first child, but he was gone.

Where, and for how long? Forever?

Hot tears flowed down my face. My arms lost all strength, and the child almost slipped from my grasp. Hastily Eurydike took the babe.

"My lady queen, you're weak. You should drink this." One of the midwives handed me a cup of herbed wine. I brought the mixture to my lips, and swallowed as much as I could. But my nerveless fingers dropped the vessel; it fell to the floor with a dull thud, its contents mingling with the blood that stained the straw beneath me.

"She must lie down," said Rhodia. Merope came instantly to my side. The two women, their hands gentle but strong, all but carried me over to the bed at the corner of the room. I collapsed onto it, exhausted and drained.

Eurydike, crooning over my little daughter, looked anxiously at the senior midwife. "Shouldn't she suckle the child?"

"My lady, if you can," said Rhodia. She took the swaddled bundle from Eurydike and positioned the babe at my breast. The infant opened her tiny lips and sucked; warm life drained from me into her mouth.

At last she seemed satisfied, and I pushed her slightly away.

"Don't you want to hold her, Jocasta?" asked Eurydike.

I shook my head, salt tears bitter on my lips.

My sister-in law hesitated a moment, looking puzzled. Then she said, "You're very tired." She picked up the baby – already asleep – and began humming again.

Light began to seep in through the curtains Rhodia had drawn to cover the window. Carts rumbled past the palace, and cocks crowed their morning greeting to Apollo. My city was waking, preparing for the day.

If only Oedipus would come!

I stared dully at the door, hoping against hope.

In time my eyelids slipped shut and I slept.

"Jocasta?"

The voice was low and familiar, but was I dreaming?

I turned over and saw my husband sitting on a stool by the bed. "Are you really here?" I asked hoarsely.

The sky was azure through the open window; it had to be well past noon. Bright sunbeams brought a copper glow to Oedipus' russet hair. "Yes, my love, I'm here."

Tears of relief welled in my eyes. Oedipus first took my hand; then, as my sobs continued, he lay down beside me and gathered me into his arms. He rocked me, kissing my brow, stroking my hair, until my shuddering stopped.

We were alone, but others must have come and gone while I slept. The blood-soaked straw had been swept away. The room smelled clean, and someone had put fresh linen sheets around and under me. On a small table near the bed was a basin of water and a sponge; on the far table stood a pitcher, goblets, and a tray of cheese and olives.

Oedipus pushed a strand of hair out of my face. "I'm sorry I wasn't here when the baby came."

"You're here now," I said, clutching him with my feeble strength.

Oedipus ran one hand down my back, then locked his eyes with mine. "Jocasta. Did I kill Laius? And did you know?"

Here were the questions I had feared, the questions I should have answered earlier. My voice shakier than before, I answered. "Yes, love. The man you killed outside Delphi was Laius. I recognized him from your description, our first night together."

"I killed your husband? Apollo's chosen king of Thebes?"

"He was not my husband. And he was no true king of Thebes."

For a moment Oedipus did not speak. "I don't understand."

"Then I will tell you." I bade Oedipus fetch me a cup, for my mouth was dry as dust, and while he poured I composed my thoughts. Wetting my lips with barley water, I told him of my life with Laius: his drunken outbursts, his failure to perform his kingly duties, his gluttonous lethargy. How his impotence had begun on our wedding night, and afterward he refused to share my bed. Finally I described the wealth he had robbed from Thebes each year, and sent in tribute to Pelops.

"Why did you not tell me this before?" asked my husband.

"I didn't want to remember. Living with Laius was miserable; with you, life is so wonderful. Why look back? I can't change it."

Oedipus' shoulders relaxed, and he kissed my forehead. "My dearest! How you must have suffered." He held me tight for a moment, then drew back, his blue eyes serious. "But why did you hide the truth from me?"

"I did tell you the truth that night, though not all of it: I feared that if the incident became known, it would be used against you. And – forgive me, my love, but I didn't want you troubled by the identity of the man you had killed. I was afraid you might decline the contest. I wanted you so much! I couldn't let anything stand in our way."

He smiled. "Nothing could have stopped me." Then he paused, worry touching his handsome features once more. "But it does seem ill-omened, to have killed the king of Thebes, while our two cities were at peace."

I remembered what my father the Tiresias had said, that the killer of Laius must be brought to justice. But I recalled many other things as well.

"There was a prophecy about me, a long time ago," I said, and told him of the old Tiresias' words: my husband would be the greatest king Thebes ever had; I would love him dearly; we would have many children together. "That king *must* be you, my love. It certainly wasn't Laius! You freed Thebes – and me – from a terrible situation. How could the gods be anything but pleased?"

Before he could reply, a knock came at the door. Merope entered, carrying a linen-wrapped bundle. "Excuse me, my lady queen, but the babe is hungry."

"Give her to me," Oedipus said, holding out his arms.

Merope gave the mewling child to her father. Entranced, he stared at the small scrap of life. Then, his blue eyes shining, he handed the infant to me. I put her to my nipple and she began to suck.

"I'll fetch some hot food, my lady queen," said Merope, and inclined her head before sidling out the door.

Oedipus reached out, not to me, but to stroke his newborn daughter's back. Then he spoke. "You must be right: there can be no curse. How else but with the gods' favor could we have produced anything so wonderful?"

Despite my husband's words, I knew Laius' death troubled him. He went to the temple of Apollo that very day to make another expiation; as he told me, the atonement months ago at Orchomenos had cleansed him only of an arrogant stranger's blood. Now he must wash away the guilt of killing a king. At sunset he went to the temple and sacrificed a red-spotted bull, and bathed in the Kastellian spring. At my urging, he shared the reason for his atonement only with the god.

The next day he seemed more at peace with himself, but still quiet and withdrawn. Creon, perhaps realizing the extent of the damage, came to my aid. Over a private evening meal in the royal chambers, my brother argued that the gods had arranged the chance meeting on the road. "Apollo must have grown tired of Laius' drunkenness. And besides, isn't it the duty of the king to give his life for his city's well-being?"

I laid my hand on my husband's arm. "Surely the gods wished it so."

For a long moment Oedipus was silent, staring into the depths of his wine-cup. At last he said, "You were right, my love. It fits the prophecy." He looked up, his eyes brighter than they had been since Creon returned from Korinth. "The gods *did* mean me to be king of Thebes."

I didn't understand the shift in his thoughts, but heard his words gratefully nonetheless.

Creon blinked; his face showed genuine curiosity. "Certainly," he said. "You prevailed against the Sphinx. What has that to do with Laius?"

"We have long memories, in Korinth. In ancient times, a city's queen reigned all throughout her childbearing years, but kings ruled only one year at a time. Each fall, at harvest time, the year's king had to die. He would call forth the challenger, and go to meet his death. The man who killed the old year's king would be king for the next year." Oedipus paused; perhaps he feared the implications of what he had next to say. "I met Laius outside Delphi in the fall, at harvest time. And he called his death upon himself."

My brother's mouth twisted in ill-concealed amusement. "More likely, it was the same king each year – and some poor fool dressed in last year's robe got the sword."

Oedipus' brows lowered; I knew he took the story seriously. To thwart any argument over tradition I said quickly: "Those days are long gone. Beyond the memories of the oldest grandmother's grandmother." I clasped Oedipus' left hand in both of mine. "And I mean you to be king of Thebes much longer than a year."

His blue eyes met mine, and he smiled at me. "And I want nothing more than to be your husband, lady, the father of your children and protector of Thebes. Now I know beyond doubt that is my purpose in life – and that is why the gods caused me to meet Laius that day, why they fanned the flames of his anger." At that moment, seeing myself mirrored in his bright eyes, I felt more loved and more certain of him than before.

A few days later, we proclaimed the babe's name to the city: Antigone.   And through the long summer days and warm nights I nursed my daughter, rocking her in my arms. Yet I felt none of the closeness I had anticipated. She was a colicky baby, and my patience with her fussing and crying quickly wore thin. Often I found myself amazed by Eurydike's fortitude; when I tired of the baby's screams my sister-in-law would take her, walking her around until at long last the child hiccupped into silence, and even smiled. How could young Eurydike manage this miracle, when I couldn't?   Were my maternal skills weak because I had never known my own mother?

Rhodia told me if I wanted to conceive again, I should give the baby to a wet nurse. And so I did, with a pang of guilt, but also with a sense of liberation. When Antigone was offered another woman's nipple, at first she looked confused; but as she began to suckle I thought I detected relief on her face as well. Was the nurse's milk sweeter than mine? I feared that I was failing as a woman.

But Oedipus did not mind, and in fact welcomed the absence of the infant from our room at night. I remember one warm evening, the linen curtains pulled back to admit the breeze; after long session of lovemaking Oedipus lay wrapped in my arms, dozing lightly, his head between my breasts. His breath was soft and warm against my skin. I ran my fingers through his tousled russet curls, admiring his beauty in the golden lamplight. Was I a poor mother, because I cherished his peaceful, sleeping face more than the baby's? I decided not. In him I had found a true partner, the completion of my heart; our children would deepen that bond, but never supplant it.

Before long I conceived again. Oedipus and I made sure that we informed Creon and Eurydike immediately. We held a private lunch with the children to celebrate the news.

"I'm sure this time it will be a boy," said Eurydike, helping herself to a third slice of beef. "I've got a feeling." She glanced up to see that her son Haemon had toddled towards the sunlit balcony. Hurriedly she dropped her napkin and dashed over to follow him. "But you may regret it, Jocasta!" she called over her shoulder. "Boys are nothing but trouble!"

"Ah, my husband loves his little girl," I said, helping five-month-old Antigone to sit up.

"That I do," Oedipus agreed, and he lifted our daughter from my arms and swung her high into the air. Antigone shrieked with joy.

My brother took a sip of wine. "Sons *can* be dangerous for a young king."

"Creon, you're worse than Father – always finding the worst side to everything," I said. "Is Haemon a threat to you?"

My brother's son, more a danger to himself than to anyone else, was trying to scale the balustrade. Eurydike picked up the child and held him so that he could see the sights himself. Then their daughter Megara wailed and Creon had to do the same with her.

"I'm not a king," Creon called back to me.

Antigone coughed, dribbling spittle down her small round chin, and began to squall; Oedipus handed her to me. I wiped her face with a soft cloth and lifted her to my shoulder, patting her sweat-damp back in an attempt to soothe her.

"Haemon would never threaten his father," Eurydike said firmly. She kissed the top of her son's head. "Nor any sons that you might have, Jocasta. Creon, how can you think such horrible things?"

"I try to think of possible dangers, so that we can avert them. And it's not so unthinkable. Pelops killed his father-in-law!"

We all stopped to think of the many scandals in King Pelops' family. Antigone was finally quiet, and I lowered her to lie in my lap. Her face was red, and she made unhappy noises as she chewed on my finger with her pink gums.

Eurydike brought Haemon back out of the sun, and came to fuss over Antigone. "You poor little girl! What's wrong, my sweet baby? Here, Jocasta, let me take her." She gathered the her into her arms, balancing the child just above her own newly-swelling belly. "Oh, my little Tig-Tig-Tigone! There, there, nothing's wrong..." She glanced back at her husband, reproof in her dark eyes. "*We're* nothing like old Pelops and his horrible family," said Eurydike.

I had little faith in Eurydike's political acumen, but I hoped she was right.

I made my trips to the temple of Artemis, and the pregnancy progressed easily. This time, during the birth, Oedipus remained outside the door, once poking his head in to assure himself that all was well. Eurydike's premonition proved false: the second child was also a girl. Ismene was sweet-tempered baby, all smiles and gurgles, and prettier than her elder sister. Although suckling Ismene was a pleasure, I soon found a wet nurse for my second daughter. Time was passing quickly, and my womb sensed its urgent pressure. When my attendant Lilika – who still seemed scarcely more than a child – left my service to marry a wealthy pottery-trader, I felt only too aware of my advancing years. I was nine-and-thirty, and my husband the king had no heir.

My next pregnancy was an ordeal; I grew huge at once, and was constantly ill. I kept down nothing but barley bread and goat's milk; my back ached incessantly; my belly swelled ever larger but my arms and legs thinned and my face grew gaunt, as though the child within fed upon me. I had never known such discomfort; there was no respite. Rhodia ordered me to keep to my bed, for the sake of my health and that of the child. Unable to attend my duties, I yielded myself to my suffering. I was sorry to miss the building projects going on beyond the walls – the new royal tomb under construction for the glory of my family, the improvements to the temple of Apollo – but my health did not permit me to consider going. My absence from public view troubled the citizens of Thebes; common people's sacrifices to the gods on my behalf grew more numerous each day.

Oedipus kissed me, and said laughingly that I would birth a Titan, but when he thought I was not looking worry creased his features. Five months into the pregnancy Rhodia declared that two babies shared my womb. How she could tell this, I did not know; but I thought it must take more than one set of feet and fists to pummel me so from within.

As the final months wore on and I grew still larger, I began to fear for my life. I was forty, suffering through a pregnancy that would try the strength of a nineteen-year-old. At Merope's urging, I made ever richer offerings to Artemis, though I could not manage the walk to her hillside altar; I had to be carried on a litter. I was grateful that I bore this growing burden in the cool of early spring; in summer's heat I would have melted into a quivering puddle.

But one afternoon Rhodia sat at my bedside, wiping my brow with a cool cloth, and reminded me of words the old Tiresias had spoken so long ago. "Don't you remember what she said, my lady queen? You are fated to bear many children." A smile lit her freckled face and she brushed a curl, brown streaked with gray, back from her forehead. "You've just had a late start! Twins are the gods' way of putting you back on course."

But the course was so difficult! Although everyone spoke encouragingly – even Creon, who looked almost as anxious as Oedipus during his visits to my bedside – I knew that they all worried.

Even I. Although I felt ready to burst, I feared the oncoming birth nearly as much as I longed for it. Would it mean my death?

But I could neither hurry nor postpone that day; and finally, it came. The contractions began at dawn, and I was taken to the birthing-room. Time crawled by, but the babies did not come. Rhodia and her assistants made me walk, walk, walk, the scattered straw sharp and rough against my swollen feet. The pains grew worse, like knives slitting through me, like millstones crushing my overripe body, and still the babies did not come.

Eurydike gasped in horror at my worsening screams, until Rhodia told an apprentice take her out of the room. One young assistant flinched; Rhodia snapped at her, ordering her to control herself. Merope brought water to soothe my parched mouth, but it made me retch.

From time to time Oedipus pounded on the birthing-room door, demanding to speak again with Rhodia.

After a day and a night I had passed beyond the point of pain into utter misery and exhaustion. Though Merope's voice remained calm as ever I could see fear in her dark eyes, and I thought then I would surely die. I sagged limply back into her strong arms while Rhodia washed her hands with olive oil and sour wine; then the midwife cried, "Push, Jocasta! Push, by Artemis and all that is holy!" and Rhodia's strong hands reached far up inside me and grasped a pair of tiny feet. The first child was in the breech position, but the midwife finally pulled him out. When he cried lustily and the women cheered I found the very last of my strength to push out the second child, who emerged head first. As he fell from my body I felt finally emptied, hollow, and my consciousness rushed out with the blood.

I woke later in my own bed. There was a cool, damp cloth on my forehead, and comforting warm fingers caressed my hand.

"My love," Oedipus said. I opened my eyes to meet his gaze: his eyes were reddened, ringed with dark circles. "How do you feel?"

Even though I had slept I was still exhausted, and speech came only with difficulty. "Weak." I shifted a bit, and he helped me to sit up. Someone – Merope, I think – settled pillows behind my back. A wad of linen cloth was wrapped between my legs. It felt wet.

My husband leaned over and kissed me softly on my cracked lips. "I've never been so afraid," he whispered. "You were fighting for your life, and I couldn't defend you." His face was pale as unbleached linen under the growth of a day's beard. Tears sparkled in his eyes. "There was nothing I could do but pray. By all the gods, Jocasta, I love you. I should have gone mad if I had lost you."

"I'm here, my love." This time I kissed him, and he clutched me desperately to his chest. Weak though I was, he seemed to draw strength from my embrace. When he released me his face was calmer, his eyes clearer.

"The children?" I asked. "Did they live?"

He laughed then, and my soul lifted. "I've never seen two such boys! No wonder they gave you so much trouble – they're already big enough for their name-day!"

"I want to see them," I said, taking my eyes from his face for the first time since waking. I looked around the room, and saw to my great joy Rhodia and her apprentice Nysa, each carrying a small bundle. They came to my bedside, and laid a child on either side of me. Their tiny faces, looking altogether alike, were red and wrinkled. Two pairs of blue eyes wandered vaguely, while each head was topped with a shock of hair, red and shining as polished copper.

"You see, my lady," said the apprentice. "They're perfect!"

Rhodia grinned. "And absolutely healthy. As you will be, in a month's time. But you have lost a lot of blood. To restore your strength, you must eat plenty of meat and vegetables, and drink as much water as you can hold." She pressed an alabaster cup into my hand. The water tasted sweeter than honey. I drained the cup and held it out for more; Rhodia nodded approval. Then she gave me a piece of bread soaked in milk; as I ate I felt a little strength returning.

Oedipus smiled, and reached for the nearest baby. "Ah, what a fine boy you are! What shall we name you two, eh? Prometheus and Atlas, after the titans?"

I laughed, and cradled the other babe in my elbow; he made smacking sounds with his mouth, so I gave him a nipple. "He's too small to carry the world on his shoulders."

"Today he is. But he will grow." Then he looked down at the child in his arms. "And so will you, my little son."

Even by the tenth day, I was barely strong enough to stand for the ceremony. Eurydike helped me to carry the babies, but I myself knelt and laid them at Oedipus' feet. He raised the first of the two boys, elder by a few scant moments, high before the crowd in the megaron. "Citizens of Thebes! Behold my firstborn son, Eteokles!"

My knees shook as I stood, but I felt no new rush of blood between my legs; I muttered thanks to Artemis.

The company applauded Thebes' new prince, and I heard one old man in the front: "Takes after his grandfather, he does! His hair is redder than the king's – he's as flame-topped as old Menoeceus used to be!"

"If only the old man could see this grandson," said another.

"Where is the Tiresias, anyway?"

The question, asked by someone behind me, was also in my mind, for I had expected my father to attend the twins' naming-ceremony. I glanced at Creon, standing behind Oedipus, and raised my eyebrows. Creon shrugged slightly.

But I had other concerns. Oedipus handed Eteokles to me, and then lifted high the second babe. "And my beloved second son, Polynikes! As his name attests, he will bring many victories to Thebes; may he be ever a strength and a support to his brother."

Again there was applause, and the women in the hall sighed to see the second child as whole and healthy as the first. But amidst the tumult I heard one man's voice: "A twin brother for the king's firstborn son? That's trouble. He'd have done better to expose the second babe."

I whirled, seeking the source of these hateful words. Creon laid a calming hand on my shoulder. "Jocasta. You know some are bound to say it."

"Never," I hissed, clutching my elder son close. "I will never give up another child."

He slipped his arm around me, and reached his other hand across to tickle Eteokles' chin. "Of course not. But some folk are bound to see twins as a bad omen. And, superstition aside, sister, as your children grow you must make it absolutely clear to both of these boys who is heir to the throne of Thebes. Or you *will* have trouble."

Oedipus, still holding Polynikes, gave the order for the feast and then walked back to us. Glancing at our faces, he asked, "Is anything wrong?"

"Not really," said Creon, giving his attention now to the other twin. "Jocasta was wondering what happened to our father."

My husband looked down at me. "My love, you're tired. There's no need for you to attend the feast."

Earlier I had been eager to participate, in order to show off my boys to the citizens and the visiting dignitaries. But Oedipus was right; I was exhausted. I followed, climbing the stairs slowly and painfully, as Nysa and Merope carried the twins back to my private chambers. There I settled on my deep-pillowed couch, grateful for the fire, and dined alone on charcoaled beef, cheese, and barley bread. When my own hunger was sated, I picked up Eteokles and brought him to my breast.

How dare that old man suggest that I expose one of my children! The thought made me tense, and I had to force myself to relax so as not to disrupt the flow of milk.

"The Tiresias is here," announced Merope. At my word, she led my father inside.

I settled one son down into the ivory-inlaid crib and picked up the other. "You missed the naming ceremony."

"That is so," said my father, putting his staff carefully down on the floor and taking a seat. He held out his hand when Merope offered refreshment. "I have many claims on my time."

Certainly the Tiresias' life was a busy one, but the demands on the prophet of Apollo could be no greater than those on a mother of four and the ruling queen of Thebes. Yet I bit back my remark, and watched Father slowly chew his bread and dill-spiced cheese. If he was eating, I thought, he was not preparing to prophesize.

"Would you like to hold your new grandsons?"

Father smiled crookedly, showing a new gap in his teeth. "Yes."

I nodded to Merope, who picked up Eteokles and positioned him in my father's arms. "Please be careful, my lord," she said. "Mind his head." Eteokles' coppery thatch of hair contrasted vividly with the Tiresias' black robe.

"He's so small!" remarked my father.

I laughed. "He did not seem small when I birthed him!"

"No, I suppose not." He explored the infant's face with his free hand, and my stomach tensed. Just so had the old Tiresias touched me, before she made the fateful prophecy.

My tension interrupted Polynikes' suckling; he fussed briefly and I lifted him to my shoulder, stroking his warm, soft back.

But Father seemed fully engrossed in acquainting himself with his other new grandson. "A fine crop of hair, for a baby! What color is it?"

"Red, as yours once was," I told him.

"Hmph!" grunted the Tiresias, but a smile betrayed his pleasure.

At a gesture from me, Merope took my other son and placed him in the crook of Father's free arm. "Here's the other babe," she said. "His name is Polynikes."

The Tiresias sat carefully with his grandsons, unable to move. "Difficult, to hold twins."

More so to bear them, I thought, but kept my mouth shut.

"And they will be difficult for Thebes – they will bring destruction and sorrow."

Despite my weak condition, I leapt up and grabbed my boys from the blind man's arms. "I won't listen to this! Just the sort of horrible predictions you made at Haemon's birth! Can't you find a blessing for your grandsons?"

He spread his gnarled hands. "Daughter, I say only what the god tells me."

"Then perhaps you should not listen!"

"My lady –" Merope took one baby from me and helped me back to my couch. "My lady," she whispered, "you're upset, but you must not speak so to the Tiresias."

Sitting down among my cushions, I shook with anger. But my fury quickly changed to fear. After Niobe had insulted the last Tiresias, her children had been cursed with death. Could this prophet – for all that he was my father – afflict me and mine likewise?

But he did not curse me; instead his mouth softened, his shoulders sagged. The prophet metamorphosed once more into my father. "Jocasta, your sons will bring both joy and sorrow to Thebes."

"Father, let's speak of this no more. And let's not proclaim your vision to the city."

His lips trembled; he opened his mouth, then closed it again – and I could see that my father was still my father, and struggled against some of the words the god gave him to say. Then he inclined his head. "As you wish, my daughter. But I can't say now what Apollo may require in the future."

My sons would bring both joy and sorrow to Thebes. Well, was that so strange? Didn't every child bring both joy and sorrow to its parents?

Yet to me, Eteokles and Polynikes brought nothing but happiness. I needed a wet nurse once more to help feed the growing babies but still I nursed them myself, for near on two years. And whether it was that, or my age, or something damaged within me birthing the twins, Rhodia could not say; but I did not conceive again. Oedipus declared he was satisfied with two fair daughters and two sturdy sons. "Thebes has had one Niobe already. It does not need another. Jocasta is by far the better queen," he said lightly one night, and kissed my cheek. "The gods will give us another child if it's their will."

I ran my palms down his chest, then dropped my hands to his hard-muscled thighs and said: "Shall we try our luck?"

Our love-making was sweet, and I did not regret my barren womb. In truth, I was relieved: bearing the twins had nearly killed me. Besides, I had so much to do. Thebes was ever growing in size – our population tallied nearly eight thousand! – and Oedipus and I had to supervise the planting of new orchards, meet with the Master of the Herds, and provide laborers to repair the roads after the damaging winter rains. With the strength of our Korinthian alliance and the strife in the Peloponnesus, Thebes' influence increased.

In addition to my royal responsibilities, I had maternal duties, supervising the education of my children. All four learned to read both the Kretan hand and that of the mainland. They could name the cities and rulers of the lands surrounding the Middle Sea by heart and recite the history of Thebes. Antigone had a talent for weaving, while graceful Ismene had a lovely voice. The boys, of course, were most interested in sport.

My sons came into the world large, and grew quickly. They soon vanquished even their older cousins in wrestling and boxing; they were fleet of foot, and superb with both discus and javelin. Their aim with the bow was keen – and they ached to drive chariots, though Oedipus forbade it until they were older. We planned a grand celebration for their twelfth birthday: a hunt, and then a festival dedicated to the gods.

A few days before the festival, Mnesikles arrived from Korinth; he planned to report the twins' birthday festivities back to their grandparents. The crinkles around the emissary's brown eyes were deeper, but he seemed as kind as ever. And this time, besides loving messages from the king and queen of Korinth, he brought us the long-awaited word of old Pelops' death. The old tyrant's passing marked the end of an age. Thebes sighed relief in the warm breeze of spring, and with lightened spirits prepared for the princes' celebration.

The boys began their twelfth birthday with a hunt that started at dawn, and although they were eager to handle boar-spears, Demochares led them after safer quarry. Before mid-day runners informed us they were returning safe with a stag; Oedipus, my daughters and I received them at the Chloris Gate. Ismene's rosy cheeks paled at the sight of the dead beast, its black tongue protruding from its lolling head, but Antigone looked on impassively.

Unlike her sister, Antigone always held her emotions in check; she rarely smiled. I knew she meant to hide her crooked teeth, but she succeeded only in seeming dour. And lately her young face was marred with red blemishes. I could not understand it – at her age my skin had been fresh and clear, like Ismene's. I bade her scrub well, three times a day with cold water, but nothing helped much. I hoped she would outgrow it with time.

Antigone was often reluctant to appear in public, especially side-by-side with her younger, prettier sister. But today she and I escaped our usual argument: nothing could have made her miss the boys' birthday celebration, and disappoint her brother Polynikes. I could not say what it was that bound her closer to him than to Eteokles; but they seemed to share a sense of dissatisfaction with the world. Just as a common light-heartedness allied the other twin with his sister Ismene.

My sons made a breathtaking sight: robust, strong, only a hand-span shorter than their father these days; they seemed to grow taller by the hour. Their fair cheeks were flushed with exercise and excitement. Even at this distance I could see Eteokles' blue eyes, contrasting beautifully with his red cheeks and coppery curls. He grinned and waved. "See the stag I brought you, Mother!"

Polynikes frowned. "My arrow struck first!"

"But whose spear found the mark?" Eteokles laughed.

"No question that it was yours, Eteokles," said Demochares.

My husband came between the twins, and wrapped one arm around each. "Sons, sons! You are a *team* – and together you have brought down a fine stag. A fair accomplishment for grown men – quite a victory for your first hunt!" He squeezed them tightly, and his face beamed with pride. "Come now, let's give thanks to the gods!"

As I led my daughters away from the gate I heard Antigone mutter, "He thinks everything is his, because he was born earlier."

I did not like this; but, deciding to let the matter drop until later, I only shot her a warning glance and settled into my sedan chair. The pillows were soft and luxurious, gold-and-crimson linen stuffed with lamb's wool – a gift from my Korinthian in-laws. Four strong bearers lifted me to their shoulders and the crowd cheered the hunters forward through the streets of Thebes.

To celebrate our boys' birthday Oedipus and I planned a plethora of offerings: to Zeus as king of the Gods and God of kings; to Apollo as the patron god of Thebes; to Demeter, asking her blessing upon the newly-sown fields; and to Hera and Artemis for favoring our marriage with healthy children. We would make a procession through the city streets, going to each of Thebes' seven gates, before heading to the agora to offer the sacrifice.

Oedipus led the procession in his chariot at a stately pace; the twins walked just behind him, strutting proudly alongside the servants who carried their quarry, its legs lashed firmly to a pole. Then came Creon, his shy gray-eyed son Haemon at his side. I noticed that Antigone had fallen into step beside her tall young cousin; not for the first time, I considered speaking to Creon about betrothing those two. Perhaps an engagement would sweeten Antigone's temper.

Just ahead of my swaying sedan chair walked Megara and Eurydike. Ismene was helping her aunt and cousin watch over Creon's brood. The youngest, Pyrrha, toddled behind her mother, and Ismene kept the girl from straying after a brown-spotted puppy.

Flute-song swirled behind my chair, which swayed softly in the sun. My eyelids grew heavy, and I feared I would fall asleep. That would not do, for the queen to drowse in front of the whole city! I bit the insides of my cheeks, strained to keep my eyes wide as I could, and tried to attend to Oedipus' words as we approached the Ogygia Gate. "My people, rejoice! Hera has blessed your king and queen with two fine sons – let's ask her sister Demeter for a double harvest in the coming year! Hello, Metron – how many calves were born to your herd this spring?"

Creon also addressed prominent citizens in the crowd, chatting in particular with the traveling merchants, to learn their news of abroad. One man gave Ismene a string of seed beads, dyed bright red, which my daughter generously looped around her cousin Pyrrha's neck. Creon clapped the man on the shoulder, and I felt sure he had learned something interesting.

People threw flower-petals at our feet, and each street seemed livelier than the last. Soon I heard a crippled basket weaver tell his shop mates why: "Free wine, he's giving! At the end of the procession are men with amphorae!"

I chuckled and shook my head, and hoped that it was well watered. But Oedipus would have seen to that.

Then we turned and headed up a steep hill back towards the agora, where the boys would offer their prize at the altar. This street was strangely quiet, until we reached a group clustered outside the door of one well-kept building.

Oedipus called out, "Come, people of Thebes! Join me in celebrating my sons' birthday!"

A wail rang out from within the house, soon joined by another. My bearers stopped abruptly, and I rocked forward in my chair, fully awake.

"Citizens," called Creon, "what is the trouble?"

A plump woman ran out of the house, her clothing soiled and her hair in disarray. She pushed her way toward me. "My lady queen, save us! Oh, save us!"

The woman's face was unfamiliar, but I knew the voice. I peered down at her until recognition came.

"Lilika?" I asked. "Lilika, what's wrong?"

She fell to her knees before my chair. "Plague."

CHAPTER EIGHTEEN

Plague.

The news spread back through our procession quick as brushfire, and with as little sound: crackling whispers, as though none dared voice the word aloud. My own heart raced; my fear centered on my sons, my daughters. I wanted them away, shielded from danger.

But I was queen – I could not abandon my people. Oedipus and I needed to protect them, to comfort them: that was our duty. And first, we must better understand what was wrong.

May the gods protect us, I thought, signaling the bearers to lower my chair. Once they had settled its carved legs on the ground, the lead man helped me out step out onto the pebbled street.

I walked over to where Lilika had collapsed, and the people parted to let me through. She had fallen face down on the ground, her skirts tumbled about her legs, exposing calves covered with an ugly red rash. I gestured to my lead bearer that he should turn her over. Although visibly reluctant to touch her – his usually steady hand shook – he obeyed, bending over and pulling at Lilika's shoulder.

Lilika rolled onto her back; the crowd gasped as they saw her yellow skin, her inflamed, staring eyes, and a trickle of blood at the edge of her mouth.

"She's dead!" cried Eurydike.

Gazing down woman who had once been my maidservant, I saw that it was so.

Eurydike stood frozen in horror, clutching the hand of her daughter Megara. Ismene lifted little Pyrrha into her arms, as though to protect her from the evil humors. My eldest daughter turned wide blue eyes upon me, but said nothing. When I touched

Antigone's shoulder, I felt her trembling beneath the silver-trimmed jacket.

The people milled in confusion, some approaching to gawk, others edging away out of dread. "Is it a plague?" asked some. "Has Apollo cursed us?" Others cried out as Lilika had done: "Queen Jocasta, help us!"

But I did not know the answers to their questions; nor had I been able to help Lilika. I felt frightened, helpless, but these emotions I dared not show.

"Who else is ill?" I demanded, and then added: "Has anyone else died?"

Answers came: "The family of Stavros is sick," called someone, and a woman added, "I think some of the potters are ill." A third voice called, "Gods help us, they'll all die!"

"Make way for Lord Creon!" shouted Demochares. The jostling of the stalled procession before me increased. My brother and the herald made their way through the crowd, and soon Creon was at my side.

He grasped my arm. "Are others sick too?"

"I think so – I don't know how many."

"We need more information," said my brother.

"Yes," I said, as my capacity to think returned. "Is it only in this neighborhood? Or are there cases throughout Thebes?"

Creon turned to Demochares: "I'll arrange for parties to investigate the rest of the city. You stay here and look into these houses – start with this one."

Demochares turned to push his way through the crowd, but an old woman clutched his arm.

"Don't go inside! That house is cursed!"

Creon once told me that Demochares never showed fear in the hunt. But at the old woman's words, he hesitated. Then he shook her off, and with an expression as hard as the stones that formed the city walls, he entered the house where Lilika had lived.

Cries from the crowd followed him, then turned and accused Creon:

"You're sending him to his death!"

"We'll all be cursed by the gods!"

Creon raised his voice and grasped the hilt of his sword. "People! Citizens! We must find out how many are afflicted, so that we can decide what—"

But the people interrupted him, with a totally different cry: "The king! The king will save us!"

Again there was commotion before us, as my husband, leaning on his staff, made his way back to us. After the strain of the morning's hunt and the long procession through the city, his ankles had to ache, but he maintained a strong, steady gait. He came to my side and squeezed my hand, hard, as if touching me gave him strength. Despite the worry that creased in his brow, he addressed the crowd with a voice that was calm and confident: "Good people of Thebes! We must not disturb anyone's sorrow with my sons' celebration. But I offer this hope to allay your fears: we are on our way to make a sacrifice to the gods. My sons will offer the full bounty of their hunt to Apollo in prayer that you and your families may be healed. We will do whatever the gods ask to spare Thebes."

"Yes!" cried some, and "The king will save us!" called others. Creon murmured to me he would supervise the investigation of the rest of the city, while Oedipus ordered a guardsman to run ahead and inform the priests waiting in the agora that there would only be a sacrifice, no festivities – and that everyone should go to their homes once the rites were complete. I directed my bearers to find some way to carry Lilika's body to the hill of Amphion, just beyond the Kleodoxa Gate. I would walk beside my husband.

The people parted to let us through, until we reached the
ne procession. Eurydike, herding her younger children,

followed right behind. Oedipus squeezed my hand, released it, and then set a measured pace.

Instead of music and singing, there was only the sound of shuffling feet. But the people were calmer, looking to be led by their king during this catastrophe. My sons came up to walk beside me: Eteokles on my right and Polynikes on my left. Although their successful hunt was another step toward manhood, they let me take their hands. They seemed to understand that I needed reassurance that they were free from illness, full of vitality and life.

Polynikes glanced back at the servants who carried the prize of the morning's hunt and whispered, "Must we really give the whole stag to Apollo? Not just the bones and fat?"

I nodded. "Yes. It's your duty as princes. We must offer Apollo all that we have, and forget the feast. Your people come first."

Polynikes sighed, but said nothing more, which I thought good enough for a boy just turned twelve.

I only hoped the stag would satisfy the gods! Oedipus had promised that we would do *whatever* the gods might demand – but sometimes the gods exacted a terrible price. The thought chilled me.

We reached the agora at last. The space was already half-filled with people, and priests and priestesses were moving about. The runner we sent ahead had reached them, for they were taking down the festive wreaths of leaves and flowers. Acolytes tended the sacrificial animals: a pig, two white goats, and a young bull with gilded horns.

Oedipus turned and addressed our sons: "Are you two ready to offer the stag?"

Eteokles let go of my hand. "Yes," he said.

Polynikes gave a jerky nod, and released my other hand.

Phagros, the chief priest of Apollo, was a short heavy man, about the height of the twins, with only a few strands of hair on his round head. His face, large and red with unaccountable bulges, reminded me of a pomegranate. He bowed before us, then spoke: "My king and my princes, the altar is ready."

Oedipus directed the twins to take the place of the servants carrying the stag. Polynikes was the first to accept one end of the pole; he blanched at the weight, but I felt proud to see him set his face firm. Eteokles then took the front end, gripping it so tightly that his knuckles whitened.

Leaning on his walking stick, my husband led the twins toward the fire. He walked slowly, so that the pace of the boys with their burden was likewise slow. I was pleased to see that they did not falter – not simply a mother's pride, for if they stumbled the people would perceive this as a bad omen.

Oedipus spoke, his voice rich and strong: "Apollo, lord of light and healing, accept the offering that my sons, princes of Thebes, bring to you!"

Eteokles' words reached me, but certainly were not loud enough to reach all the people gathered in the agora. "We offer this stag to mighty Apollo," he said. "We pray he will find our gift worthy."

"We ask you to heei—" Polynikes' voice cracked when he tried to speak louder than his brother. His face reddened, but there were no chuckles in the hushed crowd. My son coughed and continued bravely: "We ask you to heal the city of Thebes, and drive away the pestilence."

In such dire circumstances I could not smile at my boys to show them my approval; but I nodded at each before speaking. "Bright Apollo, lord of Thebes, your city needs you! Forsake us not in the face of death. Bathe us in your healing love."

Attendant priests came to take the carcass, and at Phagros' direction threw it onto the fire that burned upon the thick stone altar. For a moment the animal's heavy flesh suppressed the flames; then they crept up the ropes that bound its legs and leapt high, higher, a cleansing pyre of yellow and orange. The stag's outlines shimmered in the heat of its consumption.

While the offering burned, the priests of Apollo began a slow, mournful hymn.

Oily black smoke rose from the offering, in the beginning a straight line pointing toward the sky. Then the wind picked up and blew smoke and ashes into the crowd; those standing near the front coughed, and Haemon and Antigone wiped their eyes. People muttered, for this could mean that Apollo rejected the offering.

The other gods then received their offerings: the pig for Demeter, goats for Dionysus, and finally the bull for Zeus. Oedipus and I, and the priests and priestesses, implored each god in turn to spare Thebes. The wind remained chancy, the omens unclear.

Then Oedipus turned to face the crowd, palms to the sky. "People of Thebes, return to your homes. Your king will seek the wisdom of the gods."

From his place behind the king, Phagros added: "Any who show signs of the plague, take them to the temple of Apollo. Our healers will tend the stricken."

Some of the people rushed away, anxious to learn if their loved ones were ill. Others moved more slowly, casting hopeful looks in our direction.

I walked over to Eurydike told her to take the children back to the palace.

She nodded quick agreement, but Eteokles objected. "I'll stay, Mother."

"No," I said, shaking my head. "You will not."

"But, Mother—"

"Go now with your aunt. Your father and I will wait to speak with the priests."

"He's Father's heir. Shouldn't he stay?" Antigone, as always, thought she knew the proprieties better than I.

"I'll hear no more on this, from any of you. Go." I gave her a sharp look and she finally relented, helping Eurydike to herd away the smaller children.

Oedipus waited patiently as the priests took care of the fire. As always with a sacrifice in the agora, the fire had to be extinguished completely; but priests of all the gods and goddesses lit their lamps from the sacrificial flames. They would carry the flame back to their own shrines, there to mingle with the altar fires. The acolytes then brushed the hearth clean, removing the ashes and any charred scraps of the sacrifices that remained. When the ritual was done, Phagros trudged over to us.

"Do you believe the gods have accepted the sacrifice?" Oedipus asked.

The priest shrugged his shoulders. "My king, it is difficult to tell. The omens are contradictory."

Contradictory omens! Was it ever otherwise? But I bit my lip and kept silent.

"The sacrifices burned," Phagros continued, "But the smoke did not go straight to the heavens; some of it stayed near the earth, and ash landed on some of the people."

"What does that mean for Thebes?" pressed the king.

The priest hesitated. "My king, I am not gifted with prophecy, but I would interpret it as meaning that Thebes – or at least some Thebans – will suffer. Remember, the future holds many things."

I asked, "What would you advise us to do?" I hoped he would be explicit.

Phagros looked toward the sky, as if seeking inspiration. "I think you should send a messenger to Delphi, and recall the Tiresias to Thebes."

So: the local priest could give us no comfort, no advice. I glanced at the palace, and prayed that my children were safe.

No one seemed willing to speak; Oedipus waited, respectfully, for the Tiresias to continue, but Father only resumed tugging at his beard. Creon and I exchanged puzzled glances.

Finally I raised my voice and said, "Thebes has already sacrificed greatly. We have lost more than forty lives, and dozens more lie ill."

Father frowned, and tapped his staff against the tiled floor. "Apollo finds an imbalance in Thebes. The city is disordered."

Imbalanced, disordered – what did he mean? Of course Thebes was disordered! We had the plague!

My father continued, slowly, as if each word caused him pain, personal pain. "There is guilt in Thebes. Blood guilt."

Guilt – blood guilt! The words lingered in the air, and the people exchanged anxious looks. I glanced in Oedipus' direction. He had killed Laius, and although he had atoned for it, we had never admitted the fact publicly. My husband's face blanched, and I knew he, too, remembered Laius.

But that was so long ago! Surely that could not be the reason for the plague now?

The Tiresias added, his words even slower: "The city must be cleansed."

Creon took a step forward from his place beside my throne. "How," he said, speaking distinctly, loudly, "may the city be cleansed? What does Apollo demand?"

"Ah," said Father, turning to face his son's voice. "That is the riddle. That is the puzzle. The price we must pay." He sighed heavily. "One of the most powerful men in the city. A son of the Sown Men must die."

A son of the Sown Men! Then – *not* Oedipus! Praise Apollo, Oedipus was from Korinth!

But many others in the room were of the Spartoi. Whispers hissed through the hall, and many of the well-born shifted uneasily. Mikhos, descendant of Chthonius, crossed his arms across his chest and jutted his swarthy chin. Plainly he did not intend to be the sacrifice. Even loyal Demochares wore a stony expression; he was descended from Hyperenor.

I looked at my brother's ashen face, and his eyes met mine.

Creon was a descendant of Echion, who sprang from Kadmos' serpent-tooth seeds.

As was I, although the Tiresias had asked for a *male* sacrifice.

But if I was a descendant of Echion, then so were my sons.

No! No! Apollo could not take my sons. They were descendants of the earthborn soldiers, yes, but not men. Not yet men.

Though they had had their first hunt...

I reached for Oedipus' hand and gripped it tight. My sons were only twelve. They were princes, but they had no true power yet. They were several years away from their manhood ceremony. Besides, the oracle had specified one, *one* son of the Spartoi. If Apollo had meant my boys, why would he ask for one and not both?

This thought comforted me, and I could breathe again, although still not easily.

Father continued: "The oracle told me what I have told you, and commanded me return to Thebes at once. Tonight I will purify my heart to receive the wisdom of Apollo. Perhaps he will speak to me more clearly now that I have arrived in his afflicted city. Now I can say only that one of the Spartoi, the most powerful in Thebes, must give his life to save the city and wash away the blood-guilt."

I sought my brother's eye again, but he evaded my gaze. Creon had killed Melanthe, and had made no atonement. Could *that* be the blood-guilt of which the Tiresias spoke?

Father went on, "That is the disorder. One of the Spartoi holds a place he should not." He swayed a bit, then placed his staff more firmly against the floor. "Apollo demands that Thebes rectify this situation. The man must die."

Creon cleared his throat, and when he spoke his voice was sure. "The oracle did not name the man?"

Father shook his head.

"Nor the position he holds?"

In the long pause before our father answered, Creon looked around the room; this time his eyes met mine. A light gleamed there, humorless and unhealthy. Chills dripped down my back as I wondered what my brother might say. Could he be so cruel as to shift suspicion to my boys?

"No," Father said at last.

My brother set his hands on his hips, leaned his head back. "Then, Tiresias, you who were Menoeceus born of Echion's line, is it possible that *you* are the most powerful of Thebes' Spartoi?"

Father! I had not considered him.

And, judging by the expressions on the faces of the others present, nor had anyone else. We all thought of him as the Tiresias, not as one of Thebes' highest-born. Yet he was of the Spartoi, of course, and as the Tiresias he occupied a position of great power.

The old man nodded, then licked his cracked lips. "Yes," he said. "That is possible."

Darkness fell upon the city. The evening meal was served but I ate little. Finally everyone left and we could retire. My husband and I went to our bed, but I could not sleep. Thank the gods, no one had suggested that my sons should be the sacrifice to save the city; but other thoughts disturbed me. The choices were terrible: my sons, my brother, my father. Given those options, I must concur with Creon, and ask our father to die. But it was horrible, horrible!

I slipped out of the blankets and pulled on my robe. Quietly I stepped out to the balcony. Out to my left, in the east, was the Temple of Apollo. I envisioned my father kneeling before the wooden image of the god, his bandaged face lit by the lamplight, his gnarled arms thrown upward in supplication. In the temple he would hear the moans of the plague victims, smell the stench of their illness. For what would he ask? Would he beg the god to spare him? Or would he ask Apollo to take his own life, and spare the lives of his son and grandsons?

I leaned against the balustrade and looked down at Thebes. To save the city from plague, the most powerful son of the Sown Men should die.

Who was more powerful, Creon or Father?

And had Father even understood the god's meaning?

Oedipus walked out onto the darkened balcony, his bare feet making little sound. He said softly, "You're afraid for him."

"I'm afraid for all of us."

"I meant your father."

"Him as well," I agreed. I reached out and took his warm hands in mine. Oedipus pulled me close, but my back remained stiff and tight. Finally I dared to say, "At least the boys are safe."

Oedipus drew me back, his hands upon my shoulders. "Jocasta! Of course they are."

I nodded quickly. Still, fear gripped my heart. "In the potters' quarter," I said, gesturing towards the city, "and by the Ogygia Gate, people are dying from this curse."

He rubbed my neck. "That's why we must heed Apollo's will."

"But how will it help, for one more man to die?"

"My love... I know you don't want to lose your father, or your brother. But if Apollo finds guilt in our city, we must correct it. Your father understands that."

Perhaps Father understood. But I did not think Creon would. I wondered whether I did.

I shivered and looked toward the heavens; stars glittered high above. "Why would Apollo ask such a thing? And what – who – is he asking for?" I wanted certainty; I did not want sacrifices made in vain.

Oedipus slipped an arm around my waist and guided me back into the bedroom, where there was warmth and mellow light. "Your father seeks that answer tonight. And, as king and queen, so should we." He picked up a lamp from the bedside table, pushed open the door, and led me into the hallway. Our bodyguards fell into step behind us. We walked along the corridor and down a flight of stairs to our private shrine.

Oedipus lit the hanging lamps, and set the lamp he carried on the step below the marble altar. There before us, each in their proper place, were the gods of the royal house of Thebes. Mighty Zeus and his wife and sister Hera, the king and queen of heaven. Beautiful Aphrodite and the warrior Ares, the parents of Harmonia. Demeter, goddess of the harvest and Dionysus, descended from Kadmos himself. Sly Hermes, hardworking Hephaestus, and wise Athena. Graceful Artemis, goddess of the hunt. And her twin brother Apollo, lord of healing. And Poseidon, who was not just the lord of the seas, but the god of horses and the dreaded shaker of the earth,

Apollo's handsome face on the small ivory statue seemed as stern to me as the great wooden carving in the temple. I felt sure Father stood before that image even now, seeking guidance and wisdom. Beside me my husband lifted his palms to the god and prayed.

"Bright Apollo, speak to us. Show us the sacrifice you demand. Show us why Thebes is guilty, so that we may cleanse ourselves and be healed."

Since the crisis began we had visited this room often, yet the gods had been silent. But my husband's voice was strong, full of love for the god, full of confidence that his supplication would be answered.

I had never had a vision, and did not expect that I would receive one now. Visions belonged to the Maenads and their ilk, who claimed to fly to the ends of the earth in the space of one night; and to the holy priestess at Delphi, whose riddling words brought more confusion than clarity to her listeners.

Perhaps that was the problem: my reluctant faith and my secret doubts. Could *I* be the source of the guilt in Thebes?

I had trouble concentrating on my husband's prayer. My back ached from standing, and the marble floor felt icy against my feet. I told myself to ignore such petty discomforts. Thinking of my children, now asleep in their beds, I offered genuine thanks for their continued health. I thought of Father, praying in the temple on the hill. And I wondered what Creon was doing, whether he slept, or paced, or if perhaps he even prayed. Again and again, I brought my mind back to the prayer: asking not just Apollo, but all the gods, to reveal what needed to be done. My stomach ached with tension and emptiness; the smell of lamp-smoke made me dizzy. I tried to think of Thebes, and beseeched the gods once more for wisdom, for clarity. After a time, Oedipus lowered his hands, his own prayers finished, and left me alone in our shrine.

The lamps burned low; one wavered, and sputtered out. I stared at the one lamp that still cast a flickering light on walls of the small room. The light began to grow, the flames reaching unnaturally high. I gasped in terror, seeing the glowing yellow tongues lick at the rafters overhead. Were we to have fire as well as plague?

I tried to move but could not; my limbs had turned to stone. I tried to call for help but could not; my tongue would not obey. We would all die in the palace, burned to death! I willed myself to move toward the flame, but then, as I looked, I saw that the palace was no longer in danger – I was somehow outside, and though the flame still danced, now it was a great bonfire, a pyre of bodies heaped high, the victims of the plague. It blazed at the altar of Apollo, before the columns of his temple. And there beside the pyre stood Creon, tall and unsmiling, a bronze axe gleaming in his hand.

I stood in a crowd of citizens, just one among their number, watching the king of Thebes bring a sacrifice to the altar. Oedipus walked slowly, his russet hair made bright by the burning bodies.

He led my father by a rope tied around the old man's stringy neck.

Father's hands were bound behind his back. He moved slowly, with dignity and sureness of step. The bandage was gone from his face, baring the empty eye sockets. But firelight illumined the deep hollows, and I felt sure he could see without eyes. His attention focused on the pyre, and on Creon; never once did he turn to the man who led him.

They stopped before the altar; Oedipus spoke. "Here is the appointed sacrifice." But his voice was different. The Korinthian accent had vanished; instead I heard a distinct Pisatan lilt.

Then my husband turned to the crowd. And beneath the russet curls his face was Laius' face.

My jaw dropped, and the breath rushed soundlessly from my body. Creon raised the axe, and it fell bloodily to the mark—

Then I did scream, and my bodyguard rushed to my side. "My lady?"

I blinked, and looked up into his bearded face. The four walls of the palace shrine enclosed me once more. In the tremulous light of the single lamp – its flames back down to their normal height – I could see my surroundings well enough. There were the gods, arrayed as before; except for the guard, I was alone.

My bodyguard helped me along the dark cold corridors back to my room. I felt chill and weak; my hand shook as I opened the door. Oedipus woke, and sat up, yawning. With an abrupt word I dismissed Merope.

"Are you coming to bed?" asked Oedipus, his voice groggy.

I set my lamp on the dressing-table and sank down onto the wooden stool. "Not yet." I had questions, terrible questions, that I needed answered but dared not ask.

In my vision, Creon killed our father; but that was not what horrified me most. Once more I saw Oedipus: with his own body, but Laius' face and voice. But this time I was awake, not partaking of some vision.

Studying my husband's features, I could see his likeness to Laius. Oedipus kept his cheeks clean-shaven because he did not like the ruddy color of his beard; but in the dim light I could imagine a beard. Dark and curling as Laius' had been, wrapping round his jaw, concealing his strong cleft chin, emphasizing the red fullness of his lips.

Oedipus rose, and came to stand beside me. I shrank from the hand he laid on my shoulder.

"My love," he said, "did the gods speak to you?"

I twisted my body so that his hand fell away. "Yes," I said.

"What did they tell you?"

I did not know how to answer. He expected something terrible, but what I had learned was too terrible to share. Finally I told him, "Father is to die."

He sat down on the floor beside my stool, looked up at me. In the lamplight, his smooth-shaven cheeks now looked like those of a youth. Young, he looked. So very young. Not yet forty. So much younger than I.

"That's hard," he said. He laid a hand on my knee; I pushed back the stool, stood up and walked away. My husband's face looked first hurt, then understanding. "It's terrible, to face such an oracle." He hugged his knees to his chest, looking ever more like a child.

I shivered, but forced myself to look at his face. His smooth, young face. His curling hair: russet, like our sons'. As my father's had been in his own youth.

"But we must accept the will of the god."

"Must we?" I whispered. "Tell me, Oedipus, did you?"

He blinked. "What do you mean?"

"You had a difficult oracle once, at Delphi. What did the god tell you then?"

He shook his head, looked at his bare feet. "That was so long ago."

This had lain secret for years; but I could let it rest no longer. "Did you simply accept the will of the god? Did you do just as the oracle said?"

"I did as the god would wish—"

"Did the oracle say, 'You must never return to Korinth'?"

"Not in so many words—"

I dropped to the floor beside him, staring intently. "I must know. What did the oracle say?"

He spoke slowly, carefully, as though I held a knife at his throat. "That I would murder my father. And..." His voice trailed off, as if he could not bear to continue.

My heart sank. My voice sounded strange, unnatural, but I made myself ask: "The oracle told you that you would kill your own father?"

"Yes. That's why I could never return to Korinth. That's why I came here, my love, to make a new life."

The king of Korinth was safe on his throne. But Oedipus *had* killed a man. Laius, my own first husband, cold in his grave these eighteen years.

My stomach churned.

"And – and – what of your mother?"

His voice was barely a whisper. "The oracle said I would marry her, and get her with child."

I clutched at my belly. I wanted to retch.

"My darling, I know it sounds horrible."

He tried to put his arm around me, but I moved away.

"But I didn't! I married you, the most beautiful, wonderful woman in all of Hellas: Jocasta, queen of Thebes!"

He had married me. He was my husband, and together we had produced four children.

I gagged, controlling myself just long enough to reach the chamber-pot.

Oedipus waited until I was done, and covered his hand with mine. I stared at that hand, realizing that the fingers and nails were precisely the same shape as my brother's.

Again I shied from his touch.

"My dear, my love, I know how you must feel. That you accepted a man so cursed for your husband. But I didn't return to Korinth. For some reason – I don't know why – Apollo decided to release me. To lift the curse, before it happened. And instead he granted me a life with you."

A life with me.

I retched again, but my stomach was empty.

"My love, are you all right? Is it the plague?" There was fear in his voice. "Should I send for a healer?"

"It's not plague," I croaked. I pushed the chamber-pot away. "I don't need a healer."

He poured a cup of water and handed it to me.

I accepted it. The water rinsed the foul taste from my mouth.

Water: refreshing, cleansing, clear.

Clear. My own life was suddenly clear. The threads, once so twisted, so tangled, now wove themselves into a distinct pattern. The long-ago nod from Pelorus: he *had* given the child away. His lies had been meant for Laius, not me. And Laius, casting me out of his bed! *This* was the curse the old Tiresias had revealed to him.

What had we done?

"My dearest, can you forgive me? I'm so sorry. I should have told you long ago. But I wanted so much to deserve your love, to forget I had ever been cursed."

I sipped the water, holding the cup with both hands: trying to think, wondering what to say. Should I tell him? Or would he solve the riddle himself? He knew he had killed Laius; he knew he had married me. But he also believed his parents were alive and well in the palace at Korinth.

"Say something," he begged. "Say something, please, to show that you forgive me."

I watched a tear slide down the face I had loved, cherished, for so many years. I thought my heart would break.

"The gods can be cruel, Oedipus," I whispered.

Even his name – swollen feet – could be understood! Laius had bound our son's feet with a cord…

"It seems that way. But Apollo spared me. He spared me, so that I could come to Thebes and be your husband. We haven't been cursed, have we? We've been blessed."

So many wonderful years together. Four healthy children. He was right; we had been blessed.

"I love you," I told him, for it was true.

"I love you too," he said, his voice cracking. "The gods! Sometimes merciful, and sometimes cruel. I don't know why my father should be spared, and yours must die."

My beloved husband. I would not, could not, give him up. He must never know. No one must ever know.

"You're right, love," I whispered. "I'm sorry I asked you about something so painful. I was only looking for a way to escape, as you escaped the fate foretold for you. But from this oracle there is no escape. Father must die."

CHAPTER NINETEEN

During that sleepless night, I realized how many predictions had been fulfilled: the one that brought about my betrothal to Alphenor; the curse for which Laius threw me out of his bed and abandoned his son to die; Oedipus' fate as revealed at Delphi; Father's prediction of Laius' impending doom. Any doubts about prophecy I had harbored were gone. My one sliver of hope was that the terrible vision would prove true, and Father's death would keep Oedipus safe.

But if Apollo had revealed the truth to me at last, wouldn't he also share it with his servant the Tiresias?

Somehow I got through the hours of darkness, managed with the help of my maids to bathe and dress. In the early morning light I leaned heavily against one of the red-painted columns in front of the palace, as we waited for the Tiresias to return from Apollo's temple.

Oedipus came to stand beside me, but I edged away. I could not look up at him, dared not meet his eye.

The great doors opened and Creon and Eurydike joined us on the palace steps. Creon's face looked white and pinched; dark circles shadowed his wife's eyes.

"When will they come?" she asked.

"Soon enough," Creon snapped.

She twisted her hands together. "I can't bear this waiting!"

The rest of us made no response.

Others filed into the agora. I saw more bloodshot eyes and grim expressions, especially on the faces of the well-born. Each man among them must have wondered whether he would be singled out as scapegoat; each woman feared for her husband or son. The common folk, realizing they were but spectators, stood apart, murmuring among themselves.

Finally a youth in a tattered kilt ran into the agora. "They're coming!"

I scarcely breathed as the Tiresias and his guide made their way into the marketplace, their pace agonizingly slow after Father's long night of prayer and fasting. The guide helped the old man climb the palace steps, then turned him so that he faced the people.

May the gods forgive me, but I wanted Father to stumble and choke before he revealed anything Apollo might have told him during the night. If I could have tripped him without anyone seeing, pushed him down the marble stairs, I think I would have.

Oedipus cleared his throat. "Tiresias—"

"I am no longer the Tiresias," the old man interrupted. "I relinquish that position." And with that pronouncement he removed the blindfold, revealing his empty eye sockets, and let the black cloth drop to the ground.

A shocked gasp arose from the crowd.

"I am Menoeceus," he continued, "descendant of Echion. I have been the most powerful of the Spartoi."

I felt my shoulders sag, and heard Creon let out a long breath. Relieved sighs could be heard among the well-born; the common folk talked quietly but with animation, pointing at my father, at various of the nobles, at my brother.

Nearly four decades had passed since I had seen my father's face unobscured. Then a man in his forties, healthy, vigorous, his face had been stern but dignified, its lines indicating experience and strength. Now toothless, eyeless, sunken, his face was an object of pathos. Without the blindfold, he seemed to lose all his power. Or had his power fled when he declared himself no longer the Tiresias?

Oedipus pressed his hands together. "What must we do, Menoeceus?"

"Take me to the Astykratia Gate," the old man said. "And help me to climb to the top of the city wall."

341

That point near the gate was where the hill, cut by the Chryssorrhoas stream, sloped most steeply. The furthest drop from Amphion's proud walls.

Father's usual guide stepped aside, making room for my husband. The king himself took Menoeceus' arm and led him gently down the palace steps.

As I stared at the two men, my mind flashed back to the vision from the night before. I stood transfixed with dread, unable to move.

Creon tugged my arm. "We should follow, don't you think?"

"Of course," I said, and willed my leaden limbs to move. When we reached the foot of the stairs, a few paces behind Father and Oedipus, the people stood to either side, watching noiselessly as we passed. Some of the faces in the crowd looked desperate: I wondered if they had family members who had been struck by the plague.

"You look dreadful, Jocasta," murmured Creon as we crossed the agora, breaking into my thoughts. "Did you sleep last night?"

I looked up at him. "Did you?" We walked on another several steps; ahead of us, Father never paused. So thin he was, so fragile! "I wonder what Apollo revealed to him last night," I said, unable to keep my fears completely hidden.

"Father has always believed that to be chosen by Apollo was the highest possible honor. That would make him the most powerful descendant of the Sown Men."

If only that were true!

But then, Father, not I, was the one trained in the mysteries. He might have seen what I could not. "How can we be sure, that he really *is* the one the god meant?"

He lowered his mouth to my ear and hissed, "Jocasta, what are the alternatives? Me? One of your sons?"

My heart skipped a beat and I slipped on the steep path.

Creon put out his hand and kept me from falling. "Careful; you don't want to break your neck."

I grasped his arm, wondering if he could possibly know. No, he could not, I decided. If he had, he would have used that knowledge to protect himself.

"Still," I said quietly, "what if the gods meant someone else?"

His face hardened. "Father is convinced he'll save the city. Perhaps he's right."

From then on we remained silent. But my mind kept swirling around a single question: just what *had* the god shown Father last night? I could not believe that Apollo had revealed the truth about Oedipus. Even though he loved me, and Oedipus was his own grandson, Father would never have allowed such sacrilege to go unpunished. Perhaps he saw only Creon as a reasonable alternative to himself, and sought to protect his son.

I wondered, then, if the god had spoken to him at all. Father's second sight had never seemed as keen as that of the female Tiresias of my youth. He had been correct predicting Laius' death, true, but compared to her, he had made far fewer prophecies. Could it be true after all, that Father was the man who held a position he should not?

Besides – besides – how could my marriage be a sacrilege? The gods had sent Oedipus to me!

My mind argued thus, but my heart pounded, for I was about to let a man – my own father! – sacrifice himself in my husband's stead. Would the gods now multiply their curses, punishing us not only for the crime unwittingly committed, but further for a false atonement?

In silence I watched my husband lead my father to the Astykratia Gate. Oedipus, the handsome and virtuous king, determined to do whatever the gods might demand to save Thebes, practically glowed in the fresh morning sunlight. As did Father, assuredly inspired by the selflessness of his intentions. For the first time I saw the resemblance between the two. Not just their shared reverence for the gods but the well-carved nose, the wide shoulders, the red hair Father once had: all these bespoke a close relationship. Only the veil of Father's years and the blindfold he had worn had hidden this from me before.

Father groped his way up the steep stairs, pressing his bent body against the wall, careful not to fall before his time. Oedipus followed him, and for a moment the two stood shoulder-to-shoulder on the guards' walk atop Amphion's high wall, bathed in the sun's golden rays. The old man paused there a long moment, his face turned up to the sky that he had not seen for so many years.

Then Father's deep voice rang out over the crowd, clear and confident: "By the will of Apollo, may Thebes be cured!"

And he stepped off the stones onto nothingness.

He did not cry out, as he fell.

The hush was so complete that I heard the thud his body made when it struck the stones outside the city walls.

Later that day we buried his broken body in a cave on the hill beyond the Astykratia Gate. It was only fitting that he be laid to rest near the site of his sacrifice; after the city healed, we would build a monument worthy of him.

With Thebes still under quarantine, few attended the funeral; but Oedipus spoke eloquently of Father's dedication to Thebes and to the gods. Eurydike wept openly. Creon and I stood mute while Apollo's priests carried the linen-wrapped corpse into the dark cavern.

As we climbed the hill back to the palace, thick gray clouds moved across the sky. A good omen: cleansing rain? Or a sign of the gods' displeasure? I did not know, but as we reached the agora the clouds burst, and cold water soaked us all. We shivered in the palace until servants stoked the fires. I sank deep into private thoughts before the warming blaze.

"Well, Mother?" Antigone's voice was sharp. "Are you going to answer me?"

"What?" I asked, having no idea what my daughter might have said.

Before she could speak again, Oedipus hushed her. "Antigone, your mother is grieving. The Tiresias was her father."

At this rebuke from an unaccustomed source, Antigone's mouth snapped shut and she slumped back in her seat.

"My dear, why don't you retire?" Oedipus suggested gently. "You hardly slept last night."

I nodded and went upstairs. Merope, her eyes more reddened and swollen than my own, readied me for bed. I did not think I would be able to sleep, but the combination of warm blankets, the sound of the pounding rains, and my own exhaustion led me immediately into oblivion.

And so I was asleep when Oedipus came to bed that night, and gathered me into his arms. At first I moved closer, out of habit, but then I fully woke and edged away. When he bent to kiss me I turned my head, so that his lips met only my cheek.

"I'm sorry about your father," he said. "But he lived a long life, and he was willing to make the sacrifice. And it won't be in vain."

I stared over at the lamp burning on the bedside table. "I hope you're right."

"You must trust the gods," said Oedipus.

I mulled his words and thought: trust them for what? To treat us well? Or to prove that they were more powerful than mere mortals, however we might struggle against their will?

"Everything will be fine. Everything will be as it is meant to be."

"Will it?" I asked, and began to cry.

He tried to pull me close; again I pushed him away. And yet I did desire him, and loathed myself for it; the tears I shed on my pillow were bitter with shame, confusion, fear. Oedipus stroked my hair, speaking words of gentle understanding, and I hated myself all the more for letting him think I wept for Father.

One part of me did grieve; though I could not have done other than what I did, the guilt tormented me. I kept seeing Father, his dark robes silhouetted against the bright sky. Over and over I seemed to hear his body striking the stones.

Day after day I continued in this nightmare state, asking myself how I could live such a terrible lie but not knowing what else I could do. Unable to face my husband and children, I avoided them all, spending my time reviewing the palace inventories or working my loom. Because of the quarantine, the other women stayed home; in the weaving room I could be alone.

My brother came to me there one afternoon. "Jocasta, why do you keep hiding here? If you had been in the megaron just now—"

"I can't. I can't be there," I interrupted without looking back.

Creon hesitated. "You haven't been yourself since Father's death."

I continued moving the shuttle through the hanging threads.

"Why do you grieve so?" Creon moved to the edge of the loom so that he could look into my face. "He was our father, yes, but he was also an old man – Hermes would have come for him soon anyway." He reached out to catch my arm and stop me in my work. "Listen—"

Shrugging off his hand, I pushed up the crossbar to tighten the new row of thread into place. "I just wish there were some way to be sure about what we did."

Creon sighed. "Jocasta, if there must be guilt here, it should be mine. But Father chose this himself."

Yes, I thought bitterly. He did. But there was guilt enough to go around.

My brother lowered his voice: "Do *you* think I should have done it?"

Finally I looked over at him. I could not tell him the truth; grasping for a response that would make sense, I ventured, "You did kill Melanthe – the priestess of Dionysus – and then claim she killed herself. That could be the blood-guilt Father meant."

Creon paced across the room, his words pouring out furiously. "Her death was a blessing for the city. The Maenads are content – they have a home in Orchomenos. What I did helped Thebes! Everything I have *ever* done has been for Thebes!"

I dropped my shuttle. "I'm sorry, Creon. Of course you've served the city well."

He whirled back to face me. "And what is false about my position? I am brother to the queen – only that!"

I stretched out a hand. "That's a lot to me."

"Nothing compared to son or father! You think it should have been *me* up there, instead of Father!"

"That's not true!" I took a small step toward him. "I'm just afraid we let Father kill himself for nothing."

"But, Jocasta, his sacrifice was *not* pointless! That's what I came to tell you! I don't know whether his death healed the city – but it bought us time. Phagros and Rhodia just made their report. No new victims have been brought to the temple, and they've found no new cases anywhere in the city. In fact, people are getting well. The plague's abating."

A weight seemed to slip off my shoulders. "Is it? Is it really?"

He nodded curtly. "Oedipus plans to open the gates, and he wants to hold a festival of thanksgiving to Apollo. He wants to consult with you about it."

If the curse was ended, then all was forgiven! For if I had aggravated my sin in the eyes of Apollo, why would he release his grip on the city?

Relief flooded through me.

"I'm sorry I said anything about Melanthe. I was just thinking about the sacrifices we all make for the city. I know what you did was for Thebes."

The frown lingered on his face another moment; then he shrugged. "These have been difficult days. For all of us."

He started for the door. Turning back to my loom, I saw that the last part of the work was flawed. I began to unravel my errors.

Two months later the new Tiresias was initiated.

There had been no more cases of plague, and we had opened up the gates some time before. At first visitors to the city were few, as people waited to be certain that the curse was truly lifted. But after Father's self-sacrifice we had no more deaths; and one summer day the last invalid, a herdsman, finally walked home from Apollo's temple unassisted. Phagros praised the god for his mercy; but one day as they made their report Rhodia, who had spent long hours working alongside his healers, maintained that her use of hot water, sour wine, and olive oil to bathe the stricken was the source of their return to health. Phagros granted that the sick began to heal after Rhodia and her midwives instituted this practice, but insisted that Apollo was the one who inspired her.

Rhodia, dark circles under her eyes after many days and nights of caring for the sick, snapped at the priest. "I don't remember Apollo bringing me towels or hot water!"

"My dear, how would *you* would recognize the god if you saw him?" Phagros shook his large, misshapen head.

Rhodia twisted her mouth tightly, deep lines showing around her lips. I had heard her complaint before in private: the temple healers were all too ready to let her midwives do the real work. But Phagros had also aired his annoyances, grumbling that the women who served Artemis showed insufficient respect to the priests of Apollo.

But that matter was past. Looking at Apollo's temple now, one would not guess it had been recently filled with suffering plague victims. All reminders of illness were gone: the pallets on which the afflicted had groaned, the basins and towels, the braziers for heating bathwater. The white marble tiles of the forecourt had been swept clean.

Oedipus and I stood in the shade of a large parasol held aloft by my bodyguard, sheltering our eyes against the harsh summer sun. Near us were the most prominent citizens, a few dignitaries from neighboring cities, and the Korinthian ambassador.

"What a glorious day," said Mnesikles. "Surely a sign that Thebes has regained the gods' favor."

"Yes," I agreed, hoping that he was right.

"I'm glad you could join us for this ceremony," said Oedipus.

"So am I," said the Korinthian, watching the acolytes pouring steaming water into the large bronze basin before us. "This happens so rarely; to witness the rite is a true privilege."

"They're beginning," I said, and the men hushed.

The ram, its gilded horns gleaming, was led forward and sacrificed; Phagros examined its entrails. "The new Tiresias is acceptable!" he announced.

So many years had passed since Father came forward as the candidate; still I remembered the shock and horror I had felt. But now, when Phagros led Pelorus forward, the choice only made sense.

Since losing his sight, Pelorus lived almost exclusively at Delphi, his reputation for wit and wisdom increasing with time. Now in his middle sixties, he was heavier than he had been as a young man. Perhaps he enjoyed the pleasures of the palate more in compensation for the loss of sight; and, being not just blind but also lame, he had trouble taking exercise. His face – the usual blindfold had been removed for the ceremony – was smooth, even youthful, as if lack of squinting had kept wrinkles from forming. His sightless eyes wandered aimlessly; the injury long ago had not been to the eyes themselves, but to his head. Rhodia told me once that head wounds were unpredictable; they could render a man deaf, or blind, or paralyze him – if he were so fortunate as to recover at all.

"How strange," Mnesikles muttered behind me.

I wondered what prompted Mnesikles to make that comment – Pelorus' pitiful eyes? The ceremony itself? But I could not ask him, for at that moment the priest began the hymn. The priestess of Athena shed her gown and stepped into the bath. Pelorus turned his face her way; but his useless eyes could not see her pale creamy flesh, her rounded hips. Phagros sang the story of the hunter who chanced to see the goddess and so had to be punished. Then the flaxen-haired priestess from Athens stepped out of the basin, took the ceremonial dagger and went to stand before Pelorus, droplets of water glistening on her bare shoulders.

But for this initiate no blood was shed. She gently touched the point of the knife to Pelorus' eyelids, reminding us all that he had been chosen long ago.

Phagros continued the ritual song, and temple servants came to wrap the black cloth back around Pelorus' head. When he stretched out his hand to receive the cornel-wood staff of the Tiresias, I suddenly knew the truth of the ceremony deep in my heart, in a way I never appreciated the first time.

Pelorus was gone. The man before us was the Tiresias, by the choice and will of Apollo. I realized that who he had been before mattered very little to the god.

I glanced over at Oedipus, his face alight with wonder at the transformation he had just witnessed.

How handsome he was! A familiar wave of heat washed over me. But this time I did not curse myself and thrust away the feeling, as I had done time and again the last two months.

My husband was the man the gods had sent me. Oedipus, son of King Polybus of Korinth. Perhaps my fears were wrong after all, my sense of foreboding unfounded.

What did it matter, who he might have been before?

I ran my hand down the length of his arm and twisted my fingers with his. He glanced down at me, for I had not touched him so in months; then he smiled and squeezed my hand, hard.

That night he found me a willing bedmate once more, and I discovered that after all he was the same man I had loved, and made love to, and borne children to, and ruled Thebes beside, for so many years.

When we had taken our fill of one another, and lay spent together in the warmth of each other's arms, I brushed a damp curl back from his forehead and kissed his brow. My heart overflowed with love, washing away my shame. He was mine, and I was his. The gods had arranged it so.

Pelorus' months in training at Delphi were a time of healing for the city. The plague was gone, its victims mourned and buried. It seemed that the great heat of that summer baked out the last of the evil humors as fire cleanses away poison, bringing us back to health and happiness. Despite my return to Oedipus' arms, Thebes remained healthy, and I relaxed back into my duties as queen, mother and wife.

The only problem was Creon, who never seemed to fully forgive our exchange in the weaving-room. It seemed absurd that he could think I had wanted him dead in Father's place, but there it was. I had denied it; but still his voice carried a cold edge, and he treated Oedipus and me with exaggerated formality. My husband and I discussed what we could do to mend the breach, and so I approached my brother with the proposal that my eldest daughter should wed his eldest son. At first he said it was too soon, even though Haemon had just had his manhood ceremony. But upon reflection, Creon pronounced idea a good one. We fixed their wedding date to coincide with the harvest festival. When I told her Antigone blushed, and then could not repress a smile, crooked teeth or no.

And so we announced the betrothal, and promised the city a harvest festival better than any in living memory, a celebration to wash the last bitter traces of grief from the city streets.

Pelorus, or rather, the Tiresias, returned to Thebes not long afterward, and Oedipus immediately invited the prophet to the palace. His wife Chrysippe having died six years before, the Tiresias arrived on the arm of his elder daughter Daphne. Manto, the younger girl, born at Delphi, walked at his other side. As the trio entered the megaron, every man in the room turned to watch them pass; the girls were lovely, each with wide dark eyes and magnificent chestnut locks falling unadorned past their slim waists.

Oedipus greeted them formally. "Welcome, Tiresias."

It was strange to hear that title addressed to any but my father.

"I thank you, King Oedipus. Queen Jocasta." Pelorus, like the servants of Apollo before him, had mastered the knack of turning his blindfolded head in the direction of those he could not see. I tried to recall whether he had done that before his initiation, but memory failed me.

"Will you dine with us?" Oedipus offered. "The evening meal will be served soon."

"With pleasure," said the prophet. And so he and his daughters joined our family and Creon's at the royal table. The twins were quieter than usual, their rowdy joking subdued in the presence of Pelorus' girls. Eteokles blushed as Manto questioned him about hunting in the hills, and Polynikes stammered when Daphne asked him about chariot racing. I covered my mouth with one hand to hide my bittersweet smile: my babies were growing up.

But the new Tiresias was the true center of attention. Unlike his predecessors he had a gregarious personality, and amused us with stories of visitors from near and far, all seeking fate's edict at Delphi. Remembering how Pelorus had loved to travel, I guessed he had found a substitute in the pilgrims' tales of their journeys.

"Why is Delphi so important?" asked Ismene.

I was pleased that she spoke up, for my younger daughter was usually shy around strangers. But the Tiresias' open manner broke down reserve.

"Delphi is important because it is the center of the world," the Tiresias said promptly, answering the question as easily as his fingers found the roast fennel and spiced duck.

"But how do you know it is the center of the world?" Antigone pressed him.

The Tiresias took a bite and chewed. "Zeus wanted to answer that very question. So he released two eagles, one from the east and the other from the west. They flew towards each other, and met at Delphi." He took another bite. "Excellent! Your palace cooks are most skilled, my lord king."

"It's my pleasure to provide for you, Tiresias," Oedipus said. "We're honored by your presence." He paused. "Seer, you must know that my daughter Antigone is betrothed to Creon's son Haemon. Can you offer them a blessing?"

He who had been Pelorus tilted his head and pursed his lips, as if waiting for inspiration. When he spoke his tone was earnest. "Yes, indeed. Haemon and Antigone will demonstrate great devotion to each other."

Eurydike clapped her hands together. "Oh, that's wonderful!"

My elder daughter gave a small laugh of delight and glanced over at her cousin; Haemon's cheeks reddened and he busied himself with dipping his bread in olive oil.

Creon grunted. "Will you be staying long in Thebes?"

I paused with my goblet mid-air. No matter how jovial he might be in comparison with my father, this Tiresias was still the servant of Apollo. How could I know what secrets the god might divulge to him?

Pelorus was too entwined with my hidden history. He knew I had borne a son; he had delivered that son to safety. He had taken part in the skirmish between Laius and Oedipus. And during his many years at Delphi, he might have learned the prophecy concerning the Korinthian prince. As agreeable as this Tiresias was, as entertaining as his anecdotes might be, he was still a threat. I did not want him in Thebes.

"I walk only with difficulty, my lord, and of course I am blind," said the Tiresias. "I find travel difficult. So I plan to make Thebes my home now."

I swallowed my wine wrong and began to cough. With difficulty I regained my breath, but still my cheeks felt hot and flushed.

"I trust the queen is all right?" asked the Tiresias.

I croaked an affirmative through my burning windpipe.

"As I was saying, I intend to stay in Thebes," said the prophet. "With the permission of the king and queen, of course."

"Of course you're welcome here, Tiresias; your decision honors our city," said the king.

It was impossible for me to protest.

As the harvest-time neared, Oedipus and I sat one evening in our small study, reviewing the reports on the crops. "Several barley fields have been badly scorched by the heat. They'll have to be plowed under," said Oedipus.

"How many?" I asked.

"At least three," he said, showing me a wax tablet.

I glanced at the figures. "And how are the other fields?"

Before he could answer a visitor was announced: Mnesikles. Just arrived from Korinth, he was dusty and tired. We bade him sit and offered him food and wine.

"What's wrong?" Oedipus asked, for the manner in which Mnesikles rubbed his eyes and the sag of his shoulders signaled that not all was well.

"My dear Oedipus," said the Korinthian, "your father is ill."

A frown crossed my husband's face, and he set down the tablet he had been reviewing. "What ails him?"

"The healers call it the wasting fever. They don't think he will recover. He could live a few days more – a month or two at most. Not longer."

"Merciful gods." Oedipus shook his head; a tear swelled at the corner of one eye. In a choked voice he asked, "And my mother?"

"She grieves. She, too, is getting older – and she's lonely. She misses you terribly. Both the king and queen beg you to end this exile, and visit them before it's too late."

My husband's shoulders stiffened. For a moment he inclined his head, staring at the tiled floor. At last he looked up. "I can't," he said. "The oracle won't permit it. I can never go back, Mnesikles. You must tell them I am sorry. And I love them."

The ambassador sighed, but did nothing more to express his disappointment. "As you wish."

Oedipus set his hands on his knees. "If you will both excuse me, I must go to pray for my father."

When he had gone, Mnesikles swallowed a mouthful of wine and stared into the fire. "I wonder what terrible prophecy keeps him from Korinth."

"The gods can be hard," I said.

"Especially when they keep families apart." He leaned toward the hearth and murmured, "They love him as much as if he were their own true son."

A chill ran down my back.

I hesitated, then decided I could not let the Korinthian's words pass unnoticed. "Do you mean Oedipus is *not* the son of the king and queen of Korinth?"

Mnesikles frowned and swirled the contents of his goblet. "Did I speak aloud? By Poseidon, I'm more tired and upset than I thought. Curse this wine!" He looked over at me earnestly. "Lady, I must ask you to forget my indiscretion. The adoption of Oedipus is a secret known to but three people: King Polybus, Queen Periboea, and myself."

I folded my arms, my stomach queasy. "And how is it that *you* know?"

"About forty years ago, I was a young man in King Polybus' bodyguard, and a trusted messenger." He rubbed his bald pate. "The king and queen had been so long without children that when she finally quickened it was like a miracle. But the babe was born too soon; he died the second night in his mother's arms. My lord feared his lady's heart would break. He swore me to secrecy and sent me out to find a baby boy they might raise as their own. After a few days of searching, I encountered a young man carrying an infant in need of a home. I told him I was in the employ of a rich family from Athens, seeking a boy-child to adopt. The fellow refused to name the babe's parents but he assured me the child was of good birth. I took the babe to the queen of Korinth, who immediately claimed him as her son."

"I see."

"Queen Jocasta, I beg you not to mention this to anyone. Polybus made me swear to keep the secret. Even Oedipus does not know. There are those who would use it against him – to deny his claim to the throne of Korinth. And with Polybus dying, and the trouble being made by Pelops' sons, Korinth needs Oedipus as her king."

"I will keep the secret," I assured him.

"Even from your husband? All his life he has believed them to be his true parents."

How convenient, I thought, to have Mnesikles begging *me* to keep silent!

I nodded gravely. "You may depend on me," I told him. "I would never do anything to hurt my husband."

"Bless you, my lady," he said, and kissed my hand.

Oedipus stayed late in the palace shrine, praying for the man he believed to be his father. I also had trouble sleeping: Mnesikles' words echoed in my ears. But the man seemed determined to keep the knowledge to himself; that thought was reassuring.

After the night was half gone, my husband entered the room. When he slipped into bed I put my arms around him. "I'm sorry about your father," I told him.

"I wish I could visit him. I sometimes think the oracle can't matter any more – but what if I were wrong?"

A pang of guilt went through me, because I knew there was no reason he should not see the king and queen of Korinth. Perhaps I should have told him the truth, that he was adopted; but I did not think he could bear it. Besides, I had just promised to keep silent.

"I'm sorry," I said again, and kissed his cheek.

"I know you understand." He held me tightly, his face against my shoulder. "You know what it's like to lose your father – and to *know* that you will lose him, and there's nothing you can do."

I ran my fingers through his hair, and listened to the stories of his boyhood that spilled forth: how Polybus had brought him a sleek brown puppy for his fifth birthday, which grew into a faithful hunting dog; how his mother sang him ribald sea-chanteys that well-born ladies were not supposed to know. His father had taught him wrestling and chariot-driving and shipbuilding; his mother, poetry and writing and the lyre. I felt in my heart that, the accident of birth notwithstanding, these people were my husband's true parents.

At last he talked himself out and fell asleep in my arms.

The next day Oedipus' spirits were improved, but mine were not, for I had slept little. Our private concerns were one matter; but word from the vineyards and orchards grew no better. The summer's baking heat had perhaps driven out the last evil humors of the plague, but it had also wilted our crops.

That morning Oedipus and Creon rode out to inspect the fields with Haemon, while I brought the twins along to help Demochares and me supervise an inventory of what remained from previous years' bounty. My sons needed to learn the responsibilities of ruling Thebes.

Dried peas and lentils lasted for years, as long as the house-snakes kept the mice in check; these we had in fair amounts. Raisins and figs filled baskets stacked ceiling-high in many of the storehouses, and we had hundreds of jars of olives stored in brine. But the heat had soured thirty-two amphorae of our best wine, and eleven of the great oil-casks had gone rancid; their contents could be used for nothing more than lamp fuel – and a foul-smelling flame they would make.

Most importantly, barley and emmer wheat were in very short supply.

Eteokles turned to me. "But we can import grain, can't we, Mother?"

I leaned back against a huge terracotta storage jar. "Grain from Aegypt will, as always, be available. But this year it will certainly cost something dear."

"Hmm." Demochares frowned. "We have gold enough to keep the people in bread this year, my lady. But last year's harvest was no better than average."

"Worse, in fact," I said, worried. "And the one before that as well." I stood to go; the soldiers standing guard outside the granary pulled shut the heavy wooden door as we left, and drew the great bronze bolt.

"It's true, my lady," Demochares said. "Last year and the year before we paid well in leather and wool for Aegyptian grain."

Worry darkened my younger son's face. "We can't keep that up," he said.

"No." I ducked my head in thought. Then, remembering my duty as mother and queen, I straightened my back and slipped an arm around his shoulder. "And surely we won't have to. Thebes is rich and her lands fertile."

Polynikes looked up at me, his eyes bright. "So we shall still have a wedding feast for Antigone?"

I smiled. "A feast? A banquet! Without question, Son!" I looked up at the palace. "Your father and uncle – and Haemon – must be on their way back by now. Let's go see what they have learned."

But the news was not promising. Four of the barley-fields would have to be plowed under, not three. The grapes were doing poorly, and the olive crop would be meager too. Oedipus decided that tomorrow we had best consult with the priests and priestesses of Demeter about how best to preserve this year's harvest, and increase results next year. Creon said grumpily that he would rather talk further with the peasants who actually worked the fields.

A servant announced that the evening meal was ready. "Even if we're going to be hungry later, there's no reason not to eat now," said Creon.

We went to dinner. I was tired, and still immersed in the discussion with my brother and my husband regarding the best way to keep the city fed through the winter. I did not notice until the meat was served that Mnesikles and the Tiresias were seated next to each other at the far end of the room.

Their conversation seemed spirited; although I could hear the tone of their voices, I could discern no words. Was the Tiresias recounting another entertaining tale? Or were they recalling a long-ago meeting, in which one of them gave an infant to the other?

And then the man who had been Pelorus seemed to know I was staring at him, for he turned his blindfolded face in my direction. He nodded pleasantly. Then his sightless gaze seemed to fall upon Oedipus, and back to me.

The morsel of bread in my mouth tasted like sand. I could hardly swallow it, for I realized he knew too much.

"Excuse me," I said to Oedipus and Creon, and left the table for my private audience room.

I paced back and forth in the small space. Worry and fear built within me as though in a kettle heated on a tripod, until toxic bubbles surged in my soul. I could stand it no longer. I sent a servant to fetch the Tiresias. Alone.

Waiting for him to arrive, I picked at loose threads on my skirts, readjusted the short cape that covered my breasts, shifted uncomfortably in my ivory-inlaid wooden chair. The room seemed too dark; I called out to Merope to fetch another lamp. She brought a large one, with five wicks – which soon smoked unpleasantly, stinging my eyes. I sent Merope away again, wanting no one else there when Pelorus came; so I snuffed the flames myself, then went to the window and shifted the curtains aside to admit the breeze. I felt, more than heard, the door open and close behind me. When I turned he was there.

He inclined his head. "My lady queen," he said. "You wish to speak with the Tiresias?"

I leaned back against the window-sill. "Or with my old friend Pelorus," I said at last. "I'm not sure which."

He limped forward, his cornel-wood staff brushing the floor only lightly. "Not sure? The wise and ageless queen of Thebes is not sure?"

"I am not."

He set both hands atop the staff, and leaned against it. "Can I tell you a secret?" he asked.

I stepped forward and gripped the back of a chair with both hands, my knuckles looking white and brittle as old fish-bones. My heart raced at what he might say.

"All right."

"The Tiresias isn't always sure, either."

My mouth twisted at the corners. "That was not the secret I expected to hear."

"Is there one in particular that interests you?"

I did not like this dancing around the topic. I felt like a mouse being watched by an eagle – never mind that this eagle could not see. "A Korinthian secret," I said at last. "I noticed you speaking with Mnesikles this evening."

"That's true," he said, and stopped. But I would not let myself be pushed. If Pelorus knew nothing dangerous, I would certainly not reveal it.

After a few sighing breaths, the prophet tapped around with his staff. He reached my chair, and, without asking a word of permission, sat.

I walked around to face him. The tiled floor was chill beneath my feet.

His head swiveled to follow me. "The training of a new Tiresias is fascinating," he began. "Of course I'm not at liberty to speak of the details, and it differs somewhat for each candidate. But I can say that I learned a great deal." He sighed, and leaned his chin against the knotty head of his staff. "Even one thing that the priests and priestesses did not realize they had taught me. I discovered that, forty years ago, what seemed an unimportant but merciful gesture was in fact a grievous mistake."

The draft from the window was now too strong. I strode across and jerked the curtains shut. "How so?"

He sounded wistful. "It seems it was a terrible thing, after all, to spare the life of a child."

My knees trembling, I leaned against the wall.

He knew.

What could I do?

Now, right now, I had to keep him talking while I thought this through.

I tried to keep my voice calm. "How could it possibly be wrong, saving a child?"

My mind racing, I realized that he had to die.

The next Tiresias might learn of the curse on Oedipus, but would not know that the babe I bore forty years ago had not died on a rocky hillside. Would not have heard Oedipus' voice raised in anger outside Delphi. Would not have been maimed by Oedipus' sword.

Pelorus nodded like a foolish old grandfather. "You wouldn't think so, would you? It's done all the time, giving away infants who would be otherwise left to die. Someone else always wants a son, a daughter... a servant. And for such a sweet young mother, with a drunken lout for a husband – why shouldn't I take pity on the girl, and save her child?"

How, I thought, could I kill him?

Like a fool, I had brought no dagger. I searched the room with my eyes, and saw nothing I could use. But the pin holding my cape in place – it was long as my hand, and sharp as a needle.

"But how was I to know the nature of the curse?" he said.

I silently unfastened the fibula, and noiselessly placed my cape on the floor.

"How was anyone to know?" I said cautiously. "Laius refused to tell. Maybe there was no curse."

Now that I held the fibula, its jeweled head secure in my fist, what should I do with it? If I stabbed him in the throat, he might still have the chance to scream. His heart? Again, I wondered how quick the death would be, whether he might struggle. Perhaps if I pushed aside the blindfold and struck him in one eye, driving the end through into his brain, he would die instantly.

"Oh, Jocasta," he said, dropping the last pretense of formality, "there was certainly a curse. And this Tiresias knows these secrets."

My hand shook as I surveyed my intended victim. How I regretted the squeamishness of all my years, which had kept me from leading sacrificial rites at the altar. If I had done the duty of a priestess in the past, I would have the experience I needed now.

"And Laius was right," continued the prophet, "to fear the son who would kill him, and marry his widow – the boy's own mother."

Pelorus' voice sounded strangely detached, almost amused. But mine was cold, bitter cold. "What are you trying to say, Tiresias?"

The throat, I decided. I would have to strike the throat.

There would be blood. And a body. How would I explain it?

Creon. Creon would help me. He had done this himself before.

He smiled, showing the gaps in his teeth. "I am saying that the curse on the son you bore Laius is the same as the prophecy young Prince Oedipus of Korinth received at Delphi more than twenty years later."

My bare feet made no sound as I went to stand behind the chair. "What difference does that make, if neither is true?" With my left hand, I would grasp his thin hair and pull his head back as I struck with my right.

Then the prophet twisted in the chair, his face turning up to me as guileless and trusting as a child's. "But Jocasta, they are one and the same, and true as the fact that the king and queen of Korinth adopted the babe I rescued for you forty years ago." He sighed. "It's all my doing. Now put down that fibula. You have nothing to fear from me. If I were going to reveal your secret, I would have done so long before now."

My trembling fingers let the cloak-pin clatter to the floor.

"Do you really think you could have done it?"

"I... I..."

He reached out and grasped my hand. "Strong fingers. And you've always been a determined woman. But your heart is soft – and besides, there's no reason."

The room swirled around me. With my free hand I grasped the back of the chair.

"I am not the means the god has chosen, to bring your secret to light."

Drawing a shuddering breath, I digested this. "You won't tell?"

"Why should I? This is my sin, as much as yours, for defying the will of the gods." He touched his fingers to his blindfold. "I've paid the price."

"You don't blame Oedipus for that?"

"For this? No. My lady queen, I've lived without the use of my eyes these many years. I've learned to accept my blindness as the will – nay, the gift – of the gods. And if now I learn that it was my king, your husband, your—" Mercifully, he stopped. "Now I learn that it was Oedipus who took my sight. So be it. It's my fault as much as his, for allowing him to live." His plump hand tightened on mine. "I've paid the price; that was my fate. And you will pay yours as well. But I won't bring it upon you."

"How, then?"

"That's in the hands of the gods."

CHAPTER TWENTY

The man who had once been known as Pelorus swore to me, by his holy oath to Apollo, that he would remain silent unless the god commanded him to speak; but in that I found little comfort. Each time he opened his mouth I caught my breath, terrified of what he might say. I had him watched at all times, his every word reported back to me.

Until he took me aside one day in the agora, where traders from the east were displaying their wares, and asked that I cease.

"You can persist in this behavior," he said, sniffing a stick of cinnamon incense and then handing it to me, "or you can stop it and enjoy your life. Remember Laius."

"Laius?" I asked.

"He let a prophecy spoil twenty years of his life."

As the bustling crowd eddied around us, I searched the Tiresias' blindfolded face and saw earnest concern. Then he turned and limped away.

The Tiresias was gone, but his words stayed with me. I remembered how the words of the old female Tiresias influenced Laius: how Laius spent his time either drunk or drinking to get drunk; how his rages had ruined feasts with dignitaries; how unreliable he had been in fulfilling his duties.

Although I still appeared at every function, my days were filled with fear instead of joy; I could not concentrate on my duties.

But the gods had let my secret lie silent these many years. Why would they betray it now? What would come, would come. And for today at least, the scent of incense was sweet in my nostrils.

From that day on I willed myself to relax. I tried to slow the racing of my heart each time the prophet spoke. I no longer had him watched. And I threw myself into preparations for my daughter's wedding.

Meanwhile Antigone bloomed like the autumn wildflowers scattered through the hills. Her cheeks glowed; the smile scarcely left her face.

"You've become beautiful, Antigone," I told her one afternoon, as we sorted golden rondels to sew onto the skirts she would wear for her wedding, two days hence.

"You sound surprised!"

"It was just an observation," I said, holding one of the spangles up to catch the sunlight. Its stamped pattern was flawed; I set it aside. "I know such things aren't important to you."

"Not important!" she exclaimed. "Do you know what it's like, having *you* for a mother? Everyone always praises your beauty! Then they look at me with disappointment. And pity."

I blinked. "But you're not yet full-grown, my dear. When I was young, I discovered that a woman of thirty can be more alluring than a sixteen-year-old girl. Your best years are ahead of you."

"But you're over fifty! And yet everyone still praises your beauty."

This was true. My hair was yet dark, with only a few strands of gray – my figure still slender and firm. Only a few lines appeared at the corners of my eyes when I smiled. But I thought it better to keep my vanity to myself. "They flatter me because I am queen, and because I wear the necklace of Harmonia. I promise you: tomorrow, all eyes will be on *you*."

Antigone relaxed, smiled, but then her face resumed a worried expression. "What about the harvest feast? Will there be enough?"

"Let your father and your uncle worry about that."

"But, Mother…" Antigone did not like to be excluded from any responsibility.

"We've always managed to feed the people; we'll manage it now. You will have your feast."

My daughter stared at me another moment, as if she intended to argue, then went back to examining the golden disks to adorn her skirts.

Yet Antigone was right to be concerned. The harvest had been meager, scarcely enough barley to make it worth the reapers' while – and no matter how hard the men shook the olive trees, there was little fruit to gather. Just that morning, in the palace storeroom, I discovered fissures in eleven amphorae, allowing rivers of our best wine to seep into the earth. Creon and Demochares began an investigation immediately; I did not envy the potters whose earthenware had cracked. I ordered new inspections of all the storerooms.

In the cool of the following evening Oedipus, Creon, Demochares and I met in the king's audience chamber to review the inventory.

"Rats and mice have gotten into the lentils in the storerooms out by the Phthia Gate," I reported. "It seems some of the house-snakes died."

"A bad omen," said Oedipus, forming with his fingers the sign to ward away evil.

"Those stores were old anyway," I pointed out.

"But still edible," said Creon. He tapped his stylus impatiently against his wax tablet. "The pomegranates and olives in the northern groves have been harvested; yields are poor."

Oedipus folded his arms across his chest and sighed. "This summer was hotter than any I have known here."

"And it ruined the wheat crops," added Demochares.

"Tell me," said the king, "is there any good news?"

"The vetch growing west of the city wasn't scorched," Demochares offered.

"But there are only one or two seeds per hull," said Creon. "Sometimes, none at all."

"It seems inappropriate to have a feast tomorrow," said Demochares.

"Especially to give Demeter thanks," Creon said.

My husband shook his head. "We certainly must make her an offering – if not in thanksgiving, then to ask her pardon. Thebes must have offended her somehow."

"As you say," said my brother, his tone subdued. He glanced warily at Oedipus, then at me.

"All cities experience difficult times," I said, squeezing my husband's arm. "We still have the herds. And the swine and fowl." I looked at Creon. "Remember how much bean stew we ate, that winter behind closed gates?"

Creon grunted an ill-tempered assent, twisting his stylus between his fingers. "It's too late in the sailing season to obtain more Aegyptian grain," he said at last. "Can we can count on Korinth to deliver fish?"

A frown crossed Oedipus' face.

"What is it?" pressed my brother. "Is there any reason to think Korinth would refuse assistance?"

"Korinth will help, if we ask," Oedipus said, running a hand through his auburn curls. "If the seas grow too rough, they can send wagons across the isthmus road – under heavy guard, of course." He glanced toward the window. "It's just that I was expecting Mnesikles to be here by now – it's not like him to miss the wedding."

Through the west-facing window, we could just see the last of the sun as it slipped below the horizon.

"Perhaps he'll arrive in the morning," I said. "I'm sure he'll come if he can."

Oedipus stood; taking up his staff, he limped to the window. "You're right, he would be here if he could. That's what worries me."

As we went through the final preparations the next morning, Mnesikles had still not arrived. It was strange, not to have the bearded Korinthian as a guest in the palace. He had attended every important ceremony throughout Oedipus' reign. Surely the king and queen of Korinth wanted their envoy present at their granddaughter's wedding? Fearing that he had encountered bandits on the way, Oedipus and I sent three parties of soldiers to scout the likeliest routes.

The morning passed in a whirl of perfume and cosmetics, curling-tongs and sandal-laces, golden hair-ornaments and finger-rings. My younger daughter Ismene would lead her cousins and the other well-born maidens in her sister's bridal procession; I would serve as priestess of Hera, and receive the gifts offered to the goddess of marriage.

"Will it rain?" Antigone asked, glancing out the window. Dark clouds were gathering on the western horizon.

"Certainly not," said Eurydike, straightening the folds of Antigone's cloak. "You'll have a beautiful day for your wedding."

I wondered at Eurydike's sudden ability to command the weather to her liking, but even though Thebes needed the rain, I hoped she was right. "It's time to go," I said.

Merope gave each of the girls their offerings to carry, and we made our way through the palace. Gusts of wind lifted loose strands of our hair when we stepped outside, but the autumn air was dry.

Oedipus and Creon waited on the palace steps. I greeted them in passing, giving my husband a quick kiss; my place was across the agora, at the altar decorated in Hera's honor. I examined the vines and dried roses twisted around the shrine; surely the goddess would be pleased.

The altar was lovely, but from my spot I could see little of the bridal procession. Though I stood on a small dais, the other priestesses and the gathering citizens blocked my view. But I could hear the joyous music of flutes and cymbals. The crowd fairly simmered with excitement and happiness: a royal wedding for Antigone, princess of Thebes!

The last such event, I realized, had been my own wedding to Oedipus.

Twice I had married comparative strangers, during times of political uncertainty and great upheaval for the city. My daughter's marriage could hardly be more different. Did she know how fortunate she was? I doubted it: for all Antigone's cleverness, she was still young and inexperienced. I whispered a prayer to Hera that my daughter's marriage would be spared turmoil and strife.

Abruptly the musicians and the crowd fell silent. Phagros posed the ritual questions; my daughter and her father gave their answers. Then Antigone made the bride's traditional objection: before the wedding could continue, she must make her offering to Hera. My daughter arrived before me in a rush of brightly colored skirts and glittering jewelry, leading her attendant group of maidens. She knelt before me and placed her bouquet of wildflowers on the altar.

How peculiar it felt, to see my own daughter the young woman at the center of all attention. So very strange to hear her voice intone the ritual words! It would feel odder still to see – as surely would come soon – her breasts swell with milk, her belly with child. I felt too young to be a grandmother.

And yet—

I drew a sharp breath, pronounced her gift worthy and offered Hera's blessing.

Despite my misgivings about the meagerness of our winter supplies, the feast following the ceremony was a success. As the servants poured the second round of wine, Antigone and Haemon returned from the nuptial chamber. Antigone's hair was disheveled, her face flushed; she held her new husband's hand and said little, bearing the inevitable ribald jokes with stony dignity –

even when Merope and Eurydike appeared to flourish the blood-stained bridal sheets, she barely flinched.

I thought of my first wedding-day: I had been full of hopes that were destroyed so quickly. With relief I saw that the Tiresias kept his distance from the newlyweds, and that Haemon, after he and Antigone had eaten a little, accompanied his new wife back to their private apartment.

"Our children seem happy together," said Creon.

"May they stay that way," I said, and suppressed a yawn. Though the hour was not late, I was tired. The last few days had been filled with anxieties: the problems with the winter stores, the wedding preparations, Mnesikles' troubling absence. Now that the ceremony was over, exhaustion reigned. I told Oedipus that I was going to bed.

"I'll come with you," he said. "Creon can supervise the rest of the meal, can't you, Creon?"

My brother raised his goblet in agreement and wished us good night.

Together Oedipus and I climbed the stairs to our chambers. He wandered out onto the balcony while Merope removed my makeup and helped me to disrobe. When I was in my dressing gown, I joined him. The moon was out, but clouds scudded across the starry sky. The wind had grown stronger.

"And so our daughter is married," said Oedipus, slipping an arm around me.

I leaned against him. "She had to grow up someday."

He brushed his fingers across my cheek. "Time touches all of us, except you."

"If I can see the gray strands in my mirror, you can see them too."

He ran his free hand through my unbound hair. "Silver, never gray. And there is nothing about you that is not beautiful."

"But—"

He pulled me close and stopped my speech with a kiss, his mouth sweet with wine. "Hush," he whispered, his breath warm against my neck; and I pressed myself against his hard chest.

We were making our way to bed when a knock interrupted us. Oedipus squeezed my hand and called out permission to enter.

It was Demochares, looking embarrassed. "I'm sorry to disturb you so late, my lord. But Mnesikles has just arrived, and says he has important news."

"Ah," said my husband, and his expression settled into the lines of concern that had graced his face so often of late. "Send him here at once. And a platter of hot food, too."

I called for my maidservants; Mnesikles arrived before they had finished lighting all the lamps in the antechamber. Never before had I seen him look so pale, so haggard. He seemed to have aged twenty years since his last visit.

I sent the servants away so we could speak in private.

"My father—?" Oedipus began.

"King Polybus is dead, my lord."

Oedipus turned away for a moment, then looked back. "Sit down, my friend. And tell me what happened."

I poured Mnesikles a goblet of wine and settled on the couch; the Korinthian took the offered chair and began to talk. He told of King Polybus' final days: slowly weakening, unable to eat, finally coughing up blood, but his mind agile to the end. "His last words were of you, my lord."

My husband nodded, his face solemn. "I'm sorry that I could not see him again," said Oedipus. "But – although I grieve for his death, it's not a surprise." He gave me a sad smile; coming to stand beside me, he took my hand. "How's my mother?"

"She weeps, my lord. And she begs you to journey to Korinth for the funeral." He stretched out a hand. "If you would come see her, my lord, you would help her spirits immensely."

"No," he muttered. "I can't, not while she lives."

"My lord?" The man's expression was quizzical.

Oedipus waved his hand, as if to rub out what he had just said. "Mnesikles, you know I love my mother. But I dare not return to Korinth."

"Not return! But, my lord, you are its king!"

My husband shook his head, then spoke firmly. "Listen to me. I cannot return to the city. The oracle at Delphi forbids it!"

"But, my lord, you must! How can a king shun his own city? You've been gone almost twenty years, and there are those who would challenge your right to rule. The sons of Pelops are eager to annex the city, and take control of the isthmus and its ports." The Korinthian looked at Oedipus, then around the room, his gaze lingering on the closed cedarwood door as though to assure himself of its thickness. When he spoke his voice was barely more than a whisper. "My lord, I never asked – I know it is not my place even now, but forgive me, I must. What were the exact words of the oracle?"

"You're right," Oedipus snapped. "It's not your place."

"I have a suggestion," I interposed, attempting to divert the conversation, and hoping my voice sounded normal. "We have two sons—and now we have two cities. Why not send Polynikes with Mnesikles to Korinth?"

Both men looked at me. "Brilliant!" said Mnesikles. "Your wisdom exceeds even *your* reputation for it, my lady."

Oedipus lifted my hand in his and bent to kiss it. "Long ago I came to see the famed beauty of Thebes' queen. Her wisdom is the reason I stayed, and what has made me happy all these years."

I called for a servant to show Mnesikles to a guestroom, so that my husband and I were alone once more. Oedipus stretched out on the couch, his head in my lap. He stared a while toward the brazier, then spoke: "If one part of a prophecy fails to come true, does that mean the rest is false as well?"

I brushed a lock from his forehead. How handsome he was! "My love, I don't know. Perhaps. But I don't understand the gods."

"Could the gods have revoked their curse?"

A flash of lightning followed by an enormous thunderclap kept me from having to find a response. The wind rose, and we heard branches rustle in the distance.

"Do you think it will rain?" I asked.

"My ankles say not yet."

"Let's go to bed," I said, and he followed me into the bedroom. He fell asleep at once in my arms, but I remained awake, listening to the wind.

I woke late the next day; Oedipus was already gone. While I took breakfast and dressed, Merope told me how the wedding feast had ended, and the morning begun. Even Merope could not repress a smile as she reported that Antigone and Haemon were still abed. She informed me that Creon was tallying the cost of the celebration and Demochares was supervising the cleanup in the agora. I asked after my husband. My maid thought he was with Mnesikles, but not sure what they were about. Oedipus' manservant said I would find them in the king's private audience room.

I nodded to the guards and they opened the door for me. "Jocasta!" my husband exclaimed, surprise in his voice.

"Who were you expecting?" I asked, taking a seat in one of the guest chairs. This room had once been Amphion's conservatory; the chair-backs were lyre-shaped, their ebony arms carved with images of flute players. Mnesikles sat on one of the couches.

"The Tiresias, actually – ah, here he comes."

We heard the light tap-tap of the prophet's staff; soon he appeared at the door, accompanied by his younger daughter, Manto. She flicked a glance at each of us, but said nothing.

Her father spoke: "My lord king, you sent for me?"

"Yes; I have a question. If one part of a prophecy does not come true, does that mean one may ignore the remainder?"

I clenched my hands. I should have known Oedipus would not let this rest!

The Tiresias pursed his lips and turned his blindfolded head to my husband. "Prophecy is difficult to interpret, my lord. An oracle may mean something other than what it first seems to portend. Some deeper truth may be hidden beneath the surface."

I bit the inside of my lip to keep it from trembling. Pelorus had promised to keep our secret – *unless the god commanded him to speak.*

"That's not a clear answer," said Oedipus.

"My answer was as clear as the question."

Mnesikles said, "Perhaps if you told the Tiresias about the prophecy."

I stared at Oedipus. *No,* I longed to shout. But I could not; my mouth, my tongue would not work.

"There is no need," said the Tiresias. "Either the gods wish me to know the prophecy of which you speak, and have already revealed it to me – or they have not told me, and do not want me to know."

For such a satisfactory equivocation I could have embraced him; I struggled to keep the relief from my face. The seer turned his head in my direction, and gave a small shrug.

Before anyone spoke again, we heard a booming thunderclap, even louder than last night's had been; Manto jumped. The Tiresias shook his head, and said, "I am sorry, my lord. But unless Apollo speaks to me, I can offer no better wisdom." He reached his hand out toward his daughter. "If you will excuse me, my lord," he said.

The king nodded. They left, closing the heavy door behind them.

Oedipus stood and paced across the room, then turned back to Mnesikles and me. "We must plan a sacrifice to honor my father."

"But that sacrifice should be in Korinth," the envoy argued. "Please, my lord, reconsider your decision, and return at least for the funeral. You need not remain long, but your attendance would unify the city – and secure your son's claim."

My husband shook his head. "You heard the Tiresias. The gods have their own plans; their oracles have hidden meanings. I dare not go against their will." He folded his arms across his chest. "To return could endanger my mother, and tarnish my father's memory. I can't."

Mnesikles rose, and went to Oedipus. Speaking softly, he said, "My lord, you have not told me the words of the oracle, and I will not ask again. But if the curse endangers your parents – would it help you to learn that King Polybus and Queen Periboea are not your true parents?"

The color drained from Oedipus' face; his mouth dropped open. "What?" he cried, grabbing the Korinthian's shoulder. "Not my parents? What do you mean?"

The envoy had sworn me to silence on this matter! Why did he speak of it now? "Mnesikles!" I choked, but my throat constricted, and the word was scarcely audible.

Mnesikles looked up at Oedipus and continued: "Haven't you ever wondered how I, the son of a shipwright, became such a close friend of the king and queen? It's because I brought you to them. You were an infant, rejected by your true parents – they had tried to cripple you, so that no one would want you even as a slave! I carried you to Korinth myself. Queen Periboea's newborn had just died; she concealed the fact, and buried the small body in secret. King Polybus claimed you as his own. No one knew you were adopted except the three of us – and the young man who handed you to me."

"Adopted!"   Oedipus' fingers sank deeper into the Korinthian's flesh.   "But then – the young man – do you remember—"

But before my husband could complete his question, the door flew open.

It was Creon. "The storerooms!" he shouted. "Out by the Astykratia Gate – they're on fire!"

Oedipus whirled.

Then, setting his jaw, he grabbed his walking-stick and called for his chariot. He and Creon rushed off to do what they could.

Mnesikles and I were left alone. He turned to go, but I grabbed his cloak.

"Why did you tell him? You said you weren't going to tell him!"

His eyes widened. "My lady, King Polybus is the one who demanded secrecy. He's dead, and the succession to his throne in danger, unless Oedipus returns to make his claim. I did what I thought best for Korinth, Oedipus, and your son Polynikes."

"But you swore to keep silent! You should have kept your oath!" I was shaking, frantic, knowing it was too late. And then Ismene appeared in the doorway, gasping for breath.

"Mother – the eastern storerooms are aflame – they say the harvest is burning!"

"The harvest?" I asked, releasing Mnesikles. Stunned by what the Korinthian had done, I had hardly heard Creon's words.

"You can see everything from the balcony." Ismene said, then turned and darted away. I lifted my skirts and ran after her.

We rushed down the hallway, through the royal bedchamber out onto the balcony. Ismene and Eurydike were already there, with Creon's younger children.

"Jocasta!" Eurydike came to me, her eyes brimming with tears. "Lightning struck the eastern storerooms! The olive oil, the wheat and barley, it's all burning!"

"Lightning?" I accompanied her to the rail and looked out to the east, toward the Astykratia Gate where my father had hurled himself to his death. Black smoke hovered above the highest part of the city wall, lifting sooty fingers to the cloud-curdled sky.

"Just a short while ago. You must have heard the thunder! They say a guard was struck dead, and the oil began to burn!"

I could smell the smoke. Our winter stores, burning!

Below, in the agora, people were gathering. Some moved purposefully, carrying pots and buckets of water from the wells out to the scene of the disaster; but others milled about, talking, crying, shouting. They sounded worried, fearful.

As was I.

How much of the harvest would be destroyed? Already we were expecting a lean winter; now it would be leaner. Would Oedipus and Creon and their men be able to put out the fire? Would it spread to the houses nearby?

And – what was Oedipus thinking?

My eyes swept the streets down below; but I could not spot his cream-colored cloak, and his chariot was nowhere to be seen. Where was he?

He knew now that he was not the son of Polybus and Periboea. But had he guessed anything more?

I looked at Mnesikles, leaning out over the balustrade. How dare he do this to me – to Oedipus? Bitter anger tightened my throat, and for a wild moment I imagined pushing him off.

Then I remembered he was Oedipus' mentor and our old friend. He had done what he thought was best for my husband, and for Korinth. My fury melted into shame.

"Mother," said Antigone, her voice quavering. She pointed down at the agora. "Do you hear? They're saying the gods are angry – that Thebes is cursed!"

A chill touched my heart. "Are they?"

Antigone put a trembling hand to her lips. "Could they be cursing us? My marriage with Haemon?"

"Of course not," I snapped. Then I softened my tone, and said: "The Tiresias said that you and Haemon are just right for each other. The gods are not angry with you."

Antigone chewed her fingertip. "How can you be sure?"

I drew a breath to calm myself. "I'm *not* sure. If you want another opinion, ask the Tiresias."

The prophet had left the palace not long before; I searched the crowd for his dark robes, but could not find him. Then again, why would he be standing about? Blind and crippled, he could not see the flames; he could not fight them.

We stayed, watching the people down below. People hurried back and forth; smoke continued to billow upwards. As time passed I grew numb to the ceaseless shouts, the sounds of wailing women and children; it was as though these awful sounds had always been, and would always be. At last Haemon and Polynikes came to us, their kilts stained with smoke. Antigone ran to embrace her new husband; he smoothed her hair, and assured her that he was fine.

"The fire has spread to the houses nearby," Polynikes reported. "It's moving towards the Phthia and Eudoxa gates. We need more people to help fight the blaze."

"I'll come," Mnesikles volunteered.

I sent my bodyguards along with them; my determined eldest daughter decided to go, too.

Watching them go, my heart quickened. I knew I should go as well, and help my people. Yet I was afraid: not of the fire – but of Oedipus, and what he must be thinking.

A bright bolt of lightning streaked through the southern sky before us. Thunder cracked. It was close, close.

"Is there anything we can do?" asked Ismene.

"Pray," Eurydike said. "We should pray for rain."

I looked up at the threatening sky, remembering how Eurydike had assured us the day before that there would be no rain.

"That's a good idea," I said. "Why don't you go to the palace shrine and offer some incense?"

Ismene and Eurydike herded the young children back into the megaron. Eurydike turned back. "Aren't you coming, Jocasta?"

"No," I said, for I did not think the gods would welcome me. "I'll go join the people."

Alone I descended the palace stairs. Outside, all was confusion: people running back and forth, some carrying children or baskets, others with barking dogs trotting behind. Two women were struggling over the same water-jar, shrieking curses at one another. When they saw me they stopped.

"Queen Jocasta, help us!"

"Now that you're here, Thebes will be saved!"

"No, you fool!" shouted a third woman. "Thebes is cursed! The fire started in the very place where the old Tiresias died!"

"Calm yourselves!" I called out. "Your king and his men are fighting the fire!"

"Fires!" one man yelled. "Zeus has struck us twice!" The old basket-maker went on to tell me that the storerooms at the Eudoxa Gate were now burning as well. I shivered, for it did seem as if Thebes were cursed. Unless some evil mortal had put the city to the torch.

But I had no time to worry about the cause. There was work to be done. I organized a water brigade to carry water to the southeastern gate, from the wells and the Chryssorrhoas stream. I sent palace servants to evacuate the imperiled homes, and ordered my cooks to bring food and water for those who were working. I went myself to help direct the citizens of the southeastern neighborhoods to safety. Not once did I see Oedipus or Creon, but I heard they were still working out by the Astykratia Gate, where the great storage jars of olive oil blazed on like the fires of Hephaestus' forge.

By late afternoon we had conquered the fires at the southeastern gates. But the damage was terrible, terrible. The storerooms were utterly lost, and many homes as well. The beautiful house my father had built so many years ago by the Eudoxa Gate had been reduced to a smoldering ruin. I walked through what had once been the courtyard, remembering a lovely green place but seeing only fire-blackened stones and drifting ash. I tried to recall the fragrance of the laurel leaves, but with the scent of smoke in my nostrils, I could not.

Wiping my face with a grimy hand, I started back toward the palace. Along the way, people informed me that the original fire was still burning in the oil-stores. I considered going to help the fight there, but knew I was too exhausted. I needed a bath, and sleep.

At the well in the agora, I saw Rhodia drawing water to wash her hands. Her gown was smeared with ash, her face weary. The lines at the corners of her eyes stood out pale against her soot-streaked face.

"Have you been out by the Astykratia Gate?" I asked her. "How is it?"

She looked up at me and shook her head slowly. "Oh, Jocasta," she whispered. "How could you?"

I looked at her blankly. Then Phagros strode over from the direction of the palace, pointing at me. "You have brought a curse upon Thebes!" He raised his voice, turning to face the people passing through the agora: "This woman and her husband have offended the gods and brought down their wrath upon us!"

The two soldiers posted to keep order at the well lowered their spears. "How dare you insult the queen!" one shouted.

The little man stared up at him, his round face reddening. "I'm the high priest of Apollo! You will address me with respect!"

"My lady," asked the other soldier hesitantly, "shall we arrest him?"

I was so tired. I lacked the strength to deal with Phagros. I rubbed my face with both hands. "No," I said softly. "He's the priest of Apollo." I turned and started over to the palace steps, feeling the priest's angry gaze on my back.

Just inside the main doors stood Creon, his arms folded across his chest. He stepped in my path, blocking my way. "I'm not going to be able to fix this one for you, Jocasta," he said.

I shook my head, confused. "The fires are coming under control."

"I'm not talking about the fires. I'm talking about your *husband*."

A chill ran through me. "Oedipus? What—"

"This afternoon he sought me out. Asked about the circumstances of Laius' death. Asked about the child you bore Laius, the one Pelorus exposed on Mount Kithairon." His mouth twisted sourly. "Or so I thought."

Creon knew. Sweet Leto, he knew!

I tried to push past him, hardly thinking, wanting nothing more than to be away from my brother, to be in my room, to wash away the soot and ash and even the day itself, to undo everything that had gone so horribly wrong.

Creon caught my arm, squeezing painfully tight. "You knew it!" he hissed. "You great fool, you knew, and you kept it to yourself—"

I twisted in his grip. "Let me go!" I cried, tears coursing down my cheeks.

"How long have you known?"

I shook my head. "Creon, stop it!"

"Stop what? Stop making you look at the truth? How did you ever think you could get away with this? By all the gods, Jocasta, this is the most appalling—"

"Stop it!" I shrieked, pummeling him with my fist. Surprised, perhaps, he loosened his grip and I darted away.

As I ran down the hall he called after me: "Where do you think you can hide, Jocasta?"

I went to my bedchamber. Merope was there, refilling and lighting the lamps for the evening. "My lady," she said, "can I get you anything?"

"No!" I snapped, and then, more quietly, "No. Just go, Merope. I must be alone now."

The maidservant hesitated, then nodded and withdrew.

Numbly I went to the wash-basin. I rinsed my hands, splashed water on my face.

Thebes was cursed, and the people were rebelling against the royal house. My life was going up in flames: like the year's harvest, like a sacrifice demanded by the gods.

But Oedipus meant more to me than any of that, and by now he must know the truth. What would he do?

I dried my face with a cloth. Stepping to my dressing-table I picked up my comb and drew it through my hair, then put it back down.

If I could explain – maybe I could make him understand. We had lived together, laughed and loved together so many beautiful years. Whatever else, I was still his wife.

I had to find him.

I went to the door of my room. A soldier, a swarthy fellow I recognized slightly, blocked my exit.

"Lord Creon has given orders that you are not to be allowed out of your room."

"Creon! What right does he have to put a guard on the queen?"

I looked around for my usual bodyguard; he was nowhere to be seen, but a second soldier stood outside my door, his sword drawn. He spat on the floor before me. "Queen? Not for long!"

"How dare you!" I raged, and raised my hand to slap him.

The first soldier caught my arm and shook his head. "Please, my lady, go back inside, and don't try to leave. Lord

Creon says it's for your own safety." His other hand fell to his dagger; his broad shoulders nearly filled the doorway.

I glanced at their faces: the one impassive, the other looking at me with pure revulsion. "I want to talk to my husband," I told the swarthy one. "Send word asking him to come here."

And as I re-entered my room and shut the door behind me, I heard a snort from the other guard. "Husband!" he exclaimed.

A chill began at the back of my neck and spread through my body like an icy torrent. Trembling, I crossed the room to a brazier and knelt before it, holding out my shaking hands.

There was no mistaking the sarcasm and contempt in the soldier's voice. He knew; he had to know. But I did not care what the foul-mannered guard thought of me. I did not even care what my citizens might say.

I could think only of Oedipus, my husband, my beloved. Had he fled Thebes – and me – in disgust? Would I ever see him again?

I poured myself a cup of wine and tried to drink, but nearly gagged. With difficulty I forced myself to swallow, then went out onto the balcony. Though the sun had to be setting, it was invisible, hidden by the smoke still hanging over Thebes and the low clouds darkening the sky. A large raindrop landed on the top of my head; a second splashed on the balustrade; then they fell thick and fast.

If the fire still burned, this rain would put it out. Perhaps the gods had heard Eurydike's prayers; at any rate, not all of Thebes would be reduced to ashes. But the vital stores for the coming winter were already lost.

Wet, shivering, I went back inside. Then I heard the creak of the door opening.

"Oedipus!" I cried, my heart swelling with relief, for it was he who crossed the threshold. "I didn't think—"

And I fell silent, seeing the dagger in his hand.

"You deserve to die," he said, stepping toward me. His face contorted with rage, and more than ever I saw the likeness between him and Laius. "You're unnatural – you've made me do monstrous things. *You* are the reason Thebes is cursed. *You* are the reason for the plague and the fire."

"Oedipus, please—" I begged, but he kept coming toward me. I backed up, my skirts knocking over a small table and a jug of wine, until I was against the wall.

"You are my mother, yet I took you to wife! The children you have borne me – my sons and daughters – are also my brothers and sisters! Woman, you are the source of the curse that has followed me my whole life!"

The wall scraped against my back, his familiar once-loving body pinning me there. I watched him raise the dagger.

"Are you going to kill me?" I whispered.

"Yes," he said, and drew back his hand.

I closed my eyes and waited for him to strike.

And waited.

"I should kill you," he said. "Nature demands it – the gods demand it. Thebes demands it. You should be destroyed."

And still I waited for the dagger to slash my throat.

But the blow did not come. Instead I felt the tension slowly drain from his rigid muscles, and he stepped away.

I opened my eyes.

"I can't do it," he said dully, and handed me the dagger. "I'm sorry."

I took the weapon. I wondered if he were sorry for having threatened to kill me, or sorry because he failed to do it. I did not ask; I thought he might not know himself. Shaking, I walked across and sat down on the bed.

He sat down on my dressing-stool. "Why did you never tell me you had a child?" He shook his head, and in the lamplight I saw tears sparkling in his eyes. "Why did you never tell me that you and Laius had a son?"

"Because the memory was too painful. I never spoke of it." Even now, it was hard to force out the words. "My son was ripped from my arms just after his birth. I was told he was eaten by a lion."

"You said Laius was impotent from the day you married. If he was, then how—"

"His problem began half a day after we were married, when the old Tiresias arrived, and told him of the prophecy. But by then…"

"…by then," he echoed, his face ashen. He nodded understanding.

He dropped his face, looking blankly at my dressing-table, running his hands across the scattered objects as though seeing these ordinary items for the first time: my comb, my perfume-vials, the fibulae and bracelets.

Outside the rain roared down.

My heart ached till I thought it must fall to pieces.

How beautiful he was. My gaze lingered on the streaks of gray at his temples, the lines of laughter around his eyes; his broad chest and long-fingered hands, his scarred ankles. My beloved, my husband… I wanted to drown his anguish, the way the pounding rain was drowning the flames outside.

But I did not know how.

Oedipus finally spoke. "You knew of this – this sacrilege, didn't you?"

"Not at first. Not for many years."

"But *you knew*. How could you bear it?"

How had I borne it? I put the question to myself, for at first I did not know. And then the answer came to me, like a ray of light in the gloom.

"I could bear it because I love you." I reached out my hand toward him.

He jerked backwards, staring at my arm as if it were a poisonous snake. "How can you talk of love?"

"You loved me – before you knew. Why does that knowledge make a difference?"

He looked at me a long wordless moment, and for an instant I saw the love there in his eyes. He stood and moved toward me, still holding one of my cloak-pins in his hand. Its pointed tip glittered wickedly in the lamplight. "It makes *everything* different," he said softly. A choked sob broke from his throat. "Gods, Jocasta, how I have loved you! And still, even knowing the truth… still I find you beautiful…"

And with one swift movement his hand flashed to his face, stabbing the bronze point of the fibula into one eye. Bright blood streamed down his cheek and I screamed, leaping toward him to prevent him from wounding himself again. But he turned and shoved me away with his other hand. Before I could stop him he had destroyed the other eye as well. Only then did he let the pin fall to the floor.

"Oedipus!" I sobbed. I tried to take his hands, but he twisted away.

He groped toward the stool, sat down, and covered his ravaged face with his hands. I threw myself at his knees, weeping; but again he shoved me aside, this time violently, so that I fell to the floor, the wine staining my skirts.

The door opened again. Antigone rushed into the room.

"Who is it?" he asked.

"Antigone," my daughter said hesitantly. "Mother, Father, they are saying the most terrible—" She gasped. "Father! What happened?" She ran across and took his hands, and pulled them away from his face.

I did not want to look. There was so much blood.

"Antigone?" he asked, groping for her, and I heard relief in his voice. "Antigone, is that you?"

"Father!" she shrieked with horror. "Father, what has she done to you?"

"Nothing," I cried.

"You mean, everything! Come, Father, come with me," she said. She pulled him to his feet and put his arm around her shoulders. And together they departed, leaving me alone in my room.

EPILOGUE

The fire in the brazier is nothing but embers, but the room is not growing darker. The day's first light seeps in at the window. I hear people gathering down in the agora: the rumble of a crowd turning into a mob. Already there are angry shouts; insults and threats reach my ears.

I unwrap my arms from my daughter's form. "You must go," I tell her.

Ismene shakes her head in protest but I pull her to her feet.

"*Now*," I say firmly.

"Mother—"

"Leave *now*."

Dark shadows beneath her eyes, my daughter stumbles to the door. "I love you," she whispers.

"I love you too," I whisper back. Then she is gone.

I turn next to Merope, lying silently in the shadows. I shake her but she does not wake. "Merope, you must leave me now," I urge, but still she does not stir. And in the increasing light I see the vial Creon brought last night. But now the top is gone and the tiny flask is empty. Merope remains inert, unmoving.

"Did you drink it?" I ask, kneeling beside her. "Oh, Merope, why?"

Her inert body does not answer.

Perhaps she was too horrified by what she had heard, what I had said. Or – perhaps she did not want me to die this night, so she has done what she can to stop me, swallowing the poison herself as her last act of service.

But my maid's devotion cannot save my life. As Creon said, my choice lies only between a painful death and a less painful one. Merope has removed my best option.

I must act quickly, for the people are coming. My people! Will they ever regret their anger? Creon said they would remember me as the best queen Thebes has ever known. I only hope that will be true.

I search the room for a means of leaving my body. There is a dagger on the bed; I lift it and press it against my breast. I feel the edge, but death this way is difficult. I put it down.

And then I see the rafter up above me. The beam is sturdy and not beyond my reach. I pull a stool beneath it, then fetch a belt – the one from Harmonia's robe. Amazing, that the cloth, after all these years, is still supple and strong. But, then, it was made by Aphrodite herself.

I have been queen of Thebes for nearly forty years. I have four – nay, five – children. A husband I adore, who has adored me up until yesterday.

I climb back onto the stool and tie the belt with fingers that are surprisingly quick and sure. In moments the knots are ready.

To die is not to fail, for all lives end in death.

My life has been full of love.

I place the belt around my neck.

Made in the USA
Lexington, KY
23 August 2013